CLAIM DENIED

Claim Denied

DIANN SCHINDLER

Diann Schindler

CLAIM DENIED

DIANN SCHINDLER

CLAIM DENIED

Diann Schindler

This is a work of fiction. All the characters, organizations, and events portrayed in this novel are either products of the author's imagination or are used factiously.

Cover by Kabir Kamaldeen Tope
www.fiverr.com/pro_design190

ISBN: 978-0-9991375-2-9

To my father,
SPENCE LEDFORD, with love.
Despite his death in 1997, we continue our conversations.
To my mother,
HELEN RUTH LEDFORD, with love.
At ninety-five, she is still embracing her dancing spirit.

ACKNOWLEDGEMENTS

I have so many people to thank for helping me finish what turned out to be two years of writing, trashing, starting over, trashing, rewriting, and editing so many times I can't begin to count.

And that was before my fabulous editors, Ritta Basu and Jenna Bagnini, showed me the way, helping me polish thousands of words into a cohesive story. Thank you for your patience and kind words, Ritta. Thank you for the relentless attention to detail, Jenna.

A special thank you to Darryl Bollinger and Dr. Donna Jennings of The D³ Literary Salon. They nagged me. They challenged me when I **knew** I was right. Hate and love are so closely intertwined! Ultimately, they inspired me. I love you.

Thank you to Heather Whitaker for teaching me all about writing a novel, from the beginning to the end and everything in between. You are phenomenal.

My Beta Readers deserve my special thanks, too. They were faced with a very rough manuscript. I sensed their efforts to be gentle. Thank you, Dr. Carrole A. Wolin, Darryl Bollinger, Debra Trumpy, Dr. Donna Jennings, Frank Santry, Marilyn Shea, and Sherry Bushue.

Also, thank you, Frank Santry, for the grand title and for listening to me for hours, trying to make sense of this thriller. I sat on your front porch, and you and Donna put me through intense, often difficult discussions, day after day. I always went back for more.

And Sherry Bushue, international traveling buddy, and bestie, thank you. You are always there for me.

A special thank you, Marilyn Atlas, talent and literary manager and award-winning producer, for your continual excitement and support.

Thank you, Avia Venefica for permission to publish your quote... perfect for the blackbirds in "Claim Denied."

I am truly blessed.

"Our friends with black feathers claw open the veil of secrets.
When we seek their help in devotion and meditation,
they can help us fly behind the veil
to discover uncommon wisdom."
~Avia Venefica,
Author, Writer, Intuitive, Interpreter of Signs and Symbolism
www.Whats-Your-Sign.com

~ 1 ~

CHAPTER ONE

January 19, 2013

Michael arrived at the Tetovo, Macedonia, bus station at 6:15 p.m. It was sprinkling, and the damp settled in his leg, penetrating the tissue surrounding the rod and nails in his femur. He could handle more pain, but his leg slowed him down. The fifteen-minute trek to the Violimçel Hotel took longer now, although time was not the issue. He wanted to get this job done and get his money.

This Dugal person who hired him yesterday said his guy would deliver a gun. Michael snarled at himself for failing to ask what guy, how, and when.

In an instant, some idiot bumped hard into Michael's shoulders and shoved a paper bag in his gut. Michael kept moving, assuming the gun had been delivered. To be sure, he felt for the metal shaft.

He tucked the bag under his arm, skipped a puddle of standing water, and dodged into an alley. He confirmed he was alone, then tore open the sack.

A loaded Sig Sauer with an Aurora silencer. His heart soared as he ran his fingers over the smooth barrel. The gripped panel fit his palm perfectly. Damn, he could hardly wait to shoot it.

He recalled Dugal's warning: "Don't kill him."

Michael told Dugal not to sweat it. After all, he was a U.S. Army-trained sniper. He'd experienced combat, including two tours in Afghanistan. He slipped the gun in his duffel bag and pulled out a scarf, twirling it around his neck and readying it to cover his face at the right time. The drizzle was now a steady downpour. He pulled his jacket collar up to his ears and with his gimp leg headed toward the hotel.

When he arrived at the entrance, he secured his duffel on his shoulder, pushed through the glass doors, and stepped inside. The lobby was vacant except for the clerk at the reservation desk, who was engrossed in whatever was on her computer screen.

Michael limped past the elevators and headed straight to the stairs. Two young kids, shouting and laughing, bopped down the steps. Teenage boys out for a night of fun. Michael pivoted to the other side of a partition just as one kid stumbled and slipped to the floor.

"*Budalla!* You are a fool," the boy said as he punched his friend's arm.

Michael, ever the trained surveillance operative, noticed a silver wheat chain around his neck. The other had a small red tattoo on his hand. He watched them continue through the hotel exit.

After lowering his ball cap over his eyes, he climbed to the second floor, retrieved the Sig Sauer, cracked open the door, and peeked into the empty hallway.

With his scarf positioned, key in one hand, and gun in the other, he made his way to Room 221. He delivered a crisp rap on the door, then waited.

Just as he prepared to slide the key into the door, he heard the door from the stairwell open and bang shut. A man walked toward him. Michael slipped the scarf to his neck and was ready to stroll down the hall in the opposite direction when the man spoke.

"Michael? Michael Gorkey? Is that you?"

Who the hell recognized him here? In Tetovo? In this buttfuck hotel?

"Hey, buddy. It's Andy," he said. "What are the chances of running into you?"

Michael hid the key and turned, straining to recognize him.

"Man, Michael, it's been years. What are you doing here?"

Stunned, Michael grappled for words. "Stephen? Er, what are you doing here?"

"I asked you first," he said, laughing at an attempt at high-school humor.

Sweat drenched Michael's armpits. "I think I'm on the wrong floor."

"You staying here too? This is crazy. Let's have a beer. I'm right here in 221."

As Andy turned toward the room, Michael slipped his gun into the thigh pocket of his cargo pants. The barrel and silencer just fit.

Andy unlocked the door and held it open for Michael to enter. Michael hesitated, trying to figure a way to handle this surreal situation. He checked his surroundings to be sure he was in the right place. Dugal said Room 221, and this was the right room. The file must be in this room. Andy's room. This simple job had turned complicated in a flash. He needed time to regroup.

"What are you waiting for? Come on in."

"I'll take a beer," Michael puffed, and plopped in a chair. He eyeballed the room, searching for the disk, doubting it'd be sitting out in plain sight.

"It's been a long time, Michael. I haven't seen you since our little job in Croatia. I just talked with Grey Valentin. You remember him. He asked about you and said you served in Afghanistan." Andy looked at his feet and lowered his voice. "Had to be tough, man."

Michael rubbed his thigh, gritting his teeth and racking his brain, trying to develop an alternative plan.

Andy shifted his feet and changed the subject. "Here's your beer. Grey will crack up when he hears we ran into each other. God, that was a monumental project."

"Course I remember you two. How could I forget? You treated me like shit."

"What? I didn't see it that way." Andy furrowed his brow. "Sorry. I thought it was a fun project. Good money, for sure." He turned to Michael, nodding for some reassurance that all was good between them.

Michael took a swig of his beer, staring at him as anger seared the nape of his neck. He settled in his chair and thrusted his crotch at Andy.

Andy's jaw muscles rippled, and he retreated two steps. "Damn. What's going on?"

"What are you doing in Macedonia?" He drank again, glaring at Andy. "Everything on the up and up?"

"Hell, you know me, Michael. I've always colored inside the lines," he said, swallowing.

Michael realized he'd have to ask for the disk and risk confrontation, the last thing he wanted.

"No. No, Andy." He repositioned his weight, preparing to attack. "I don't know you or Grey, except that you were condescending bastards."

"That's not true."

Michael jumped and grabbed Andy's shirt at his throat. He pushed him against the wall and knocked the wind out of him. "You got a disk I want."

Andy's legs and arms quivered, and his eyeballs bulged as he struggled for air.

"Where is it?"

Still holding Andy, Michael suddenly stopped when he heard a familiar noise. He struggled to identify it. He felt strange, dizzy, and his vision fogged. The taste of old pennies filled his mouth. Finally, the sounds registered: gunshots.

He cocked his ear toward the reports coming closer. Through the blazing Afghan sun, he spotted six tangos on the top of the building, hovered behind the ramparts with their automatic rifles aimed directly at him. The fuckers were waiting for a clean shot.

A tango on the ground ran and, in a flicker, appeared directly in front of him. His ebony eyes were fierce with deadly terror, face slick with perspiration.

Michael butted him with his head and tackled him to the ground. The little guy fought hard as a monkey on cocaine, clawing and spitting. They wrestled and rolled until the asshole gained strength and slipped a leather strap on Michael's neck. He twisted it tighter and tighter.

Michael gasped for air and growled. Gradually, maneuvering his hips and legs, he got on top and pinned the tango. He flattened his knee into his shoulder. The monkey's clavicle crunched, cracked, and snapped, and his frantic breath burst powdered soil into the air. Drool trickled from his lips.

Michael jammed one knee into the small of his back and planted his other boot on his neck. The tango was in a perfect position for the kill.

As he placed the tip of the silencer on his skull, Michael's groin flooded with fiery lust, and he waited for his dick to stretch full.

"Michael. Please—"

A gunshot blast interrupted them.

The monkey rolled over in a soft thud, with blood spurting two inches high, pooling on the ochre-colored dirt.

Done.

Michael tried to put his gun away, but he couldn't find his holster. He patted around his belt. Where was his carry? Suddenly, the desert floor pitched and yawed, and he lost his balance, squeezed his eyes shut, and toppled to the turf.

When the earth stopped rolling, he opened his eyes, looking for the dead tango. "Shit. goddamn it." No tango, just a dead man.

Michael lay next to Andy's crumpled body. The gun slipped from his hand as he scrambled up and hopped around like a wild savage. "Dammit. Dammit."

He caught his image in the mirror and stood fixed, watching his chest heave as he fought for air.

You killed him, you sick motherfucker.

Michael's hands trembled. Not because he had murdered, but because he'd wigged out.

Find the file and go.

He dug into Andy's pockets, found his wallet, and emptied everything on the bed. No disk, just credit cards, money, and a photo of Andy with a girl.

A quick scan of the table revealed a few coins. Most importantly, he saw Andy's passport and when he turned to the first page, Grey Valentin's business card fell to the floor. He also noticed a Prishtina address penciled on the inside of the passport. With his cell, he took pictures of the card, passport location, and the photo of the girl.

Michael got a towel from the bathroom and wiped every surface. He also checked himself for traces of blood in the bathroom mirror. I'm clean and I erased the evidence, he thought as he adjusted his hat, put the key in his pocket, and the gun in the duffel.

Using the towel to grab the handle, he pushed the door just as a phone rang from inside the room. He let the door close again and pulled the cell from Andy's back pocket. The caller ID read unknown. He pushed decline and jammed it in his bag, thinking he ought to lose it in case Andy still had his number stored.

Again, he shoved the door, stepped into the hall, and descended to the first floor. It was empty. He exited the glass doors and crossed four blocks to the Pena River. The rain had picked up and people rushed for shelter.

Michael tossed the piece and Andy's cell into the center of the river and hobbled along with the others escaping the rain. Two

blocks later, at the back of the crowd, he peeled off and ducked under an awning outside a café, stomping his feet to release water and
mud from his boots.

While he waited for a break in the weather, he remembered
Andy calling him "buddy." A sorrowful twinge jolted his stomach.
He didn't mean to kill him, and wasn't even sure how it happened.
Michael clinched his jaw as he watched the standing water splash
and ripple into vanishing circles. He wanted his PTSD to disappear,
too. "Fuck it. I'm a trained killer," he whispered, mopping spittle
from his mouth with his fist.

The rain stopped, and he pulled out his phone to check the photos. Especially the one with the girl. Young, attractive, quite a nice
smile. She looked American. They looked pretty damn cozy. He took
a chance the passport address was the girl's.

Michael wondered if he'd find the disk at her place.

~ 2 ~

CHAPTER TWO

January 1, 2013

Margot had slept little, if at all, last night. She twisted and turned her pillow over repeatedly, trying to tuck it under her head in a perfect position to avoid stretching her neck muscles. She never did get it right. Her neck ached and her head hurt, too. Of course, it wasn't the pillow. And it wasn't her neck.

"It's nothing physical, you idiot," she whispered aloud. "It's your stupid, relentless brain. You're reaching back into the hidden corners of your mind to find, revive, and force you to relive the worst experience of your life."

Unspeakable images of her little sister, lying dead in the snow, had seeped into her dreams and snapped her awake, drenching in sweat, and relentless regret.

Did you have to make Sam go home with Alice in a snowstorm? Why didn't you take her yourself?

Always the same haunting questions. Of course, she had answers, but none of them were good enough.

Margot gave into her familiar insomnia and sat on the side of her bed, legs dangling, chin on her chest, shoulders curled over her heart. Her chest felt bruised.

That's what happens when you don't control your thoughts.

It made no sense to wallow in her family's past, especially now, just as she was embarking on an incredible future. Of course, why would logic stop her from dwelling on Sam, killed in a violent car crash, followed by her father's unforgivable behavior. He ran away ten days later, causing Margot's mother to plummet into a major depression.

The coward left his wife. And he abandoned Margot, the only child he had left.

What kind of man does that?

So there she was. Her baby sister was dead. Her father had fled. And her mother....Well, her mom was trying to survive and pretty much unavailable. She hated her dad for all of it, although, admittedly, he didn't tell Sam to go home with Alice that night.

Unlike her mom, Margot didn't get depressed. Her grief was more visceral. Her father and his narcissistic choices stuck to Margot's ribcage, clogging the arteries to her heart. When the images in her head were too vivid to bare, she convinced herself her father was a mere annoyance, same as those No-See-Um bites on her ankles. True, the stinging nibbles created an excruciating itch, so much worse when she raked her fingernails across her skin. It felt so good to scratch. Until it didn't. That was when bright, moist blood surfaced, and she couldn't stomach it. So, she refused to give into the itch. And, three or four days later, when she had ignored her prickling skin and after the sores had healed, she forgot all about those insects. Till the next time.

Margot took in and let out a long breath to rid her body and mind of this same old negativity. She scratched her ankles, then turned on the lamp on the nightstand and stared at three family photos. First, a picture of her and Sam a few months before she died. Mouth wide open, eyes flashing with excitement, she was pointing to a single front tooth just poking through her gum and hugging her new ice skates.

Margot looked closer at Sam's face and wondered where all that enthusiasm went. Seemed like one minute Margot felt Sam's bubbly joy and the next, nothing. That was it. Sam was gone.

Margot didn't cry as much anymore, and she promised herself she wouldn't cry today. Crying, sobbing, blubbering was futile. It didn't change a thing. So she focused on trying to recapture that same feeling she had when they were together ice skating, playing checkers, or just sitting next to each other. The closest word to describe it was bliss and sometimes, for a fleeting moment, she had it. She got a whiff of Sam's sweet breath or the sound of her tiny voice calling Margot's name.

Bliss.

She kissed her finger and touched Sam's face.

The next picture was her and her mom at Afton Alps Ski Resort about two years after Sam died. Her mother had changed. Margot saw sadness in her eyes. A year after this photo was taken, and after three years of counseling, her mom said she could finally talk about it. *It* meaning Sam and her husband, their father. Her losses. She also admitted depression had continued to torture her, rumbling just below her consciousness.

Trying to help, she told Margot she needed to talk too, repeating her favorite Rumi quote: "The wound is the place where the light enters you."

Talk, wound, light, whatever. No matter what she said or how hard she tried, nothing changed for Margot.

Learn to live with it best you can.

The last photo on the nightstand was of her and Andy at the University of Minnesota on her graduation day. Margot had put this one in a shiny silver frame. A gift from Andy. She enjoyed running her fingers along the birds perched across the top.

Truth was, she had plenty to be grateful for, especially her Andy. Andrey Orlo Stephen, that is. In two days, she and Andy will arrive in Kosovo. He'd work for the State Department. She'd teach. To-gether, they'd make a difference in peoples' lives throughout the world, one country at a time, starting in Prishtina, Kosovo.

Today, on New Year's Day, Margot wanted to ski, burn off her funk, and say goodbye to Afton Alps before leaving her home. She put on her university sweatshirt, stained and ragged with wear, and the secondhand ski pants she bought in Uptown, the bohemian side of Minneapolis.

These ski pants were quite the steal because they were long and fit her lanky, high-waisted torso perfectly. Even though she was five feet six inches tall, her legs were more suited for women as much as three inches taller. She hated her too-long legs, of course, but her mom said she could be a high-fashion model.

Margot chuckled to herself as she looked in the mirror and smeared Burt's Beeswax Balm over her lips, noting her eyes were too deep set and close together. She never got the hang of wearing makeup except for a quick wisp of mascara on a special evening out. Besides, her freckles congregated on one side of her face, leaving the other side virtually freckle free.

Her mom thought Margot was beautiful because she was her mother. Simple as that. Margot didn't argue. She just let her see and believe whatever she wanted, always grateful to have such a loving mom.

Rather than waking her mom, she left a note.

Off to Afton Alps. Love you, M.

She texted Andy and told him to meet her on the slopes, adding she wanted him with her this last time.

When she got outdoors, she tossed her gear in the trunk of her beater car, her beloved Myrtle, a 2004 Honda Accord. She was a rusty blue, mangled with minor fender benders. That's why she loved Myrtle. They were kindred spirits. Bitchy survivors.

After clearing the ice and snow from Myrtle's windshield, she grinned, patted her hood, and climbed inside. She glanced at her phone. Nothing from Andy. Heat flared between her shoulder blades, her body's typical response to frustration.

She heard her mom say in her head. "William Langland said, 'patience is the greatest virtue.'"

She sighed and rattled her shoulders as she turned the ignition. "Come on, Myrtle, help me out."

Myrtle sputtered before sounding a long *vroom*. She took time to warm up, too. Cold was nothing to Margot because she had lived her entire life in Denver. Until Myrtle brought her along with her mom cross-country to attend the University of Minnesota.

They had two weeks of great conversation with crazy fool laughter, singing their favorite songs over and over again. "Blackbird" by the Beatles, "My Girl" by the Temptations, and especially Don Henley's "The Heart of the Matter." They weren't just mother and daughter. They were best friends. She needed her mom. In the same way, her mom needed her.

Margot's heart hurt, imagining 5,158 miles, the distance between Minneapolis and Prishtina. She recoiled at the thought of leaving her mom alone to fend for herself in a big city where over 23,000 thefts and assaults had taken place the previous year. Way more than in all of Kosovo.

"Honey," her mom had said, "kidnapping, sex trafficking, and armed robbery are rampant in Kosovo, especially in Prishtina."

"Andy and I get that. We'll be smart. I agree with him: nothing worth achieving is without peril." She flipped her chestnut brown hair in defiance and said, "Don't worry, Mom."

She bit her bottom lip as she remembered her mother's response. "I'll worry. That's what I do. God, I'll miss you, honey."

She had arrived and pulled into the ski resort parking lot. She opened the trunk, changed into her boots, got her gear, and schlepped inside to get her pass.

"Hey, Margot. You're early. You by yourself today?" Brooks said from behind the ticket counter. He was a handsome kid, good-hearted, and everyone loved him. She had told him repeatedly he should be a star in public relations and make oodles of money instead of wasting his time and talent at a less than stellar ski resort. He'd always shied away from her compliments and said he loved the Alps. Margot had done all she could do to push this boy into making a good living.

"Yeah. Tsk. I doubt Andy will make it today." She crinkled her eyes and gave him her credit card.

"You and Andy off for Kosovo tomorrow?"

"Day after tomorrow. Hey," she said as she rubbed his sleeve. "Is this a Helly Hansen jacket? Love to have one myself, but even at eight hundred bucks on sale, it's not happening. How do you dress so well, Mr. Brooks Pap, on minimum wage?"

The corners of his mouth turned up as he returned her credit card and handed her a locker key. "It's been great getting to know you guys. Jana and I will hate missing those dinners at your house."

He didn't answer her, and because she thought Jana might be supporting him and his expensive tastes, she didn't press. It might embarrass him. Skinny introverted Jana, the intellect, had a thriving accounting business. Margot never knew what was going on behind her onyx eyes, except that she idolized Brooks. "When are you two getting married? Is her father still giving you fits?"

"Yeah, Mr. Mihailovic. He's old-school Serbian. Be not concerned, however. I'm going to crack that nut." He laughed.

"Serbia is right there next to Kosovo. Have you visited?"

"Oh, no need. There are so many Serbians right here in Minnesota. I get a genuine sense of their culture. Anyway, I want to keep in touch with your mom, if that's okay."

"She loves you. Says you're the son she never had."

"Aw. That's nice. Have a great run."

She found her locker and checked her phone one last time. No text. She rammed her cell into her backpack, shoved it inside, slammed the door, and turned the key. Her frustration morphed into fury.

Let it go, Margot.

With a deep breath, she rushed to catch the lift to her favorite black diamond: Rosa's Run. Afton was no Breckenridge, yet these hills belonged to her. She had learned to conquer every trail in the last four years.

At the top, Margot adjusted her helmet and goggles, rattled the tightness out of her knees, and took two deep breaths, holding the third for three seconds. Then, growling an extended exhale, she propelled forward toward the toughest moguls at Afton.

After a breezy fifteen seconds, the treacherous exhilaration began. She attacked each mound with peak perfection, topped each apex, recovered, and prepared for the next. She loved dominating the steep run with her muscles pumping a slow burn, and icy wind ripping past her ears. Nothing was better than this passion and physicality, wrapped in exploding endorphins.

She skied five runs. On the sixth, she stopped halfway and looked up the hill. Green pine trees blanketed with snow framed the run. A lone cirrus cloud punctuated the ultra-blue sky. She slowly inhaled, soaking in the artistry as goosebumps raised on her back.

"Awesome," a voice said from behind.

The familiar tone sent tingles throughout her body. Still, she held her gaze. "For sure. Especially this time of day."

"I'm talking about you, my love."

She turned around and faced Andy. Her heart fluttered, as it did every time she saw him. He wore his mishmash snow gear and camouflage sweats. A dingy yellow sweater peaked out from under his plaid blue-and-green jacket. No helmet, no goggles. His frayed New York Jets stocking cap accentuated his dazzling blue eyes.

"Those stupid gloves," she said.

One-size-fits-all cotton gloves, his Walmart specials were useless in Minnesota winters and a total contradiction to his top-of-the-line Black Crow skis. Same for his geometric-patterned scarf designed by Russian artist Kazimir Malevich and his David Yurman watch, valued at $5,000. All gifts from his wealthy father.

"What? What a steal for three bucks."

Andy always said he detested his dad along with his super rich elitist friends who were self-absorbed and oblivious to the rest of the world outside their personal orbit. Margot loved Andy's liberalism, yet his keeping those expensive gifts puzzled her. Maybe they represented hope he and his dad could resolve their differences someday.

"Whatever. I'm glad you're here, but I'm not happy with you. Why didn't you answer my text?" she asked in a nasty tone.

"I bought a new phone with a new number. It's been transferring data throughout the night. I couldn't make or receive calls. I went to your house and your mom said you were here."

"Another new phone? Didn't you get a new one last month?"

"Did. I wanted a few more bells and whistles. Anyway, sure wish I could get you in a body hug. This'll have to do, given our ski paraphernalia." He placed the end of his pole on her shoulder. "I'm sorry I upset you. I'm lucky to have you in my life."

Despite her best efforts, she seldom could resist his charm. Plus, she didn't want to fight on their last day in the States. She let her disappointment melt as she placed her pole on his shoulder. "I'm the lucky one."

"Come on. Let's have some fun." He dropped his pole and dug it into the snow.

"Aha! Wanna race?" She tucked her poles under her arms and snickered.

"Oh God." He belly laughed. "Okay. Let's do it. I don't mind getting beat by a girl." He scooted next to her, bumped their hips, and aligned their skis. "Ready. One. Two. Three!"

They left together then. In an instant, he took the lead. She told herself he'd fade after the fifth mogul. He stayed ahead longer than expected.

Wait for it. Patience is the greatest virtue.

Then, at mound seven, his pole work got sloppy.

"Go!" Margot squealed and lowered her center of gravity. She leaned forward with her upper body motionless and knees bobbing like cylinder heads in a finely tuned car. Once she breezed past him, she slid into a 180 and threw an arc of snow four feet into the air.

Andy teetered on one ski, arms flailing to stay upright. She giggled and covered her mouth.

He screamed past her and crashed into the out-of-bounds barriers.

"Gawd, you could have hung yourself," she said, skiing to his side and crouching next to him.

"I'm fine. Just another ass kicking." He howled.

"And you got snot everywhere. Ick."

Andy used his Walmart specials to clean his face and reached over, trying to rub Margot's mouth with his sticky glove.

When she jerked to stay out of his way, she lost her balance and keeled over into the yellow plastic tape, landing on her back beside him. She pulled at his knitted cap and his blond-streaked hair fell to his shoulders, brightening his dazzling blue eyes.

Andy slipped her goggles over her helmet and nuzzled snow in her face. "Damn, you are fearless, girl." He planted a wet, playful kiss on her.

"I always say, competency banishes apprehension." She puffed and expanded her chest, adding a boastful grin.

"God, you're beautiful."

Her body turned fuzzy. "You are, too."

He paused and perched himself on one elbow. "I planned for just the right time. This is perfect."

Her chest pumped as she sensed what was to come.

"Can you hear my heart pounding? I hear yours. And your eyes are sparkling."

Speechless, she nodded as a soft hum filled her throat.

"Will you marry me? You are my everything. We are exceptional together," he said as his eyes glistened with moisture. "I love you beyond description. I know I must sound silly, but it's true."

"Doesn't sound silly. I don't care if it does. My entire body is buzzing, singing. I love you."

"Rats. I'm getting a call. Damn poor timing." He tossed his gloves, struggled to unzip his jacket pocket, yanked his cell out, and scrambled up to a standing position.

"Who has your number already? You'd think I'd have it first." She snarled and gnashed her teeth, waiting for his answer.

"Sorry, I need to take this." He skied toward the clubhouse.

~ 3 ~

CHAPTER THREE

January 15, 2013

"Come on. You can do it," Andy said.

Margot doubled over, panting, "Okay. I must be out of shape. Tell me again, what's the name of these steps?"

"Two hundred thirty-three steps up to the Dragodon section of Prishtina. Most people call them the Dragodon steps. Can't wait to see the view from the balcony at Valbona's Restaurant. It's supposed to be breathtaking. Careful, though. A few risers are crumbling."

"Why don't they fix this? It's dangerous."

"This is Kosovo, darling," Andy snickered.

"*Përshëndetje Zonja*," a tiny voice said.

Margot spotted a small child two steps above them. Shoeless, her little toes had to be freezing. She wore a filthy pink hat perched above her sad eyes. She cupped her little hand and reached out to Margot.

Margot gasped as images of her sister Sam filled her head. She lowered her voice to a whisper. "She's adorable."

"*Ju lutem*, nice lady?"

"What'd she say?"

"She said 'please.' Ignore it. Let's go." Andy jammed a coin in the child's hand and motioned for Margot to keep climbing.

The girl slid off the steps and scampered away, disappearing into the bushes.

"Is she alone?"

"I'll bet the mother is hiding with another baby at her tit. She uses her kids, trains them to look pitiful. You've traveled. You've seen this before." Andy took Margot's hand and pulled her up the steps.

This wasn't the Andy she knew, and how could they not help this baby? Guilt filled her chest.

When they reached the top. Margot said, "Wait. You called her 'it.' What's got into you? I don't understand the hypocrisy. Unlike you, I cannot ignore homeless children."

He exhaled, folded his arms tightly across his front, and leaned on one leg.

It was a standoff. And she jammed her hands on her hips, glaring at him.

Finally, Andy said, "Okay. I give. Please, let's sit."

"Better be good because so far, you sound heartless," she said as she sat on the step.

Andy's voice was gentle, almost placating, as he explained that the children may have come to Kosovo from Albania. He said their parents may have paid unscrupulous border patrol officers a lot of money to enter the country illegally. The Dragodon area was a perfect place to find unsuspecting western tourists to give them money, he said, trying hard to keep the judgment from his voice.

"Then, they are exploited in unspeakable ways. And everyone, from local police to top Kosovo leadership, turns a blind eye."

Andy's voice carried the exasperation of years of witnessing this kind of heartbreaking injustice.

Margot, though, wouldn't be swayed. "True, and seeing them up close is heartbreaking. Where's your compassion?"

"Exactly where yours is: with the children. Still, I focus on the larger picture where I can make positive, systemic change."

"Really?" she said, cocking her head. "I hope that child doesn't starve to death before benefiting from your macro approach to addressing fraud. Obviously, we can agree to disagree. Understand, I do what I want, Andy."

He hugged her and smooched her forehead. "That's why I love you. You are such a bleeding-heart hard-ass." He tilted his head. "Tonight is our first chance for quality time together. You and me."

His eyes held hers, and she saw all the exhaustion of his week in them. He had been working hard to get them settled in and to get himself settled in at the State Department. He had just been pushing hard.

"We got off to a poor start. Be warned: I want to have an adult discussion regarding this child and her plight at another time." She inhaled. "And I admit, I'm a sucker for your blue eyes. A charming touch, Mr. Stephen."

"Why, thank you, my sweet," he said with a grin.

When he opened the double doors to Valbona's Restaurant, Margot's mouth fell open. The restaurant was a stunning contrast to the treacherous steps of Dragodon and the raggedy beggar child.

She scanned the massive room filled with twenty or more tables covered with soft pink tablecloths and surrounded by floral pink and green wingback chairs. Landscape oil paintings and vintage photographs of Prishtina decorated the brick walls.

A young man in black pants and a crisp, white long-sleeve shirt greeted them with a toothy smile. "Good evening. Welcome to Valbona's Restaurant. I'm Elion. I have a table for two on our enclosed veranda. Come with me, please."

They followed him up the worn wooden steps to a small patio and sat in front of an enormous window that filled the entire external wall. The view was breathtaking, although a stack of boxes displayed on a shelf to Margot's left distracted her attention.

"Those are our traditional filigree boxes fashioned with fine silver mined right here in Kosovo. Note, they are for sale." He handed two leather-bound menus to Andy. "Our special today is the fish. I'll return for your order shortly."

"Incredible, heh?" Andy touched her knee under the table. "I'm sorry. The little girl, I mean."

"Yes. It's just that—"

"She reminded you of Sam."

Margot nodded and dropped her head.

His cell phone rang and interrupted her thoughts of her dead sister.

Andy checked the caller ID. "I need to take this. Sorry."

"Shall I order the fish?"

"What did you say?" he said into his phone. "*Chto proiskhodit?*" He waved her an apology and descended the stairs.

She noted tan lines on his wrist, outlining his father's expensive watch. She'd ask him where it was when he returned. Meanwhile, she wanted to examine the boxes.

"Excuse me, madam," Elion said, "There's a gentleman below who says he's an old friend of yours. Your husband's, rather. May he join you?"

She glowed with pride when Elion said *husband*. They weren't husband and wife. No need to correct him. "Yes, of course. And Elion, two orders of the fish special, please."

Elion nodded.

Whoever this "friend" was, she hoped he didn't linger. Hence, two dinner orders.

A stout, bald man with wettish eyes approached the table. His suit stretched across his round body and his pink shirt clashed with his ruddy complexion.

He reached to shake her hand. "Hello, you must be Margot. Andy told me everything about you. We haven't talked for months, though. I didn't expect to run into him here in Prishtina. Please, I hope I'm not intruding."

That's totally what he was doing. "Hello. And your name?" She shook his hand and found it sticky and chilly. "Sit, please. Tell me how you know him," she said, wiping her hand on her pants to tamp her revulsion.

"Thank you." He sat across from her. "We met at Stanford and spent a semester together at Koc University in Istanbul when we were seniors. We also worked together in Croatia."

"And your name?" she said again, tossing her hair back this time. He was either anxious or low wattage. Whatever it was, he annoyed her.

"Oh, sorry. Greyson Valentin. Please, call me Grey."

"Odd, I don't remember Andy ever mentioning a Grey." She raised her eyebrows at him.

"Ah. Ahem. We were college chums and then we worked together in Croatia."

"Yes, that's what you said." She let out a long puff.

Neither spoke and she let the silence build, hoping he'd get her message and leave.

With a thin chuckle, he said, "I couldn't help noticing your admiring the boxes. They're filigree, an ancient metalsmithing art made with silver from the mines right here in Kosovo. Artisans spend hours curling wire into those lacy shapes."

He was an encyclopedia, on the other hand. The filigree artistry piqued her attention. "This one with the bird is my favorite." She lifted it to the light.

"It's my favorite, too. Kosovo, a Serbian name, comes from the Slavic word for blackbird. More plausible, the bird design replicates a jackdaw, birds that are very prevalent here. They are a cousin of the blackbird, or crow family."

Okay, she had to admit he was intelligent.

"They often flock in the thousands, wheeling and turning in formation with such unity and precision they resemble one huge beast swimming in the sky."

"Grey." Andy said, climbing the stairs. "Oh, my God. Great to see you."

Margot cringed at Andy's high-level response to Grey and, to her surprise, one side of her nose crimped, unmistakably an involuntary reaction revealing her embarrassing envy. She covered her nose with her hand.

Andy slapped his shoulder, and they hugged. Grey winced at Andy's intensity.

"Margot, this is my outstanding friend, Grey." Andy practically cooed when he said his name. "Grey, this is my lovely Margot." He turned to Grey. "What in God's name are you doing here?"

"I'm working with the United Nations. I'm here often. It's my favorite restaurant."

A violent pang of jealousy smacked at her insides as they laughed and reminisced.

Andy said, "I'm at the State Department working on sustainable development goals and governance. My job is technical stuff. I'm re-designing systems to enable tracking."

"I see. Cyber security. Is it classified?" Grey said.

"Andy, who called?" Margot's question had nothing to do with their conversation. She wanted attention.

"They classify everything. Kosovo is still recovering from the war," Andy said.

"Hello?" Her lower lip pouted.

Andy snapped back. "My supervisor."

His tone stung her, and heat radiated between her shoulder blades.

He said to Grey, "I got to go to Macedonia. Tetovo for a few days—"

"I'll go with you," she said.

"Someone said Michael Gorkey was in Macedonia," Grey said. "You remember him."

Now Grey was ignoring her, too.

"Hell yeah. He's a very weird dude. I haven't talked to him since Croatia."

"Yeah, me neither. I heard he's done a couple of tours in Afghanistan. Anyway, how's your mom? Is she doing okay?"

Margot leaned back and folded her arms. She despised being excluded. And, no matter how hard she tried, she couldn't squeeze into their conversation.

Surrender.

"Yes, I got a letter from her in July. She's still in New York City." Andy sipped his wine.

"That's it? Nothing since then? That's six months ago."

"Of course, we've chatted since then."

"And, how's your dad?"

Andy shrugged and didn't respond, creating an awkward silence.

"Oh, I'm sorry. That was rude. Didn't mean to dredge up old wounds about your mother," Grey said, pursing his lip and shaking his head.

"Forget it."

"Well, Margot, it has been a pleasure." He said with a nervous grimace. "Here's my business card. One for each of you. Call me if you need anything."

"Don't leave. Have dinner with us," Andy said.

Margot's eyes widened at the excruciating thought of spending their evening with Grey.

"Oh, no, thank you. I'm sensing this is a special evening for you two."

She breathed easier.

"Let's get together when I return. Here," he said, writing on a napkin. "Our phone numbers. And thanks for your cards. Margot will be here by herself while I'm gone. I'm glad she can reach out to you if need be."

"Of course." He bowed and descended the stairs.

They were alone at last.

Andy raised his glass, urging Margot to do the same.

They sipped their wine.

"We just arrived here and you're off to Macedonia?" she said with a slight whine.

"I'm sorry. I wish you could go. Don't be mad. We'll go another time. The two of us." He moved closer to her.

"I'd love that." She took his hand. "Oh. Where's your watch? God, hope you didn't lose it."

"It's too ostentatious for these parts. I put it in safe keeping." He relaxed in his seat and looked away.

He appeared distracted. "Are you okay?"

He nodded and smiled. "Sure, I'm thinking how much I'll miss you."

"Me too. Thank you for saying that. It warms my heart."

Their mood had shifted into sentimental romance by the time Elion brought their entrees.

Famished, Margot took a mouthful of fish and instantly fought her gag reflex. She hated black olives, and capers weren't her favorite either.

"How's the fish? I love capers."

"Great," she lied. The brine was too much for her palate.

"I'm shocked," he said, shaking his head. "It's salty. You prefer clean food."

She dropped her fork on her plate. "True."

"Margot, you don't have to eat it on my account."

"I spewed enough negativity tonight, arguing over the beggar child and mistreating your friend. The fish was way beyond what even I could tolerate. So. I lied, but not about the potatoes. The potatoes are great," she said, trying to make up for her stupidity. She shook her head and blushed an apology.

Andy grinned. "I know. It's okay. Honest. Let's move on. I saw your interest in these boxes." He picked up one box she had admired.

Just then, Elion appeared with the check.

"I love these boxes with the birds," she said.

"I do too. We'll take two, please," he said, handing Elion his credit card.

Elion thanked them and said he'd have them wrapped and ready at the exit downstairs.

"You must know, Margot, Grey is a fantastic guy. We've had great times together. And yes, you were damn rude to him." He frowned at her. "I'm surprised. Disappointed, actually. Tsk. You'll love him when you get to know him."

He hit a nerve and her palms turned damp. "I'm sorry. Truth is, he interrupted our time together. And now you're leaving. Besides, you two excluded me. Why?"

"I didn't mean to. Honestly, I'm stressed, you know, Macedonia." He tugged at his ear. "And leaving you," he said, shaking his head and pursing his lips. "I was thinking. Let's have that adult discussion."

"That's sweet of you to say. Thank you. So you mean an adult discussion about the child on the steps? Now? An adult discussion? I see. It feels like you want to shift from one uncomfortable topic—ignoring me—to an opportunity to be critical, Andy." She felt angry, with the same heat rising in her stomach, and glared at him just as she did on the steps earlier in the evening. "I have my opinions," she said, folding her arms across her chest.

He will not change your mind about homeless children.

"You really think you're wasting your time tending to a child who is suffering right in front of your eyes?" she asked.

"It feels that way every time I see a homeless child," he said, lowering his voice.

"Imagine how she must feel, Andy?" She tightened her arms.

"God, I've never seen this look on your face." He reached for her elbow, and she twisted her arm away. "Come on, babe. I know, I know. You're right."

"Of course you do. Don't try and charm me. This...these children are way too serious. I'm stunned that we're in disagreement about basic....Well, this is about girls, children, and human rights." A single tear streamed down her cheek, but her stern stare did not waver.

The tension between them was the greatest she had ever felt, and it scared her. Could she lose him over this? She didn't move, willing her lip not to quiver.

"You know, you may find this hard to believe but the truth is I was thinking all during dinner, how can I ignore what I hate the most? Governments are not taking care of people." He rubbed his palms on his thighs. "Yeah, sure, I can say I'll change their lives for the better by working with the leadership." He breathed a long, disgusting sigh and rubbed his forehead. "It's a long, tedious battle—"

"If you are successful. That's a big if in this country. I mean, have you even established allies to help? You cannot do this alone and even finding the right people to help you will take time. Maybe years." She tilted her head and softened her face. Pleading with him she said, "In the meantime, what will have happened to the children? Listen, you know I want to support you, Andy. I do. But, we met this little girl for a reason. To wake us up to the realities of Kosovo."

"For sure. Reading about the plight of Kosovars and seeing photos does not compare to sitting next to a poor little girl, scraping for food. And, it really doesn't matter how it's happened to her. Whether we blame the mother, politics, the war, or...whatever the myriad of causes. And they are complex. It's a single child and you, Margot, forcing me to rethink. I don't want to go to Macedonia without our coming to some common ground. With this negativity between us."

Margot unfolded her arms and relaxed her shoulders, realizing she didn't need to gird herself for an argument any longer. She put her hand on his elbow as the angst in her stomach dissipated, replaced with a warm, soothing glow. "Seems like we're in agreement. That's certainly great common ground, for starters."

Andy leaned his shoulders back and sat up straight. He frowned but his eyes were bright, hopeful.

"You have an idea?" she asked, grateful for the shift in mood.

"While I haven't thought this out at this moment, I want us, you and me, to start an NGO." He raised his eyebrows. "What do you think?"

"Wow, Andy." She swallowed. "Yes, but to do what, exactly?"

"Well," he chuckled, "not sure I have all the details. But, I'm thinking of ways to get kids off the streets. Find them homes. I don't know. Save them from becoming prostitutes."

"Slaves." She bit her lip at the thought of seeing that little girl caught up in trafficking.

Andy nodded slowly and closed his eyes for a moment before smiling at her.

"I think you don't listen to me...or you don't hear me," she said in an apologetic tone.

"You're wrong."

"I am. You always surprise me, thank God. I think he sent you to me to fill my heart because it's overflowing right now." Her face flushed, and she kissed his cheek.

How can your life get any better than this moment with this incredible man?

Andy squeezed her hand. "I want you to think about it while I'm gone."

"Have you? Have you been thinking about it? I mean, you came to this idea over dinner? Seems so sudden."

"I have. It's been simmering for a long time. I was afraid to say it out loud because it's an enormous commitment."

"For sure. So, let me quickly jump to reality. Could you manage a business, an NGO, and work for the government at the same time?"

"Nope, I couldn't," he said, as his face lit up. "I'll resign."

"Are you being funny or are you serious?"

"I'm serious, of course!"

"Oh, I see." Her voice grew bubbly. "You think this is exciting because you'll quit your job and we'll be broke."

"Nothing worth achieving—"

"Is without peril. I know," she said as her voice cracked with emotion.

"Those aren't my words. I'm paraphrasing Theodore Roosevelt. He said, 'Nothing in the world is worth having or worth doing unless it means effort, pain, difficulty.'"

"God, I love who you are, Andrey Orlov Stephen." Her entire body tingled with contentment, knowing he was hers and she was his.

~ 4 ~

CHAPTER FOUR

January 18, 2013

After his first tour in Afghanistan, Michael Gorkey signed up for U.S. Army sniper training because he was eager to use his skills on another tour. Get back with his buddies. He figured he'd been acting weird cause he had trouble getting clearance. He lied to the docs and said he'd never got confused or lost reality during the day. Sometimes at night.

"Come on, doc. Yeah, I have some nightmares. Name someone, any asshole in combat —I'm talking Afghanistan—who says he doesn't dream at night. Well," Gorkey huffed. "that son of a bitch is feeding you some fucking bullshit."

Michael must have been convincing because he got authorization and returned to action. Trouble was, he was setting up his sniper gear in a combat post in Kandahar Province when some tango shot him, nearly shattering his thigh. Although he had treatment in Germany, the limp was lifelong.

The pain came and went. Nothing he couldn't handle.

The Army wanted to send him home. Not him. He wanted to travel the world. He'd done some civilian work in Croatia a few years ago. Traveled around Montenegro, Bosnia, and Kosovo.

R & R in Kosovo sounded outstanding. Kosovo women were crazy sexy. Big black eyes, long black hair, tight jeans, and clingy tops. The ones he had in Prishtina drove him wild in ways no American woman ever had.

He headed for Stripe Depot, a few blocks from Mother Teresa Boulevard. The Depot had been his favorite bar the last time he was in Prishtina. Damn hot strippers were contortionist pole dancers. It was a private club where military guys could ogle and drink all they wanted without mixing with the general public who'd tell stories on them.

The Depot had been a hangout for the NATO Kosovo Force who had fought in the Kosovo War. Bombs blasting for seventy-eight straight days had to be hell. Over 13,000 civilians died before the NATO Kosovo Force stopped it in 1999. Everybody wanted to be around these guys. They were genuine heroes.

Now, fourteen years later, he saw the Americans in the Force as pussies. The only gunfire they'd ever seen had to be on their daddy's chicken farm in some Midwest redneck state.

Michael wanted a few drinks with a hardass he could shoot the shit with. a real combat fighter who had battled like he had. Plus, could be he'd get lucky and go home with a Kosovar broad.

Live music was playing when he stepped inside the Depot and after his eyes adjusted to the darkness, he sat at the end of the bar between two empty seats, making sure he had an unobstructed view of the strippers. He'd pick out the sexiest one for a lap dance as soon as he had surveyed the place.

Satisfied all was safe, he ordered a beer and grabbed a handful of peanuts from a small bowl while ogling a skinny girl with big tits riding a pole. She was hot. He shifted his weight to accommodate his hard on.

Then, Michael's attention diverted to a guy coming through the door. A bad actor? No. Peculiar? Hell yes. He wore military fatigues, but he was no soldier. Had the buzz cut. But his pants dragging the floor over his filthy tennis shoes were a barefaced, cockeyed clue. If he'd ever been in the military, they'd booted him out.

"Hey, all right if I sit here?" he asked with a heavy brogue. He dragged on his cigarette and sat before Michael answered.

"Guess so." Michael huffed.

"Thanks. Name's Hetrick. Dugal Hetrick. I go by Dugal." He scoped the people at the bar.

"Name's Gorkey. Michael. You Irish?"

"Fuck no. Scottish." He took another drag and blew smoke out of the side of his mouth. "Hey, bartender. Give me the same as my buddy's drinking."

"Blow your smoke somewhere else, fella." Michael pushed out his chest.

He butted his cigarette. "Afghanistan?"

"Two tours. You?"

"Fuck no. Royal Regiment. I didn't last."

"Yeah. What'd they kick you out for?"

"None of your fucking business." He put his hand on the side pocket of his jacket, looking squarely at Michael for the first time.

Michael didn't look away. "Take it easy, buddy. Didn't mean to hit a nerve." Aware that something was off, Michael was glad he was packing, and planned how he'd react if this idiot went ballistic on him.

Things simmered a bit though. They sipped their beers.

As he fiddled with the label on his beer bottle, Dugal said, "Hey, wondering if you can help me out."

"You're shitting me. You sat here to tap me for some money." Michael wiped beer from his lips.

"No, no. Got a job in Macedonia. I can't cross the border because I got passport problems. It's easy and great money."

He checked Dugal up and down. "No offense, my friend, you're damn pathetic looking. Why should I listen to you?"

"A thousand euros now and three more when you finish the job."

Michael took a swig of beer and pumped out his breath. He squinted. "Why can't you cross the border?"

Dugal shifted in his seat and chuckled. "Bet your government's paying you big bucks for that leg. What, two hundred bucks a month? Here, have another peanut."

He was right on the money. How'd he know about the leg? Michael waited for more information. "Hmm. Got to assume your silence shows an interest," Dugal said, with a sickening chuckle. "Hey, two more beers. Me and my friend are taking a corner table," he told the bartender, raising his empty beer bottle and throwing five euros on the bar. He nodded for Michael to follow him.

Michael didn't move.

Dugal nudged his arm. "Come on, my friend. Let's talk."

No harm in hearing him out. Plus, four thousand euros would go a helluva long way in Kosovo.

They moved to a small table in the corner. The bartender followed with two beers.

"What makes you think I'd be interested? Why me?"

Dugal leaned his chair back and grinned, "I spotted you on the Boulevard. You limp. You've survived some bad shit. You're big, mean-looking. I figure you for a real disciplined soldier, a stickler for rules, with a lot of rage going on. Exactly what I need for this job."

"So, you followed me, eh? I have to say, Dugal, you look like a psycho. What makes you think I'd do business with some fuck up like you?"

Unfazed, Dugal retorted with an evil laugh. "Takes one to know one." Michael's impatience set in. "Ok, prick. Stop with the bullshit. Tell me what you got."

"So, short on funds?"

"Humph. What kinda robbery? No banks and I don't do stores."

Dugal leaned in closer, "Perfect. A thousand now. Got to get something in Tetovo. Get it and bring it to me. You'll get the rest, three thousand."

"Who's the guy? What's the something?"

"He's a fucking weenie. No clue he's in over his head. He's—"

"What is it?"

Dugal sneered at him, "You want the job? Commit and I'll tell you."

Hot anger seared the back of Michael's neck. In the past when his body reacted this way, he'd go wild, but not anymore. His sniper training had prepared him for every situation, even more when he had used his M2010. Awesome rifle. He could take out enemy personnel at 1,200 yards. Now, that heat was sensual. Made his dick get hard. When his shot hit whatever or whoever, it was better than the best sex. In fact, sometimes he creamed.

Michael shifted in his seat, adjusting his cock, "A robbery? Cause if I have to take this guy out, four thousand euros won't cut it."

"Shit no. Not asking you to kill anybody. Damn, you're a demented asshole. It's a file. A disk, that's it."

Michael blew out a long breath, "When?"

Dugal pulled an envelope out of his inside pocket and handed it to Michael under the table. "Everything you need is inside. Get the disk."

Michael peeked inside and counted one thousand euros and asked how he'd get the rest.

"Give me your number," he said, handing Michael a small tablet and pen. "Bus ride is three hours and leaves for Tetovo at three p.m. tomorrow. Take it. I'll contact you tomorrow night. Catch the bus back the next morning. Leaves at five-fifteen a.m. Don't miss it. One bus a day back to Prishtina."

"Got to show my passport to get a ticket. I'll be leaving a trail. I'm taking all the risks. So, four thousand won't cut it. Anything can go wrong. No weapons on the bus. They'll do a search. I'll need a gun with a silencer.."

"My guy will give you a gun when you get there."

"The money?"

Dugal shook his head and lit another cigarette.

Michael rose from his seat and handed the envelope back, "No deal."

"Shit. Sit. Quit flashing it." Dugal jammed the envelope back into Michael's hands. "You idiot. This is serious shit."

"Who's paying you and how much?" Michael sat again.

Dugal wriggled in his seat and took another drink. "The less you know, the better off you are."

He didn't want to know more, he wanted to pressure Dugal. Test him. "All right," he said, pointing his finger. "Five more when you give me the disk and check in the guy's computer."

"Check for what?"

"It may be in the computer disk drive. I'll be labeled Magpie."

Michael leaned back, folded his arms, and cocked his head, looking his eyes on Dugal's. "You fuck with me? I'll kill you," he said in a low, controlled voice. "Ever kill anybody, Dugal?"

Dugal folded his hands over his head and nodded.

Michael believed him. "Question before I take off. What's the tattoo on your hand? Looks pretty girly," Michael grinned.

"It's a Scottish thistle, you asshole. Stands for bravery. Means no one attacks me without impunity. Don't forget it."

Michael stood, stuck the envelope inside his jacket and left the bar.

Hell of a way to shoot the shit at Depot. Dugal Hetrick brought an unexpected change of plans. He'd have to wait for some Kosovar pussy until he got back from Tetovo.

~ 5 ~

CHAPTER FIVE

December 15, 2012

Cass got up early. By the time she got to Jer's back door it was 6:55 a.m. The conference call didn't start till 7:45, which gave her time to discuss her trip to New York City. More importantly, she needed Jer's help to smooth her jangled nerves.

She brought along her most treasured book, Alderfer's "National Geographic Complete Birds of North America." This book was her solace, her place to hide whenever she felt her most apprehension. She'd earmarked "magpie." The magpie was highly intelligent, the most murderous fiend of the entire avian world.

They had named their project Magpie, a fitting title for the massive cyberattack designed to obliterate the United States' health insurance industry. This attack will lay open the industry's systemic fraud and corruption. Brilliant, efficient, and comprehensive, Magpie will incite revolution throughout the masses. The entire world will be watching, and, as a result, the stakes were incredibly high.

Cass clutched the four-hundred-plus-page book so tight her knuckles were colorless. Her hands froze in the below zero temperature in Brinnell, Iowa. Truth was, she was plain scared.

She forced her fingers to uncurl and snapped her wrists back and forth to get her blood moving. She scrunched her shoulders to warm her neck and shoved her hand in her flannel-lined jacket pocket. Pain stung her fist when she knocked on the kitchen window.

Mrs. Bloom waved to her and opened the entryway into the vestibule, "Why Cassandra, you're back. Come in out of the cold, child. I was making coffee. Want some? Bet your trip was beautiful. Wow. New York City. You're a lucky girl, darlin'."

"Good morning, Mrs. Bloom." Cass loved Jer's mom. Her chatter was warm, sweet.

Cass removed her green, knitted stocking cap and stuck it in her pocket. She rubbed her head to loosen her short brown hair from her scalp and stomped the snow off her boots before stepping inside to the kitchen. "Hope I'm not too early," she said, closing the door.

"No, no. You know you're welcome in this house anytime. This has been your second home for years. You know, I think you started coming here—"

"In seventh grade." She snorted in embarrassment.

"Don't be silly. That's over fifteen years ago. You followed my Jeremy around, a puppy after its momma. No, wait. You printed on him. Is that the word? Ah. Birds do it."

"Yes, still mortifying," she chuckled. "It's called imprinting. Birds do it when they see their mother. It's called species identification. Nature's way of—"

"That's right. It was cute, and Jeremy...oblivious. His daddy and I used to laugh at that. Funny." Her voice trailed off.

Cass watched Mrs. Bloom fade into a memory. She had seen her do that hundreds of times in the last two years since Mr. Bloom died. The loss was still fresh. And most egregious, Mrs. Bloom knew her husband could have lived longer if IowaHealthCare hadn't denied their claim for treatment.

"Mrs. Bloom, I'd sure love that coffee," Cass said to bring her back to reality.

"Oh, yes, of course."

"Jer up?"

"Lord, yes. That boy's been up. In the cellar for hours. You two love playing with those machines. Can't imagine what you do all day. And sitting in front of those screens with those numbers jumping around. Crazy." She smiled. "Here you are and a fresh cup for Jeremy. Go on, honey."

"Thank you. Can I give you a morning hug?"

"You're a darlin, Cassandra." They embraced. "You're as smart and sweet as you are pretty. You always know when I miss my Raymond. Oh, how he loved you. The daughter he never had. I promised, I'm not going to get started. No use in it. What's done is done."

Mrs. Bloom pivoted to the kitchen window. She folded her arms across her ample breasts and gazed across the cornfield. Stiff yellow stalks blanketed with February morning snow stood defiant against the harsh winter wind.

With her glistening eyes wide open, Mrs. Bloom stared into the piercing sun inching above the horizon and reflecting off the silvery snow. The bright light had to hurt her eyes.

Cass didn't totally grasp grief and what it does to the mind and body. She wondered if Mrs. Bloom welcomed the pain to punish herself because she couldn't do anything except watch her husband die.

Cass's heart ached for her.

"What's done is done," Mrs. Bloom sighed.

"Thank you," Cass said, even though she knew Mrs. Bloom was too far into her own thoughts to hear her.

When Cass opened the entrance to the cellar, kitchen light flooded the wood steps, carved with wear. The door clicked shut, and the room turned dark except for the red and green flashes streaking across the walls and floor.

Fixated on his computer, with lines of green code pullulating on the black screen, Jer didn't move. He was hunched over, squinting into the huge monitor, hair disheveled. She had adored him since the eighth grade. An intelligent and nerdy introvert, everything about him had appealed to her.

Cass set his cup within his reach before taking a sip herself. She watched him, waiting for him to take a break from his intense concentration.

He'd never shown the type of interest in her that she actually wanted. Their connection was one-sided and limited to technology, the web, and having fun breaking codes. And, now with Magpie, he was more distant, less personal. No fun anymore.

"Morning," she said.

He nodded, added additional lines of code, and looked up with half a smile. "What did you find out?"

Cass exhaled a long breath, "And hello to you, too."

The cellar door opened. "Jeremy, did you feed the chickens?" his mom said.

He reached for his coat and jerked his head toward the door. "Come on. I want an update on the money."

Once outside, Cass said, "We've been over this a hundred times, Jer. I told you. Funds are secure. With every deliverable, they've deposited the correct amount in our Singapore account. I checked and rechecked. Maureen did, too."

"And tell me again. We can absolutely trust your cousin Maureen?" he said, as they entered the coop. He shut the wire gate and filled the bucket with feed.

"Yes. Maureen has connections. In Serbia, Russia, and Kosovo."

"Did she tell you who they were, their names?" He raised his voice. "Give me names."

"Got two names for you. I don't know who they are. If you try to reach them, you'll face dire consequences. It could end Magpie altogether."

He glared at her, demanding an answer.

Her frustration level peaked. She unzipped her jacket as anger raged in her chest. Every conversation turned into an argument, and he escalated into a power struggle. "Maksim Nikitin in Russia and Eris Hoti in Kosovo."

"What do we care about people in those countries? We need Macedonia connections."

"See. Nothing is good enough for you. Names are useless information unless Homeland Security investigates you. God help us all if that happens! Let's stick to our job. Let Maureen do hers."

He didn't answer, throwing feed pellets across the dirt floor.

The chickens went wild, screeching, fighting, pecking each other for their share of food. The flapping wings caused fine dust to go airborne. Shielding her eyes didn't help. Dust caked her eyelashes.

She hated chickens. They were Machiavellian creatures. She exited and watched him fling food.

Jer was particularly harried despite their experiences with Anonymous, the *good guys* of the cyberattack global community. She and Jer had been in on Operation Payback. They leveled Payback to the tune of $5.5 million in losses. With Operation Anti-Bully, they had forced those perverts to their knees.

Then, Cass and Jer soured when Anonymous refused to take on the powerful, corrupt organization that ripped off thousands of people. They took off on their own.

"Cass, you piss me off. If we're caught with this one, we're in for prison time. We cannot let a single question go unasked. We must be immaculate at every step. I told you, it ain't personal."

He was right. Their relationship hadn't been personal for years. For some stupid reason, she had stuck with him. As a result, when Jer got stressed, she did, too.

She folded her arms. "Yeah, your job is leading the cyberattack, not challenging Maureen. Without her, we wouldn't even have this project. She's our conduit. We want to keep her happy."

He pitched the last bit of feed, threw the bucket back in the food bin, and exited the pen.

"I want nothing to do with Hoti or Nikitin or anyone else who she's working with," she said. "When we discuss the dangers we face, it's about getting caught and going to prison."

"Yeah?" He closed the gate.

"That's not the half of it. Think of it. The last thing I want to do is piss off the deep pockets from Russia, Serbia, whoever, wherever. These are powerful people. They want to screw with the United States, create chaos. We're nothing to them. We are the worker bees. Easily replaced. Then, they can, they will eliminate the evidence on a whim. The evidence? That would be us, Jer."

He looked at her, cocked his head and puffed. "You know, the U.S. Department of Labor reported last year insurance companies rejected approximately fourteen percent of medical claims. That's one in seven, over two hundred million a day. A fraction of those are legitimate denials."

"Right. We are fighting for those who have suffered mightily because of fraudulent denials." Cass stuffed her hands in her jacket pockets. "We gotta choose our battles. Maureen isn't one of them and I'm not the enemy either, Jer."

They stood silently facing each other as the minutes passed.

"You need to trust me, Jer. Let me take some pressure off."

He put his arm through hers. Before, she'd seen this as affection. Not now. It was his feeble way of apologizing.

"You're shaking," he said. "Are you sure you're cut out for this? Get out right now. No questions asked."

"Who are you saying? You or me?"

He tipped his head toward the house, "It's time. Conference call is going to start."

"You didn't answer me, Jer."

Suddenly, a black crow landed on top of a cornstalk. It had flown so close Cass had to duck for fear he'd crash into her head. He flapped his wings to gain balance, then peered at them.

"Damn! Scared the crap out of me," Cass whispered, "What's he doing here? It's February. Crows are long gone by now."

He turned his head as if he were listening or getting a closer look. His inky eyes glinted in the sun.

They stood mesmerized.

At last, Jer waved his arms, "Shoo!"

The crow let out a shriek, assaulting her ears. Wings thudding, he pushed off and flew away, skimming the dead cornstalks. His call echoed in the distance.

Her National Geographic book on birds was factual and didn't wander into the subject of birds and symbolism. But she had read somewhere that crows were associated with messages from beyond and represented dark omens and death.

Suddenly Cass was cold. She zipped her jacket up to her neck. "That was beyond disturbing."

"We're going to be late," he said.

Her jangled nerves provided a constant distracting hum in her ears.

~ 6 ~

CHAPTER SIX

January 21, 2013

Margot swore she was done waiting. Andy said he'd be back from Macedonia in 3 days. Day 5, and she had yet to hear from him. No calls, no texts.

What could she do? Honestly, she was scared, and her fear had mutated into self-inflicted fury.

She talked to herself in the bathroom mirror. "What an idiot! You fall for a guy and let him talk you into coming to a third world country. Then he leaves you alone, thousands of miles from family and friends. What if you need help?"

She spit at the mirror and her chin quivered as she watched the phlegm slide toward the sink. "The one person you know in Prishtina is Andy's college buddy. What's his name? Grey something or other. Sure, he's going to reach out and help you after you treated him like shit. Way to burn bridges, Margot."

Her eyes darted around the room, searching for her cell. The fourteen calls to him in the space of thirty minutes this morning had gone straight to a recording: "This voice box has not been set up."

There it was, peeking out at her, lodged between the sofa cushions. She dialed for the fifteenth time. Nothing, no ring, and no recording. It went dead.

Even your phone has deserted you.

She plunked herself down on the sofa, preparing for her head to explode, when someone pounded on her door with such force, the hinges jangled.

When a voice said, *"Përshëndetje,"* her entire body turned to stone. "Hello? Mr. Andy?"

Margot shook her body loose, tiptoed to the door, and opened it just enough to see a huge, rugged man with a scraggly beard and a broken front tooth. His threatening, narrow slits for eyes telegraphed danger, and sweat trickled on her spine. "Who are you?"

"Me Ismet. Ismet Lokaj, landlord. Excuse me, madam. My rent, please."

She checked to see that the door chain was intact before responding. "You are the landlord? My God, did you need to bang so hard? You scared me. And, no, the State Department pays our rent."

"Sorry. Here is contract." He pointed his fat, hairy finger to the bottom of the page. "See? Andrey Stephen. Said call him Andy. He responsible to pay."

She took the paper from his massive hands. "Wait," she said, shutting the door.

Andy's signature, all right. Due date: 20 January 2013. Four hundred euros.

This time she talked through the door. "Come back later, in an hour. I'll have your money." She gulped, wondering if she had four hundred euros.

"Faleminderit. Thank you. Please, Mrs. Stephen. Must use peephole before open door."

His assumption Andy married her was fine with her. At least he'd think she had male protection. He was right, though. She should've used the peephole, and she did. She saw him scratch his beret and turn toward the stairs. He looked less ominous, and Margot thought he might be authentic. And Andy usually offered his first name.

She needed to relax because everything set her off and spitting and screaming at herself only made her feel stupid.

The rental contract made no sense. Had to be a misunderstanding. For now, she'd resolve one hassle by paying the landlord and getting reimbursement from the State Department later.

She dug around and found four hundred and ten euros in her purse. That was every euro she had. After rent, she'd have a mere ten left. She rolled her eyes. "Andrey Orlo Stephen, where the fuck are you?" Andy's note on the refrigerator caught her eye. His State Department contact information: Donna Edwards, Human Resources. The minute she dialed, her phone rang, and she disconnected to accept the incoming call.

"Andy! Thank God," she said, blowing the foul air out of her lungs and body. "Where have—"

"It's me, Grey."

"Grey? I thought you were Andy. You're killing me. How did you find me and why are you calling me?"

"On my way up." The call ended.

She didn't have time to entertain him. No, correction: She didn't want to entertain him or even talk to him. If he had been merely semiconscious at Valbona's Restaurant, he had to know how much he annoyed her. His showing up unannounced was incredibly rude. She gritted her teeth, opened the door, and looked down the stairs, "God. What's taking you so long?"

He didn't answer, because he was struggling to breathe. Every time he lifted a foot, he wheezed and groaned.

"Shit, Grey, it's only two flights. And, listen, if you tell me Andy called you, I'll be livid."

He came inside and flopped on the edge of the sofa with his knees spread apart and his face a flaming red.

She slammed the door shut.

"I don't," he said, twisting and fidgeting with his fingers. "I can't do this." He dropped his head and his shoulders quaked as he began to sob.

Why was he crying? Whatever it was, she'd stay out of his drama. "Do what?"

He was in a pitiful emotional state, and she figured she ought to show a modicum of compassion, even if she didn't feel it. She sat across from him. Faking empathy was hard work, and to release the steam suffocating her skin, she ripped off her cardigan.

"He's gone, Margot," he said in a high-pitched tone.

"Who? Gone where?"

"He's. Andy is dead."

Margot's back stiffened. "What? Can't be."

He kept talking, but nothing registered because buzzing chaos clogged her brain. She shook her head, grasping for order. "What on earth are you saying?"

"Somebody killed Andy." His swollen, bloodshot eyes stared at hers.

"No. He's in Tetovo." She covered her ears to stop the buzzing. "He'll be back. I expect him today, for sure."

Grey loosened his shirt, drenched with sweat. "Tetovo police found him in his hotel room."

"It's not him. Got to be mistaken identity." She swallowed. "Nobody, er, no one wants to hurt Andy. Everybody loves him."

"I know. I can't believe it either," he said, raking his fingernails over his bald head. "Tetovo police chief, Officer Dime Pavlovski, said someone had ransacked his room, looking for something. It was not money, though, because Andy's wallet with credit cards and money were in plain sight." He stood. "Pavlovski found my card and called me. He warned me. Said whoever killed Andy might come here trying to find what they didn't find in the room. They might come to the address written inside Andy's passport."

"Where? Here? I don't believe it."

His eyes fixed on her, he said, "Pavlovski read the address to me. That's how I found you here, Margot. The address he read was right here, your apartment."

Her mouth dropped open. She stopped breathing.

"*Përshëndetje?*" a voice said from the hall.

~ 7 ~

CHAPTER SEVEN

January 21, 2013

The voice from the hallway startled Margot. Grey shuddered.
"*Përshëndetje?* Hello. I'm landlord. Andy available now, please?"
Wide eyed, Grey grimaced at her. "Who is that?" he mouthed.
"Whew. It's okay. Give him the euros on the kitchen table."
He rubbed his chin. "Are you sure?"
"Check the peephole. He's huge. Hairy. Front tooth missing."
Money in hand, Grey edged forward and squinted through the hole. He nodded to her then opened the door, "Yes?"
"Oh. You not Andy. Please, I here for rent money. Mrs. Stephen home?" He craned his neck, peeking inside. "Everything okay?"
"Yes, thank you, sir," Grey said, handing him the money.
"What wrong? I help?"
Grey shook his head, shut the door, and turned to her. "It's true, Margot."
Her face twisted, her eyes filled with tears, and she chewed her bottom lip.

Grey put his hand on her shoulder. She jerked away, rocking back and forth.

He handed her a roll of paper towels from the kitchen counter.

She tore one off and wiped her face. "What are we going to do? I mean, I don't believe it...."

He wiped the sweat off his bald head with his handkerchief, then staggered to a chair. "Police want to talk, face to face. Oh. Shit," he said, looking at his watch. "Gotta catch the bus."

She jumped up. "I'm going, too."

"No. No. You need to stay here. I'm barely capable of handling this myself." His voice quaked. "Frankly, you'd be a distraction. I'll fill you in as soon as I know more."

She wanted to protest. Instead, unsure she could cope with any further trauma herself, she kept her mouth shut.

"Call me if you need me. Keep your apartment locked. Don't let anyone in—"

"It's always locked, dammit," she said in a loud voice and scowling at him for bossing her around. She hoped shouting at him would release the fear vibrating in her hands.

"I'm saying do not let anybody in. I mean, this is crazy stuff."

"Stop scaring me."

"I know. I'm sorry."

"Stop apologizing."

He took a deep breath. "You need to understand how they killed Andy to grasp the danger. It wasn't random, according to Pavlovski."

She dropped her jaw. Not random? What the fuck could that mean? She held her breath.

"They shot him. In the back of the head."

She covered her mouth with both hands, stifling a monstrous scream fighting to get out. Grey rushed to put his arms around her.

"Stop it. I don't believe you. I don't believe any of this." She shoved Grey away, repulsed with what he was suggesting. "You've already let yourself believe Andy is dead and that he was involved in some sort of illegal maneuvering, but I don't. I won't." She forced herself to swallow the anguish and anger stuck in her throat.

"But, Margot," Grey said, pleading for her to listen to him. "I'm trying to tell what I know. That's all."

"But nothing! You think Andy was doing illegal stuff. Well, I don't and nothing you can say to me can change that." She stomped both feet and wiped the sweat off her forehead.

"I don't believe it either. Andy had big dreams and got involved in high-level government stuff. He was smart. Savvy. I cannot see him breaking the law."

Margot dropped to the sofa as if surrendering to a great weight atop her body. She brought her hands to her face and dug her fingers into her scalp. "None of this makes sense. It feels all wrong. It cannot be happening."

He touched her shoulder. "Don't tell anyone anything. Do you understand?"

She nodded, barely listening, trying to find order in the frenetic thoughts clanging around her head.

"If I'm not back in five days, go to the police," he said as he walked toward the door.

"What?" Suddenly she heard what Grey was saying. "You gotta come back. You can't leave me here. What'll I do if you—"

"I'll be back." He rubbed his head. "I may have to identify a body. I'm afraid the image will be seared in my mind forever."

"Grey, it's not him. It isn't." She held her breath and covered her mouth.

He blinked. "Let's hope you're right." He blinked a second time before he pulled the door open and stepped outside. Looking at the doorknob, then at Margot, he said, "Lock it."

The door clicked shut.

She secured the dead bolt, hooked the chain, and pulled the drapes. Sitting cross-legged on the floor, she racked her brain, trying to remember anything odd or unusual about Andy. To help her think, she got up and paced, circling the living room and kitchen.

Then she stopped at the fridge, remembering Andy's note: Donna Edwards, Human Resources.

She dialed. It rang twice and shifted to a reorder signal. She disconnected and tried the number again. Same thing. She ended the call, went to her computer on the kitchen table and googled the State Department, Prishtina, Kosovo. She found the main number under Find Us. Even though her fingers cramped as if they had a mind of their own, she powered through and pressed each number.

"State Department Mission, Kosovo. How may I direct your call?"

"Andy Stephen, please," she said, shaking the tension out of her hands.

"Thank you. May I tell him who is calling, please?"

Margot jumped up and down in place. "Yes, it's Margot Hart." Her heart soared at the thought of hearing his voice.

"Thank you, Ms. Hart. One moment."

He got back late, so it made sense he'd go straight to work.

"Hello, Ms. Hart? Can you spell Stephen for me, please?"

She swallowed and slowed her words. She spelled out Andy's first and last names letter by letter, giving the woman on the other end of the phone Andy's full name this time.

"Hmm. We don't have a listing for anyone with the last name Stephen. This is the State Department. Are you sure you dialed the correct facility?"

"Donna Edwards? She's in HR." Buzzing started in her ears again.

"Let me see." The woman on the other end of the phone paused, then clicked her tongue. "No, I'm sorry, Ms. Hart. No Donna Edwards. Would you like me to connect you with HR?"

Margot ended the call without answering. Her entire body rattled. Had Andy lied to her? He must have. Why? How? Who is he? No, who was he?

Saliva filled her mouth and her stomach muscles curled, forcing bile into her throat. She ran to the toilet and emptied her guts.

Back in the kitchen, she swallowed two glasses of water and headed for a shower when she heard someone in the hall on the stairs.

Who could it be? Was Pavlovski right?

She froze, praying, willing the footsteps to pass her door. They sounded like regular steps. No tiptoeing. She loosened her chest and breathed easier, still listening. The boots grew louder and shuffled to a stop exactly at her door.

He was within two feet from her on the other side of her door. She covered her mouth in case he could hear her breathing. Too afraid to look through the peephole, she slinked six feet backward as blood gushed through the veins of her neck, thumping on her skull.

The footsteps shifted in place, then continued up the stairs.

You're overreacting.

Margot dismissed her panic and continued to peel off her clothes. She gingerly laid down on the couch, afraid if she left the living room, she wouldn't hear if he returned. As much as she wanted to sleep, she couldn't.

Go outside, get lost in a crowd.

At home, that'd be Lake of the Isles in Minneapolis.

You need your mom.

The footsteps returned, passed her door and descended the stairs. Safe at last, she exhaled and proceeded to her bedroom chest of drawers, pulling out a top, her favorite jeans, and socks.

Wait. Hear that?

She cocked her head toward the front of the apartment and stopped breathing to listen.

The boots thudded, pausing at her door again.

Eyes bulging with dread, she pursed her lips and waited.

A loud rap shook her every bone. More raps, louder. When her knees buckled, she grabbed the drawer to stay upright. "Ah. Who is it?" Her throat had dried and made her voice weak and hoarse.

"I'm here to see Andy. Open the door."

Margot's hair on her head bristled. This wasn't a request; it was a demand.

"Andy called me this morning, he said to meet him here."

If Andy was dead, this guy was a liar.

"Ah. He's still at work. What did you say your name was?" She crept to the door and peered through the peephole. It was no use. He was too close. All she saw was a blue hat.

"I don't mind. I can wait inside."

She watched the doorknob turning.

Thank God she had locked it. "Oh. No. Sorry. I cannot receive guests. He'll be back in an hour."

"Look, I've been walking a long time. Let me in, please. I need water."

She thought it best to use her kindest tone. "Please, you understand. He'll be here in an hour." She closed her eyes, praying the dead bolt would hold if he attempted to crash through the door.

He shuffled his feet, heavier this time. "In an hour." He clomped away.

Margot fell onto the sofa, trying to breathe.

Get the fuck out of here.

She wasn't sure if the voice in her head was speaking to her or to the unwelcome visitor.

~ 8 ~

CHAPTER EIGHT

January 21, 2013

Margot jammed her purse and a bottle of water in her backpack. After sneaking a look through the peephole at an empty hallway, she glided out the door and secured the dead bolt.

Before descending the stairs, she noticed she'd stepped in damp soil on the landing, and it had wedged in the crevasses on the bottom of her tennis shoes.

Typically Margot paid little attention to her shoes. But, today her sensibilities were heightened, and she was bombarded with minor details, adding to the confused mass muddling her mind.

She banged the back of her heels on the step and released some clumps of mud. Confident the rest would naturally fall away as she walked, she raced down the steps to the street.

The cool, fresh air helped to untangle her thoughts and her instincts told her to find anything mildly pleasant to lift her mood. The child she'd seen outside Valbona's came to mind. Her sweet, tiny voice. But, the truth was, seeing her again with her ragged clothes and those troubled eyes could shift her state of mind from one calamity to another. She groaned, straightened her back, and, right or wrong, decided she'd take that chance.

Keep a lookout for that blue cap.

Three blocks later, she found herself among a crowd of strangers laughing and talking while strolling along Mother Teresa Boulevard. It seemed chaotic to her, and she realized she had never felt so alone. She picked up the pace to escape the sense of despair and made her way to the Dragodon steps. As she got closer, the aroma of freshly baked bread wafted through the air and her empty stomach clenched. She followed her nose and stepped into the nearest bakery. Two girls with bright, open faces greeted her with curtsies.

Her shoulders relaxed. She curtsied back. "Hello, *për...shën...de-tje.*"

They both giggled. The taller one said, "Hello, madam, well done. How can I help you? We have savory pastries, or do you prefer bread?" She waved her arm over the display behind her.

Margot had never seen this many loaves of bread, all shapes and sizes, stacked four or five deep on five rows at least fifteen feet wide. "One loaf, sliced, please. You pick for me."

A girl pulled a sliced loaf and shoved it in a thin, white paper bag. "One half euro, please."

"Your English is perfect," Margot said, delighted that her mood was shifting.

"Thank you. My name is Lindeta, and this is Agnesa. We learned by watching television. And in our classes at Sars University."

Margot placed a five-euro banknote on the glass counter. "I'm Margot. Thank you, er, *Faleminderit.*"

"*Bye e mire,*" they said in unison.

"Here's your change. You are beautiful," Agnesa said. "You should be our teacher at Sars. Dr. Zekolli would love you."

"Very kind of you. Thank you," she said just to be polite, thinking this would be no use to her, because she and Andy would be establishing an NGO. But she had a second thought. Who knows what lies ahead? NGO or not, Agnesa's suggestion could be useful. She made a mental note: Sars University and Dr. Zekolli.

Back on the pavement and ten minutes later, Margot stood at the bottom of Dragodon, sipped her water, and began scaling the steps.

As she climbed, hordes of people came in single file, to keep from falling off the edge into the weeds. She noticed flat landings appeared every thirty steps or so and when the crowd thinned, she stopped and turned around to enjoy the view.

A tiny voice said, "Nice lady, euro, *ju lutem?*"

"It's you again." Margot smiled, sat, and patted the spot next to her, encouraging the little girl to sit, too.

"*Faleminderit.*" She scooted up from the brush.

Margot was careful not to touch her or get too close, although she felt the warmth of her body. She was filthy and the ammonia stench took her breath away, forcing her to sputter and gag.

The girl didn't seem to notice.

When she found control, Margot said, "Want a piece of bread?" She reached in the bag for a slice.

The child glanced toward the weeds before she took it.

It pained Margot to see her sad eyes circled in drab gray, and her dingy baby teeth. She looked to be four or five, a year younger than Sam when she died.

After a quick bite and an uneasy smile, she cupped her hand. "Nice lady. Euro, *ju lutem? Per familjen time?*"

Margot thought she recognized the word family.

"*Po. Familjen,*" the child said as her eyes darted toward the weeds and back again. "Euro, nice lady?" She stood and grinned.

Margot pointed to herself, "Margot." Then back to the girl. "You?"

She put her grubby finger on Margot's chest, "Margot." Then, back to herself, "Nora."

Margot had never been so close to feeling or smelling a child scrounging for money. Exchanging names made it even more personal now. Nora would haunt her day and night. It was a small price to pay for helping this poor child. "Nora, it is nice to meet you." She dropped two euros in the girl's hand. She noticed littered breadcrumbs sticking to the sweaty palm.

Nora jumped off the steps, disappearing into the weeds.

Could've been you or Sam, if not for the grace of God. Don't forget that, Margot.

With Nora out of sight, anxiety reentered her head. It had been a couple of hours since she left her apartment, but the thought of returning terrified her. The stranger could be lurking in an alley or hiding in the apartment stairwell.

Her jaw muscles tightened and pain shot through her gums, probably from gritting her teeth throughout the morning. Quickly dismissing the minor discomfort, she considered the stranger had possibly removed his hat and was following her this whole time. No matter. She decided to return to Mother Teresa Boulevard, and let go of her angst. Mingle with the crowd of people from all over the world. Revel in hearing the variety of languages. Try to change her perspective. Her feeling alone—that state of mind—served no purpose. Besides, who'd attack her in a public place?

Buck up and soldier on.

When she reached the bottom of the Dragodon steps, she drank the rest of her water just as her phone vibrated inside her backpack. Once she dug it out, she checked the caller ID.

Mom.

Margot swore she and her mom shared a psychic connection. A comforting smile filled her insides and spread across her face. Her mom's timing was perfect. And she was dying to talk with her, tell her everything. Her mom always knew what to do, and she'd make it all better. That's what mothers do.

Hey, sweetie. How's Prishtina? Having fun? Chat? Luv u.

God, she needed that, but if she told her about the stranger banging on her door, she'd have to tell her everything else. It made no sense not to, but she also knew her mom would ask questions that Margot wasn't ready to answer because she didn't know the answers herself.

She ducked into a narrow, empty street and stared at the call button, wondering how to begin without mentioning Andy or the blue cap guy? If she spoke the words, the mess would be more real. Plus, she'd scare her mother out of her senses.

Another text: **Miss u. Call me, honey.**

No avoiding it now. She sucked air and pushed the call icon.

"Margot. How are you?"

Margot's face locked into an involuntary ugly grimace and her lungs emptied, making it impossible to utter a single sound.

"Margot? Honey, what's wrong?"

She chastised herself for all the buck up soldier on self-talk.

"Take your time. Breathe, sweetie. I'm here." She sniffed.

Her throat squeaked but gradually, Margot found air and took three deep breaths.

The truth without the whole truth.

"Hi, Mom. Whew...sorry." She took her time and carefully spelled out the last few days: Andy's reaction to Nora, how his friend Grey barged in at dinner, and his unexpected trip to Macedonia.

"Well, what else? So far I don't understand why you're this upset."

"I know." She remembered, once again, her mother had great instincts and always saw through Margot's effort to skirt a problem. Shifting the focus, she said, "Nora reminds me of Sam. God, I miss her."

"Tell me."

"No, I can't go through it and, Mom, I know you can't do anything."

"I can listen."

"Who listens to you?"

The silence that followed said everything. Sherry epitomized emotional reservation, exactly the opposite of Margot's distress, which, at this moment, was literally tormenting her every thought, clamoring to reveal itself.

"It's okay, Margot. You have to grieve."

It was obvious her mother was doing what she often did: slip by her own grief, only to help Margot, her poor emotionally inept daughter, deal with hers. Well, it pissed her off on so many levels, all of which they had discussed *ad nauseam*.

"Margot, we've been over and over this. You have not allowed yourself to face Sam's death. Until you do, you'll be damaged."

Margot was in no mood or condition to repeat the old, tired truth: Sherry's need to counsel, or mother, was greater than her need to commiserate with her daughter, her friend, who had experienced this trauma along with her. And, even more unsettling, Sherry wasn't being honest with herself. Her mother hid behind her academic knowledge instead of facing the loss of Sam herself.

Margot regretted bringing up her sister, because it only served to paint herself into another familiar sorrowful corner.

"You know I'm right."

Margot caved into Sherry's insistence and breathed resignation.

"And you, Mom?"

She exhaled. "Every day, I miss her. I smell her baby skin, her hair. I'll never heal completely. I'm working through it."

"You didn't see her. I did. Her mangled, limp body. Her slashed face. The blood."

"My heart breaks for you. And for me. I've lost both of my wonderful daughters. Samantha to death. And you. I see you dive into self-loathing. It does not serve you."

"Please, not now. I'm in a strange country. And Andy. Well. I'm alone."

"I hear the anguish in your voice. Talk this out with Andy when he gets back."

Margot didn't respond.

"Sorry, Margot, I have to scoot. Let's talk again soon. I love you."

"I love you, too, Mom." Of course, she really did love her mother despite the complicated relationship that had developed owing to loss and grief. In her heart, she understood that they grieved, or denied grief, in their own individual ways. Sometimes Margot swallowed her difference with her mom. Other times, she just wasn't capable. This was one of those times, and it hurt. She let her tears flow in silence.

"Give Andy my love and promise me you'll have a long talk with him."

"I promise." She dropped her head and covered her face with her hands, flooded with shame for thinking poorly about her mom, and sadness for herself.

The call ended.

Promise.

~ 9 ~

CHAPTER NINE

January 21, 2013

Margot leaned against the brick wall and allowed her body to slide down, her butt landing on the broken asphalt. When she had ended the call with her mother, her cell went black for a nanosecond before returning to the home page: her favorite picture of Andy, laughing with his mouth wide open.

She wanted to cry. For Andy, for her sister, for withholding information from her mother, and for the promise she had made, which wasn't a promise. It was her passive agreement to avoid telling the truth. Translation: a lie.

But crying was too easy a release. She'd hold off; she wasn't finished punishing herself.

Her cell hummed, and a text popped up: *Forgot to ask. Seen the Cathedral yet? Have a great day. Love u.*

She texted back: *On my way. Great talk, Mom. Thnx. Love u miss u.*

As a single tear rolled onto her cheek, she wiped it away with the back of her hand, stood, packed her cell, and headed toward the Cathedral of St. Mother Teresa.

When Andy had first said he wanted to visit the Cathedral, Margot asked him why Catholics built a church in a Muslim country.

He had explained, before the Ottoman Empire ruled Kosovo, it was all Catholic and there were over ten cathedrals. Now, just the Mother Teresa Cathedral remained. During the Ottoman regime, most people converted to Islam, but some did not. He said Kosovo, with 1.8 million Muslims and around 60,000 Catholics, prided itself on having an open heart to everyone.

She remembered his exact words: "Let's embrace that philosophy. I want to open my heart to everyone, don't you?"

To agree with him was simple, and she had repeated his words to herself many times, hoping to open her heart. She swallowed hard.

If Andy is dead, you'll never get there.

Margot worked through the crowd, maneuvering around holes and loose tiles on the pavement. Soon, she was standing in front of the Cathedral, still under construction. Cloth mesh and scaffolding covered the unfinished portions. The brick, the red roof, and contrasting white stone were a refreshing contrast to the worn, unkempt, and damaged structures Margot had passed along the way.

The inside was magnificent, with gleaming white marble and intricate wood beamed ceilings framed by rows of stained glass windows. Additional enormous windows on the ground floor allowed gorgeous light to flood the vacant hall. And, most impressive, it was cloaked in total silence.

No pews, just rows of black folding chairs. She picked one, sat, lowered her head, closed her eyes, and focused on her breathing. Eventually, she was immersed in reverent grace.

Soft music, a flute and singing, flowed into the hall from the street. It reminded her of the time she, her mom, and her little sister attended church every Sunday, and sometimes Wednesdays.

The last time they were together, Sam was five. She recalled Sam's sweet, innocent face with her front teeth, barely pushing through her swollen pink gums.

It had been five years and Margot could still hear her voice. Her thoughts gravitated to their last conversation, their squabble, at the Eden's Ice Rink in Minneapolis. Despite the torment, Margot couldn't stop reliving it. She deserved to remember the horror. It was all her fault.

"Margot, please. I wanna stay," Sam said. When Margot saw the hurt in her little sister's big brown eyes, stained with tears, she was riddled with guilt. But she pushed it out of her mind. There'd be other times when Sam could stay.

"Come on, Sam. The scrimmage is over—"

"We won." Sam jumped up, sending her knitted hat askew.

"Look at yourself." Sam was her sweet cheerleader and very feisty, no more than forty pounds and less than four feet tall. She could be quite a force to deal with when she put her mind to something.

Margot fought back the proud smile working at the corners of her mouth and forced a stern face. "I mean business." she said with a cough, as she adjusted Sam's hat and stuffed her long brown curls in the back.

"Please? Please?"

Margot stooped, face to face with her. "Listen. I promise, there will be other ice hockey games—"

"I don't want to go. Let me stay." Her voice pitched to a pathetic, annoying wail.

Irritating stress rippled up Margot's spine. She lowered her eyes and her voice. "Stop it. You can't come with me; we're going to a bar. Now, you know my teammate Alice. She'll take you home."

Sam quieted her cries.

"Yeah, Sam," Alice said. "We'll stop for ice cream on the way. Let's go, honey."

"You sure it's okay, Alice?" Margot whispered. "I can take her home."

"No, no. You were the top scorer tonight. Go, celebrate. I love spending time with Sam."

"Thanks, I appreciate it. Okay, Sam, go on with Alice."

Sam pouted her bottom lip and didn't move. "Come with us, Margot," she pleaded.

"No. Now, I've enough, little girl. I'm warning you."

Sam stomped her boots in the crusty snow.

Margot raised her voice and pointed to the door. "I said go."

Alice took Sam's hand and started toward the exit.

The sound of her sobs echoed through the hall and were fixed in Margot's brain.

These years later, she still played that night repeatedly, trying to change it.

You could have let her stay. It would have been so easy. Why didn't you?

She teetered back and forth in her folding chair, trying to stifle Sam's voice.

"Are you all right, madam?" The man's voice stirred her from her memory. Margot wiped her face with her sleeve and bobbed her head as Sam's image faded away. She blinked a few times and looked up to see a thin, distinguished looking man, dressed in a black suit and tie.

"I'm sorry to disturb you," he said with a British accent. "However, I could not help but notice you. I heard you from the street. You appear distraught. Do you need medical attention?" He put a handkerchief in her hand.

"Oh, deep in thought, I guess." She stood and staggered.

He took her elbow and helped her sit again. "Are you alone? May I call someone for you?"

"No. Please. I'm fine," she said, forcing a narrow smile.

"Of course, forgive me, I am intruding. Please, my name is Edgar Leeds and here is my card. I will be outside if you need assistance now or even in the future. Perhaps I can help." He turned and walked away.

She waited for her bleary eyes to return to normal. An earthy sandalwood aroma filled her nose when she used his handkerchief to clean her face.

Who carries a cloth handkerchief anymore, and who gives it away? Especially white linen with black embroidered initials: EBL. "The charming Mr. Leeds," she said as she read his card: Edgar Bernard Leeds, Barrister. Beatrice Place with two locations: London and Prishtina. She stored his handkerchief and card in her backpack.

Her breath was effortless now. Guess she needed to remember and cry again, just as she had done many times since Sam died. Unfortunately, reliving it often made it worse.

When she got to the street, Edgar Leeds greeted her again, "My apologies. I waited, thinking you may need a ride home. May I call a taxi for you?"

Margot thought it was odd bumping into Mr. Leeds again, especially since he said he had been waiting.

She pursed her lips and frowned and opened her mouth to decline his offer when he shook his head. "Please," he said, "I can see my effort to provide assistance has caused you pause. Just let me say, we are here," he said, opening his arms and smiling gently, "and look, surrounded by many people. I promise you no harm." He cocked his head. "Just a small gesture of kindness and I'll be on my way."

He made sense and seemed very kind.

"Perhaps you can 'play it forward,' as they say."

She decided she was overreacting to Mr. Leeds because, at the moment, she was fearful of everything. And rightly so. But, she liked his smile. She did plan to walk home, but she realized she was too tired, physically and emotionally. A taxi ride sounded good. She breathed a surrendering thank you and smiled.

Without a word, he raised his arm, motioning for a nearby taxi. The driver pulled up to the curb. Edgar opened the rear door for her, and she scooted inside.

"Do you need change?" Edgar asked.

"No, thank you."

"It is my pleasure." He shut the door and stepped back from the curb.

"How much to Objekt, Vicianhum?" Margot asked the driver.

"Two euros," he said as he pulled on to the street.

Margot leaned back in her seat and breathed a long relief-filled sigh, glad to be driven home. The taxi was a good idea. She had made too much of accepting help from a stranger.

God, another stranger. If this keeps up, you are going to need a friend. You will need to ask for help. How will you know who to trust?

~ 10 ~

CHAPTER TEN

December 15, 2012

Cass and Jeremy prepared for their first conference with the Magpie team members. She wanted a video call to see faces, read expressions. Jer said calls were audio only, for security purposes and this was a professional group, not a social gathering. After their argument earlier this morning, no doubt they'd have lots of battles and she'd need to pick and choose. Video versus audio wasn't one of them. Still, she felt Jer's icy attitude, and it created tension that filled the entire basement.

"Good morning," Jer said. "Our purpose today is to get acquainted. I want to answer questions that are project related rather than technical details, unless you have problems you want to discuss. So, we've been working independently for...how many months now, Cass?"

Cass said they had been working day and night for ten months.

"Yeah, I've talked with each of you individually and now, it's time to come together as a team, get to know each other. I'll start. I'm Jeremy, former Anonymous project manager and superintendent. My cyberattack experience is comprehensive: Slowloris, Havij, Acunetix, and more. I'm the Magpie project manager. Juan?"

"Hello. Former Anon with expertise in networking and programming. Excel at problem solving and glad to be here."

"Hey, Juan!" a voice said. "You legal? I hear an accent."

"Yep, second generation, American-born Cuban," Juan said.

"Did you check that out, Jeremy? We can't have no illegals."

"Who's speaking, please?" Jer said.

Cass sensed Jer was treading lightly with whoever was being a jerk. She might have responded differently, without the please. Nip this crap in the bud at the get go. But she waited to see how Jer was going to handle this squabble, so soon in his effort to bring people together.

"It's Peter," the voice said. He went on to say he had been with Anonymous for thirteen years, starting on the ground floor. "I got more experience and expertise than all you put together. Now, my question: is Juan legit?"

Jeremy took his time to respond.

Cass had seen Jer do this before, pausing to create tension and demand order. He was pissed, and he wanted everyone to know it. His face had flushed to a rosy pink.

He straightened his back. "Well, Peter," Jer said, "I thought I had made this obvious during our individual conversations. Allow me to repeat: We are professionals. I handpicked you. I expect you to rise to the level of professionalism this job deserves. I require respectful questions and comments. If not, you'll be history—"

"Yeah—"

"Yeah, I'm not done. Do not interrupt me. Do you understand?" Although he raised his voice, it sounded calm and reverberated throughout the cellar.

Peter coughed and said, "Yes."

"Are you committed to this project and the decorum I require?"

"I am."

Cass felt her temperature rising. She wasn't sure she liked Peter.

"Juan is on board. We are lucky to have him. I don't care if he's purple. He's got what we need and if you want to question my judgment, we'll do that offline. Anybody got a problem with Juan, say it now."

No one spoke.

Jer held the silence longer, increasing the pressure.

"Cass, you're up."

She drew a deep breath and said her expertise included reconnaissance and the application attack phase.

"Cass is my comanager," Jer said. "She's very knowledgeable and has a good head on her shoulders."

Cass wasn't no damn *co*. They had never discussed that. Besides, Jer treated her as his subordinate, and further, he micromanaged her every move and questioned her judgment, working to knock that good head off her shoulders. Whipping boy was a better descriptor.

"All right, Claudia?" Jer said.

"I'm an Anonymous defector. Similar to Cass, I'm experienced in reconnaissance, networking, and programming."

"Excellent."

"Excuse me, this is Peter. I honestly don't mean to interrupt, but I got a question."

"Go ahead."

"Well, since you say you handpicked us, I want to know your criteria. Specifically, how did you do it?"

"Fair question, Peter. I contacted a former Anonymous colleague and asked her to find seasoned people with specialized hacking skills. People with experience in complicated schemes and with a willingness to commit to a high stakes project. Each had to be a team player, trustworthy, and squeaky clean with no prior arrests. I also accessed Hacker for Hire with the same criteria. I got ten names back."

"Yeah, question is how could you be certain the ten people truly met those criteria? I mean, for one thing, I didn't submit any information regarding arrests. And, how do you determine our risk tolerance? That's real psychology stuff."

"Yeah, I'm curious," Claudia said. "While I understand risk aversion in the financial world, it escapes me in this arena."

"Okay," Jer said. "I didn't have the time or wherewithal to test trustworthiness. So, I went to the top."

"Who is that?" Peter said.

"Prominent individuals in Russia. They scrutinized everything: your background, personality, family. Five made the cut, and I followed up with personal conversations and chose you three."

It was so quiet Cass swore she heard the electrical current running through the basement. Sweat pooled at the bottom of her feet.

"Shit! I'm overwhelmed," Peter said. "I'm steeped in my portion of Magpie, and when I got deeper into details, I realized this project was massive. Well, I didn't even consider it. Damn. I don't know what to say."

No one spoke.

Finally, Juan said, "What's this about family? That sent chills up my spine."

"Each of you has had family members who have had serious health issues. And, the health insurance companies denied their claims. My dad, he died while trying to get the insurance company to agree to pay for immunotherapy." His voice cracked. "They refused his appeals. I believe his stress level contributed to a quicker death." He choked. "Give me a minute."

He turned off his mic and dropped his head.

Cass bit her lip and put her hand on his shoulder. She watched him close his eyes and shake his head, trying to get control of his emotions. As pissed as she had been at him all morning, she had to do something to help. "I got this," she said.

She turned the mic on. "Cass here. To be clear, we are attacking the United States' health insurance industry. They're making millions and sucking the lives out of the rest of us. They're our common enemy. You got burned, bad. You've lost fathers, sisters, brothers, nieces, nephews." She was out of breath. "Which speaks to your motivation and ultimate commitment."

Even though no one spoke, Cass sensed anguish emanating from the computer screen.

A voice said, "I hate them. I watched my newborn nephews die. A simple operation could have saved them. It wrecked my sister's family. She couldn't live with her pain and guilt. They are responsible for her suicide, and I'm the one who has to live with it."

"That's you, Peter," Jer said, having found composure. "Let's turn hate into action and destroy their billing systems. They'll lose millions of dollars every single day, day after day."

Silence.

"Juan here. Peter. Man, I'm sorry. It shouldn't be this way. I say let's do it."

"Okay. If you're ready to move on, we can go to updates."

"I'm for moving on, and note, at some point, I want to hear from Juan and Claudia. About your families," Cass said.

"I'm not ready to share," Claudia said.

Juan said he wasn't either.

Cass said she'd put it on the agenda for their next meeting.

"Let's review where we are," Jer said. "We'll use a link that will automatically transfer our required files to the system and a toolkit that will conceal our files."

"Further," Cass said, "The virus can transmute itself and we'll recognize how and when that transmutation trigger takes place."

"It's designed to go dormant and will appear eradicated," Jer said. "Questions?"

No one responded.

"Updates," Jer said.

"Claudia here. I'm seventy-five percent done with the transmutations."

"Perfect," Jer said.

"It's Juan. I'm working on facilitating dormancy. That is, when finding nothing viable, the virus changes its course and disappears. Then it's undetectable. I'm around forty percent complete."

"Regarding payment," Cass said, "we're getting big bucks, deposited in a Singapore bank. They haven't determined the total dollar amount because we're also set up for bonuses and incentives to complete early. It'll be at least a hundred thousand dollars."

"Each?" a voice said.

"Yep, for each deliverable, to each person," Cass said.

"Damn," Peter said.

"Big job. Big money," Jer said.

"Excuse me. Claudia here. I want to go back. It's Cass. How did you choose her? Just curious."

"Cass and I have worked together for years. She meets the criteria. That's it. Thanks, you guys."

The call ended.

Jer said, "That went well."

"Peter is going to be a problem. Got a horrible attitude and his comment about Juan was bullshit."

"Not everyone is as perfect as you." He chuckled.

"God! What is your problem and why do you think that's funny?" She boiled inside.

"Sorry, that was uncalled for. Delete. I meant to say he'll settle in."

"Deleted. Let's be honest, your attempt at humor is caustic and disrespectful. Stop it. Besides, we don't laugh together anymore." She glared at him. "Anyway, do racists settle in?"

"At one hundred thousand dollars a deliverable they do."

"I disagree. Make a note of it." She grabbed her coat and scrambled up the stairs to the kitchen door.

"Wait, Cass."

She stopped.

"This morning, our spat. You're right. I got to trust you and Maureen. I'm sorry." He smiled at her.

"To say you're sorry is a start, assuming you're sincere, though I'm not convinced at this point because I'm still smarting from our *spat*, as you call it. Look, as your pseudo *co*, I remind you: I'm not the enemy. We have to come together, despite your lack of confidence in me, my work, or our contacts." She opened the door and stepped into the kitchen.

"You're off too soon. Can you sit?" Mrs. Bloom said.

She nodded.

"Before you leave, dear."

This sounded serious and her shoulders tightened. She hoped Mrs. Bloom hadn't been privy to conversations from the cellar. "Sure."

"Listen, honey. I see you're on edge. Don't worry, I'm fine. Sure, I miss my Raymond."

"Me, too." Cass's shoulders softened. "I love you, Mrs. Bloom."

They hugged and said their goodbyes.

On her way home, she revisited the conference call. While she agreed the call had gone well, her gut said Peter was trouble and Jer's blind spot. If he proved to be a weak link, how could she make Jer see?

CHAPTER ELEVEN

January 21, 2013

The street was empty when the taxi pulled up to Margot's apartment building. She remembered how she loved sitting shoulder to shoulder with Andy on the sofa with their feet intertwined on the coffee table, sipping red wine, and musing about their exciting future together. His muscular arms safely surrounded her. He made sure her legs were on top of his to keep her comfortable, because these conversations went on for hours, with high-pitched enthusiasm, laughter, and, ending, of course, with sex.

Dear God, please bring Andy home to me.

Now, since the stranger had threatened to enter their apartment, she dreaded entering it again, and she hated that.

The cab stopped. Her knuckles bulged as she grabbed the door handle, worried she'd see a blue baseball cap. Or worse, worried she wouldn't see it because the stranger was hiding in the shadows.

Her bladder burned and if she didn't get to a bathroom soon, she was sure to wet her pants. So, she gingerly wriggled in her seat, positioning herself to scan the street. Holding her breath, she leaned forward toward the front seat and peered through the windshield first, then the passenger side window. The sound of the front car door opening and closing startled her until she realized it was her driver.

He glanced at her with a comforting smile, and he clicked her door open. "*Falminderit*, madam," he said, extending his arm.

She put two euros in his hand and grabbed his wrist at the same time. With him still in tow, she stepped up to the front door and said, "Wait, please."

He nodded.

Margot let go of his wrist and dug in her purse for her key, chastising herself for not retrieving it earlier. At that moment, someone from inside the building pushed the door open toward her. She frowned at the driver, signaling him to stay.

"Hello, Mrs. Stephen—"

It was Ismet, her landlord. "Thank goodness, it's you." Relieved to see a familiar face, she released a puff of air, lips quivering.

"Ok to leave, madam?" the driver asked.

"Yes, thank you."

"Sorry to report. Someone in your apartment," Ismet said. "Come. We take elevator."

His words *someone in your apartment* stung her. Her legs wobbled as she steadied herself on Ismet's arm.

He said he had heard unusual noises coming from her apartment earlier in the day. When he stood at her apartment door, he said, he heard banging, thumping sounds. "Not lady. Too strong. Must be Andy, I think."

He added he knocked, and the commotion continued until he rapped harder a second time, when the apartment went quiet. "I say loud, Mrs. Stephen? Andy? No answer. I use my key, open door. Man jump to fire escape and run."

"Did you see him?" She trembled. "Was he wearing a blue baseball cap?"

"Didn't see. Please, sorry. My apartments, very safe. In ten years, only happened three times. I wait for you, tell me what he steal. Then we call police."

When Ismet opened the door, the sight stunned her. Dishes, pots, pans, and flatware covered the floor. Clothes were strewn everywhere. Her favorite white silk blouse, a gift from Andy, was twisted and caked with muddy footprints.

She gasped, "I have to go," she said as she ran to the bathroom, slammed the door shut, yanked her pants down, and sat. Perspiration drenched her body as she waited for her bladder to empty. As she leaned forward on her knees, sweat dripped from her nose and top lip. She had never known this level of intense angst. And she was here, facing this completely alone. With no one to help her through it or comfort her. Finished, she washed her hands. splashed her face with water, inhaled, and returned to the front room.

They had emptied the closets and drawers. The pillows and mattress were sliced open, and pulled off the box frame onto the floor. Trails of cotton batting entwined with overturned lamps, canned goods from the pantry, and her framed pictures of Sam and her mom.

"God, how can I tell what's missing?" she said, covering her mouth and sliding to the floor. At the same time, she scanned the debris for the photo of Andy in the silver frame with the birds.

Ismet took off his beret and shook his head. "So sorry. Look terrible. Don't be sad. It will be okay." He opened his mouth to speak again, then didn't. "Okay, I be quiet and wait for you."

Margot heard his words but not their meaning, because her mind whirled with thoughts of Andy and her world tearing apart.

Finally, Ismet broke the silence. "I bring new mattress and pillows from storage," he said, as he put his hat on his head and began grabbing clothes and putting them on the flat boards of the bed. Hangers fell loose and dried clumps of mud rattled on the floor. "Mr. Stephen be home soon?"

Margot tightened her lips and shrugged one shoulder, staring at the pile of dresses and pants jumbled into a ball of colors and textures. She recognized Andy's Stanford T-shirt coiled around his brown corduroys. The sight added to the feeling of despair settling under her ribs.

No one was going to be home soon.

"Not good to sit and look at mess," he said as he took her elbow and gently pulled her to her feet. "Come, work together to clean up. Better for you."

"I suppose so. Thank you, Ismet."

"Mrs. Stephen, where is Andy?"

"He'll be back soon," she said, as she struggled to hang a skirt in the closet, missing the rod several times. Frustration roared through her body as she jammed the hanger inside with such force, it got stuck. When she jerked it and it refused to come out, she resorted to violent yanking and growling.

"Please me." Ismet pulled his flashlight from his tool belt and pointed it inside the closet. "I see." He dislodged the hanger and chunks of debris fell to the floor. After dusting himself off, he reached in and pulled out a bundle covered in white dust. "Is yours?" he said, handing it to her.

She tilted her head and grimaced. It was Andy's scarf, the Malevich from his father, wrapped around a hard object.

Ismet cleaned off the coffee table, Margot set it down, and they squatted to get closer to the object.

"New hole. New plaster. See? Soft," he said, holding a piece between his finger and thumb.

Silence.

Margot drew a deep breath with her eyes fixed on the bundle, knowing she needed to decide what to do at this very moment. She was alone. She didn't know if Andy would be back. Grey was gone and she wondered if he'd actually return, and besides, she detested him. She had no one. The only person she might trust and perhaps ask for the help she needed immediately was standing in front of her. She had known Ismet for two days and under normal circumstances, she'd never call anyone a friend within forty-eight hours. These, however, were not normal circumstances. At that moment, in the face of untold risks, she made her choice. "You must promise me, whatever this is, it is our secret." Her voice shook.

He blinked, perplexed. "Why? You in trouble, Mrs. Stephen?"

She was clammy now, and her breathing turned sharp with quick, shallow pants. "I don't know. A chance I could be."

"Andy do this? Hide from thief?"

She shuddered.

He rubbed his face and eyes, and rose to his feet, spreading them wide apart. He pumped out his chest and folded his arms. "Mrs. Stephen, I help till Andy return. Whatever trouble is, I protect you."

If Margot hadn't been so terrified, she might have laughed. He looked like Superman without the cape. Unfortunately, this was no comic book story, and Ismet meant what he said. She needed help and thanked God for Ismet. "Bless you, my friend."

She began removing the scarf.

"Ah. Lovely filigree," he said.

It was the box Andy bought at Valbona's Restaurant. She dusted it with her hand, blew on it, and bits of plaster buried in the crevices flew to the floor.

Locked, she turned the filigree box over, hoping to find the key taped to the bottom. "No key. Shit. Where could it be? I'll never find it in this mess."

Ismet pulled a knife out of his pocket, "I open?"

With her voice quaking, she said, "Go ahead."

With a quick flip of the blade, the lock broke. Margot rushed to turn it over. Two tightly folded notes fell to the table. One had milky blue ink stains melted at the corners. The other was plain.

Her hands trembled as she unfolded the first one. It was a handwritten letter dated 20 July 2012, signed, *Lyubov*, Mama. Margot pointed to the signature, "Is this Albanian?"

Ismet shook his head. "Russian, possible."

"Makes sense. His mother and father are Russian, second generation."

Margot had spoken with Andy's mother once over the phone after Andy's proposal. They were planning to meet her in New York City on their first trip back to the States.

God, what will you tell her?

The second note was taped and labeled "My Margot" in Andy's handwriting. Margot held it to her chest and brought the scarf up to her face. Smelling Andy, his body, his musky cologne, she tottered back and forth with muffled sobs.

A minute passed.

"You must move from here," he said. "You say State Department. Maybe they help?"

Margot didn't respond; it was too complicated. She put both letters back in the filigree box. She'd read Andy's letter by herself, after she had time to prepare for the worst.

"Not to push you out. New locks can make safe. Truth, man get in if he want. Understand?"

"I'll stay here tonight but I have no place to go."

"Don't worry. I know a place. Not as nice," he grinned. "Different location."

"Yes, another location." Her mind spaced out.

"Okay. Sorry. Come. Back to work?" he said, helping her up to standing.

They worked for hours until most everything was in its place. Ismet brought in a new mattress and pillows. "Okay. Finished. Please, my number." He handed her his card. "Call for anything. I here immediately. I stay in the apartment below. For your safety. Or better, I stay here, and you sleep in the apartment below?"

"No, no. He wouldn't dare come back. Ever. You scared him," she said mostly to convince herself, denying the truth to calm her rattled nerves.

He nodded, dropped his head, and blushed.

"*Faleminderit*, Mrs. Stephen."

"Thank you, Ismet. Please call me Margot."

"*Faleminderit*, Margot." He beamed. "Good night."

As soon as she locked the door, she got the scarf, sat on the mattress, and opened Andy's letter.

Dearest Margot,

If you are reading this, you have found me out. Maybe you cleaned closets. More likely, I'm late coming back from Macedonia, and you became impatient, digging for answers.

Yes, I hid this box in the closet. I wasn't ready to share its contents, especially the letter from my mother.

Well, you probably know by now, I don't work for the State Department. My work in Kosovo and Macedonia is compelling and of greater importance than any work I'd do for the government.

I'm sorry. I couldn't tell you the truth. Not until I completed this task in Macedonia.

You might think you deserve better than me. Dear God, I pray not.

Please don't do anything rash. I promise, when I return, I will explain everything, and we'll get started on that NGO to get those children off the streets into safe homes. You inspire me, Margot.

All my love,

Andy.

P.S. Shall we get married in Mother Teresa Cathedral? I hope you have visited it by now.

Margot tucked his scarf under her pillow and cried herself to sleep.

~ 12 ~

CHAPTER TWELVE

January 22, 2013

The time stunned Margot when she woke: 8 a.m. Sheer exhaustion caused her to sleep through the entire night. She peeked out of her bedroom window and saw the alley teeming with people. Margot envied them. They were going on with their lives, oblivious to her trauma.

Would her life go on?

The break-in was devastating—it was the act of a stranger intruding into her personal space and pilfering through her possessions. It was a psychological violation. It shook her world, leaving her in a constant state of worry with a clouded sense of self, wondering if she could handle her wrecked reality and survive.

Andy said he loved her because she was a strong, self-reliant woman. Could he love her now, if he were alive?

Margot reached for his letter on the nightstand and read it again. His words were tinged with concern, and yet full of hope for their future together. She put it away, pulled Andy's scarf from under her pillow, and pressed it to her nose, breathing in his memory again. She'd never tire of his scent.

"Morning, Mrs. Stephen?" Ismet said through the door, followed with a quick tap. "Good news. I find an apartment. Excellent location."

"Give me a few minutes, please?" After folding the scarf and storing it and the box in her backpack, she rushed to the bathroom, brushed her teeth, splashed water on her face, and pulled her chestnut-brown hair streaked with subtle blond highlights into a ponytail, catching her reflection in the mirror. "Good to leave this apartment and start anew where you'll be safe. Remember to smile, Margot. It can lift your mood."

"Come in," she said, opening the door and shoving her feet into her tennis shoes. "This is great. When can I move?"

"Today. I work fast. Truck and movers come soon."

As she started to shut the door, she heard a familiar voice from down the hall. "Hello. Top of the morning."

Margot turned and was shocked to see Mr. Leeds. He'd showed up unannounced, and it was definitely unsettling. "Hello. Ah. I'm surprised to see you. How did you know where I lived?"

"Well, Margot." He leaned on one foot and smiled. "I was present when you gave the taxi driver your address last night."

She covered her face with her hand at the thought of unknowingly revealing her address to anyone within earshot. "Oh. This is embarrassing. You heard me and committed it to memory?"

"I sense I have made you uncomfortable. Forgive me."

"Well, yes, to be honest." She swallowed.

"Excuse me." Ismet squinted his eyes at her. "You know Mrs. Stephen, sir?"

She sensed Ismet's distrust. "Mr. Leeds, this is my landlord. Actually, he's my good friend, Ismet. Ismet, this is Mr. Leeds."

They shook hands.

"Please, call me Edgar. You as well, Margot."

"Someone broke into my apartment yesterday." Margot exhaled. "I'm a little afraid to stay here now." Even though "little" was an understatement, she wasn't willing to reveal her vulnerability in front of Edgar.

"Of course you are. This is terrible, my dear; are you all right? What can I do to help?"

"Ismet found me a new place."

"Thank you, Ismet. We need to help our Margot, do we not?"

"Our Margot" sounded too familiar to her, but she let it go.

Ismet didn't answer.

"You could not have known, Margot, but I am familiar with excellent apartments near USAID. I am aware of one that is currently available. It has a lovely view of Dragodon and Prishtina."

"Well, Ismet. He's—"

"Mrs. Stephen, these apartments, better for you. Suitable location. USAID security guards always there. Very good choice."

"Ah, then," Edgar said. "Give me a moment to confirm. Pardon me." He stepped on to the street with his cell at his ear.

Confident that Edgar was far enough away he couldn't hear her, Margot lowered her voice and spoke to Ismet, reminding him he'd lose rent money.

"No worries. Is good for you. We are friends. Stay friends. I get boxes from storage now."

Edgar returned. "I arranged it, and I took the liberty of requesting grocery delivery, within the hour. With your permission, I will help you pack before Ismet's truck arrives."

"This is...I can't thank you enough," she said, swallowing hard. How was she to pay for everything with less than ten euros?

"Now, now, my friend," Edgar said.

"Andy have new apartment. Big surprise when he return." Ismet said. "He will be happy, yes?"

Ismet's words jolted her, and her eyes brimmed with tears. Andy may never return.

"Why women cry when happy, Margot?" Ismet chuckled.

"'The most efficient waterpower in the world is women's tears,'" Edgar said. "That's a line from playwright Wilson Mizner." He tipped his chin, with an air of confidence.

Margot didn't comment, even though they both were wrong.

"Hmpf." Ismet wheezed and sneered. "We have work."

They entered the apartment, packed clothes in her suitcases, and loaded the cardboard boxes.

When the truck arrived and Edgar busied himself supervising the movers, Ismet took Margot aside. "Need anything, must call, please. This Edgar Leeds, a good man?"

"I think so. Look what he has done for me this morning. Why?"

"Hmm. We say *kontrollin*. You say pushy?"

"True. I think he means well. He's kindhearted."

"Maybe we give him chance. Pushy not always bad, correct?"

"Correct. Pushy isn't always bad. Thank goodness. If that were true, I'd have no friends. I've been known to be very pushy." She chuckled for the first time in days.

"You have me."

"Yes, I do." She wanted to kiss his furry cheek but thought better of it. So she grabbed his hands, squeezed, and looked into his eyes. "You have been terrific to me."

"You, as well. Here, refund," he said in a soft tone, placing a roll of euros in her hand.

"No—"

"Yes. I not accept 'no.'" His face brightened.

"This is sweet, you two, and I am sorry to interrupt," Edgar said with a hint of disapproval. "I am afraid I must go. It was lovely to meet you, Ismet. Is it all right if I drive you to your new apartment, Margot? The truck will follow."

"It's fine." She didn't feel like she could decline his offer. After all, he had found her a new apartment with groceries. Besides, Ismet had done enough for her today. She tossed her backpack over her shoulder.

"Here," Edgar said, grabbing her pack, "let me—"

"No." She jerked backward.

Edgar frowned and wrinkled his nose.

"Sorry, Edgar."

"Wait, please. With permission. Address of new apartment please?" Ismet said.

Edgar narrowed his eyes. He gave a look to Margot for permission.

"Of course. Thank you, Ismet," she said, sensing the tension between them and ignoring it. She had enough problems of her own.

"It's ninety-eight Ismail Qemali, apartment two-oh-two B."

"*Faleminderit.* Please, check when you unpack, what missing. I report to police."

As they drove away, Edgar said, "I offer a bit of friendly advice. Ismet may be a delightful person, however, you do not know who you can trust in Prishtina. Or in Kosovo, for that matter. I am not confident he is credible."

She didn't respond.

"Accordingly, he was responsible for your safety. He is accountable. You must understand, that is the reason for his not calling the police. That is, he owns the building, and the authorities will cite him for negligence."

Unless this was Kosovo law, she'd have to file a complaint against Ismet for this to occur.

Never.

"I know," she said, acquiescing. She didn't agree but was too tired to debate with him.

~ 13 ~

CHAPTER THIRTEEN

January 23, 2013

It seemed all was right with the world when the morning sunlight streamed through Margot's window, tickling her eyelashes. As she opened her eyes, reality set in and her momentary bliss gave into a high-pitched frenzy. She jolted out of bed and opened her backpack, wondering where she could hide the filigree box and scarf in this new apartment. Her suitcases and boxes stacked against the bedroom wall waited for her, compelling her to unpack and create order. An organized environment might help to straighten the havoc in her head.

She zipped the backpack closed and tucked it in the vanity under the bathroom sink. As she reached for her toothbrush, she stopped, amazed at the luxurious bathroom: gray ceramic tile, two sinks, plump towels.

Her mind had blurred with exhaustion last night, and she remembered falling into bed as soon as she had locked the door. Nothing else. She hadn't even looked at her new apartment. The suitcases could wait until she checked out her new digs.

The wood floor in her bedroom carried through the hall beyond the kitchen and living room. She stopped to admire the floor lamp next to the sofa. It looked to be an authentic Tiffany with a large multicolored glass shade and a massive base.

After checking out two more bedrooms and a guest bathroom, she went back to the kitchen and opened the refrigerator to find it chock full of every food she could imagine. In addition, she found a loaded pantry, including peanut butter, her favorite gluttonous comfort food.

The boxes could wait until she had a bite of peanut butter.

She grabbed the jar, found a tablespoon in the drawer, and dug out an enormous scoop. When she plunked on the sofa, air escaped from beneath the cushions, blowing a small piece of paper off the coffee table to the floor. She picked it up and turned on the lamp for more light.

Welcome to your new home. The Wi-Fi info is in the top drawer of the desk. Take your time to get settled. Let's have dinner soon. Ever yours, Edgar.

"Dear Mr. Leeds," she said, as her heart warmed. The apartment was near the USAID, with armed guards and surveillance cameras, 24-7, according to Ismet. She was safe thanks to him. To admit the appearance of Mr. Leeds was divine intervention seemed dramatic. Her meeting him was a stroke of luck, no doubt about it. She brushed her forehead to smooth the last remnants of a frown.

Peanut butter jar in hand, she stepped to the balcony, looking for guards. They were incognito, and she hoped never to see them, knowing if she did, she'd feel like a prisoner.

The Dragodon steps were within her view and no doubt Nora was on the job, begging for money. Margot had her rent refund, but no coins. She swallowed another scoop of peanut butter, thinking Nora probably loved peanut butter as much as she and Sam did. She returned to the kitchen looking for bread to make sandwiches for Nora and found none.

**

The bell jingled as Margot opened the door to the bakery. Lindeta and Agnesa greeted her with wide smiles and began chattering right away, lifting her spirits higher.

Margot pointed to a loaf of bread and asked where they had taken English classes.

"Elementary school." Agnesa said, pulling the loaf from the shelf.

"Not at Sars University?"

"They waived our English language classes because we both scored in the ninetieth percentile on the TOEFL. Our English improved when we started classes at the University," Agnesa said with an air of pride.

"Classes, textbooks, our homework, everything is in English, and students must learn fast to succeed. Why? Do you want to teach there? Agnesa and I agree you would be a wonderful teacher," Lindeta said, placing the bread in a bag.

She scratched her head and handed Lindeta a five-euro banknote. Teaching at a college intimidated her, and besides, she didn't have English as a Second Language certification. "*Faleminderit*, sweet ones."

Lindeta giggled and returned her change.

Margot pushed the door open, and the jingling bell caught her eye just as she stepped on to the pavement directly in the path of another pedestrian. The collision almost knocked her off balance. Her quick footwork saved her. "Oh, sorry," she said as she checked her squashed loaf of bread.

"No, no. *Më vjen keql.* I'm at fault."

It was Edgar Leeds.

"Margot. This is a lovely coincidence. Do you have time for coffee?"

"Of course." As hard as it was to put off seeing Nora, coffee with Edgar was the least she could do to show her appreciation.

"Excellent. Come with me to my favorite spot for coffee in Prishtina." He took her elbow and steered her down two blocks to a small café. "Macchiato?" he asked, urging her to sit.

She nodded and watched him walk to the counter. He was an attractive man, dressed to perfection with a luminous white shirt, starched and flawless, and classic black shoes buffed to a high sheen. He reached inside his suit coat breast pocket for his wallet. No saggy back pocket in his pristine and finely creased slacks. He turned back to her and smiled.

"Here you are," he said, placing her coffee in front of her. "Tell me, how are you?"

"Good, I'm good. The apartment and food...Well, I cannot thank you enough."

He shook his head and smiled.

"Please," she said, "tell me about you, your work."

"Of course." He explained his law practice began in London, then he became involved in an NGO that focused on psychosocial treatment and rehabilitation for women in Prishtina.

"What does that mean?"

"It means we assist women who are suffering with long-term illnesses and other maladies. We offer housing, healthcare, counseling, transportation, training, and employment. At Beatrice Place, we strive to be a one-stop shop. However, we are often limited due to lack of funds. Therefore, I devote much of my time to friend raising and, of course, fund-raising. Frankly, I am good at it and as a result, we have generous sponsors. Here in Kosovo, I owe my success to my friend Eris Hoti. Other countries support us, as well. Of course, there is never enough; therefore, I am constantly looking to acquire additional money."

"Only women? No children?" she said, thinking of Nora again.

"We allow children, of course, only a few, unfortunately. Many of the children stay with extended families. Our lack of space precludes us from offering childcare."

"I see. Question: What is the London address on your card?"

"Beatrice Place began in London, and we opened a similar service in New York City. Eris Hoti was instrumental in my coming to Kosovo. You might say we are an international organization; however, currently, Beatrice Place, here in Prishtina, is our only facility. We measure our success by the number of women who leave Beatrice Place and live healthy, independent, productive lives. We have done well and hope to expand to Serbia and Russia."

Unfortunately, his chatter had turned into droning and, meanwhile, her mind had shifted to counseling. He could be helpful and suggest a grief counselor. Dare she confide in him?

"Yes. Mr. Leeds, I'd—"

"Margot. I am British, however, I'm truly much less formal than you might think. Call me Edgar, please. What if I called you Ms....Oh my, I don't know your last name."

"Crazy, eh? With everything you've done for me. It's Hart."

"Hart? Perfectly fitting. I believe you have a big heart."

They laughed.

She was more at ease now. "Well. Edgar. This may be totally inappropriate," she said, pressing her lips together.

He tilted his head and smiled, sipping his coffee.

Margot hesitated, then blurted. "It's my sister, Sam. She died in a car accident when she was five years old."

Edgar's eyes widened, then he leaned in closer, with a concerned frown.

Margot told him the entire story, from the argument after the ice hockey game, to her shouting at her sister to leave with her teammate Alice, including the shocking call from the police. She spared him the intimate details for his sake and because she didn't know him well enough to share that level of vulnerability.

"Oh, Margot, how dreadful," he said, eyebrows knitted with concern.

"Sam was on the ground," she said. "I can't describe it now. Too horrific." Her stomach turned, and she closed her eyes to stop the image from entering her head.

Edgar reached across the table and took her hands.

She pulled away.

"Let me, please. A gesture to comfort you."

She thought back, trying to remember the last time she let anyone console her. Other than her mom or Andy, she had refused compassion. She was the one asking for Edgar's help and refusing his kindness was simply rude.

"All right," she said. His light touch turned tender, and her stomach settled into an easy purr. He offered his handkerchief, and she dabbed her eyes and wiped her nose. "I have dreams. It just happens, without warning. Always the same: Sam's looking at me, pleading for my help."

"Did this happen at the Cathedral?"

She nodded.

"I'm sorry. I see the depth of your grief and I hear the pain in your voice."

"Yes," she said, clearing her throat and sitting up straighter. "Can you recommend a grief counselor? Seems you would know people."

"Indeed I do. I know superior grief therapists. The Kosovo War touched so many and rather than dealing with their emotions, they repressed them. Pain hemorrhages until people face the truth. I experienced this when my wife, Loretta, died. I think this is where you are."

She nodded. This was her mother's message, too.

"Are you here alone?"

His question jolted her insides. She couldn't discuss Andy. Not yet.

"No, my boyfriend is here."

"Very good. I'm honored you shared this with me, Margot. I hope you consider me a part of your support system."

She breathed a long sigh and grinned.

"Brilliant. Now, finish your macchiato. I'm sorry, I must go. Until next time, you have my card. Call me and we will talk more. I sense you need to share with your boyfriend. And I want to meet the lucky man who has stolen your heart, Ms. Hart," he chuckled at himself. "Can I meet him soon?"

"Of course, when he returns from traveling," she said squirming in her seat. "He's off to Croatia on business."

"Dubrovnik?"

"Yes," she said with a cough.

"I love Croatia. The Dalmatian coast is stunning. And, so, with your permission, I will gather names of the best counselors for you to consider." He politely kissed her hand and dashed out the door.

Margot took a deep, cleansing breath and residual heaviness left her body, replaced with a sense of well-being, despite her lies. She had no choice but to lie.

As she drank her macchiato, she opened the bread and pulled the jar of peanut butter from her purse and made two sandwiches, while smiling at the curious servers. Just as she prepared to put the sandwiches in her purse, a waiter brought paper napkins. "Madam. For wrapping."

"*Falminderit*," she said as she wrapped the sandwiches and stored them in her purse. She smiled and rushed outside, careful not to crash into another pedestrian.

Within a few minutes, Margot stood at the steps, searching for Nora. It wasn't long when she found her perched on a landing approximately 10 feet away. Margot skipped below and joined her.

"*Përshëndetje*, Nora."

"Hello. Euro, nice lady?"

Two girls with bright faces hopped up from the bushes.

Margot's heart soared when she saw the other children. "Hello. And yes, euro. I have food for you first." She pulled out the sandwiches, ripped both in half and handed three to the girls.

Her friends began eating right away. Nora, however, only smelled the peanut butter.

"She no eat," one girl said, devouring her sandwich and reaching to Margot for the last half. She looked to be five or six years old and wore plastic purple flip flops, a pink-patterned skirt, plaid T-shirt, and a coat, at least two sizes too big.

"Yes, here, sweetheart. You can have it. What is your name?"

"Me, Arita. She, Vlora," she said, pointing to the other child. "Nora sick."

After Margot gave Vlora a banana she tried to give Nora a banana, too, but Nora pushed it away.

When Nora allowed Margot to cup her tiny face in her hands, she realized how sick and listless Nora was. Her eyelids drooped, and when Margot pulled her on to her lap, her skin was hot. Perspiration drenched her filthy hair, and her panties, soaked with urine, dampened her jeans. Margot didn't care. She was too distraught and didn't know what to do. Nora needed to see a doctor, but Margot couldn't just take her.

Suddenly a stern female voice shouted from the weeds. "Euros."

The children jerked and Nora, startled with newly found energy, slipped from Margot's lap.

Margot gave Vlora every coin she had, and the kids retreated into the brush.

Before she had a chance to think, her cell vibrated. It was a text from Grey.

~ 14 ~

CHAPTER FOURTEEN

January 23, 2013

Michael's cell rang. Dugal, again.

Dugal said he'd call when Michael returned from Tetovo with the disk. Well, he didn't have the fucking disk. So he'd been ignoring his calls, all twenty of them. He decided to hold out longer before answering his twenty-first call because he wanted to enjoy a beer at the Soma Café in peace.

The ringing stopped.

Michael preferred the Stripe Depot, but he didn't want to run into Dugal, so he chose the upscale Soma, knowing this was the last place Dugal would drink.

He took a swig of his beer just as his phone rang again. Twenty-two calls was one too many, so he answered the twenty-first. With a disgusted sigh and a swig of beer, he answered. "What's up?"

First, Dugal swore at him for not answering his phone, and Michael ignored that crap. Then, Dugal said he had an important message from the boss.

Michael had no idea how he'd explain his screwup. Steal a disk from a guy in a hotel room in Tetovo, Macedonia, and get four thousand euro when he delivered the goods. How the fuck could he know the guy was Andy Stephen, his college buddy?

Andy had recognized him, even called him by name. He could've fingered him, so Michael didn't have a choice. Of course, he hadn't considered the identity excuse until after he shot him. Killing Andy to protect himself from incrimination was a hell of a lot better than the truth: admitting everything had gone to shit, his brain turned haywire, and he found himself fighting to the death in Afghanistan.

At least that's what his fucked-up brain told him. He was back in Wardak Province, sweat plastering his fatigues to his body and stinging his eyes. Suddenly, the gun blasted and jolted him. Everything changed right in front of him. No blaring sun, no sand, no buildings. He found himself in the hotel room again watching the blood pool from Andy's head.

Michael rubbed his forehead with his fingertips, trying to erase his memory. Not the murder so much. Honestly, he never liked Andy anyway. No, he wanted to fix his brain somehow and never return to war again, real or imagined.

He sipped his beer to cool his throat.

To make matters worse, Michael couldn't find the disk. He thought he'd scored when he found the Prishtina address in Andy's passport. Once at the location, the girl refused to let him in. He had to leave. When he returned, the apartment was empty, and he tore the place apart, finding nothing. The third time, he climbed the fire escape and peeked in a window. Wrong again. She'd left for good. He should have crashed through the door the first time.

You'd have your cash and be long gone by now. Idiot.

"Listen," Dugal said. "We know what happened because the Tetovo chief of police said his officers had found a dead body. I told you not to kill him. You are in real deep shit with the boss."

Michael didn't answer.

"You there? Don't hang up on me. We'll find you, man. Tell me, did you get the disk?"

"Tell him he'll get his money back."

"That's bullshit. You can't expect to walk away from this, free to spill your guts in a drunken stupor somewhere. No way. You're on the hook and the boss says you have two choices. One, join with him and become a part of the team. An essential part, the boss said. Let me tell you, its great money. Or two, take the next bus to Tetovo—"

"The hell you say. I ain't doing that." Michael growled.

"Okay, perfect. Because, just to let you know, Dime Pavlovski, the chief, he's close friends with the boss. The boss said Chief Pavlovski won't bother arresting you. You get my drift?"

Michael had figured he'd get offered a deal, yet nothing on this order. Dugal had his head in a vice and twisted it tighter, irritating the hell out of him. He opened his jacket to cool off.

"What's this team doing?"

"The boss thought you'd ask that question. Let me read what he told me to tell you, his exact words. 'It's an international project. And the mission, while seemingly unlawful, is worthy of tremendous admiration and is designed to benefit millions of people.' The boss says it's humanitarian. You can tell, these aren't my words." He chuckled.

"No kidding." Michael scoffed. "Your boss is a real pussy."

"He's smart, educated, and powerful."

"If he's so damn powerful, why does he want me?"

"He knows your background, your tours in combat. I told you at the Depot, you got the skills and the right attitude. You're full of rage."

Michael didn't believe this was as big as Dugal let on. True, he had made it a massive problem; he killed Andy. Plus, he couldn't take a chance on misjudging and ending up dead, entirely possible in a foreign country. Kosovo was no exception. He scratched his head, and he exhaled.

"Oh, I hear you, buddy. The boss says he'll give you time to make your decision...a couple of weeks."

Michael didn't answer.

"Listen to me, my friend, and this is me talking. Wait for my call and another thing, don't try to skip. He's got people watching you from every angle."

"If that's true, why call me twenty-one times? Why not just nab me? Don't blow smoke up my ass."

"The boss has better things to do than nab you, you asshole. Besides, don't be a fool, he's always got a plan."

"Yeah? I need to meet this guy?"

"You'll meet him when he wants to meet you. And, oh yeah. Hope you are enjoying your beer. Soma is too highfalutin for my taste."

The call ended.

Dammit.

Michael planted his boots hard on the floor, ready to pounce or exit, his eyes darting to every corner of the room, scanning and rescanning. He didn't detect anyone suspicious. It was obvious, however, someone had to be watching him, and it pissed him off. Rivers of sweat ran down his forehead.

His view of Dugal had changed in an instant. Despite his appearance and the stupid talk, Michael agreed murder in Macedonia meant he'd be executed. Maybe on the spot. After all, he was a foreigner, and the law was questionable for noncitizens.

No doubt about it, this wasn't combat, where he provided surveillance from a concealed position and covered the soldiers on the ground. Seldom was he under surveillance and to his knowledge, he had never been a target of reconnaissance till now. No denying it, Dugal's boss was gathering evidence against him.

Paranoid? Maybe. Shaken? His heart pounding in his chest was proof, and he fucking hated it.

Stop what you are doing. Look around. Listen to your surroundings. Smell your environment.

Michael paid for his beer and went to the street, clenching his fists. He had to get a gun for self-protection and for anything in his way.

~ 15 ~

CHAPTER FIFTEEN

January 23, 2013

Margot barely had time to say goodbye to the girls when Grey's text came.

I'll be at the top of Dragodon in ten minutes.

As she watched them hop off the steps and disappear into the bushes, she worried for Nora. She looked so sick and Margot hoped it was nothing serious. Margot realized there was nothing she could do except pray Nora had a more caring mother than those Andy had described.

Let it go.

She rushed to the street and caught a taxi. Ten minutes later, the taxi dropped her off and she held onto the railing at the highest Dragodon step, craning her neck to see Grey. Then she saw him, trudging and sucking air.

Margot's gut quaked because she knew the truth. Grey would have called her at once if he had good news, if this was a mistaken identity, or if he thought there was a chance, somehow, Andy was alive. He hadn't called and only texted once in the four days he had been in Macedonia. Denial had been her constant companion. That was over now. Terror settled in her chest.

Grey's face, more flushed than usual, was greasy with sweat. Dark rings circled the armpits of his jacket. His wrinkled and stained shirt hung out on one side of his belt.

"Grey," she said, as he got closer, "You look awful."

He stopped and bent over to catch his breath. "Been to hell and back. I ran into Ismet on Mother Teresa Boulevard, and he gave me your new address. And, now these damn steps."

"Well, Grey, did you think of taking a taxi instead of these steps?" she said, instantly regretting her smartass remark.

He didn't answer.

An awkward silence followed them into they were inside her apartment.

Finally, she offered him a glass of water.

"It's terrible, Margot," he said, gulping his water. "I don't understand any of it."

She refilled his glass and sat across from him with her hands over her mouth, bracing herself.

"I met with Officer Dime Pavlovski." He drank the second glass and released a long, deep breath. Margot watched as his complexion turned a soft pink again. She had so many questions, but she waited for Grey to settle himself and talk in his own time. That's the least she could do.

Finally, he said Pavlovski denied it was a robbery because Andy's passport, money, laptop, and credit cards were on the table in plain sight. "Untouched."

Margot coughed as phlegm filled her throat.

"You okay?"

She nodded and bit her bottom lip.

"Okay. Tell me if you want me to stop."

She cleared her throat and waved her hand for him to continue.

"Chief said there was no damage to the door lock. Whoever it was, Andy let them in."

"Fingerprints?"

"I thought the same thing. No fingerprints. Well, they didn't look for any. They think Andy got involved with work in Veles, a town about ninety minutes southeast of Tetovo." Pavlovski didn't tell Grey what the work in Veles was, so he researched Veles himself and found it's a very poor community.

"God, it is beyond disturbing. Makes me furious," he said.

Margot watched Grey's face grow a deep red color as he described Macedonia as an extremely poor country, so much so that people are literally starving.

"And, get this: high school kids in Veles have learned technology and they are brilliant at it. They're making websites, blogging, and doing the social media stuff. Mostly, they're hacking."

"I don't understand. Isn't hacking illegal?" Margot frowned in disbelief.

"Illegal or not, it's extremely profitable, and generates money for food, houses, cars, everything. So, everybody, including the government, the police, the parents ignore it. It's Macedonia's solution to survival."

"A bunch of kids? Why kill for that?" She rose from her chair and paced as she spoke. "Especially if they embrace hacking. Makes no sense."

"Can't answer. I'll tell you, though, the police won't investigate. They're going to let Andy's murder go like it never happened."

"How? Andy is a U.S. citizen. Don't they follow his movement when he enters the country?"

"No. Border patrol doesn't track people once they enter the country. No one would know about the murder unless someone reported it to the U.S. Embassy."

"Perfect, I'll do it." She glared at him and pounded her fist on her chest. "I want to know what happened, Grey."

"I get it. Think. If you go there and threaten to call the police on their fraud, you'd be putting yourself in danger. You'd be an enemy and dispensable, just like Andy."

She rubbed away at her forehead with her palm. "I have to tell you something, Grey, and given what I know now, it's worse than I thought." Her breath quickened. "On the day you left for Macedonia, a guy pounded on my apartment door. I didn't open it because I was petrified, and you told me not to." She stopped talking to read Grey's facial expression.

"Go on."

She swallowed. "This guy said Andy had told him that morning. That morning, he said." She stomped her foot to hold back tears. "He said Andy told him to meet at my apartment."

Grey tugged at his neck and frowned at her. "That's impossible. Andy couldn't have told him."

"Right." She shook her wrists and bounced up and down on her toes to release the tension building in her body. "I said to come back later when Andy would be home. Then, I got the hell out of there. I guess he came back, I'm not sure. Anyway, somebody broke in. Ismet caught the guy in the act, and he ran off. The apartment was in shambles, Grey."

"Dammit. Remember, I told you Pavlovski read the address penciled in Andy's passport? That's how I knew where to find you before I left for Macedonia. Could be this guy...."

Her mouth dropped open. "Give me a minute." She went to her bedroom, shut the door, and leaned against a wall, struggling to get control. The last thing she wanted was to fall apart. Not now. Her knees buckled, and she grabbed the doorknob to catch herself from falling.

Hold on. Breathe.

After two or three minutes dialing down her emotions, she was ready to dig into this nightmare again. First she got the filigree box from her backpack, then returned to the kitchen.

"I remember that box, from Valbona's Restaurant," he said.

Margot told him how she and Ismet had found the box and scarf hidden in the closet ceiling. She gave him the letter. "Here. I think it's from his mother. Can you read it?"

"Hm. Looks Russian, I think. I can read a few words. Let me see. It's from his mother and she's apologizing...something to do with Andy's father." Grey squinted and put the letter on the table.

Margot gulped and searched his face. "What?"

"Nothing. I mean, it's a love note, from a mother to her son. At least that's what I think it is, but I can't read it. Frankly, it's too personal for me to read. I'd be intruding." He rubbed his forehead. "I don't get it. Why not put it in a drawer for safekeeping? Why would Andy go to such extremes to conceal it? A box, a note? This stuff can't be worth somebody killing Andy or breaking into your place."

"Another thing." Margot marched around the kitchen table. "Andy doesn't. Oh God, didn't...work for the State Department." Her voice cracked. "I called. There's no record of an Andrey Orlo Stephen. He lied to us, Grey." Her chin quivered, and she chewed her bottom lip.

Grey slowly shook his head. "This is nasty shit, Margot. You're not safe here. I think you should leave Prishtina. Go back to Minneapolis."

She glared at him. "Yeah, and you?"

"Andy didn't lie to me, and no one has come knocking at my door."

She huffed. "You said the police found your card in the hotel room. This goon could be looking for you, too."

"Yes, I agree, and I considered leaving, then when I saw Andy, his body—"

"Please, I don't want to know. I'm so sorry you had to be the one, Grey." She had never seen a man fall apart like this. Even her father, when Sam died, didn't allow his emotions to spill out in her presence. She was ashamed to admit she was uncomfortable watching these unbridled feelings.

God, Margot, must you make this about you?

Margot knelt next to him, putting her arm across his shoulders. "I'm so sorry."

Grey, coughing, struggled with his words. "I should've. Gone there, too. With him. To Tetovo. If I had gone. I mean."

"No. Stop it. Come on, now, don't do this." She squeezed his shoulders tighter as he moved to put his arms around her. Both on their knees, their cheeks rested against one another as they breathed together. She felt his heart pumping.

They stayed that way without speaking.

Then Grey gently let go and stood. "I'm not ready to leave here. But you—"

Still on her knees, she looked up at him. "Wait a minute, I've been in limbo, first waiting for Andy to return, then for you, and reeling from the intruder. The entire time asking myself how can this be happening? Yet, leaving Kosovo never entered my mind."

He didn't answer.

"I have too many questions. Listen, Grey, Andy was a wonderful person, kindhearted, compassionate." She gulped, preparing to say the harsh truth. "He lied to me. And to you." Standing, she put her hands on her hips. "I want to find out why. There has to be a reasonable explanation. I'm determined to find the truth. I owe it to him, to myself. We had planned our lives together." Her voice cracked. "A future in Prishtina."

"I know. I loved him, too."

Margot didn't know what else to say, and it appeared Grey was at a loss for words, too. As the minutes passed in silence, the living room air felt thick with regret and sorrow.

Finally, Grey shuffled his feet. "I'm sorry. I'm exhausted."

His comment made her realize they had been delving into the trauma, working hard to put sense around this nonsensical catastrophe, for what seemed like hours.

"Of course," she said, her voice filled with gloom. She motioned for him to sit again as she poured him another glass of water.

Grey dipped his head in gratitude and emptied the glass.

A long pause seemed to lighten the heaviness in the room.

"This is hard," he said, placing the glass on the coffee table.

Margot's expression showed her agreement. She realized, beyond the emotional harangue they had just put themselves through, that Grey had endured a three-hour bus trip from Tetovo, followed by climbing the Dragodon steps. No wonder he was exhausted.

Grey inhaled and followed with a long exhale before he spoke with an apologetic tone. "I need a break. I'm done talking now. It's too much and I need...I dunno, a shower."

"You can get cleaned up here. Please don't go home." Her voice was rushed, panicky. "Don't leave me alone, not tonight. Use the spare bedroom and shower—" She stopped herself and took a breath. "It's a totally selfish request, I know."

"Well, maybe," he said with a gentle smile. "I am tired, and it would take more effort to go home than crashing here. So I appreciate it."

"No, actually, I have you to thank. So, go, take your shower. I'll do the same. Let's agree, no conversations on this topic. Let me know if you need anything. Anything at all."

He nodded.

Once in the shower, Margot tipped her head and let the warm water stream through her hair, over her neck and back. She took comfort in Grey's kindness and imagined tension, like glue, pulling away from her bones and tendons, melting and disappearing into the drain. Her back released and softened, opening her lungs. She breathed deeper and extended her breaths until she became aware of an odd sensation growing at the bottom of her ribs, settling at the base of her lungs, trapping the air. She grabbed the ceramic soap dish on the wall to keep from keeling over, waiting for this demon to subside. When it didn't, she slid to the floor and hung her head between her knees, panting quickly. She heard her inner voice droning. *He's dead.*

She stayed on the shower floor whispering, pleading for the voice to stop. When the water turned a numbing cold, she heard Grey call to her from the living room.

"Margot? You okay?" Grey shouted from the living room.

She took a moment to steady herself, made sure her voice was strong and clear, and lied. "I'm fine."

~ 16 ~

CHAPTER SIXTEEN

January 24, 2013

Margot and Grey walked to Mother Teresa Boulevard, passed Skanderbe Square, and crossed the promenade to the Union Café. Edgar had called her earlier in the day, inviting her to dinner. Grey agreed to come along, eager to meet Edgar for the first time.

She spotted Edgar sitting outside at a lone table surrounded by tall potted trees and waved.

As they got closer, Edgar stood. "Hello, you must be Grey."

Grey smiled and shook his hand.

"Lovely to meet you," Edgar said. "Come. Sit, please."

Edgar kissed Margot's hand, and they took their seats.

Margot immediately thanked Edgar again for the beautiful apartment, replete with lovely furnishings and a stocked pantry.

"Please, it is my pleasure. You needed help, and I could accommodate. That is what friends are for."

Margot stumbled on his calling them friends. She didn't quite see them that way and would have agreed they were acquaintances. Maybe Edgar viewed all his acquaintances as friends.

Let it go.

Edgar didn't skip a beat, delving into conversation, first talking about Beatrice Place, then turning his attention to Grey. "This is delightful. I am happy to meet a friend of Andy's, this man of Margot's I fancy meeting someday. Now, tell me, Grey, what brings you to Prishtina?"

"I'm working for the United Nations. So, I—"

"What sort of work?"

"Job creation."

"Brilliant. Unemployment throughout Kosovo is dreadful. I imagine it is rewarding, however, it is government work with meager wages. I'm very sorry about that, of course."

Grey shifted his shoulders slightly and darted an irksome glance at Margot.

A server approached the table and interrupted the awkward silence.

Margot vowed to stay quiet, knowing that Edgar's condescending remark had irritated Grey. She didn't want to get involved and perhaps add to the tension. Besides, Grey could take care of himself.

They placed their orders with the server and the conversation turned to the typical pleasantries, weather and travel. When their food arrived they ate, drank, and discussed Prishtina and Kosovo.

"Tell me, Grey, how long will you be in Prishtina? When does your contract end and do you have plans for work elsewhere? It is possible I will need your services."

"No plans." He tapped Margot's foot under the table.

She responded with an uncomfortable smile, trying to interpret Grey's curt comment and his private nudge. Edgar didn't seem to notice, because he moved on to another topic.

"Did Margot tell you about the invasion? My God, how frightening for her."

Grey nodded but did not comment.

Margot felt his discomfort with Edgar and figured he was sizing Edgar up.

"Did you find out anymore, Margot? Did your landlord alert the police? My apologies, I have forgotten his name," he said, raising his nose in the air.

"His name is Ismet," she said, thinking Edgar probably did remember his name. He was being a real shit tonight, and she didn't know why. "No, no need. Nothing missing, and I doubt they'd investigate in any case."

"Ismet. That's right. Ismet. I do not trust the man. Then, again, who am I—"

"Why not?" Grey said in a challenging tone.

Edgar stretched his neck toward Grey and said, "I cannot say precisely, it is a general sense I have. To be sure, he is the responsible party for keeping the apartment secure. In my estimation, he failed and must be held accountable."

"He said exactly the same thing to me, Edgar. He knows he's responsible, and safety is his highest priority," she said, rubbing her temple, completely annoyed at Edgar's continual posturing.

For what reason?

"Ah, yes, it is the litigator in me," he said, steepling his hands. "As you know, I am an attorney. Correction, barrister. I apologize. I am pleased you are in a safe place near the USAID complex and surrounded by security guards and surveillance."

"That's true, thanks to you, Edgar," she said, trying to get him to be more civil like he was when they first met. "I looked out my balcony to see the guards—"

"You must be cautious, and I encourage you not to draw attention to yourself. It is best to be anonymous."

"Anonymous?" She blurted with an incredulous tone. "Oh, God, Edgar, what is with you tonight? You're so...so dramatic."

"Dramatic, I am not. I am realistic, experienced, and knowledgeable. Women are not treated well here. They are expected, often required, to behave in a shy, apologetic manner."

"And when they don't?" Grey asked, raising an eyebrow.

"They draw attention to themselves, unnecessarily. As a result, of course, people consider them antagonistic, disrupting the so-called *balance of power*. Men are superior to women in Kosovo."

"As in many countries," she said, squeezing her eyes and curling her brow.

"Yes. I have learned this to be the case from my previous experiences with my safe houses for women in London, New York, and, currently, in Prishtina." He raised his chin and narrowed his eyes. " I know from where I speak," he said, pushing his chest out and sipping his wine.

Edgar's superior attitude was relentless, and way more than she could tolerate. Trouble was, she didn't want to debate with a man who displayed such deep conviction. It'd be a waste of time. Besides, she had had enough of Edgar, and she sensed Grey felt the same way. "I'm sorry, I'm exhausted," she said.

"Yes, Edgar. Nice to meet you," Grey said, reaching for his wallet.

"Thank you for joining me on such brief notice. And, please, this was my invitation. My gift to you." He rose, clicked his heels, and bowed, kissing Margot's hand. "This was lovely. Please, come visit Beatrice Place. Grey, we should discuss your job creation work, given job placement for the women at Beatrice Place is our ultimate goal."

"Perhaps," Grey said, without genuine conviction.

"Good evening," Edgar said.

Grey and Margot nodded as they left the café and walked toward the Skanderbe statue.

"Let's take a moment," she said, sitting on the nearby bench.

"Did you know," Grey said, sitting beside her and putting his arm in hers with his nose in the air. "Did you know Gjergj Kastrioti, aka Skanderbe, was the Albanian nobleman who led a rebellion against the Ottoman Empire in what is today Albania, North Macedonia, Greece, Kosovo, Montenegro, and Serbia?"

"Oh God, please don't. I've had enough grand pontification tonight."

"He had three older brothers, Stanisha, Reposh, and Constantine, and five sisters, Mara, Jelena, Angelina, Vlajka and...rats...let me think—"

"Mamica."

Grey jerked his head. "You know this?"

"Yes, honestly, I don't give a shit," she said, chuckling.

"Me neither. My feeble attempt to be funny."

"Speaking of funny, lovely dinner, don't you agree?"

"Lovely is not a word I'd choose," he grinned. "No. I'd choose stiff. Pompous."

"He's so British."

"Bellicose, perhaps."

"Why, Grey, how dare you mock him," she giggled. "Good word choice, though. Edgar would never use a simple word such as aggressive."

They burst out laughing, gleeful in their clever jabs at Edgar.

"He knows a lot of people here. Now, I'm serious, Grey, we should ask him to recommend a translator for the letter."

"Oh, you mean for the letter from Andy's mom. Humph. No way. I don't trust him."

"Yeah, he's strange yet, in a way, gallant. You are reacting to his British heritage. Don't deny it," she said.

"I have many British friends. That's not it. I don't want him in our business. We can get an excellent translator. I have a few connections." Grey smiled at her and puffed out his chest. "Okay. What is the real reason?" she asked, returning his smile not so much at his silly pride. She asked because he referred to the business as *our business*. A warm, comfortable feeling swelled in her chest.

"What was he saying, the anonymous crap? You have no reason to be anonymous. Cautious? Yes. Still, anonymous is over the top."

"God, Grey, he's an attorney. He's trained to be suspicious." She squirmed, rethinking her decision to confide in Edgar and hoping she wouldn't end up regretting it.

He didn't answer.

"All right, you don't have to respond. Just listen," she said, readjusting herself on the bench. "I admit, Edgar raised my anxiety level. He did, and now I'm really nervous. Scared." She stared at him, wondering how to proceed, because a thought had just occurred to her, and she hadn't thought it all through yet.

Grey tilted his head down and looked up at her. "Do you think he did that on purpose?"

She ignored his question because she was focused on saying what she needed to say. Any delay might cause her to lose her nerve. She put her index finger on her top lip. "Grey. I want you to stay here, with me in my apartment," she said, dropping her hand and sitting up straighter. "You have your own place, but I'd be more comfortable if you stayed with me."

Grey instantly raised both eyebrows, jerked his head forward, and blinked slowly.

It was clear to her, he was utterly shocked. She gritted her teeth, waiting for him to say something.

"Wow. I hear you," he said, taking his arm out of hers and turning to face her. "But, have you thought about this? I mean, I know I irritate you."

Margot lowered her head, embarrassed that she had been terribly rude to him when they first met. Guess she was paying for that now.

"It's an important question," he said. "I don't want to ruin our friendship, and I certainly don't want to cause you to feel uncomfortable."

"Well." She adjusted her shoulders and cleared her throat. "Do we have a friendship? Maybe not."

"Let me correct something. When I said that I irritated you, that didn't quite capture it. We both know you were a total bitch."

The word bitch stung her and even though he was telling the truth, it seemed out of character for him. She looked closer at his face and detected a slight smirk. "Wow, you go straight for it, don't you? I'm crushed."

Laughter flowed easily then.

Both Margot and Grey knew they were in uncharted waters and living together would help her feel safe.

"Okay, Edgar might say this is a lovely invitation."

She noticed Grey's chin had a deep dimple unless a genuine smile filled his face.

"That he might. What does Grey Valentin say?" she asked.

"It's risky business. But, I'd say I'm up for the challenge."

Convincing Grey to move in had been easier than she had expected. She gave him a peck on his cheek. "Oh yeah, there's one minor detail: I'm going to need help with the rent."

She looked directly into his eyes, needing to understand what his genuine response would be to this open expectation.

"Oh, I get it. I'm your meal ticket." He laughed.

"Well, there's that." She raised a soft fist and tapped his bicep.

"Ouch!" he said, pretending he was injured and laughing all at once.

"Truth is, I need to work to stay in Prishtina. Meanwhile, I'll have you to supplement my income," she said with a grin spreading across her face.

Grey hummed an acknowledgement and put his arm back in hers.

They were silent.

Margot enjoyed these pleasant few minutes, but then Andy entered her thoughts again.

Grey stood and looked down at her. "Are you ready to go?"

"No. I'm feeling guilty, sitting here, laughing and joking with you while the horror of Andy's death swims around in my head. I shouldn't be doing this. I should be—"

"Stop dwelling on shoulda's. Laugh, cry, think what you will, Margot, mourning will be a constant companion for a long time. A moment of humor doesn't negate Andy's death or your grief. Don't deny yourself an opportunity to enjoy a moment of levity."

Margot heard Grey's words. They were wise, but they didn't touch her. She couldn't seem to access her feelings. Yet she felt her chin quiver and heat rise behind her eyes as tears gathered, ready to fall. "Can we sit for a while?"

He sat down so that his legs and torso were against hers. He wrapped his arm around her but didn't say a word. He regretted he had tried to quash her emotions. She was entitled to feel the pain of her loss. He had just gotten wrapped up in the moment. It felt good to laugh with her, to see her smile, to feel at ease with another human. He hadn't felt that in a long time. He put his arms around her as they sat on the bench.

"Forgive me. You are entitled to feel everything you are feeling without me quashing your emotions." He wrapped his arm around her.

Margot didn't respond because it was such a sweet moment. She wanted to savor it, uninterrupted.

They sat in silence, watching children riding their tricycles and scooters around the Skanderbe statue until the cool air chilled them. She put her hand on his thigh and looked at him. "I'm ready now."

"Thank you, Margot. I appreciated our fun tonight. Can't remember the last time I laughed. You made it happen." He pulled her shoulder closer and pressed his cheek against her head.

***

They opened the door to her apartment, Margot froze and sucked in a deep breath. She whispered, "Someone slipped a note."

As she leaned over to pick it up, Grey pulled her arm back. "Shh. Or, someone dropped it from inside."

She held her breath and moved to search inside. Grey signaled to her to stay put.

He peeked around corners and disappeared into the bedroom. When he returned, he shook his head, pointing to the spare rooms, and disappearing again.

"Whew. Okay. We're fine," he said, his voice echoing down the hall. He locked the door and fell on the sofa. Beads of sweat glistened on his bald head.

Perspiration had drenched her body, too. Even her fingers were wet. She picked up the paper, read it to herself, then plopped next to him and howled. "Lord. It's a bill, due in fifteen days. Our rent."

They burst out laughing.

As the laughter subsided, Grey shifted in his seat, picking at his fingers. "Hey, all kidding aside, what happened? Earlier. This has been nagging me and wanted to clear it up. When you came out from your shower?"

She tossed her hair. "Everything finally came crashing in on me."

He pursed his lips and nodded. "Can I help?"

She breathed in. "Nope," she said, breathing in and tugging at her earlobe. "Actually, you have already." Her breakdown in the shower was deeply personal, and she wasn't sure she could talk to him about it. "But I'm not ready to discuss it right now. Besides, there will be a time to talk about it in the future because it'll happen again and again."

CHAPTER SEVENTEEN

January 25, 2013

"Hey, roomie, want some coffee?" Grey shouted from the kitchen.

The sound of another person's voice in her apartment startled Margot at first, then she breathed easier when she realized it was Grey. She put on a robe and paddled in her slippers to the kitchen. "Morning. Look at you, all dressed up."

He handed her a cup of coffee, waved the rent bill in the air, and grinned. "Leaving for work. Need to earn my keep."

She chuckled. "Me, too. I'm calling Edgar today to see if he can help me find a job."

Grey pursed his lips and rolled his eyes.

"He can help. Let's go easy on him."

Grey rolled his eyes again, even more pronounced this time, and shook his head.

She didn't answer him. No need, Grey knew she agreed with him. It was difficult to ignore Edgar's annoying habits. She knew it'd happen again, and she promised herself she'd bite her tongue, be civil, and power through it.

She secured the dead bolt, poured another cup of coffee, found her cell, and called Edgar. When he answered, he said he had a lovely time at dinner. Of course, Margot thought otherwise, but she didn't go there. They exchanged a few pleasantries and then she got right to the point, asking him for help to find work.

"Do you want to work at Beatrice? That is out of the question. We aren't even accepting volunteers at the moment, my dear."

In no way did she want to work at Beatrice Place and have Edgar over her shoulder every moment. That would surely ramp up her unease around him. It was important to experience Edgar in small doses for fear she'd grow to dislike him altogether. In her heart, she thought he was a good person. But he could be a real shit. She covered her mouth to avoid laughing out loud and to chastise herself.

Stop it. You need him.

She explained that although she preferred to teach children, she'd take what she could get. Edgar clicked his tongue a few times. "I know of a potential opportunity to teach ESL. Allow me to make a call."

"Great. But, I'm not certified in ESL."

"Details, my dear, mere details. Now, I must run. Watch for my text. Ta ta."

He made it sound as if she'd get around the details. She hoped so.

Margot spent the next hour straightening the apartment. When she got to Grey's bedroom, the door was closed. She hesitated to go inside, wanting to respect his privacy. But the image of him trudging up the steps, shirttail out, sweat stains under his arms nauseated her. He must understand, she refused to be his maid because of her gender. She opened the door a few inches and peeked in.

Surprisingly, the bed was made and there were no clothes outside the closet. Even his shoes were put away. Everything was in place. She checked his bathroom. Same. He had even folded the towels and hung them perfectly over the rack.

Grey would be a good roommate. Now she felt competitive, and no way could she allow him to beat her in the tidiness department. She laughed to herself.

Margot had one foot in the shower when her phone vibrated. A text from Edgar.

Brilliant news. Meet me at Casa Rita Restaurant at 10:45. Taxi will know Casa Rita. University appointment at 11:15. Please confirm.

How did he get this done so fast?

She texted back a quick confirmation.

***

Margot hired the first driver available in the line of taxis next to USAID. When she said Casa Rita, the driver said, "Yes, madam. Casa Rita near Sars University and Germia."

They drove fifteen minutes to the outskirts of Prishtina and he dropped her at the curb in front of the restaurant. The entrance steps were practically in the street. She tightened her grip on the railing and as she passed a terrace on her right, Edgar, already seated, bobbed his head, acknowledging her.

Her hand quivered when she waved because she worried she'd have to lie if Edgar brought up Andy again.

The maître d', dressed in a black suit and colorful cummerbund, greeted her, "Welcome to Casa Rita, madam. Mr. Leeds is on the terrace. Come with me, please."

The sound of dreamy jazz, played by a muted trumpet, filled the air. Gradually, she relaxed and stopped shaking.

The maître d' led her to Edgar's table, covered with a white linen cloth and flanked with fica trees and red and yellow flowers. He pulled out a chair for her and she sat. He stepped a few feet back from the table, hands clasped behind his back, and waited at attention like a soldier.

Edgar kissed her hand. "So good to see you. It is splendid here, wouldn't you agree?"

"Yes. It's elegant, the flowers, and I love jazz. Thank you again. Seems I'm thanking you every moment."

"It is my pleasure. Indeed, there is beauty and elegance in Prishtina. You must know where to look. And Margot, please meet my friend, Lavon."

Lavon, the maître d', stepped closer. "Madam," he said with a slight bow and a soft tapping of his heels. "Care for a beverage?"

"A Coke, please."

Edgar glanced at this watch. "We have only a few minutes. With regard to the assignment, it is English as a Second Language. Ten to twelve hours a week, a six-month project, teaching writing to adults, native-Albanian speakers, who work at USAID."

Had Edgar found her a job or an interview? She was dying to know.

"USAID near Dragodon?"

"Yes. They want an American teacher, and it pays thirty euros an hour."

Lavon brought her drink to the table.

"Thirty? You're kidding." She sipped her Coke.

"I seldom kid, my dear. No, we can walk to the University. You will meet with Dr. Zekolli. He—"

"Dr. Zekolli? I know that name. The two young girls at a bakery mentioned him."

"Ah, yes. Agnesa and Lindeta. Prishtina is similar to a small town. Word gets around, as they say. Now, we must go. Please."

When Margot awkwardly gulped down her Coke, emptying the half full glass rather than sipping, she felt coarse, unsophisticated. This was no way to behave at Casa Rita restaurant, especially in front of Edgar. He was always so proper, which caused her to question her own manners. She paused and blotted her mouth with the napkin, resolving never to embarrass herself again.

When they were on the street, Margot had to contend with the narrow, uneven pavement littered with broken concrete and sickening trash thrown everywhere. She watched her every step. Meanwhile, cars zoomed through the street, in contrast to the traffic gridlock in Prishtina proper. They walked past an upscale hotel.

Across the street she spotted four cows lying under a tree, slowly chewing their cud.

"Cows?" she asked. Those gigantic eyes looked human. The cows eyeballed her as if they knew her secrets, but not in a threatening way. They comforted her. And she thought it was weird until she remembered reading somewhere that cows symbolized power and nurturing.

"Yes, cows. They are resting now and often walk in the street. Welcome to Kosovo." He smiled.

"I love it." She giggled, reveling in her relationship with these cows, knowing Edgar would certainly think it odd. She was open to finding comfort...nurturing...anywhere she could.

Once at the University, they approached a guard house, perpendicular to a red and white striped horizontal pole blocking the vehicle entrance. A guard stood at the house door and tipped his cap to Edgar.

"*Përshëndetje, kemi një takim* me Dr. Zekolli, *ju lutem*. Edgar Leeds *dhe Znj*. Margot Hart," Edgar said.

The guard said, "*Mirësevini, Ai është duke Peter për ty, dhoma dyqind e dyzet e tre.*"

Margot strained to decipher the words. To teach Albanian speakers, she needed to learn the language.

"*Falminderit*," Edgar said.

"Welcome, Ms. Hart," the guard said with a nod and a welcoming smile.

She smiled, "*Faleminderit*."

"Very good, Margot. You are learning the language."

"Beautiful Albanian yourself, Mr. Leeds. Can you teach me?"

"Of course. People will appreciate your zeal to learn their language. We are to go to Room two forty-three."

When they arrived, a professorial-looking man with wire-rimmed glasses and a tweed vest motioned to them to enter his office.

"Hello, nice to see you, Mr. Leeds and Ms. Hart. Thank you for your interest in our ESL program. I am well aware of your interest already. Lindeta and Agnesa speak very highly of you."

Margot liked his face and his warm style.

"I met them at the bakery. They love it at Sars. To be honest, I'm not certified to teach English as a Second Language."

"Edgar told me as much. You have a college degree from an accredited institution in the United States, no?"

She nodded.

"We are good, then. You'll be teaching writing to native-Albanian speaking employees who work at USAID, and I assume you will have approximately thirty students. The contract is open regarding the number of classes; however, it indicates a maximum of fifteen hours a week. You will need to complete an application, a formality, you understand. Email it to me right away," he handed her his card. "Stop in the business office. They have a packet for you with all the details, English as a Second Language manual, and contact information for your liaison, Ganna Hoxha, USAID's human resources officer."

"USAID is close. I can walk from my apartment."

"Excellent. Another point. You will need paper and access to a printer. We have that here. Even so, it's a waste of time, back and forth. Plus, we can't pay for your travel."

"Margot can buy a printer. May I suggest you consider a reimbursement for a printer, paper, and any other office supplies. Actually, we can spare some supplies from Beatrice Place."

"Perfect. Thank you. Questions?" Dr. Zekolli stood up, signaling the meeting had ended.

"No. Ah. Well. The pay and when do I start?" Margot breathed.

"Of course. Forgive me. Thirty euros an hour, an exceptionally good wage here considering the annual income in Kosovo averages six thousand five hundred dollars in U.S. currency. As far as the start date is concerned, I agreed with Ms. Hoxha. You will begin with assessments in two weeks. This will give you two weeks to bone up on ESL."

Edgar nudged her elbow and raised an eyebrow, signaling he had told her as much.

"And my students speak English?" she said.

He nodded.

"That's a relief," she said, brushing her hand across her forehead.

"Congratulations and welcome to Sars University." He handed her a bag with the Sars University logo and papers.

"Thank you, Dr. Zekolli. It's beautiful and will come in very handy." She draped it over her shoulder and patted it, smiling at him.

"Edgar, always a pleasure. Let's explore additional student internships at Beatrice Place." They shook hands.

After picking up the packet in the business office, they went outside and sat at a picnic table in a grassy area. She enjoyed watching students mill around. It felt like being back on the university campus back home. She spotted the girls from the bakery waving to her and walking toward her.

"Hello. Remember us? Lindeta and Agnesa. From the bakery?"

"Yes, of course, lovely to see you."

"Hello, Mr. Leeds," Lindeta said. They shook hands. "We haven't seen you for a while. We hope you will come back to the bakery soon."

"Yes, of course," Edgar said.

"Oh, I didn't realize you all knew one another," Margot said.

"As I said, it is a small town, Prishtina," Edgar said.

"Oh, let me introduce you to my friends," Agnesa said as two young men joined them. "This is Vis and Bestar."

"Yes. Our web and mobile computing class. My apologies. We're late." Vis leaned forward and shook Margot's hand.

She noticed a tattoo on his hand. "Oh, I love your tat. Is that a flower?"

"Yes, the Macedonia poppy. Thank you. My mother loves it too." He beamed. "Sorry, we must go now." He nodded to Edgar before turning and walking toward the building.

"Wow. Nice kids. Do you know those boys? Vis acknowledged you. I'm surprised you were silent, Edgar. You pride yourself on British correctness." She giggled.

"No, I do not know him at all," Edgar said, frowning and clearing his throat.

"Sorry, I didn't mean to offend you. I was just teasing."

Edgar shrugged.

Margot sensed he was annoyed. Certainly, for no reason in her mind. She changed the subject. "Do all the students speak English so well?"

"I think so. Sars is an English-speaking university, although students are from all over the world. By the way, you made an excellent impression on Dr. Zekolli, my dear. Andy will be very proud, I'm sure."

She wished she could tell Andy. She folded her arms on her stomach to contain the emotions bubbling inside.

Suddenly, a dense cloud of birds swooped down from the top of a building, whirling over their heads, casting a gloomy shadow. Margot flinched, covering her head with her university bag.

"Jackdaws," Edgar said.

Then as quickly as they came, the birds returned to the rooftop, clearing the sky again.

"They are from the crow family and extremely intelligent. Do not worry, they reportedly love people. They say a jackdaw on the roof proclaims a new arrival."

"That would be me, I guess," she said, still holding her stomach.

"However, jackdaws on the roof might also foreshadow a premature death," he scoffed. "If you believe in that sort of folklore."

A chill rippled up her spine, causing her shoulders to shudder. Suddenly, she received a text notification. It was her mother.

"Your Andy?" Edgar asked.

"My mother, and I need to call her. Do you mind?"

"Not at all. There are taxis near the entrance. Let me know if you need assistance navigating the details for USAID."

They approached a taxi parked at the curb at the university exit. Edgar opened the taxi door, helped her inside and handed her a 3x5 card. "And here is the list of grief counselors I promised, my dear. Congratulations and give my best to Grey."

She waved to him as they drove off and giggled to herself when she thought how Grey might react to Edgar's best. It had been a good day and she couldn't wait to tell her mother the exciting news: she had a job and a list of counselors.

Most important, and what she couldn't share completely, she had an income allowing her to stay in Prishtina and solve Andy's murder. A bittersweet plan.

~ 18 ~

CHAPTER EIGHTEEN

January 25, 2013

Margot returned to the apartment, called her mother right away, and told her the good news.

"And thirty euros an hour. How about that?" Margot said.

"Wow. Bet Andy's happy you're helping with expenses."

Change the subject.

She paused before answering, telling herself not to revisit the angst from their last conversation. "Yes. What's going on with you? I miss you. How's work? Classes?"

"Good. More fun, tell me about your job. I'm short on time though. I need to go to work."

Margot quickly went over her morning, Sars, USAID, and Edgar Leeds.

"Wow, this Mr. Leeds sounds fabulous."

"Yeah, and you'll love this: He gave me a list of grief therapists."

"Oh, Margot, I'm glad, honey. He knows what happened to Sam? You told him?"

"Yes, I did."

She wanted to tell her about Grey and the new apartment but didn't know how to explain it without discussing Andy.

"Talk about Sam as often as you can, especially with Andy. He's such a good listener, and he needs to know how you've struggled with this. Is he there?"

Margot choked. She hadn't considered that question. "Ah, no, he's, he's—"

"Of course, it's the middle of the day there. He's at work. Next time, let's chat when I can catch him on the phone. Listen, honey, I'm going to be late for work. Thanks for calling and I'm proud of you. I love you."

"I hate hanging up too soon. We barely had time."

"Oh, I know. Me, too. Work calls. Bye."

The connection ended.

It was hard being here, so far away without her mother, even in the best of circumstances. Margot wanted to talk more, but nothing could be done about that. She'd have to buck up. To shed her disappointment, she went to the window to watch the setting sun cast a pink hue across the empty steps of Dragodon.

The front door lock jiggled, and Margot gasped, realizing she had forgotten to turn the deadbolt.

Despite beads of perspiration on her forehead, and her throat trying to lock, she mustered up the courage to speak. "Who is it?"

"Margot? It's me."

"Grey. Thank God."

He let himself in. "Yes, it's me, lucky you. I'm sorry I scared you, but you deserve to be scared, dammit." Grey glared at her, pointed to the door. "You left it unlocked," he said, raising his voice.

"I'm sorry, I forgot. I called my mom—"

"I'm shocked you were careless after all that has happened." He shook his head in anger.

"Please, don't yell at me."

He threw his briefcase to the floor and marched to his bedroom.

Grey was right, and she was disgusted with herself. She plopped on the sofa. She was so embarrassed. How could she be so stupid, thoughtless? She deserved his wrath. After a long ten minutes, he returned to the kitchen.

He jammed his hands on his hips. "You cannot be negligent, Margot. I'm worried for you."

She bit her top lip.

He opened the refrigerator door. "Okay, let's move on. Took me a few minutes, but I got that off my chest," he said, exhaling. "Want breakfast for dinner?"

She was relieved because she did not want to fight. "Sure. Eggs, bacon, toast. By the way, I have lots to discuss."

"Me, too. Let's decide who we need to tell, you know, Andy stuff."

She dropped her jaw to stop her chin from quivering. Not the time for despair now. "Do you know his parents?"

With his face buried inside the refrigerator, he said, "Yeah, well, his mom, for sure. Did you tell your mom?" He got eggs, bacon, and butter out and shut the door.

She shook her head and pulled bakery bread from the drawer.

"Tough conversation for sure. When you do tell her, she's going to want you to go home. And your father? Maybe talk to him first? Sometimes men react differently." He opened the bottom cupboard and took out the iron skillet and a small frying pan.

Grey struck a nerve, bringing up her dad. Her plot to view her father as a minor annoyance, an insect, a No See Um, had been working just fine for a long time. Now, Grey's interference was changing all that, and she didn't like it. "My dad is nowhere in our lives. Mark him off the list." She scratched her ankle.

"Really?" He frowned at her and pursed his lips.

"Yes, anyway, you are right. I never thought she'd say to come home. Got to think about that. Who do you need to tell?"

"Nobody. I told you, my parents died."

"No, you didn't tell me. I'm sorry," she said, scratching her neck, realizing how little she knew about him.

"Nobody here in Prishtina needs to know. I prefer my eggs scrambled the best. You?" he said.

"Yes. And that reminds me, Edgar got me a job." She unwrapped the bacon and placed four slices in the skillet.

Grey turned a burner on, sliding the skillet over the flame. "Why would it remind you of Edgar?" He reached for a small bowl in the cupboard and cracked two eggs open on its edge, dribbling the yolk and white inside. "Three eggs?"

"Four. For a moment today, I considered telling him—"

Grey's eyes widened. "I cannot believe you thought that for a nanosecond. What the fuck is wrong with you?" He cracked two eggs with a loud bang, hurled the shells in the sink, and whipped the eggs with a fork.

"I didn't tell him, and if you'd let me finish a sentence, you'd know. You cannot talk to me that way." She turned the flame under the skillet higher.

"The hell I can't if you screw up." He reduced the flame.

"No, you cannot." She stomped her foot and turned the heat back up.

"You can't even remember to lock the door. You're burning the bacon." he said, turning the knob to off.

"I said I was sorry—"

"Yeah, after the fact. Listen to me." he said, shaking the fork dripping with raw yolk at her. "You cannot tell Edgar. He's trouble as far as I'm concerned."

"Stop it. You aren't listening. I didn't and I won't. Understand, Edgar is my friend. He got me this apartment, stocked it with food and he got me a job today, Grey. A fantastic job with excellent money." She glared at him and wiped the spittle off her lips. "You are jealous of my relationship with him. Damn, you piss me off," she said, crossing her arms and secretly applauding herself for saying exactly what she thought to her new roommate.

Grey's face went blank, then he tilted his head and opened and closed his eyes three times, deliberately.

"What are you doing?" she wrinkled her Greta Garbo nose as she held her lips together as if she were thinking of something hard to grasp. "That looks very weird, Grey."

He straightened his stance. "It's my way of gathering my thoughts to avoid conflict. Obviously, I have failed." He threw his fork on the counter. "So, let me put it this way. I don't want to tell you what to do. However, I will tell you when I believe you are doing something that puts you in danger," he said, with his neck veins bulging. "You are not alone in this and it's keeping us safe."

"Well, I—"

"You can choose your friends. It's none of my business. I'm asking you, do not tell Edgar. Yes, I could be out of order. I prefer to err on the side of caution." He drew a deep breath, grabbed his fork, and went back to stirring his eggs, more violently now.

When he said it wasn't his business, it hurt her feelings and her heart twinged. That both confused and surprised her. "I prefer my bacon burned. Watch my lips. I didn't tell him. What else can I say?" she said, lighting the fire under the skillet again.

"And your toast?"

"I'll do the toast. I won't tell him. And, just so you know, I prefer my scrambled eggs soft."

"Gotcha." He wrinkled his forehead and with his eyes fixated on the bacon, he shoved the hardened, dark strips around with a fork.

Margot had said all she wanted.

They cooked and ate their breakfast for dinner in complete silence as tension gradually subsided.

"Bacon burned perfectly," he said, his face void of expression.

"Eggs were perfect too," she said, leaning her chin on her knuckles.

"Tell me about your job," he said.

She sat up straight. "Thirty euros an hour. Even at twenty hours a week, it's excellent." Margot explained everything that had happened: Casa Rita, Sars University, Dr. Zekolli, and USAID. She said little regarding Edgar, just that she was grateful to him. "Let's get back to the question. Who should we tell?"

"Yeah. I guess nobody. Not until we know we're safe."

"How will we know?"

"When no one breaks in here."

"Damn." Her mind went back to images of clothes and dishes strewn throughout her apartment. And the damaged framed photos of Sam and Andy. "Not sure I could handle another invasion."

Grey put his hand on her shoulder. "It's going to be fine. Our decision, commitment to stay and find answers doesn't mean we won't have occasional doubts. Right?"

She closed her eyes and bobbed her head in agreement.

"You can change your mind, Margot. Leave anytime, you know."

"I do know that, yet I'm determined to work through the doubts and fears. But, let's talk about Andy's mom. What are you going to say? It'll help me when I tell my mom."

"Like you said, I need to think." He rubbed the back of his neck and looked around the kitchen. "We sure made a mess."

"Yes, we did," she said, snickering. "Let's make a house rule: no fighting while cooking."

"Hmm. Don't know if I can promise that."

They chuckled softly.

"What I started to say before the shouting. Listen. It's funny, especially now. When I left Sars today, Edgar said his goodbyes and told me to give you his best."

Grey gave her a blank stare.

"Rats. I thought you'd love the irony: best eggs and his best? Get it? I doubt you think Edgar even had a best."

"Yeah, real funny."

"I try. Come on, Grey, lighten up. We got other important matters to wrestle with."

"That we do," he said, twirling his fork. "I've been playing with the idea of taking a leave of absence with my project at the UN. Understanding Andy's murder will require all my time. My colleagues can do without me for a while."

"Well, okay, if it's what you want. My part-time teaching will bring in enough money to cover the rent. Don't forget, it's only a six-month contract."

"God, I hope we're not still doing this in six months. Anyway, I've put money away. We'll be more than fine. Your working part time is perfect."

"Yeah, twenty hours a week and once I get up to speed, I'll have plenty of time."

"You can always go home, Margot."

"Even so, I don't see that as an option, Grey," she said, gritting her teeth. "I'm committed." Her chin quivered again. "God, I miss him."

He leaned closer and took her hand. "I know," he said, with soft, comforting eyes.

She squeezed his hand and smiled. "One thing?"

He raised his eyebrows, listening.

"I have no idea where to begin."

He sat back and took a deep breath. "That makes two of us."

~ 19 ~

CHAPTER NINETEEN

February 11, 2013

The thought of her first day at work caused butterflies to tangle in Margot's stomach. While ecstatic about her new job, she worried because she was teaching for the first time.

When she entered the USAID security building, she found herself standing in a vacant room with nothing on the walls except a clock, which read 8:40, five minutes slow, by her watch. Two uniformed guards, heavy in discussion, sat behind a large glass panel, enclosing a small office. After two minutes without the guards noticing her, she rapped on the glass. They both looked up, and she made a note of their name tags. She'd call them by name, her first opportunity to make new friends. She saw Saban leave the office through a back door. The other man, Guzim, spoke to her, his words muffled behind the thick pane.

"I'm sorry, I can't understand you," Margot said, cupping her ear with her hand.

He nodded and pushed a shallow drawer, which emerged from below the glass, toward her. The top opened automatically, and he moved closer to the glass and said something with exaggerated lip movements and facial expressions. She still couldn't decipher his words.

"Good morning," she said, raising her voice.

He tilted his head and lifted his eyebrows.

She shrugged and placed her Kosovo identification card and Minnesota driver's license in the drawer.

Guzim pulled the drawer back inside. He glanced at her three times, comparing ID photos to her face, followed by scribbling notes on a clipboard and dialing a black rotary phone.

At the same time, three people entered. She assumed they were employees because they had badges clipped to their coats. They walked up the ramp toward an inside door, and the first man swiped his badge across an electronic pad. An alarm blasted so loud that covering her ears did little to soften the jarring noise in her head. She watched him strain to open the metal door, which turned out to be at least six inches thick.

When they crossed the threshold, the massive door began creaking closed. Margot counted five seconds before it shut with a heavy clacking sound, shaking the cement floor and taking her breath away.

The blaring alarm stopped, but the ringing in her ears didn't. She dropped her hands and her breathing returned to normal just as four sharp raps on the glass startled her again. The guard mouthed unrecognizable words and pointed to the door.

She mentally prepared herself for the deafening onslaught again, approached the door, grabbed the handle with both fists, and pulled. It didn't budge. A tap came from inside. She stepped back. The alarm sounded again, rattling her body, and the door groaned open.

Saban stood in front of her. He was tall, and extremely thin, with a sharp, straight nose and serious dark eyes. The sight of his gun and the stick on his belt caused her spine to ripple.

CLAIM DENIED ~ 139

He must have known she couldn't hear over the alarm because he spoke deliberately, exaggerating his enunciation with grotesque lip movements.

She watched his lips say, "Good morning, Miss Hart. Welcome to USAID."

The alarm stopped, and the door slammed closed with a reverberating clack, the walls rumbling.

Margot forced a smile. "That's crazy loud."

Saban didn't answer. He simply jerked his head. She followed him until he halted and turned, raising his palm to her. She froze in place.

He passed through a metal detector and perched himself behind an adjacent table. "Everything on the table. Coat, handbag, laptop. Sars University bag."

Now she knew how criminals felt. She was confident he'd arrest her, or worse, if she didn't do precisely as he said. She obeyed and waited for further instructions.

"Cell phone, please." With a glum expression, he pointed to a pink plastic basket like one you'd get at a dollar store in the States. A sweet baby pink color, a perfect dainty gift for a four-year-old girl. Certainly not a government issue.

Saban motioned for her to move through the metal detector. No buzzers or bells sounded, and she breathed easier, assuming she was home free and would have no further inspections.

Wrong.

He instructed her to spread her feet apart, shoulder width, with her arms out to her sides. He moved a wand over her body, front and back.

"Please," he said as he pointed to a space next to the exit.

She moved as directed and stood on the spot.

He left her laptop, phone, and Sars University bag on the shelf and placed her coat and purse on a conveyor belt connected to a huge X-ray machine.

Her watch said 8:58 a.m. She'd never make her 9 p.m. start. Her chest became hot.

Saban pushed a button, and an engine hummed as the belt rumbled forward. He examined her items through a display screen as they moved through the machine. He stopped and reversed the belt twice, leaning closer to the screen. Finally, her belongings emerged from the conveyor on the other side.

"Permission, please?" he said, pointing to the zipper on her purse.

"Of course. And don't you want to X-ray my Sars University bag?" She used her most cheerful voice, trying to be helpful.

"No." he said, with his face buried in her purse.

Her effort to be friendly had failed. She was inferior, not worthy of his attention, and worse, he suspected her. It would have been a grave error to address him by his first name.

Still digging in her purse, he said, "USB? Electronic files?"

"No."

"Not permitted."

This was ridiculous, and it peeved her. "I said no."

He yanked the zipper closed. "Ms. Hart, please."

His reprimand embarrassed her, reminding her not to fuck around. USAID did serious work, international stuff, with X-ray machines; and had stoic guards with guns and sticks. They could damn well arrest her in Kosovo, a poor country and unrecognized by European Union because of corruption and organized crime. She'd rot in prison and no one would even know.

Inhale. Exhale. Repeat.

She picked up her purse and held her coat tight to her chest.

Saban retrieved her laptop, cell phone, and Sars University bag from the table.

"Your Sars University bag, madam."

"My laptop, please?"

"No. No computers inside. We will keep for you here, along with your phone."

"I need my laptop to teach." She kept her voice low and calm for fear of agitating him.

He ignored her and knocked on the exit door. Another alarm rang, thankfully not as loud as before. She didn't know if her nerves could take much more jarring.

Once inside, they faced more glass. Saban slipped her cell and computer through yet another narrow drawer. Guzim tucked her items on a shelf, placed two laminated cards into the drawer, and pushed the drawer toward Saban.

He handed the badges to her. "Keep this yellow card clipped to your clothing and visible at all times. The white is your receipt for your belongings. You will return it for your phone and laptop. Do not lose it if you want to claim your possessions."

She nodded.

"Ms. Ganna Hoxha, our human resources officer, will be your escort. Wait here."

Margot checked the time: 9:10. The security procedures had taken twenty minutes, causing her to be late on her first day.

A perfect first impression.

She sucked her teeth in frustration.

The tedious process had zapped her energy. She closed her eyes tightly and inhaled deeply, hoping to free her emotional tension and regain strength.

An attractive petite woman with fashionable gray hair opened an external door and welcomed her. "Good to meet you. We are all glad you are here. Come with me."

Margot questioned her choice of the word *all*. It likely didn't include the guards. To them, she was an irritant.

"I'm sorry I'm late."

They walked outside.

"Yes. The security process usually takes twenty minutes."

"Every time? Or can I get a pass?"

"Security is tight here. I'm sorry, it is how it is. You must arrive earlier in order to start promptly at nine o'clock."

"I understand," she fibbed. In fact, she couldn't imagine what secrets they could be protecting. It seemed silly. Still, there was no reason to start off on the wrong foot with the human resource officer.

Swallow your pride. Be pleasant. You can do it.

They entered another building. Thanks to Ganna's wave, they whisked past another security station.

"Twenty-four employees have enrolled in your classes. We will go to the conference room, and you can test them for placement. Their skills vary. I think you will teach three classes a day for three to four days a week, based on how you group them. One or two may ask for individualized instruction, and you can choose to accept or deny their requests. It's solely your decision. We can adjust the hours and classes as you proceed. Will that work for you?"

"Yes."

"Follow me. I'll take you to the room and you can get started."

"Ganna? May I call you Ganna?" Margot wanted Ganna to warm up to her.

"Of course."

"Ganna, your English is perfect. Where did you learn?"

"I learned here in Kosovo. You'll find your students, most of them, speak English very well. A few are multilingual, but they have difficulty writing. That's why we hired you."

"Everyone is from Kosovo?"

"Yes, all your students are Kosovar. However, the executive staff, the upper echelon, are from the United States. You have two hours. When you're finished, ask an employee to accompany you to my office. Note, you must always have an escort inside the facility. Even to use the restroom. I'll escort you to the security building."

Ganna opened the conference room door, and Margot faced twenty-four people, all of whom were staring at her without even a glimmer of a smile. All of a sudden, her chest was under enormous pressure.

"Good morning. Thank you for coming. This is your instructor, Ms. Hart." Ganna turned to her. "Two hours."

As soon as Ganna left, the mood in the room shifted dramatically. Shoulders softened, faces relaxed, and tense expressions turned gentle and welcoming.

The pressure on her chest disappeared, and her throat opened.

A pudgy, short man with sparkling blue eyes rose from his chair. "My name Illir Goxilli. Individualized instruction, please. Because of work." He grinned.

He had a thick accent, and poor verb choice or no verb choice at all. She made a mental note, although she was drawn to his kind demeanor and the way he cocked his head, as if he was shy and apologizing for his request.

"Illir, don't be rude. Let's at least welcome her first. Ms. Hart, I am Albert Zefi. We are happy you are here." Albert was slight, with a lovely, open face. He spoke perfect English, with minor Albanian inflections.

"Thank you, I'm happy to be here," she said with a wide smile.

Illir sat. "Yes, I sorry. Welcome, Ms. Hart. Please, I don't want to be rude. I want to be best student. Your best student. I work hard for you. Can you help me?"

"Yes, Mr. Goxilli, I can help you."

"Excellent. Please. Call me Illir."

Margot nodded, with a smile, and was pleasantly surprised how his few words calmed her and made her feel much more welcome.

A plump woman announced, "My name is Vlora. I won't bother you with my last name. Not yet." She dipped her head, tittered, and flipped her hair.

"You can teach me how to pronounce your names—"

"And you teach American writing." Illir said.

"Excellent. Let's get started."

They scooted their chairs closer to their tables and everyone sat up straight with eager, beaming faces.

As the tension drained from her body, she recalled Edgar's words. "There is beauty and elegance in Prishtina. You need only to look." She had him to thank for finding beauty in the faces of her Kosovar students.

~ 20 ~

CHAPTER TWENTY

February 11, 2013

Margot sat at the kitchen table sifting through paperwork and revisiting those first two hours she had experienced in the USAID conference room earlier in the day. Meeting each student, evaluating skill levels, and deciding how to group students together had not been easy. Add to that enduring the ridiculous security procedures and coming to realize this would be a daily occurrence.

Studying the ESL manual every day for the last two weeks had given her a great knowledge base, but classes started in a week. She had to create lesson plans, design individualized instruction, develop a class schedule, and the list went on. And this was only the beginning and the cause of a small part of her anxiety. Further ominously, how could she teach writing with no experience?

As she stood to take a deep breath to settle her nerves, she heard someone cough at her front door. She froze, waiting, wondering if she had imagined the cough, especially since all was now quiet.

Suddenly, a cough sounded again, and the image of the stranger with the blue cap flashed in her head. Her knees locked and perspiration drenched her face as she approached the door.

Then a knock. "Margot? You home?"

"Ismet, is that you?" She cocked her ear toward the door to listen more closely.

"Yes."

"Oh, my gosh. I panicked," she said, opening the door.

He politely removed his beret and smiled, bowing at his waist. "Happy to visit with you. I have mail for Andy." He handed her an envelope.

"Andy?" In an instant, memories of the past five weeks that had been simmering in the back of her mind came forward, flooding her brain. She mopped the sweat glistening on her neck and chin as her mind lurched back in time. Once again, she was trapped in that fear, the ransacked apartment, Grey's confirming that Andy was dead. How can this be happening again?

She held her breath and looked at Andy's name and the previous address on the envelope.

They sat at the kitchen table as she slowly opened the seal and slipped out a letter.

"See?" he said, pointing to the return address. "I know *Kampion i Sigurte*. In English, Champion Safe Company. In Peja."

"Hmm," she said, bringing her mind back to the present. "What does this company do?"

"To keep safe. Furniture or machinery, for example, when people move or have no room to keep themselves."

"A storage company?"

"*Po.* Yes. Important?"

Tension gripped her body as she remembered Grey saying Andy's murderers were looking for something in the hotel room. Ismet couldn't know important it may be.

"Man, it would be crazy if—" She heard footsteps in the hall.

Ismet stiffened and his eyes riveted to the door.

When she heard keys rattling, she closed her eyes and tilted her head back. "It's Grey."

"Hello," Grey said, opening the door. He halted at the sight of Ismet.

"This is Ismet. My former landlord."

"Of course. We've met. It's just," he said slanting his eyes, "I warned you not to let people in."

"I apologize. I here only for letter. I leave."

"No, Ismet, I'm sorry. Grey, please, he's my friend, and he has mail addressed to Andy."

Grey dipped his head. "Of course. Margot's right. I'm a bit on edge these days."

"Is okay. From *Kampion i Sigurte*, Champion Safe Company."

"Read it, Ismet," Margot said.

"Two papers. First, letter. Date eight February two thousand thirteen. Second is contract. Date seven January two thousand thirteen. Signed Andrey Orlo Stephen. Okay?"

Margot bobbed her head and put her arm through Grey's, reassuring him and preparing herself for whatever was in the papers.

"Is late notice. I read."

Dear Mr. Stephen,

Thank you for renting the storage Unit 326.

This is a LATE NOTICE.

We could not reach you by phone after many calls.

See the contract agreement enclosed. Agreement is for one year. Payment is required monthly. Thank you for deposit (€100) and one-month rent (€100) received on 7 January 2013.

Payment was due 7 February 2013. If you do not pay by 4 March 2013, contents become property of Kampion i Sigurte and we will sell at auction.

To continue the agreement, we must receive payment in the form of a bank transfer or cash. If you choose bank transfer, please call our office for assistance.

Office hours are Monday through Thursday, 9 a.m. to 6 p.m, Friday and Saturday, 9 a.m. to 12 p.m. Sunday, closed.

Margot stomped her foot in both frustration and anger. "I didn't even know he had gone to Peja. Where is Peja? And why store anything? I can't imagine what it can be."

"Peja in Kosovo."

"You know this company? I mean, is it legitimate?" Grey said.

Ismet dipped his chin. "Yes."

"We have to go, Margot. It's February 11." Grey said.

"I agree. But I have classes. I have to get through these first classes. I could lose my job if I cancel. I'd have both Ganna and Dr. Zekolli on my case. It's their contract."

Grey raised his eyebrows and glared at her.

"Shit! This is frustrating. I want to go this very minute," she said, exhaling. She sifted through her papers, looking for her calendar. "Okay, Ah. March fourth? I know it's cutting it close. I can't screw up my contract with Sars. How far to Peja, Ismet?"

"Peja, seventy kilometers. Ninety minutes by auto."

Grey paced.

Ismet said, "Excuse please. We go. I drive. Or Andy return before fourth March?"

Margot chewed the inside of her cheek and shook her head.

Grey faced her, squeezing her hands. "Margot, what do you think?" he said, squinting his eyes.

Margot understood Grey's question completely. He wanted to know if they could trust Ismet. "Yes," she said, squeezing Grey's hands back.

She looked at Ismet, "Wait. I don't have the key to the unit and no identification for Andy. Will they let us open it?"

"Have letter. Have contract. We pay. They open for sure. How you say? Money talks." Ismet snickered.

"Okay. We're set then," she said. "I have something important to tell you, Ismet. We'll talk on our way. Meet us here on the first of March?"

"Yes," Ismet said, raising his eyebrows. "Important bad? Important good?"

~ 21 ~

CHAPTER TWENTY-ONE

March 1, 2013

Margot and Grey piled into Ismet's car, an older model Yugo. Grey sat in the front passenger's seat; Margot in the back. No one spoke as Ismet pulled away from her apartment.

Once they were out of Prishtina and coasting on the highway, she said, "Ismet, Grey and I discussed this at length over the last two weeks. We agreed to tell you what has been happening. You have to decide if you want to listen. It affects you because they broke into your apartment in your building."

"You know who did this?" Ismet said.

"No," Margot said. "What is important, when we tell you our secret, you cannot reveal it to anyone. We are in an extremely dangerous situation. You must either promise to forget it, or—"

"Or, consider helping us. You know Albanian and you understand how things work in Kosovo," Grey said.

"Americans are safe here. Because of President Clinton and Mrs. Albright. NATO, too. They stop the war and save lives. Kosovo love America. But if very big trouble, I don't know. Please, yes, tell me."

"Are you sure you want to know? You could be in danger, too."

"Yes, when you victim in my country. This not right," he said, slamming his hand on the steering wheel. "I victim and almost die in Kosovo War. I promise God, if I survive, I help others treated bad."

"Thank you. We're going to need you," Grey said. "Margot, you want to start?"

Margot told Ismet everything about Andy, including someone tearing through his hotel room. She said this same person might have ransacked her apartment.

Ismet was silent at first. Then he said, "Andy kind man. I know that for sure. Kind to me. Terrible story. Margot, you too young for widow. You okay?"

"I'm coping, sort of. I...." She choked and burst into tears. Retelling the story brought it back to life for her again. She covered her face.

Ismet and Grey didn't speak.

"It's hot in here," she said, opening her window, thrusting her face into the wind.

Grey turned around and leaned over his seat. "What can I do?"

"Nothing," she sniffed. "I'm okay. Thank you, Ismet." She reached forward and caressed his shoulder.

"Hey," Grey said, pointing out the back window. "A car's coming."

"Okay," Ismet said. "I slow. He pass, maybe."

Margot swallowed hard.

Ismet reached across Grey's lap, pushed the glove box button, and the door plopped open.

Margot gasped at the sight of a huge, black handgun.

Ismet took it out, placed it on the floor behind his right foot, and slammed the door shut.

No one spoke.

As the car got closer, Margot rolled her window back up. Margot saw a woman in the passenger side. "A Toyota and he's right on our tail," she said in a whisper. As she watched the Toyota move to the passing lane and come up alongside the Yugo, she recorded every detail in her mind. The woman faced forward. She had disheveled mousey brown hair and a broad burn scar on her chin.

Kids bobbed up in the back seat and waved. She waved back. "Phew. Scared the hell out of me."

"Try not worry."

"Oh yeah. Don't worry. That's why you have a gun at your feet," she said.

"Aren't guns illegal in Kosovo?" Grey said.

"Yes." Ismet laughed.

"Glad you're on our side," she said.

"Look. We here."

Kampion i Sigurte was visible from the highway, approximately a quarter of a mile down a parallel service road. Ismet exited the highway, got on the service road, pulled into the company parking lot, and stopped the Yugo between the two vehicles: a company van and a blue, late model BMW.

Grey and Margot got out of the car, leaving Ismet sitting in the driver's seat. When Margot motioned for him to come, too, he shook his head and folded his arms. She gave him a thumbs up.

As they entered the building, a skinny twenty-something man who was perched behind the counter grinned at them. Margot handed him the letter and the contract.

"Good morning. I am Driton," he said, as he reviewed the papers.

Grey explained they wanted to end the contract and retrieve the contents from the storage unit.

"You can end, however, you must pay for the remainder of the contract. One year is twelve hundred euros, subtract two hundred paid, that is, the one hundred deposit and one hundred January rent. I will waive the late fee. Your balance is one thousand euros. Identification, please?"

While Margot bristled at having to pay for the full year, she didn't protest, because she worried without the proper identification they couldn't get into the unit.

Grey gave him his passport.

"Mr. Valentin? Where is Mr. Andrey Stephen? The contract is in his name."

"He had to work today. He sent us," Grey said, as he pulled his wallet from his back pocket.

"Hmm. Need his permission."

"I'm his wife," she said, yanking her cell out of her pocket and holding it up ready to dial. "I can call him at work, but I doubt he can come to the phone."

At the same time, Grey placed a one-thousand-euro banknote on the counter.

Driton's eyes widened, fixating on the note. "No, no." He swallowed. "Unnecessary. Key, please?"

Margot watched Driton salivate. "Sorry, he lost his luggage on an Arian flight from Vienna, along with his key."

"Oh, I hate Arian Airlines," Driton said, as he picked up the note and licked his lips. "They lose my luggage all the time. Okay, you must pay for the lost key, because we must change the lock. Please, another fifty euros," he said, with an arrogant smirk.

Grey gave him a fifty.

He stamped the contract *paid*, with a loud thud. "Okay, follow me. You can use my master key. If there is damage inside, you must pay more." He grabbed a hand truck leaning against the wall. "I'm in business to make money."

Margot and Grey rolled their eyes at each other as they followed Driton. He led them through a narrow hall to an elevator, which they took to the third floor.

When the elevator door opened, Driton handed Margot the key. "I am alone today, and I must return to the lobby. Note, the only exit for you is by my desk. All other exit doors have an alarm. So do not try to steal my key." He glared at her. "Understand?"

"Yes." She was tempted to ask him the fee for a master key just to be funny, but thought better of it. She doubted Driton would share her sense of humor.

"Take the hand truck, please. Unit three twenty-six is straight ahead." The doors squeaked closed.

They walked to the end of the corridor and Margot inserted the key into the lock. The door opened easily. It was pitch black inside, and Grey reached around on the left wall and pushed the light switch to *on*.

Intense fluorescent lights flickered on and filled the room, causing her eyes to sting. She squinted.

They faced a space that was empty, except for a cardboard box in the far-right corner.

"Wow. That's it?" Her body shook, from cold or nerves.

Grey shut the door and stood over the plain cardboard box. It was wrapped with thin, brown plastic tape.

"Open it," she said.

Grey nodded and paused as if to gather his thoughts before lowering himself on one knee. He searched for the loose fringe of the tape. No luck. The edges were sealed tight. Even so, he found a weak spot on a corner and pulled out a writing pen, working to penetrate the tape. It was futile. "My hands are sweating. Dammit. Let's go back for scissors."

"Wait." She burrowed in her purse and removed a metal fingernail file.

Grey used the pointed edge to snap through and release the tape. He signaled her to open it.

She lifted the top and saw Andy's David Yurman watch and a music box hand-painted lemon yellow with tiny red flowers. And another Kazimir Malevich, a duplicate of the scarf Andy had used to wrap the filigree box. Last, a tin box labeled Albred Tea.

When she picked up the tin box, it rattled. She handed it to Grey. He popped the lid and emptied the contents into her cupped hands. Two flash drives.

Her mouth dropped open.

"Damn. Could this be it? The reason for ransacking Andy's hotel room and your apartment?"

When her words didn't come, she winced and let out a groan.

"Do we need to hide these?"

Margot stared at Grey, and stuffed both drives into the front pocket of her jeans.

Grey snapped the lid back into place and hesitated. He took it off again. "Put your lipstick in here. In case someone finds it, they'll hear something inside and assume they have what they need."

"Who?"

"God, I have no idea. I'm not making sense."

"None of this makes sense." She dropped two tubes inside. "Two for extra measure, I guess. I'm putting the music box and the scarf in my purse. I'll wear his watch, ostentatious or not." She wanted something of Andy's on her body, and slipped it on her wrist.

Grey pressed the lid in place, returned the tin to the cardboard box, and closed the box. He placed the box on the hand truck.

When they were back at the front desk, Driton said, "Everything out?"

"Yep, want to check it? And your master key, sir," Grey said, handing the key back.

"No, no. I'm sure it's fine. Please come back. We're always looking for new customers. And tell your husband we thank him for his business."

Margot's heart hurt when she heard *husband*. They would never be married.

As they strode toward the parking lot, Ismet stood outside the vehicle, leaning against the passenger door. He had turned the car around with the rear end facing the building and the trunk wide open.

Grey put the cardboard box inside, slammed the trunk, and hopped back in the passenger side. Margot got into the back seat and pulled her seat belt tight.

Ismet slid in behind the wheel, turned the engine on, and rolled the car off the lot.

***

"Hey. Ismet. Faster." Grey said, looking closer at his side mirror.

Margot turned around to see the blue BMW closing in on them.

Ismet hit the accelerator, and the Yugo responded with a loud rumble, shaking everyone.

To steady herself, Margot held on to the front seat. "False alarm. The car made a U turn and drove to the storage company parking lot."

Grey clicked his tongue.

"Is good. You watch for autos. I drive."

"Margot, you look left and back. I'll look right and forward," Grey said.

The Yugo roared forward and dirt from the road flew up behind them, obscuring Margot's view.

Finally, as they entered the paved highway, the dust disappeared. She saw they were alone on the road.

Ismet slowed down, and they sighed in unison.

Grey readjusted his sitting position, craning his neck to look farther to the right. Margot did the same, checking the roads that veered left.

Margot said, "Not sure why I'm so nervous. How could anyone know about the storage unit? I didn't even know."

"Call me paranoid," Grey said.

"Must be cautious," Ismet said. "Why I have weapon."

Margot's shoulders shuddered.

"Car behind," Ismet said. He pointed at his rearview mirror and slammed his foot on the gas pedal. The engine strained and made a high-pitched scream, wobbling the whole car. Margot was positive the fenders were falling off, and even though the engine's sound was deafening, she still heard the blood coursing through her ears.

"Close now. Get down." Ismet grabbed his gun and put it in his lap.

Grey bent over, hiding under the dash. Margot tilted onto her side, grabbing her knees to her chest. She heard the car gaining speed, getting closer, louder.

As it pulled alongside the Yugo, Margot couldn't help herself. She shifted to her knees, and peeked out of the bottom of the window to catch a glimpse of the driver. He had crow-black eyes, a mole high on his cheek, a scruffy beard, and short hair. When the driver turned his head and locked his eyes on hers, she couldn't move. He took a deep drag of his cigarette and slowly exhaled smoke with a repulsive grin.

The Yugo slowed, allowing the creep to pass.

Margot sat up and squealed. Her face dripped with sweat. "What the fuck? I can't do this. Did you see him look at me? What an evil asshole."

Grey said, "It's okay. I didn't see him as evil. We're too keyed up. We see the worst when we are fearful."

"Bullshit. He wanted to scare me, and it worked."

"Make note. License plate. Oh four nine oh two FD. Car from Prizren area," Ismet said.

"Got it," Grey said as he punched the numbers in his phone. "And why are we recording this number?"

"Like you say, call me paranoid. Oh, oh. Now I see van. Don't worry. I think *Kampion i Sigurte* van."

The storage company van raced toward their rear and darted into the passing lane. The driver, mouth open, pointed to the shoulder of the road.

"That's not Driton." Margot put her hands over her eyes. "Please, this has to stop."

Ismet pulled off to the side, and the van stopped behind them. The driver got out and approached Ismet's window.

"Po?" Ismet said through the window.

"*Ke harruar faturën tënde*," the driver said, pointing to a piece of paper.

Ismet nodded, opened his window, and took the paper. "*Fale-minderit.*" He drove back onto the highway, rolled his window up, and handed Grey his pistol. "Please, put away."

Grey opened the glove box and held the gun from the edge of the handle with his fingertips, as if it were a piece of dog shit. He put it inside and clicked the glove box shut.

Ismet rolled his window up, exhaled, and snorted as he handed the paper to Grey. "Receipt for storage unit."

Grey cracked up.

"Don't know how you can laugh." Margot sniffed. "My heart is still pounding from the asshole blowing smoke at me."

As the laughter trailed off, they were silent for a few miles.

Then Ismet spoke. "Find what you want?"

"Not sure," Grey said.

"Oh, forgive me. Not my business."

"No, no. We found sentimental stuff belonging to Andy," she said.

"Aha. Leave box in trunk. Very secure. No worries."

"Speaking of worries, let's get away and leave our worries behind."

"Hmm. Where?" she said.

"Everybody love Albanian beach. Dhermi is beautiful even in winter," Ismet said.

Margot leaned into the space between the two front seats. "Count me in."

"I just remembered," Grey said. "I have a friend we should visit: Wila. Dr. Wila Lewis. She's smart, fluent in many languages, and could be helpful to us. She owns a condo in Dhermi. I'm thinking—"

"Can you call her?" Margot said.

"Let me see." Grey checked his phone, then dialed. "Hello, Wila. It's Grey Valentin."

Grey listened.

"Yes, good to hear your voice, too. And you're in Dhermi now?"

Grey turned to face Margot. His eyes brightened and his brows raised, matching his wide grin. "My dear Wila, I have a special favor. Can I come visit you for a few days? I want to bring two friends along if it's all right."

He listened.

"Are you sure? I don't want to impose. I mean....Yes....Excellent. It'll be great to see you too."

He ended the call, "We're set. You will love Wila. And I think she knows Russian."

"The letter?" Margot said.

Grey nodded. "Besides that, we've spent a lot of time together. I know we can trust her."

Ismet said, "You take Yugo—"

"Ismet, you come, too. We're a team now," Margot said.

"Right," Grey said.

"No. Thank you. Yes, team. But I must work."

"We can rent a car," Grey said.

"No, no rent. Leave trail for sure. Use Yugo."

"Ah. Ismet. Forgive me, but your Yugo, I mean, the engine. The fenders are about to fall off. I appreciate it but—"

"Yugo is shit. Yes, of course. I not thinking."

Margot giggled.

"Yes, yes. Have different car for you. I sell Yugo."

"Forgive me, again," Grey chuckled. "Honestly, who'd buy it?"

Ismet howled with laughter. "Correct. Good question. Don't worry. I have good auto for you."

Relaxed now, Margot leaned back against her seat, lifted her wrist, and ran her finger across the face of Andy's watch. He loved this watch.

She pulled his scarf from her purse. As she laid it across her lap, she caught an image of his smile in her mind's eye, just long enough to tug at her heart and cloud her eyes with tears.

~ 22 ~

CHAPTER TWENTY-TWO

January 5, 2013

On their third conference call, Cass looked forward to catching up with everyone. She had good news regarding payments and Jer had planned to do some "team building." To her, it gave proper attention to hard-working daredevils, Magpie's heroes, as they risked everything to better the health and the lives of American citizens. A noble calling.

Jer glowed as he grabbed his coffee and sat in front of his computer. "This will be our best call. Mark my words."

"First time I've seen your smile in months. It's nice. Glad you and I are on a kinder footing. We should've done it first."

He didn't respond.

She sighed. "Let's hope Peter behaves."

"He will," he said, as he made the call.

"Hey guys. Welcome. A quick few notes before we get started," Jer said. "One: Be sure to include the VPN on your devices. Two: Cass says they have made four deposits in the Singapore account. And three: I got a question regarding the scope of our cyberattack.

Specifically, one of you asked if it included stealing data? The answer is no. Patient data are off limits. Our goal is to dismantle the United States health insurance companies. No more, no less. Moving on, let's get started. Cass, give us numbers."

"Morning. Every year, insurance companies deny over two hundred million health insurance claims. That's loads of money taken from patients and their families. Meanwhile, insurance company profits keep skyrocketing. One of the biggest, Unisome Health Care, raked in over fifty billion dollars last year."

"Thanks, Cass. Just a few stats to keep in mind should we waiver from our mission. Stress, pressure, and potential burnout can run roughshod over us. We'll be working day and night."

"Excuse me. Juan here. Money is a big issue, for sure. But I'm motivated when I think of the loss of lives and the destruction to families."

Cass smiled. She liked Juan.

"Tell us about your family, Juan," Jer said.

"Well, my parents immigrated from Cuba. Legally, for your information, Peter. My brother, Miguel, was a year older than me. After high school, we both got tech jobs, dealing with websites, SEO, and security stuff. We ended up working for Anonymous. Then Miguel got sick. Ah. Real sick. Cancer. In his pancreas. Died last year."

The sounds on the call stopped, except for faint sniffs.

"I'm sorry, Juan," Claudia said.

"Thanks, Claudia. My parents' health insurance refused to pay claims. They also denied life-prolonging—I'd say life-saving—services for my brother. Mom and Dad spent every cent they had. To this day, they still owe hundreds of thousands of dollars. They lost their son, I lost my best friend. What's worse: it broke my parents. They'll go to their graves with guilt because they couldn't save their firstborn son."

"Peter, here. Sad story for sure. Although the important question is, if he got the care he needed, would it have cured him? The answer is no. Pancreatic cancer is fast acting. He was a dead man as soon as he got diagnosed. Get real. You can't blame the insurance company for that."

A number of voices clamored simultaneously.

"Hold on. One at a time. Let Juan speak. Juan?" Jer said.

"Dammit. Peter. Did you hear me? It destroyed my family."

"Claudia speaking. Peter, you're an asshole."

Cass sneered at Jer, expecting him to step in and stop this negative escalation. When he didn't, she pounded her pen on the desk.

"No disrespect, Claudia. I got my own story, my dear. It's a little rougher than the Cuban's."

Cass was learning to hate Peter, beyond resenting his attitude. His racist sneer at Juan's nationality and the condescending "my dear" sparked her revulsion. Her stomach knotted.

"Okay, go ahead. How about we measure our losses against one another? Let's see who wins," Claudia said.

Cass was surprised Claudia had stepped in between Juan and Peter. It was the first time a team member had challenged Peter, and she was curious how he'd come back at her.

Silence.

"Thank you, my dear. I'll do that for sure. For now, I got a question about the VPN on our phones. Doesn't protect us, does it? It hides our IP and encrypts the online traffic, but make no mistake, there's no protection from hackers, viruses, or malware. So, why get a VPN at all?"

Cass seethed. Peter just blew Claudia off.

"It's a nonissue. TunnelSAFE solves that problem," Jer said.

Cass covered Jer's mic with her hand. "We all know this about VPNs, and we have all used TunnelSAFE when working for Anonymous. It's Peter's diversion tactic. He just likes to stir us up. So while you said today was focused on team building, he's tearing the team down and using you to do it," she said in a low growl. She took her hand away and spoke into her microphone, glaring at Jer. "This is old news, guys. More important, whatever you do, don't lose your phone. I know you got passcodes. So, there's a good chance cops can't gain access to your data. But honestly, it's not guaranteed."

"Yeah," Jer said, waving Cass off. "If you're thinking cops need a search warrant to access the data on your phone, don't be a fool. They'll bypass legalities, get the information they want, then ask for forgiveness. Meanwhile, you will have been found out."

"It's not just law enforcement. We're under the crushing fists of our benefactors, too," Claudia said.

Peter said, "Ha. Benefactors. That's an ironic word choice. It implies altruism. I doubt they're funding us out of the goodness of their hearts."

"I said this was risky, guys. You're steeped in it now. Any effort to pull out will light you up like a rocket," Jer said.

"Okay, then. We're trapped. No turning back now. Right, guys?" Peter said.

Mumbles of confirmation came through the audio.

When the sounds subsided, Peter said, "Now, let's keep on keeping on. Ah. Cass. I know we got the deliverables in. Did we get paid?"

"Yes. Got one hundred thousand dollars each, deposited in the Singapore account. I triple checked. It's there."

"How and when do we get access?" Peter said.

"The purpose of overseas banking is to keep your money hidden. It's not available for everyday use. If you need money, get a loan. It is the way it is," Cass said.

"How will we get it?" Juan asked.

"Bitcoin. Granted, they're iffy right now," she said.

"Claudia speaking. Guess we were damn naïve. This is stuff we should have discussed before, Jer. Too late now? What the hell—"

"Yeah, for sure. I am not happy!" a voice said.

Cass recognized Juan's voice, although it didn't matter who said it, because everyone thought the same thing.

"Hold on a minute," Cass said as she muted the mic. "Jer, this is falling apart. Do something."

He got up from his chair and paced around his desk. Minutes passed, and he still circled.

Finally, he sat and unmuted his mic. "Sorry, I needed a minute. I should have discussed this. Peter is raising brilliant questions. And Claudia, I hear you."

When Cass heard brilliant, she realized Peter intimidated Jer. Why else suck up to him?

Everybody talked at once, which made it difficult to hear exactly what was being said.

She watched a deep frown appear on Jer's face. His jaw muscles rippled.

"Come on." Cass said, whacking her thighs in frustration.

Finally, the cacophony dwindled.

"Jer?" Peter said.

He didn't respond.

"Hey, buddy, our fearless leader, say something."

When Jer didn't respond, Peter said, raising his voice, "Fucking mess. We've been had."

Jer's silence and smug expression confused Cass.

"Shut up, Peter. You must know, it's Claudia speaking. I'll bet Anonymous went through this, too. Unfortunately, Magpie is our first rodeo."

"First time for me and I never earned a cent," Juan said.

"I gotta think," Claudia said. "How can I protect myself and my family?"

"We all have family," Peter said.

Cass's hands quaked. The group was on the edge of aborting, and she had to break this spiral. "All right, let's hit *pause*." She checked Jer's face for approval.

He nodded.

No one talked. The silence didn't matter, because Cass felt a rush of fury blowing through the computer screen.

"I agree," Juan said. "Let's take a break. Say, two days."

"I dunno," Peter said.

"Two days' delay. Before we decide too quick and fuck ourselves up totally. Who's with me?" Juan said.

Finally, Jer said, "You are jeopardizing your futures. Don't forget our benefactors."

Cass sat back and folded her arms to stop her entire body from shaking. If the team abandoned Magpie, no way could they hide from the Russians.

Jer buried his face in his computer. "Okay, two days. Listen. Going once. Going twice. Going...."

Silence.

"Three times. Okay, it's settled. We'll meet in two days, eight a.m.," Jer said with a self-satisfied grin.

The call ended.

"What happened? Why are you smug?" she asked.

He took a deep breath and blew out, "They know all this stuff: VPNs, phones, money. They're nervous, that's all."

"That's all?"

"Yep. They gotta go through figuring this out for themselves."

"What are you saying? Are you stupid?"

"God, Cass!" He leaned back in his chair and folded his hands behind his head. "I want their total commitment. This'll get it."

"Or not. You're killing me, Jer. That was not team building. You let Peter shift the discussion to VPN without addressing his asshole comments? And, because you didn't explain how the money worked, Magpie is blowing in the wind."

He reached for his coffee. "They'll stick with it. You watch." He sipped his coffee, squinting at her over his cup.

"And, if they don't?"

"We're fucked."

She grabbed her coat. Her legs barely held her up when she climbed the basement stairs.

She headed straight for the vestibule when Mrs. Bloom spoke. "Cass, you okay?"

Cass didn't answer. She stomped out the back door and started home.

It was pitch black and silent out, except for that damn black crow cawing from somewhere in the fields.

~ 23 ~

CHAPTER TWENTY-THREE

March 7, 2013

Wila, Margot, and Grey shared a bottle of red wine on a balcony overlooking the Ionian Sea in Dhermi, Albania. The spectacular setting sun with its streaks of crimson and yellow hushed the conversation of the three of them. Margot felt blessed to be in this special place, safe with Wila and Grey, where she could let go, even only for an hour, the distress she had endured since she learned Andy was gone. Delving into the letter, the music box, and the flash drives could wait. She craved normal social conversation.

Dr. Wila Lewis, a stout woman with short auburn hair, hazel eyes, and patches of soft brown freckles, was fascinating, a world traveler and a dedicated eye surgeon.

"Thank you for having us here. It's an awesome place," Margot said.

"Of course, it's my pleasure," Wila said, with a Scottish brogue.

"I'm curious, Dr. Lewis, Grey told me you two met in Vietnam. Go on."

"Please, call me Wila. Even my patients call me by my first name. Grey and I met in Vietnam, at the Red River Resort in Hoi An. I'd recently completed a SEE project in Cambodia. SEE stands for Surgical Eye Expeditions International. We had conducted twenty surgeries over a four-day period on children and adults in desperate need of sight-saving operations. SEE has its rewards, and, yet, it can be emotionally exhausting. The Red River Resort is one of my favorite respites. Have you been to Vietnam?"

"No. I hope to go someday."

"It has everything I enjoy: history, countryside, beaches, bustling cities. But, enough of my musings, I'm thrilled you are here, Margot, with my splendid Grey. My sense is you have a special, urgent purpose. We can begin if you wish."

The word *splendid* caused Margot to see Grey for the first time, again. He appeared smarter, more attractive. She smiled to herself, remembering her mother's words: your negative attitude causes you to miss the beautiful truth right in front of you.

"Yes, we do. We have a letter. I think it's in Russian. Thought you could translate it for us," Grey said.

"I'm happy to assist. May I ask, however, why this distance for a simple translation?"

Margot sat on the edge of her seat, curious to hear Grey's response and how much he'd reveal.

Wila's eyes were transfixed on Grey as he explained that his best friend, Andy, Margot's fiancé, had been killed in Tetovo. He described how the murder was shrouded in mystery, noting Police Officer Dime Pavlovski reported someone shot him in the back of the head.

It was difficult for Margot to hear it again, and when she noticed her jaw tightening, she took time to calm herself, relaxing her jaw and parting her lips. She put effort into holding back her emotions. It was necessary if she wanted to be calm.

"No items of value were taken. His passport, wallet, and banknotes were in plain sight. The culprit was searching for something because he tore the room apart. He may have found it, although we can't know for sure."

"I see, and as a result, you are in a constant state of fear. I don't envy you. Let me ask, you said Andy was your best friend. Did you have an inkling this might happen to him? And why Tetovo?"

"Not an inkling. Andy and I were very close. At least, I thought so. I loved him," Grey said, rubbing his nose with his napkin.

Wila whispered, "I'm so sorry."

"He said he had to go to Macedonia on a classified assignment for the State Department," Margot said. "When I found out he didn't work for the State Department, it struck me like a bolt of lightning," she said, with an awkward gulp.

"He lied to both of us. It's not the Andy we knew."

"I don't know what to say. This is horrific. I cannot imagine...." Wila's voice faded.

"There's more," he said. "Someone broke into Margot's apartment in Prishtina. Thank God she wasn't home. Ransacked it, too. We think it's connected to Andy's murder. We've come this distance to avoid detection. Of course," he said with a smile, "seeing you is a bonus." He told her about the flash drives. "It's possible we've seen too many thriller movies," he said with a nervous titter, "we're too afraid to view them on our laptops for fear of malware."

"I don't think you're overreacting," Wila said. "Until we have additional information, I encourage you to be extremely vigilant. Regarding the drives, my partner, Alexandra, was passionate about technology. We were together for fourteen years before she died of breast cancer two years ago. She was the brains in the family," she beamed. "Alexandra taught me a bit of web and computer knowledge. She also warned me, repeatedly, to be aware of identity theft and outlined many other ways technology seeps into our lives. Indeed, the flash drives may very well harm your laptops. Just this past June, we began learning about Stuxnet and infected USB flash drives causing substantial damage to the Iran's nuclear program."

"What? You're kidding," Margot said. "I don't even know what that means."

Wila scratched her head, "Can't say that I do either. We're only beginning to learn what really happened. It's fascinating. But, time for that discussion later. First, it's getting chilly. Let's go inside."

"It's raining, too," Grey said as he slid the glass doors open.

"Cool and damp this time of year. Care for tea?"

"Not for me, thank you," Margot said, taking a seat on the sofa. "We have Andy's music box." Margot took the letter and the box from her purse, placing both on the coffee table. She hadn't examined the box, and she couldn't interpret the letter. Rampant anticipation caused perspiration to trickle down her back. Her hand trembled as she sipped her wine.

"I haven't finished my wine." Grey pulled the doors shut and sat beside her, his face turning crimson. "My nerves are edgy, too."

"Well, then, let's get at it, shall we?" Wila said as she settled across from them and scanned the letter. She set her jaw. "All right. I am not fluent in Russian. However, I can interpret most of it. Dated July twentieth, two thousand twelve. Here we go."

My darling Andrey,

This letter is a long time coming and circumstances are such now, I'm compelled to tell you the truth. I'll get right to the point.

First, you must understand, your father was not a financier or a stockbroker. In fact, he worked for a Russian oligarch. You were twelve when your father disappeared from our lives, young and unaware of the ways of the world. I allowed you to believe he left because he wanted a divorce.

How could I tell you he was a spy involved in espionage, hiding away to protect us? I couldn't.

He led a secret life, and I had no choice. I had to go along. The truth is your father and I have been in constant communication the entire time. I was stupid and too naïve to grasp the depth of his involvement until recently, when he confessed to an elaborate, destructive scheme.

He explained he and his Russian colleagues were planning a cyberattack on the United States' health insurance system. Initially, the attack compromised the entire industry, state by state, causing company losses in the trillions of dollars.

We both agreed these organizations have only themselves to blame and deserved our wrath. Thousands have suffered abuse put upon us by the despicable insurance companies who outright refuse to pay claims or pay after years and years of haggling and suffering, to the point of death for too many.

For us, it's personal. Kaz's sister, your Auntie Rachel, died from a rare immune deficiency. Her insurance company denied coverage for intravenous immunoglobulin infusions. We did what we could. After paying $1,200 a day for months and months, she'd spent every cent she had. She refused our help, discontinued treatments, and died within a month. Heartbroken, your father blames himself to this day.

To be sure, your father turned obsessive, even fanatical, until he learned his colleagues had hidden the truth from him. The cyberattack included sabotaging and stealing individual medical files to sell on the black market. He was convinced this created confusion. Most importantly, it resulted in delayed care. Patients would go without proper treatments or no treatment.

Kaz said the attack had virus capabilities and upon detection, it mutates repeatedly, as necessary. He wanted to stop it. Unfortunately, he was under constant scrutiny. If he took any action, they would kill both of us, leaving the attack to continue.

Please, we need you, Andrey. You are the only one we can turn to. You must stop this senseless act. Your father will protect you from the interior.

Along with this letter, you'll see the sweet music box you gave me for my birthday when you were five. I've cleverly hidden the computer virus data inside.

It's important to know, the cyberattack will activate on April 15, 2013. Kaz told me there's not much time to develop an antidote.

Soon after this conversation, he left for Macedonia, and he's not contacted me since. I'm sure he's cut off communication to keep me safe.

Now, I know anyone with a conscience would question the obvious: what parents would send such a heinous and dangerous request to their child. Believe me, this is the hardest decision I have ever made. In reality, no one is as capable as you, Andrey. And, second, our family, the Stephen family, your father, me, and now you; we have this extraordinary opportunity to create a lasting legacy by taking action to save the lives of millions of Americans.

We love you very much. Be careful, my darling.

All my love, Mother.

Wila dropped the letter in her lap and shook her head.

"My God," Margot bellowed. "It's an impossible burden." She choked as her throat filled with bitterness. "I hate this woman."

Grey and Wila were silent as Margot rocked on the sofa.

Finally, Grey said, "This is hard, Margot."

Margot sniffed and pulled her shoulders back.

"Can this possibly be true? Sounds like science fiction," Grey said.

"Not, it's not. It has been done before, at least to some degree. In March two thousand two, an American company..." Wila trailed off, curling her brow. "I think. Yes, Premera Blue Cross. They finally admitted to a breach that had compromised over twenty million medical and financial records. Further, they kept it secret for two months, then denied it had happened. Of course, the stunning truth emerged, but unfortunately, it was after thousands of identities were stolen."

"What do you mean *finally admitted*?" Grey said.

"They waited because hacking causes a loss of confidence on the part of patients, the public, and the government. No confidence equals loss of revenue. It's always the money. They tried to fix it. Of course, they were too late."

"You'd think they'd invest a minuscule fraction of their revenues in programs to protect data instead of lining their pockets," Margot said, scowling.

"This is real, I'm afraid," Wila said. "Those of us who live in Europe enjoy superb and inexpensive, often free, health care. We're fully aware of the United States' insurance company atrocities. It's no surprise people want to destroy them."

No one spoke.

"I don't get it. How does stealing patient files do anything and who buys this stuff?"

"Personal data is a lucrative market. Cybercriminals make fraudulent credit card purchases. Or, they sell it on the black market where broader networks commit identity theft or hold data for ransom. Patients pay the ransom, although few ever get their information back. Furthermore, unscrupulous organizations buy data and sell to pharmaceuticals who, in turn, develop surefire strategies to increase their market share."

"I still have a disconnect. Are the data deleted?"

"They're not deleted," Wila said.

"Okay, then, how do people die? I'm totally confused."

"The key word in Nadia's letter is *sabotage*," Grey said.

"Agreed and I take *sabotage* to mean *corruption*, which is worse than deleting because they distort data. The result: no accurate records for healthcare professionals to access regarding allergic reactions to medication, prescriptions, treatments. Patient histories are lost or just plain wrong. Understand?"

"Why? Just to kill innocent people?" Margot stomped her foot. "It's, I don't know....It's mind boggling and I don't believe it."

"You must. For years, Russia has devised plans to invade your country. Of course, they cannot do so militarily because they're ill-equipped. However, they've had success with technology. Cyber espionage is their weapon of choice in today's world. They've ravaged systems in many countries. And they'll do everything possible to weaken the worldview of the United States."

Margot jolted up and paced around the room in a frenzy.

"We cannot dispute the facts, Margot. This is fucking serious." Grey said.

"Indeed, fucking serious," Wila said. "I'm sorry. Time is of the essence. Look, today is March eighth."

Margot fell into a chair in despair. "My brain is in overdrive," she said, closing her eyes.

"Yeah, we got five or six weeks. And I do not know where to start," he said.

"Let's start with these flash drives. I have a laptop I don't use anymore. Look on the second shelf." Wila pointed to a bookcase.

"Got it," he said, placing it on the coffee table and plugging it in a nearby wall socket.

"I can review, in general." The screen lit up. "I can evaluate certain criteria; however, I cannot read the content, the code, or specifics. I don't have that level of expertise."

"If you say it's a virus, that's perfect, right, Margot?" he said.

"Sure. The blind leading the blind," Margot said, opening her eyes wide for effect.

"Aye, dear, you are correct. The question is, who can we alert to identify and stop the cyberattack?" Wila said.

"And how?" Margot said.

"You must go to the FBI headquarters in Prishtina," Wila said, "Wait, we're getting ahead of ourselves." She inserted one drive and waited for it to load.

~ 24 ~

CHAPTER TWENTY-FOUR

January 7, 2013

Cass hadn't slept or eaten in two days, obsessing over the team's decision. If anyone among them called it quits, they'd have to abort Magpie, and they'd face dangers so terrifying she couldn't fathom how they'd survive. Russians don't screw around with peons, and they were peons. Her stomach ballooned to capacity and sharp pains etched her groin.

Jer started the call and reminded everyone Cass had provided an update on their payments, explaining they wouldn't have access to their money right away. "Juan had requested a time out. Our time is up today. Are you in or out? First, Cass?"

"I'm in," she said.

"Yes," Claudia said.

There was a silent pause.

"I say yes," Juan said.

Cass breathed easier. But she was waiting for Peter. She figured him for an outlier based on the arrogant and racist attitude he made clear in their earlier conference calls.

"Peter," Cass said, holding her breath again. He shocked her when he said he was in.

Jer gave her a cocky smile. She turned red from embarrassment and forced herself to nod an apology.

She always considered herself to have excellent instincts, excelling at determining character. How could she have been so wrong? She was having a hard time swallowing her pride. But, for the good of Magpie, she decided to make a special effort with Peter.

"Glad to hear it, Peter," she said, taking her first step to accept him and smooth over their differences.

"Ok, we're a go," Jer said. "Listen up. We got to have this up and running by Zero Day, April fifteenth. You got your assignments. Trouble or questions, contact me via IRC. An emergency? Get me right here. Questions?"

"I have a comment," Peter said. "Like I said, I'm in. Plus, I'm thinking we ought to go deeper, wider. Let's go for patient data."

Cass glared at Jer and shook her head, mouthing, "No way."

Jer reminded Peter that Magpie's scope had been established. "Stealing data skews our focus. It's off the table."

"It will cause compromised scripts and incorrect treatments," Claudia said. "We're here to help people, not risk their health."

"The data are worth thousands on the black market. I'm talking about copying, not compromising the files. Juan, you could get your parents out of debt in a flash," Peter said.

"Don't drag me in on your bullshit, Peter. It's not for me," Juan said.

"It's too dangerous and can leave a trail." Cass said, cradling her chin in one hand and caressing her upset stomach with the other.

"I doubt it," Peter said.

"It's not happening," Jer said, sitting taller.

Peter answered in a calm, low voice. "I don't agree."

"Agree or get out." Jer said with such force that spittle landed on his mic.

Jer's outburst surprised Cass, but she was happy he drew the line for Peter.

"God, Jer. Don't get your Iowa bibbed overalls in a wad." He blew air in his mic and laughed.

His sarcastic humor infuriated Cass. "That's not a firm commitment."

"Whatever. You aren't getting rid of me. Truth is, you need me, bad. So, yeah. Count me in."

When Cass scowled at Jer, he flipped his hand, dismissing her. She sneered back and slapped her thighs in frustration.

Jer ended the call.

"Peter's *overalls* crap was offensive. I didn't think you'd let him get away with that. We can't trust him. He's already shown a pattern of defiance. How are you going to corral him?"

He didn't answer.

"What's your plan?"

Jer stood, towering over her in her chair. "Fuck you, Cass. I got this. I'll check in on him. He's going to be fine, and he's right. We need him. Magpie requires his expertise and experience. Nobody is near his precision."

Cass wanted to bring up Operation Malcolm, but worried it'd set Jer off even more. Still, she had a strong sense that Peter wouldn't stop pushing Jer. "He's rotten."

He plopped in his chair. "End of discussion. You're done here." He pointed to the door.

"You're quick to dismiss me. You don't want to discuss it because you know I'm right," she said, leaning on one leg and cocking her head.

Hold your ground.

His face showed no emotion.

"What? You don't know what to say?"

Silence.

Cass shifted her weight back to both feet and straightened her head to a less threatening position. "I'm just saying, have a plan to control him. Just in case. Be prepared. And, if I'm wrong and if it turns out he's trustworthy, no harm done."

He turned away from her. "Go home."

She grabbed her jacket, and stomped up the basement steps and out the back door. As she walked the three miles to her house, she hoped she was wrong. But she prayed Jer didn't slip into old behaviors and refuse to acknowledge a problem hitting him right in the face. He had done that before with Operation Malcolm, which marked the beginning of the end of his relationship with Anonymous. Jer had fallen into disturbing despair. Cass feared he was clinically depressed because he refused to talk and hadn't come out of his cellar for four months.

Surely he had learned his lesson. She dropped her head, overwhelmed with a terrible thought: What will you do if he hasn't?

A gradual sharp pain worked its way across her lower abdomen. She bent over and held her breath, waiting for it to subside. In the quiet, that damn crow called out. His familiar jeering caw sounded like a sinister warning, a suggestion that she be wary of impending doom.

When the pain stopped, the crow went silent, too.

She straightened her back and searched for him on her way home, hoping he'd flown away forever. Well, at least until spring, after Zero Day, April 15th. Who ever heard of crows in Iowa in December, anyway?

When he was nowhere to be found, she asked herself again: What if Jer hasn't learned from Operation Malcolm?

~ 25 ~

CHAPTER TWENTY-FIVE

March 10, 2013

"I agreed to do this shit, join with your boss and you on this un-known project, because you told me it'd be lucrative," Michael said, drawing out the word *lucrative* in a sarcastic tone. "Seen nothing lu-crative yet. I want money. And when you want to meet at Stripe Depot, I'm on the clock. So, you need to pay for my alcohol and whatever else interests me," he said, jutting his chin toward two pole dancers.

Dugal scoffed and took his army cap off, tossing it on the vacant barstool between them. "Listen—"

"I don't have time to sit around waiting for you. And why do you wear fake military shit? It's offensive. Where did you get the hat? The dollar store?"

"Had a thing in Peja. Anyway, I see you're dressed in black. Per-fect. Where's the ski mask?"

Michael smirked, waved the mask in front of Dugal's face, and shoved it into his cargo pants.

"Good boy," Dugal grinned and tossed five euros on the bar. "For your beer. The boss decides—"

"When do I meet the boss man?" Michael bristled when Dugal called him *good boy*, but he'd let it go for another time. Right now, he needed money. "I'm sick of you and your bullshit. I want to go to the boss man."

"Well, let's see if I can arrange that. As they say, careful what you wish for," he said, taking out his cell and walking to a corner of the room.

Michael tried to listen in, but he was too far away, and Dugal cupped his hand over his mouth. So he went back to watching the girls and finished his beer.

Dugal came back to the bar and said the boss had summoned him.

Well, la-di-da.

The meeting was in three hours. Michael asked the meeting location, and Dugal said every taxi driver knew the big house on the hill, before Germia.

***

Dugal was right. When Michael said *the big house on the hill, before Germia*, the driver nodded, and they were on their way. Twenty minutes later he stood in front of an enormous mansion, three stories high. He hoped his gimp leg would hold out if he had to go all the way to the top floor.

Someone had to be watching, because when he approached the twelve-foot-tall iron fence, the gates unlocked and grumbled open. He heard growling and barking inside. Dogs usually didn't scare him, but these dogs sounded damn vicious and he couldn't tell how many there were. He squeezed his left elbow to his side to secure his Italian Beretta handgun, unzipping his jacket for easy access, just in case.

Michael climbed the stairs to a massive porch. The dogs' snarling stopped when the front doors opened. Two pooches sat on either side of a man dressed in ironed jeans and a stiff white dress shirt.

"Welcome, Mr. Gorkey. Do not mind my blues, Gertie and Oliver."

"Blues?"

"Yes, blue, the color of my pets: Thai Ridgebacks. Please, come in." He shook Michael's hand. The handshake was quick and cold. Then he shoved an empty box at him. "Your weapons, please? I insist upon civilized behavior in my home, and therefore, do not permit firearms," he said, raising one eyebrow and tipping his nose to look down at Michael.

Michael paused and rolled his eyes. He refused to get sucked into some power play so soon. He'd wait to start that on his own terms. Besides, he was positive this guy had a gun.

Michael put his gun in the box. Since there had been no specific mention of knives, he didn't remove the Bowie blade hidden under his pant leg, and strapped to his right ankle.

"Follow me, please." The man led Michael upstairs to a balcony. "You have met my partner, Dugal Hetrick."

Dugal sat at the table, stone-faced.

Michael tipped his head.

"Dugal and I are having our favorite Rakija. It is the best local moonshine and exceedingly high in alcohol content. Care to join us?" he said, taking a seat.

Michael declined. He needed to stay clearheaded. Besides, he couldn't trust these guys. At the very least, they could spike his drink.

"We have information and are totally aware of your background and your tours in Afghanistan. You have withstood great pressures, on and off the battlefield. I consider you very resourceful, as well. Strange, I find it remarkable you failed at the elementary task of securing a disk."

The man stood like he had a rod up his ass, with perfect posture. Michael didn't respond. He took a seat and leaned back, broadcasting disrespect.

Although the man seemed to ignore Michael, Dugal squirmed and frowned at him.

"I assume when you failed to find the disk in Tetovo, you took an alternative route and pillaged an apartment in Prishtina," he said, pulling on his collar to straighten it. He glared at Michael while sipping his Rakija, and blotted his lips with his handkerchief. "Nevertheless, you didn't find it. My, my, Mr. Gorkey," he said with a cocky grin. He leaned back in his chair, puffed out his skinny chest, and crossed his legs.

Michael's neck twitched with concern when he realized someone had followed him.

"Unfortunately, Mr. Gorkey, you owe me one thousand euros. You see, I invested in you, a guarantee you would fulfill our agreement. However, you did not." His eyes narrowed.

"Want your money back? Here," Michael said, reaching around to his back pocket. The blues grumbled and bared their teeth, inches away from his calves. Michael froze.

"No one interrupts me." The boss pounded his fist on the table, rose from his chair, straightened his shirt, and pressed his handkerchief to his scarlet face. "Even Gertie and Oliver recognize rude behavior."

This guy's a nutcase.

The dogs sat again.

"Understand, we know what happened in that hotel room." His voice was higher, and he spoke faster. "The Tetovo chief of police, my close friend, said his officers had found a dead body. It shocked me, of course, and I told Pavlovski so."

"Listen, Dugal and I went over this. I said I'd work with you. Why go down that stupid road? It's history. Now, explain this mission thing. What is it?"

The man's words were measured again. "Impressive. I appreciate a man of conviction and curiosity. Good, Mr. Gorkey. Indeed, this mission thing you refer to is an international project and, while seemingly unlawful, worthy of tremendous admiration. Frankly, I consider it a humanitarian endeavor, designed to benefit millions of people," he said, clearing his throat.

"No kidding," Michael scoffed. This guy was such a pussy, and he used too many fucking words.

"I do not kid, Mr. Gorkey."

The boss' voice was stern and had a seething quality that told Michael he'd struck a nerve. He laughed to himself, proud he was figuring out this guy's weak spots to irritate him in the future.

"You must know, I have incredible knowledge and power in this country and beyond. I wield it as I deem necessary. Do not tempt me." He inhaled and raised his eyebrows. "Questions?"

Michael didn't know what the fuck the mission was, but he quickly realized the more he knew, the tighter the boss's trap. No fool, he shook his head.

"Lovely," he said, leaving the room. With his back to Michael, he said, "I shall be in touch. Dugal, escort Mr. Gorkey out, please, and explain his next assignment."

CHAPTER TWENTY-SIX

March 8, 2013

Grey and Margot stepped back from Wila's computer, waiting for the flash drive to load.

"Don't worry. It won't explode," Wila said, with a slight grin.

Two minutes passed and nothing.

Finally, the screen opened.

Margot couldn't believe her eyes.

"Who are these people?" Wila said.

"My mother. Andy. Brooks."

"Brooks?" Grey asked.

"He works at the Afton Alps ski resort. I took these photos in Minneapolis last year."

Wila shook her head and removed the first drive and clicked in the second.

Again, they waited.

"I don't believe it. More pics? No documents?" Margot said.

Wila leaned back and exhaled, "That's it. The photos are lovely. Forgive me, I know this is nothing to laugh at—" She burst out laughing.

Neither Grey nor Margot cracked a smile.

While Wila covered her mouth and continued giggling, Grey said, "I get it. Way too much tension. Something had to give. But, let's keep going. The music box. I'll get it."

Margot took a deep, cleansing breath. When Grey came back with the box, she opened it and looked inside. Empty. She turned it over and noticed the screws securing the mechanism cover were loose. She used her thumbnail to twist the screws out. The bottom released easily. Tan-colored dust covered the barrel and comb, so thoroughly caked the prongs were barely visible. She blew on it several times, releasing fine particles into the air.

Wila leaned over her shoulder. "Oh my God. Nothing. It's not funny anymore."

"No kidding. Everything I thought to be true isn't. Nadia's letter is the most valuable piece to the puzzle. For me, it's created more questions and angst than answers," Margot said, followed by a long exhale. She felt hopeless and closed her eyes, trying to block out the negative images in her head.

Wila gently closed the lid of her laptop. They sat in silence for a few minutes as a pall settled over the room.

"Wow. How about some hot caffeine to lift our spirits?" Grey said, as he went to the kitchen.

"Excellent choice," Wila said from the living room. "Bring us our coffee in the study. I have a whiteboard and we're going to need it. Come with me, Margot."

"Great idea. I want to get the timeline straight in my head. What happened and when. Can you scribe, Grey?" Margot said, following Wila.

"For sure, when the coffee's ready," he said.

Wila sat on an overstuffed chair facing the board.

"Let's start with meeting at the restaurant on January fifteenth," Margot said, sliding her chair in position to face the board. "Andy left for Tetovo the next day, the sixteenth." She removed her slippers, tucked one leg under her butt, and sat.

"Hold on, coffee's nearly ready. Do you have a tray somewhere, Wila?" Grey shouted from the kitchen.

"In the pantry on the bottom shelf."

"Grey, that's the same day you came to my apartment and told me about Andy."

"Lord, can you wait till I have the coffee ready?" he said.

Margot heard dishes rattling and the frustration in his voice.

"We can't wait all day," Wila said, raising her eyebrows with a grin. She whispered to Margot, "He's such a good man. I adore him."

She considered Grey an outstanding friend, although Margot couldn't bring herself to agree she adored him. That was too much too soon, but to be polite, she winked and signaled a thumbs up. When Wila tilted her head, Margot sensed she had disappointed her, and even though she was honest with herself, she felt a twinge of guilt.

Let it go.

"You two are slave drivers. Don't kid yourself, though, I readily accept the role," Grey said as he entered the study with a bright smile and a long exhale. He placed the tray on the desk. "Okay. Tetovo police had called the morning of the twenty-first. Still, I'm not positive which day the murder occurred," he said, sipping his coffee. "They said the hotel staff found his body and called them. So, the twentieth?"

"Yes," Wila said, "assuming they clean daily, and by three or four o'clock. They murdered him either on the nineteenth or twentieth, in the evening after they cleaned."

"Oh, my God. Does it matter?" Margot said, losing patience. "Let's not get caught up in meaningless minutia."

No one spoke as Grey wrote the information on the whiteboard.

"Somebody came to my door the twenty-first." Margot cleared her throat to stop herself from falling apart. She decided she'd list the dates with minimal explanation because her emotions were creeping in, causing her throat to tighten. "A guy knocked on my door and I got rid of him. I left, scared shitless, and when I came back, I found a ransacked apartment."

"Hope you moved," Wila said, mouthing, "I'm sorry."

Margot shrugged. "I did, the very next day, the twenty-second."

"And, today is March ninth. So, it's been six weeks?" Wila said.

Margot and Grey nodded.

"Anything else?"

They looked at each other, both shaking their heads.

"So, nothing has happened since the break in, back on January twenty-second? No threats?" Wila said.

"Wait. When we returned from Peja," Margot said, in a frenzy. "That driver, a weird-looking guy, pulled alongside us on the highway. He blew smoke at me. And, um, and the woman in another car. She had a big scar on her chin."

Silence.

"Margot, that's a stretch," Grey said. "Lots of people have moles and scars."

"No, no, it's not. You didn't see them—"

"You were frightened, Margot. We all were," Grey said.

"Fear," Wila said, "can make the most benign images appear ominous."

Margot thought, *How could I be so wrong?* She exhaled, disgusted with herself.

No one responded.

"I'm considering...this may be resolved," Wila said, raising her eyebrows.

They both frowned at her.

"God, if only it were true." Margot said in a shaky voice.

"Well, look at these dates," Wila said, pointing to the whiteboard. "Especially the amount of time we figure Andy was in

Tetovo. Let's assume he created an antidote for the computer virus even before you moved to Prishtina. Once in Tetovo, he'd have time to hand over the file. And you know Macedonia, right?"

"Yes, it's the worldwide epicenter for cyberattacks," Grey said.

"Somewhat true. Frankly, it's happening everywhere these days. Not at the same level as in Macedonia. Let me think, July twentieth. So, Andy had, what, five months? Let's assume he had time to develop an antidote," Wila said.

"Or find somebody to do it for him," Grey said. "In Tetovo."

"God, that sends shivers up my spine," Margot said, wondering if Andy had lied to her from the beginning, all along, keeping this horrendous secret to himself.

They drank their coffee.

"Wait a minute," Margot said, cracking her neck to relieve tension. "Let's suppose your speculations are correct and he had taken care of it in those five months. Why murder him, then? And how can we know that? We'd have to wait till...er...well, Nadia said the release date is April fifteenth."

"Superb point," Wila said. "Another possibility is—"

"They found the file." Margot said, bouncing in her chair with enthusiasm. "Got the antidote and destroyed the virus."

"Or worse. They found it and destroyed the antidote," Grey said.

"Wow," Wila said. "This is confusing."

"Dammit. It's all swirling in my head." Margot said, jolting out of her chair. "Let's say they found it. Have to figure they didn't find it at the hotel because they came to my place. So, back to Andy." She started flailing her arms, walking in circles, trying to attach logic to their assumptions. With a raised voice, fraught with frustration and dread, she said, "Why kill him when he could point them in the right direction? It's so fucking stupid. Why kill him....Why?" She went to the window, mumbling "Why?" She covered her mouth. Soft sobs escaped, despite how she promised herself she wouldn't cry.

No one spoke, as if they were letting Margot have a moment in her grief.

Grey put his marker down, took a drink of coffee, and peered over his cup at Margot. "To get rid of the evidence."

Margot turned to him. "Aren't we evidence?"

He looked into his cup, paused, and bit his bottom lip. "Anyone for another cup of coffee?"

"I see. My question is too much, isn't it?" Margot said.

No one answered.

"Well, all right then, I get it." Margot said, tossing her hair.

Wila and Margot placed their cups on the tray, and Grey took it into the kitchen.

"Please tell me you don't have to make a new pot," Margot said, rolling her eyes and trying to reframe the discussion.

"Nope, I do not," he said, raising his voice.

Margot and Wila stared at each other in silence. When Wila narrowed her eyebrows and dropped her chin, Margot looked at her and said, "What?" all the while holding her breath and dreading Wila's answer.

"What?" Grey said, coming back with the tray, placing it on the desk again. "Let me answer. In both cases, if they got what they wanted, either in Andy's room or your apartment, then we're home free."

"And, if they didn't?" Margot said.

"You're clean because you didn't...you don't have it." Wila said.

"And, it is?"

"One can only assume it's the information Nadia hid in the music box. She referred to it as the virus data," Wila said.

"Smaller than the flash drives. They're too big. So, I'd say a small electronic file. Anyway, the point is it's highly unlikely we are evidence," Grey said.

Margot pressed her hand to her forehead, trying to believe they weren't evidence.

"Let's go back to your question, Margot. How will we know when and if the virus is destroyed? Well, I have contacts in the States. I might find out if there are breaches before it gets to the press," Wila said. "In the meantime—"

"We take Nadia's letter to the FBI." Grey said, rising from his chair and marching around the desk.

"And tell them what?" Margot said, shaking her head in frustration.

"Tell them someone killed Andy. Show them the letter."

"Without the file?" Margot said.

"Man, you're right. It's useless. Plus, Tetovo police have covered it up by now. Besides us, no one knows Andy is dead."

Margot covered her face in her hands. "You're right. It's as if he never existed."

Wila slipped out of the room.

Grey pulled Margot up from her chair and hugged her. "He existed, believe you me. He loved you and said it every time we talked."

Margot buried her face in his shoulder and choked on her unrelenting sadness.

Wila returned to the study with three glasses and a fresh bottle of wine. Grey and Margot sat again.

"A French Bordeaux, my favorite." Wila poured a glass and handed it to Margot, another glass for Grey and one for herself. "To Andy."

They drank.

"I think you two are free from this."

Margot wanted to believe it.

"Here's what I think," Grey said with a broad smile. "We go back to Prishtina. Confident we're free, as you say, Wila."

"And damn cautious," Margot said. "Vigilant." She picked up the music box, twisted the key, and put it on the desk. It plinked out a delicate tune.

"Oh, it's 'Kalinka,'" Wila said, explaining it was a famous Russian folk song, popular throughout the world. She added the lyrics refer to red berries, strawberries in a garden, a peaceful setting.

"Wonder how many times Andy and his mother had played it. What a tender gift for a five-year-old boy to give to his mother," Margot said.

They listened to the end.

"You know, Pavlovski didn't give me Andy's belongings. I'm not the next of kin," Grey said.

"Only Andy's mother or father could have claimed the body," Wila said.

No one spoke.

Margot poured herself more wine and passed the bottle to Grey. He topped Wila's glass before dribbling the last of it in his.

They drank.

"It's been seven months since Nadia's letter. If Kaz broke his silence during this time, she might have additional information by now," Margot said.

Grey nodded.

"Forgive me, I'm compelled to comment on Andy's mother," Margot said, leaning forward with her elbows on her knees. "She should be ashamed."

"Hmm. Mothers are people, too. We are all flawed," Wila said.

"Nadia, Mrs. Stephen, is an elegant woman," Grey said. "Very smart. She and Andy were extremely close, especially after his father left. He was completely devoted to her." He put his hand on his head and pursed his lips.

"Grey, you said you'd call her. We can do it together. The question is how will we tell her Andy, her only child, was murdered while risking his life for her, at her request?" She gulped. "There are no words."

"Another thing," Wila said. "If no antidote and we go merrily along, oblivious, until April fifteenth, the time to find a solution will have lapsed."

"It'll be too late," Grey said.

"How will we live with that?" Margot asked.

They finished their wine in silence.

~ 27 ~

CHAPTER TWENTY-SEVEN

March 10, 2013

"Here's your gun," Dugal said.

Michael put it in the holster under his arm and they stepped outside onto the boss's porch.

Dugal slammed the door. "First, the boss won't forget you put us in danger when you killed that guy. Doubt he'll let you forget it, either. The good news is, you're in and we got your back. But if you fuck up again, he'll snuff you out in a flash."

Michael seized on *we got your back*...pure bullshit. And seemingly unlawful. What a fucking joke. Bound to be a law broken in some country. He could smell it.

"Listen to me. We want you to mess up this guy. Do it tonight and be back at the Depot by eight."

"What? Why?"

"Rough him up and tell him to stay away from the girl."

"Hey, now that we're in this together, I'm part of the team," Michael said, even though it turned his stomach to say it. He wanted to know what he was getting himself into. "What did you do in Peja?"

"None of your business. While you're roughing up this guy, I have to get a box from the trunk of his car. You do your job, I'll do mine."

Annoyed that Dugal didn't answer his question, Michael narrowed his eyes and lowered his voice for effect. "What's my pay?"

"First, listen. He owns an apartment building. You've been there before. In case you can't remember, here's the address and the apartment number." Dugal jammed the note into Michael's jacket pocket. "And your retainer."

"Wow, pretty fancy word," Michael said, as he pulled the note out of his pocket and counted three hundred euros.

"Boss first said three hundred euros when it's done. I put in a good word for you and told him you ought to get more since you signed on with us. He agreed. Count on seven hundred euros more when it's done."

"Wow, good buddy, I'm impressed. You can't fool me, though. There's got to be something in it for you."

"Yeah, well, I don't want the physical stuff. You can do it."

"That's it? You're a squirt, and probably damn fast. You're plain scared, admit it."

Dugal squirmed and twisted his mouth sideways.

Michael figured if he waited for Dugal to respond, Dugal would give away a dark secret. Something he could hammer him with later.

"Come on, you can tell me," he said, careful to hold back his smartass snicker.

"I can't get caught," he said, jamming his hands in his pockets and pinning his shoulders to his ears.

"Well, hell, everybody worries they're going to get caught. Goes with the territory. Stupid not to."

"Yeah, well, I can't go back to prison. Can't do it," he said, panting. "I won't." His breathing turned to guttural rasping.

Michael watched Dugal's chest heave and his body tremble.

"Hey, man, get a grip."

Dugal sneered at him and took in a sharp breath. "You'd better get going. Don't kill him, Michael." He went back inside.

Dugal's deranged, Michael thought.

Dugal said he knew the location. Michael pulled out the note and recognized the address. For sure, he knew it. He'd been there three times trying to find the damn disk.

***

The taxi driver dropped Michael two blocks from the apartment complex. He continued on foot and when he was close enough, he checked the perimeter of the building. He saw no one, and the street had no moving vehicles. Michael slipped into an adjacent alley and noted the rusty fire escapes that zigzagged on the exterior wall.

A getaway route.

Michael didn't look forward to risking jail time for leaving a message and a simple thrashing. The getting caught bullshit with Dugal started his heart pounding. He rubbed his fingers on his lips to settle his nerves. He had to think.

When he had arrived at the front entrance the prior three times, he was plain lucky because the door was wide open, and he got right in without a problem. This time, he'd walk to the entrance, and if unlocked, he'd duck in. If not, he'd be fucked, because he didn't have the code. He figured crashing through the metal door might be possible. The bad news is it'd make a ruckus. He could wait for an idiot to leave the door ajar.

His watch read 6 p.m. He had plenty of time.

From where it stood, the door opened, startling him. His breathing was less labored as he got closer and realized the door had been left ajar a few inches. As he pulled it open a bit more, his ears perked. There were people on the stairs. He bailed, dashed across the street, and looked back to see a young couple and a kid exit to the street. Michael watched the door swing little by little toward the doorframe. He held his breath, hoping the lock didn't click.

It didn't.

He ran across the street, slipped inside, and snapped the door shut, securing the lock. Then, avoiding the elevator, he tiptoed up three flights. Apartment 332 was directly in front of him. He lowered his baseball cap over his eyes and tugged his knitted mask up his neck, adjusting it to cover his face in an instant.

He reached for his Bowie and slid it, blade first, under his sleeve, resting the handle at the edge of his left palm in perfect position to grab with his right hand.

After shifting his mask over his nose, Michael tried to twist the doorknob. It wouldn't budge.

He stepped back and checked the door. Should he knock and risk people from inside checking him out through the peephole? Heat penetrated under his shoulder blades and he realized he hadn't thought out thrashing more than one person until this moment. He squinted and felt the gun with his elbow.

Shit, you don't have a silencer.

His mind went blank, and he stood paralyzed for a second.

Move!

With his feet steady, shoulder-width apart, he banged his left shoulder into the door with all his weight. The lock held, but the wood in the center cracked. Instantly, he broke through and was inside. One man stood at the kitchen sink with his back to Michael. No one else in sight. Before the guy turned around, Michael caught him in a choke hold and at the same time, he clutched his Bowie and flashed it in the guy's face. None of this came easy because his victim was at least a foot taller than him, and huge.

"Listen, buddy." Michael said.

"Grrrr." Leaning over at his waist, he lifted Michael off his feet, turning and swinging him around like a toy doll.

Michael pulled tighter, flattening his windpipe. Surely the guy couldn't breathe; he'd done this a hundred times. The guy should've died already.

He didn't.

The centrifugal force loosened Michael's grip. Another time around, Michael let go altogether, crashed into a bookcase, cracked his head, and fell to the floor. Books dropped on him and scattered across the room.

Still bent over, the hulk coughed and gagged, holding his throat with his left hand, a long knife in his right, staggering toward him.

Michael scrambled up to his feet and moved toward the door at the same time as the giant lost his balance and slammed into the wall. The entire foundation shimmied, then stopped dead.

The body didn't move. Michael got closer to check his breathing.

His chest heaved. Alive and unconscious.

In two seconds, he scanned the room, searching for money. He found a wallet on the kitchen counter, and peeled out eight hundred euros, stuffing the money in his pants pocket.

Michael ran out, pulling his mask to his neck again, and slid on the stairs. When he got to the street, he slowed up, slowed his breathing, and strolled to the alley, as though he didn't have a care in the world.

When he got under the fire escape, he bent forward, hands on his knees, mouth wide open, gasping for air.

Finally, he rubbed his head to check for blood. When he looked at his fingers, he saw blood, although there was more than he could have gotten in his run-in with the bookcase.

Your Bowie.

He had cut himself with his own damn knife. Slapping his ankles and sleeves, he searched...no Bowie.

Michael leaned against the cement wall, scooted to a squat, and wiped the blood on his thigh. Elbows on his knees, he cradled his head in his hands, and blew a long sigh.

He lost his Bowie and didn't tell him to stay away from the girl.

198 ~ DIANN SCHINDLER

What the fuck.

When Dugal heard how this mission went down, he'd shit. As he began to stand, it struck him as funny as hell, 'cause he could rankle the deranged Dugal. He covered his mouth to muffle his howls and staggered to a shadowed wall, yanking his zipper open. He peed. His liquid splashed against the wall and the smell of hot urine floated up to his face.

He snorted, realizing he didn't have to tell Dugal the truth.

Finished, he pulled his zipper closed, got his cell and dialed Dugal.

"Why are you calling me? I told you to meet me at the Depot at eight."

"'Cause it's done. Pick me up at the Union Café."

"Don't tell me you killed him," Dugal said with a growl.

"I want my money," Michael said, ending the call.

CHAPTER TWENTY-EIGHT

March 11, 2013

Grey had driven five hours straight from Dhermi when they stopped in south Kukes, Albania, near Kosovo's southern border. He said he had visited this stunning town many times and wanted to enjoy an early dinner at the Buzë Lumit restaurant on Lake Koman. The temperature was a mere 3°C, so it was too cold to sit outside. They found a table inside next to a window where they could see the snowcapped peaks of the Gjallica Mountain in the distance.

With little conversation, they ate chicken thighs encrusted with crushed walnuts, creamed spinach, and *buke shtepie*, Albanian bread. It had been a long five-hour drive after intense discussions at Wila's condominium, and winter nature was a much-needed reprieve.

Margot noticed small tufts of dormant yellowed grass poking through thawing damp spots near the lake's edge, where the earlier afternoon sunshine had begun to warm the garden. Now, the late afternoon sun illuminated the water and the sheet of new snow, reflecting a shimmering, comforting light through their window.

For a few minutes, she closed her eyes, imagining the peaceful light flooding her entire body. When she opened them, Grey was smiling at her with a loving facial expression. Rather than blushing at his observation of her private meditation, she grinned and smiled appreciatively. Her heart fluttered. She was grateful he was at her side.

They agreed they'd return to Kukes again when they had more time, but now they needed to get back to their lives in Prishtina.

"Now that we're safe," Grey said, "life will be normal again."

Life was not normal in her mind, but she kept it to herself because every time she had expressed her concern before, Grey rejected it. Who was she to continue to poke at him? She decided against challenging something he so badly believed or wanted to believe.

After dinner, it was her turn to drive, and Margot agreed to take the wheel the last couple hours through Kosovo back to Prishtina. Grey fell asleep at once, and after driving for an hour on a dull highway, her mind returned to their visit with Wila and the tedious review of details surrounding Andy's death.

She had had a question when they had reviewed their litany of facts. Truth was, though, they had so much to discuss, her question was overshadowed. Even she had shelved it at the time, but now, it nagged her, poked its way into her thoughts, as if her unconscious was trying to tell her something.

Grey was still in a deep sleep, and as much as she wanted to talk and flesh out her unsettling thoughts with him, she didn't want to disturb him. She'd struggle through on her own.

Her basic question pointed to the storage unit. Specifically, why did Andy contract for a storage unit in Peja for a scarf, harmless photos on two flash drives, a watch, and an empty music box? That was her major question. But there were more. For starters, why not simply put the scarf in a drawer, the flash drives in the desk, and his watch in her jewelry box? Display the music box, his childhood gift to his mother, on the coffee table? None of the items were worth hiding. If he was so compelled to store them, he could have done so in facilities in Prishtina.

It made no sense. Margot knew she was missing something, some clue. But what?

And why was Andy so secretive about these benign items? Why didn't he tell her? That was the worst question. Why didn't he trust her enough to tell her? It hurt her to think of it that way, that Andy didn't confide in her or, worse, that he wasn't as close to her as she thought.

Gradually she had a haunting sense that she didn't know Andy at all. Was their relationship a sham? Had Andy used her?

Her love for Andy seemed to be spiraling, fading away. Her throat caught, she stifled a breath, and a tight whimper escaped. She sobbed quietly, wondering if Andy had betrayed her.

Could you be so stupid?

Grey woke and stretched his arms behind his head. "Where are we?"

"Around the corner from Ismet's place," she said, wiping her nose with her sleeve and hoping Grey didn't realize she'd been crying. She didn't want to delve into her emotions with him just now. They didn't have time, and besides, she had beaten herself up enough. She'd bring her storage question up at another time, knowing Grey would find simple answers and continue to hold on to his safe comfort zone.

"Wow, see that coral color streaking across the sky?" Grey asked. "Makes Prishtina glow with a sweet pink color. Beautiful sight to come home to."

Margot hummed in agreement as she pulled the car into Ismet's apartment complex parking lot.

Grey scooted out and closed his door. "You okay? You're pretty quiet."

"Yeah, I'm good," she said, opening the trunk. "Let's take the luggage out and lock the doors to avoid going back and forth. We can thank Ismet and leave him the keys. We'll be back here in short order and on our way."

As they walked toward the entrance, she said, "God, this door is always unlocked." She tossed her hair back.

"There you go, again," he said, with a teasing grin. "You have a habit of tossing your hair when you're frustrated."

"I am frustrated. This open door is an emotional trigger and reminds me of when someone ransacked my apartment...in this very building. I was terrified then and here we are again...unlocked," she said through clenched teeth. When she remembered Edgar criticizing Ismet for a lack of responsibility that day, her forehead dripped with perspiration. Was he right?

As they climbed three flights of concrete stairs to Ismet's apartment, they stepped over an obstacle course of toys and bicycles. "Lots of kids are here now. Nice," Margot said, trying to put a positive spin on her foul mood.

Grey knocked on Ismet's door. When Ismet didn't come, he puckered his forehead and squinted at her.

She knocked, louder this time. "I left him a voice message—"

The door opened and Ismet peered through the narrow opening, "Hello, hello. Come in. Good to see you," he said, turning and limping to the kitchen. His left arm was in a sling with a cast from his wrist to his elbow.

Margot gasped and her heart grieved at the sight of this huge, burly man wounded and struggling to walk.

"What happened to you?" Grey said.

"Sit," Margot said. "You fell over those damn toys, didn't you? Are you in pain?"

"No. How you say? Mugged. A little pain, yes." With a loud sigh, he fell to a nearby recliner. "Thief crashed door and attacked me from behind. His arms around my throat. Choke me. I big powerful man. I think maybe he kill me."

Margot sat on the arm of his recliner, careful not to touch his injuries. She covered her mouth when she saw bruises on his neck and face and listened in horror as Ismet described a muscle-bound man grabbing him from behind in a stranglehold.

"I swing around and lean this way, that way, everything for him to stop. Then he fall. Now, I get knife, but dizzy."

Margot held her breath, anticipating his every word.

"Then what happened?" Grey said, biting his bottom lip.

Ismet scrunched his shoulders to his ears and raised his eyebrows. "I wake up on floor with neighbor shaking me. He call police and I go to hospital. Neighbor excellent friend. He install new door right away."

No one spoke.

"Arm broken. Back is sore. That's it. No problem. Good my gun in secret hiding place. Police put me in jail if they find it. Guns against law. See?" He held up a knife. "Idiot left knife." His belly bounced as he laughed.

"It's huge. One nick and you could bleed to death. He could've killed you." Her voice pitched high with anxiety and she shuddered. "Did you see his face? Was it the same guy who broke into my apartment?"

"Why you say that? No reason to think that," Ismet said. "He had mask and he take eight hundred euros. How you Americans say: shit happens?" He smiled at himself.

Margot glared at him and curled her lip. "Hilarious."

"A robbery and no ransacking? It doesn't fit the pattern; it's the opposite of the break-in here and Andy's hotel room," Grey said.

"Don't worry. Question, please. Any news in Dhermi?" Ismet said.

Holding her emotions in check, Margot took a deep breath and with a slow exhale, said, "Yes and no. It's complicated. We agreed. We're out of danger now."

"For sure?"

Margot cocked her head, signaling their safety was questionable, but Grey was quick to confirm.

"Yes. Let's have dinner together and we will explain everything. If you're all right, we're going to go home now. Thank you for the use of your car," Grey said, handing him the keys. "Oh, dammit. The luggage. I left it on the curb."

"Go. Hurry," she said, raising her voice.

Grey ran out the door.

"Probably okay. Safe community here," Ismet said.

"Really?"

"Hmm. Perhaps." His belly bounced as he chuckled.

"Luggage is still here," Grey shouted from the bottom of the stairs.

"I love you, Ismet, but listen to me." She clenched her fists. "I am furious, and I didn't want to say this, and embarrass you in front of Grey. The door downstairs is unlocked, and you have not taken responsibility to protect your tenants and yourself. There is no excuse for this, and you know it." Her voice, shaky with anger, reflected her escalating emotions from her nagging questions, the unlocked door, Ismet's injuries, and Grey's unwillingness to face what she felt was true.

Ismet had dropped his head, reluctant to look at her. She had shamed him, and he deserved it, so she did not apologize or say anything to make him feel better.

"Lock the door behind me," she said as she opened the door.

"Automatic. Just make sure it click," he said, without looking up.

The door closed and clicked.

Grey stood at the curb with his hands on his hips, as if disgusted with himself for forgetting their suitcases.

"Don't feel too bad. It took longer than we thought. Besides, Ismet said it's a safe community," she said, with a tone of sarcastic disbelief.

"You think?" he smirked. "Yeah. There's a lot of petty crime in Prishtina. And look, the few streetlights here hardly light the area. If I wanted to break into an apartment, I'd choose this place."

She pursed her lips, frowned, and shook her head back and forth, staring at him. It was her clear signal to him again: this was no coincidence. Margot had voiced her opinion too many times, and she hoped her facial expression would have a more lasting impact.

"I know that look, Margot. We have nothing, no evidence, to link this with Andy," he said, putting his arm around her shoulders. "Remember what Wila said. 'Fear can make the most benign images appear—'"

"Ominous. Yeah, I know," she said, blinking her eyes slowly. "Fear can also blind you from reality."

~ 29 ~

CHAPTER TWENTY-NINE

March 12, 2013

Soft rapping on Margot's bedroom door woke her.

"Psst. I'm leaving for work," Grey said.

"Give me a minute, don't leave." She slipped out of bed, put on her robe, and joined him in the kitchen.

"What's up?" he said, pouring her a cup of coffee.

"Are you requesting a leave of absence today?"

"Ah, no. Why?"

"Just checking," she said, wondering what other coincidences besides Ismet's mugging they might suffer. Grey had said before that he'd take off work to devote his time to solving the mysteries around Andy's murder.

He shrugged, "No need."

"So, does that mean you're giving up finding out why Andy was murdered?" she said, playing with the bowl of coins sitting on the table.

"That reminds me," he said, digging in his pocket. "I have a few coins for your little Dragodon girlfriends." He tossed in a handful of coins and took out the two flash drives. "Keep the drives in this bowl because I want to look through them later."

She nodded, noting he avoided answering her question.

"Don't you want to look at Andy's photos?" he said, putting the drives back with the coins.

With her eyes lowered she said, "It'll be hard, but yes." At the moment, she was more focused on her disappointment that he chose to ignore her question.

"Yeah," he said with a long sigh. "Okay, I need to go." He walked to the door and paused. "We're safe now, Margot—"

"So you are changing the subject...on purpose?"

He hesitated and looked at the floor.

Margot took his silence as a yes and said, "Please, let's not start bullshitting one another now."

Suddenly her cell on her bedroom nightstand vibrated. It could only be her mother calling at this hour of the morning. It was midnight in Minneapolis.

"I agree. Take the call. We'll talk later," he said.

"That's a deal," she said, rushing to the bedroom to answer the call. "Mom, what a pleasant surprise," she said, using her cheerful voice despite feeling unsettled from her exchange with Grey. "Everything okay?"

"Yes, of course. I wanted to call you early when we'd both have time to chat. And, I hoped to catch Andy. Put him on."

Margot threw her head back and stared at the ceiling, thinking how to answer.

"Honey?"

She swallowed. "He just left for work."

"Damn it. This is impossible. Can I call him at work? Wait. Scrap that. Please tell him to call me. I miss that boy. Now, listen, have you seen a counselor?"

"Rats, Mom. Pushy." She breathed hard into the phone. "Not yet, my plate is full."

"Nothing's for nothing unless you actually see a counselor."

"I know," she said, dragging out her words in annoyance and rolling her eyes. Why couldn't her mom just be a mom? Why was she always the counselor? Truth was, she hadn't given counseling another thought, and she wasn't about to reveal that information. Her palms turned sweaty with the pressure to control the conversation. Just as she had done before, she switched the subject to Nora and her sisters. "I see them as often as I can."

"Your feeding them and giving them money is easy, but you have to know you are perpetuating homelessness."

"You're right. It's hard not to." Her mind drifted back to Andy, saying the same thing. Then she heard herself blurt out. "Andy and I are considering establishing an NGO to help these kids get off the street." Slapping her hand on the bed and wincing, she couldn't believe she said it. Or why. So stupid. But it felt good to talk about Andy. Then, of course, it didn't. They'd never start an NGO. Her eyes filled with tears.

"Wow. Will he quit his job at the State Department?"

"Probably," she said, sniffing. "Sorry, mom, I need to get ready for work." True, she had to go to work. Yet, the real reason she was signing off was that she wanted to end the call before she lost control and spilled everything. She just couldn't, not yet.

"No problem. Hey, let me know when you're open for company."

"Really?" she said, hoping her voice didn't reveal her anxiety. Margot would have to come clean before her mom could ever visit. Her hands shook, and she nearly dropped her phone.

"How about an Easter visit?" Sherry said.

"Easter is March thirty-first. Oh boy, this is awkward." She searched her brain for excuses. "I'll be steeped in USAID work."

"I understand. Okay, we'll find a time. Miss you. Love you."

Margot threw her cell on her bed and stared at the ceiling again, searching for solace. She let out a long, frustrated groan. Their calls were emotionally exhausting, and she hated it. Moreover, she worried she'd start to dread talking to her mom.

Argh. Something's got to give.

The clock on her nightstand said 7 a.m., and she had to get moving. She jumped out of bed, stripped, and got in the shower. The warm water was glorious on her back. She reached for her lavender body wash, poured a few drops on a washcloth, and began swabbing her arms when she heard Grey in the kitchen.

Sweet man came back to apologize.

"That was my mom on the phone," she said in a loud voice, while scrubbing her heels to loosen dry skin. When he didn't answer, she leaned closer to the shower door. "Grey?"

Silence.

She turned off the water and stopped breathing to listen closer. "Grey?"

If not Grey, then who?

Her warm body shook as if she were freezing. As quietly as possible, she got out of the shower, put on a robe, and tiptoed toward the kitchen, stopping at the end of the hallway. The great room was empty. "Grey?" she said, creeping past the kitchen toward his bedroom.

Still no answer. She tapped on his bedroom door and peeked inside.

No Grey.

You're hearing things.

Convinced her imagination had run rampant, she blew air through her lips to release tension, ran her fingers through her damp hair, and returned to the kitchen. After turning off the coffee pot, she gasped when she noticed her purse upended on the sofa. The most disturbing thing was that someone had spread the contents across the cushions. Stunned, her mind raced back to the image of the blue baseball cap in the peephole. She stood frozen as the familiar fear filled her chest and her heartbeat gushed in her ears.

After taking a deep breath to muster courage and moving toward the sofa, her sleeve caught on the bowl of change, nearly sending it to the floor. She managed to catch it without losing a single coin. When she set it on the table again, she saw the flash drives were missing.

How was that possible?

She glanced at the door. It was ajar. The lock and dead bolt were not damaged. The chain was intact.

You didn't lock it?

She slammed it shut with her shoulder, securing the lock and the dead bolt, and hooking the chain, with her entire body trembling.

This was no coincidence.

~ 30 ~

CHAPTER THIRTY

March 12, 2013

How are you going to tell Grey? Margot asked herself before removing her coat and handing her Sars University bag to the USAID guard.

He's so hell bent on believing in coincidence.

"Hello, Miss Margot," the guard said. "No need to scan your Sars bag."

His voice was barely audible. Yet, it did bring her out of her daze and back into the USAID security building, a welcome relief from dwelling on the cunning intruder in her apartment this morning. And although she knew the guards' names and their children's names, the process remained the same. Every step was rote, from the radar machine, the scanning procedures, the purse inspection, to repeating the questions regarding USBs or electronic files. Day after day, they asked her to open her tubes of lipstick, as if they were seeing them for the first time.

"Sorry, Genti," she said, realizing she was not thinking clearly. If she were, she would have stayed home from work. Unfortunately, here she was. She told herself she could get through three classes today.

Suddenly, the door opened with a loud buzz, jolting every part of her body. Ganna stepped inside and Margot's muscles eased a bit, but only for a moment. She stiffened, sensing a dark cloud of trouble when she saw the frown on Ganna's forehead. How could she handle any more distress this morning?

Margot stood still as Genti pinned the visitor badge on her coat. At the same time, she noticed a subtle tremor stirring in her stomach.

Just as she turned to tell her she needed to go home, Ganna said, scowling, "Come. I have an important message."

Margot hesitated, thinking her message could wait for another time. But Ganna's menacing glare changed her mind. Canceling classes wasn't an option. She took a deep breath, promising herself she could power through three hours of class.

As they exited security to walk to the main building, Ganna said, "Illir has a six-week training session in Bangkok."

"He's such a delight," Margot said, trying to be positive. She also noted Illir's commitment and enthusiasm. "He often has difficulty with certain concepts but he's one of my favorite students."

"Your favorite. Far from your best, perhaps," she said with a disturbing edge to her voice. "He worries he'll miss classes while in Bangkok and has requested to meet twice a week, including a third session when he returns. His supervisor gave his approval. Your thoughts?"

Ganna's menacing mood filtered into Margot's head, and she warned herself to tread lightly and measure her words.

Don't take this personally.

"Yes, it's fine," Margot said, hoping her voice didn't reveal her unease.

"I canceled your classes this morning because the employees are on special assignment. Note, as per the contract agreement, we pay you when we cancel on the day classes are to take place. Meanwhile,

I arranged for Illir to meet for his first additional tutoring session instead, canceling out one class payment. Does that suit you?"

"Of course," she said, quietly exhaling a breath of relief.

"Follow me. And Margot, I hope this extra work with him has better results. His supervisor is very disappointed and remarked he hasn't seen significant improvement. We expect your teaching will have measurable results."

Ganna's comments stung Margot. Her body temperature rose, and her face flushed. It was personal. It was about her.

"I understand." Lying was the best she could do until she had time to consider Ganna's comments and respond more thoughtfully. Besides, she didn't want to delve into an unpleasant conversation. She'd had enough stress today.

When they arrived at Illir's office, he jumped up, grinning and flashing his sparkling blue eyes. He always made Margot feel valued. It warmed her heart, and it could use warming right now.

Ganna jerked her head sharply and left the office, closing the door behind her.

Illir rolled his eyes. Margot ignored him, choosing not to engage in office politics.

"Miss Margot, good to see you. Ms. Ganna explain Bangkok and tutoring sessions?"

"Yes, she did. And, let me correct your sentence. Repeat after me, please: did Ms. Ganna explain?"

"Did Ms. Ganna explain?" He dropped his head. "Sorry. Why I forget?"

"Why do you forget?" she said, raising her eyebrows. She explained that people who learn English as a second language omit articles and helping verbs. They also use incorrect verb tenses. "I expect improvement." She pulled her lessons from her Sars bag, and they spent the next thirty minutes conjugating irregular verbs and reviewing helping verbs.

"Miss Margot, you make it easy. Then, I always forget." He slapped his forehead and gritted his teeth. "What can I do? I worry

214 ~ DIANN SCHINDLER

about my Bangkok trip. I miss too much." He pursed his lips and shook his head.

"No. You will miss too much. Remember, will is a helping verb. We just now practiced it." His pitiful frustration touched her heart, and it pained her to continue with every correction. Truth was she didn't have a choice now. The pressure was on.

"I will miss too much. Oy. Can you make lessons? I take to Bangkok." His face darkened as he pressed his palms together at his chin. "Please?"

She paused and watched him bite his lips, hating how their lessons had turned from a positive learning experience to full-on angst. Still, she had a job to do. "Let's see. Well, I could create a series of exercises, specifically for your needs." He raised his eyebrows as his face brightened again.

"Okay," she said. "I appreciate your dedication, Illir, and I expect better results. I'll have a packet of work ready by, say, Wednesday?"

"I must leave Wednesday. Possible to come tomorrow? Early...for coffee?" His eyes widened in anticipation.

That would give her just today, but she had an entire file of lessons she could draw from in short order. "Are you buying?" she teased, glad for the opportunity to shift to a lighter mood, if only for a few minutes.

"Of course. I buy."

"Say that again?" she said, squinting at him.

"Okay. Ah. I am buying?" he asked with a wide grin. "Or, I will buy."

"Perfect. Take your time and think before speaking. You know this stuff."

"You work hard for me, Miss Margot. I will work hard for you. Promise," he said, placing his hand over his heart.

He was a sweet man, and she loved his determination. It was difficult not to rush him with a hug.

Margot left the building reviewing Ganna's nagging comment, referring to Illir: "Your favorite. Far from your best, perhaps." Indeed, Illir was not nearly her best. Had she allowed his charm to interfere with her judgment? Did she evaluate his work less critically? She didn't think so. The more looming question, was she capable of changing his habitual errors?

You can't allow your confidence to shatter now.

Margot looked up at the sky.

Suddenly, she felt weak. Her knees buckled, and she stumbled, barely catching herself on the sidewalk railing. That subtle tremor loomed larger and spread to her arms and legs. She shoved her hands in her pockets to stop them from shaking. She needed to talk to Grey. The burglar, the missing flash drives, her emptied purse, proof this was no happenstance. This was real, and they were facing unknown peril, again.

CHAPTER THIRTY-ONE

February 8, 2013

Today was their first Magpie conference call in three weeks. Cass had dug into her work and avoided any conversations with Jer the entire time. He was always a dictator, and she had said everything she could say. She hoped, by now, her words had resonated with him.

"Peter, give us an update," Jer said.

"Ok guys, you're going to love this. I got us set up with zombie computers. Really, I'd call it a zombie army. There are so many. Cass and Claudia will continue reconnaissance and find weak spots to get us inside. After my signal, you guys send an electronic connection request to the computers we've identified. These poor saps will think the request is legit and follow our orders, causing total system failures because of multiple unsolicited responses from these computers.

"This is the fun part. We'll be in DDoS attack mode with mail bombs and teardrop attacks,"

Jer said, "Once DDoS attack begins, there's little they can do to prevent catastrophe. Well, the head IT guy could try to limit the traffic. He won't because they need their legitimate connections to do business."

"We'll have spoofed our addresses with the zombie computers. So, they're SOL," Peter said.

Cass explained team members would be ready to use a key logging program. "At Peter's command, we'll track everything: employee types, keystrokes, and passwords."

"We have to make sure we get into the administrative office computers, down to the billing clerks. Once we get there, *fantástico*," Juan said. He added the billing systems will go haywire and cause a loss of revenue, which will quickly get out of control.

Peter requested a timeline update and Jer responded, noting Magpie was ahead of Zero Day.

"Once we're in there, get access to elevated privileges, and take over the networks, how long are we staying, Jer?" Cass asked.

"It's complicated because our first victims are the five largest insurance companies. To meet our goal, I think we may need two to three weeks sustainment at the most. Of course, during that time we'll incorporate trail obfuscation techniques, such as log cleaners, Trojan commands, and any other tools you guys want to use."

"I say we go for the full assault. Once we've breached their websites, they got no defense."

Without hesitation, Cass jumped in. "No way," she said, raising her voice and pounding her fists on the computer table. She glared at Jeremy and mouthed, "He's trouble."

"You're such a pussy, Cass."

At pussy, her mouth fell open, and fire filled her chest. She took a breath and glared at Jer, waiting for him to intervene.

Silence.

"Okay, we're done unless you have questions," Jer said.

No one spoke and the call ended.

Before Cass could utter a sound, Jer turned to her. "Don't start with me. I've heard your Peter crap too many times. Go ahead. Storm off in your little girl stupid huff. I don't give a shit."

It was everything she could do not punch him in the face. They had had fist fights when they were little. She was a grown woman now, so that was off limits. When she tightened her jaw and sneered, he turned away. She took a minute to think about what he said. Of course, she seized on the little girl and stormed off, but realized these words rang true. Marching off hadn't worked.

Jer was right, and that sent her mind reeling. She wanted to shove every computer in the cellar onto the floor and rid herself of the violent fury attacking every inch of her body. Unfortunately, it served no purpose except to damage equipment. She needed a novel approach.

She scratched her head, took a deep breath, and let out an extended exhale. In a low, measured tone, she said, "Listen, just talk to him in private. Reason with him." Cass pressed her palms together and tilted her head. "Can't hurt."

He paused and lowered his eyelids as if he was considering her suggestion.

She thought this approach was working and even felt somewhat optimistic. The corners of her mouth turned up in a thin smile.

Then he snorted at her.

"I give," she said, slapping her thighs. "You got it. Magpie is your baby. You have to stop Peter. If you don't, you have no one else to blame when this all goes down."

He nodded with a frown.

"Does that mean you'll talk to him?"

He cradled his chin in his hand and didn't speak.

She cocked her head, demanding an answer.

He looked at her with his mouth closed.

"It's all yours. I'm out of here." She crossed her fingers and kept them that way up the cellar stairs, throughout the three-mile walk home, still hoping, maybe with divine intervention, he'd come to his senses.

When she stood on her front porch, she dropped her chin and closed her eyes.

Lord help us.

~ 32 ~

CHAPTER THIRTY-TWO

March 12, 2013

After meeting with Illir, Margot, deep in thought, strolled a few hundred yards toward her apartment, stopping to take in the fancy homes of the affluent internationals. Anything to take her mind off Illir's grammar errors and her ability, or not, to teach him proper English. She passed through this neighborhood every day on her way to work, but never took time to enjoy the view. Mammoth solid metal doors or tall ornate gates with manicured gardens of evergreen bushes and grass hid most of the homes. Other areas were clad in gray concrete and crumbling pavement, which always depressed her. So, once again, negativity filled her head when she couldn't tolerate any more. She continued walking home.

When she arrived at her apartment, she saw a cardboard box sitting at the door. At first she thought her mother had sent her a package. As she looked closer, she saw Edgar's business card taped to the side.

She had forgotten Edgar's rude behavior toward Grey when they were together last. Maybe this was his peace offering.

After she opened her door, she pushed the box inside with her foot and tossed her coat and bag on the couch. And before doing anything else, she locked the door and hooked the chain.

She kneeled and pulled at the tape away from the cardboard. A quick flick of her hand and the top flipped open. Inside, she found four reams of much-needed printer paper, reminding her to buy a printer.

No getting around it, this was a kind gesture, and his generosity today deserved a phone call. But Edgar was an enigma. How could one person be extremely thoughtful and horribly thoughtless simultaneously? Nevertheless, she needed to take the high road and received his gift with sincere gratitude.

As she picked up her phone, she reminded herself to make it short. She'd had an endless morning, and her energy level was waning. Before she could dial, it rang.

Edgar.

She inhaled and prepared herself to be courteous. "Hello, how are you?"

"I'm fine, thank you. I assume you got the printer paper. May I stop by?"

"Edgar," she said, blowing a long, weary sigh, "can we do this another time?"

"I have a few gifts for you."

All she wanted to do was find the energy to prepare Illir's lesson plans.

"How nice, but...honestly, I can't today. Tomorrow?"

He paused, then said, "Margot, I shall be quick." His stern voice was insistent.

She dropped her head in her hand, both conflicted and frustrated. She was truly indebted to him: the apartment, the list of counselors. Now, paper. And she'd never forget his gentle compassion when she told him about Sam. As ridiculous as it sounded, she didn't know how she could bear much more of his generosity. Besides, she had said no twice, and his pressuring her only made her dig in her heels.

"I can't. Come tomorrow...in the afternoon. I must go now. I'm sorry. Goodbye." She ended the call as a guilty chill rippled through her back. Even to her, her tone sounded curt, disrespectful. If he only listened to her the first time when she politely suggested he come another time. She shook her head, thinking he had brought this on himself.

Convinced she had made the right choice to eliminate one stressor, her attention gravitated toward her baggy sweatpants and tablespoons of peanut butter comfort food. This was a perfect strategy to ease into Illir's lesson plans.

She put aside how to approach Grey, knowing it'd require her to relive her frightful morning and acknowledge their dangerous predicament. The mental preparation for that conversation was deeply unsettling, and she felt that subtle tremor in her stomach again.

Breathe. One step at a time.

***

Margot sat at the kitchen table, sifting through her lesson plan files, when she heard a knock on her door. She flinched and her eyes darted to the lock and chain. Both were secure. When she got up and looked through the peephole, she saw Edgar. His face was dark, sullen.

Margot turned and leaned her back against the wall, rolling her eyes in disbelief. Who did he think he was, ignoring her?

He knocked again. "Margot, it's me. Please."

She was pissed. On instinct, she decided to let him in, take his gifts, be courteous, and get him on his way. Fast.

She straightened her back and opened the door. "Edgar, you are a persistent man," she said, forcing a pleasant inflection. She motioned him to enter.

He came in with two boxes and when he dropped them on the table with a thunderous thud it startled her already frazzled nerves.

His eyes narrowed, glaring at her, evidence to her that his plopping the box was intentional. How could she be courteous with his intimidating behavior? She braced herself for an argument, determined to be as respectful as she could, and to show him to the door as fast as she could..

"Hello, my dear."

To her surprise, his voice was light, even playful, and no hint of provocation. He spoke as if their tough phone call had never happened. This struck her as odd, given that his facial expression through the peephole and the way he slammed the boxes down were the total opposite. She remained cautiously optimistic, hoping she could make his visit short and somewhat pleasant.

"Voilà." He flashed a pompous grin. "It's a multifunctional machine with extra print cartridges."

Admittedly, she was pleasantly surprised. "You read my mind."

"Indeed. I am a clever man." His voice was louder, and his eyes danced with wild excitement, unlike the cool, controlled Edgar she knew.

"And I have supplies from Beatrice Place. As you can see, you have envelopes, post-it notes, and pens. These are our marketing materials adorned with our new logo."

"Nice colors," she said, deciding to go with his erratic emotional state, whatever it was.

"Yes, blue and green reflect nature. Colors of the sky and grass. It's designed to be pleasing to the eye and evoke a sense of serenity." He bounced on his toes and his eyes darted around the room.

"For me?" She looked directly into his eyes and smiled, hoping he'd calm down so she could encourage him to leave.

He nodded, still bouncing, with his eyes darting.

"These large envelopes are especially nice," she said in an effort to be courteous. Truth was, she couldn't help focusing on his unusual behavior. Maybe he was high on drugs. She tilted her head. "Are you all right, Edgar?"

"I'm fine." He stopped bouncing. "I brought two envelopes. I have a box full at the office."

"I see." She paused, searching his face for some clues. Finding none, she said, "Excuse me, do you mind?" She examined an envelope and picked at the at the edge of the logo sticker. "The Beatrice Place logo comes across as advertising and, in a government building—"

"No. Stop it." he said, yanking her hand away. His voice was sharp and threatening.

She froze, wide-eyed, confused and alarmed at his strength.

"Sorry, my dear. We sealed the logo. I tried removing one and the entire envelope disintegrated," he said, tilting his head and wrinkling his forehead. "And, it's my logo, you know."

"My fault and totally disrespectful," she said, as shame twitched in her stomach. "And you should be proud. It's lovely. Plus, a torn envelope will not do. I know you prefer everything tidy."

"Yes," he said, suddenly in a calmer tone. "It's in my DNA after growing up with my auntie in London. Quite the stickler for perfection."

"Was her name Beatrice?" She wanted to engage him while he was more tranquil.

"No, no, Beatrice was my mother's name. She left me to live with my wealthy Auntie Minerva when I was six years old."

"Were you close to your auntie?" She wanted to ask why his mother had left him. Yet she didn't want to meddle, or worse, extend his visit.

"Not at all. However, we grew to love each other because we understood my mother was unwell and had made the best choice for me," Edgar said, jutting his chin forward.

He was proud or upset. Margot wasn't sure.

"Mother was a drug addict. After she took me to my auntie's, she disappeared." He settled in a kitchen chair, dropped his jaw, and fluttered his eyes.

She hadn't seen this side of Edgar. The stitch in her stomach spread to her chest, and she stretched her shoulders back for relief. "This is such a bittersweet story. I'm sad for you."

"Oh no, my dear, please. Do not pity me."

"It's not pity. It's acknowledgement of a hard life and I had no idea." She understood Edgar more completely: an extremely disciplined, steely, and caring man who had not only survived abandonment but also had taken action to commemorate his mother's life with safe houses in her name.

"Of course. Forgive me for being flippant, my dear. Now, let us move on. How are you? I stopped here twice to see you. When you were not home, I became concerned. Did you skip your classes at USAID?"

"Edgar, please," she said, folding her arms across her chest. "I'd never do that. Anyway, I'm sorry, Edgar, I really have work to do. So now you need to go." She searched his face, preparing for another outburst.

He didn't speak, and he didn't move. Obviously, he wasn't leaving.

"Listen," he shouted. "I helped you get this work. And, as a result, my reputation—"

"I'm grateful. I'm surprised you'd think I'd skip classes." And in an instant, just as Edgar's demeanor switched from ease to agitation, she had gone from admiration to exasperation and fury.

"Yes, you never know what you will get these days, I'm sorry to say. The lack of commitment runs rampant. Please, don't take my comments personally."

"Hard not to," she said, shaking her head at him.

"Dr. Zekolli relies on me to provide the best recommendations." He cleared his throat and carefully picked tiny pieces of brown paper off his arm, from the cardboard box. "Two women have besmirched my reputation and I've paid for it, my dear."

His "my dear" was condescending. The arrogant Edgar had returned. Even though she wanted to bite his head off and force him to apologize, she didn't have the energy, so she tamped down her anger. "And I appreciate everything. I do."

Edgar snapped his head, squinting at her.

She sensed something else was brewing.

"Where have you been? And Grey must stay here with you, in your bed. I see too many dishes in the sink for one person. Furthermore, those cannot be your shoes," he said, pointing at Grey's loafers.

Stunned, her mouth fell open and she could not find the words to express her utter outrage.

"I do not mean to pry. I am merely concerned for you. Grey does not impress me." He leaned forward, on his face a disturbing smirk.

Her heart pounded, and she sensed her blood pressure skyrocketing, but her thoughts had sharpened, razor thin.

"You are prying. How dare you insult Grey. Again. It's none of your business. True. You got me a job and this incredible apartment and now supplies. I am grateful. Understand, Edgar, you are fucking up this friendship."

"Your debased language shocks me. Nevertheless, I do not think you understand this country, Kosovo. It is dangerous with a great deal of fraud."

"You brought this nonsense up before," she said, pounding her foot. "The dangers here are at the administrative level, with the leadership, not the citizens. Andy explained this to me. Last year, in this entire country, there were five murders."

The word *murders* got caught in her throat and she swallowed to hold back her emotions. If she cried, showed any vulnerability, he'd meddle further. She was sure of it.

"Margot, I have upset you."

"Stop it. I've had a trying day and I have no more patience. You need to go."

"Yes, of course. However, I must ask you. Where is Andy? When is he coming back? Is it possible he has left you, Margot?"

"Oh my God, shut up." She gritted her teeth and watched Edgar calmly fold his hands and relax back in his chair.

Breathe.

In a low, controlled voice, she said, "You have interfered, and I won't have it. You must respect my boundaries, or we cannot continue our friendship."

Neither moved nor spoke.

Margot stared at him, leaning on the table with both hands, demanding a response.

He unfolded his hands and bent forward. "Yes, Margot. I appreciate your boundaries and I agree. Consider it done."

He was lying. His face was flat, emotionless. Plus, he hadn't apologized, and she detested his patronizing tone.

Neither spoke.

In the silence, it came to her. She had gone as far as she could, and it was futile to repeat demands. He'd merely recite his bullshit.

"I must go now. Thank you, Margot."

Thank God.

She nodded and opened the door for him.

He moved to kiss her hand, and she pulled away. She recognized his deceit. Looking straight at him, she opened and closed her eyes twice, with a message: he had not fooled her.

He walked out the door without a response.

As she shut and locked the door, reality set in. Edgar had been disingenuous. And the real kicker? He relished in her knowing it.

She dropped her head in her hands in a sad manner. Previously, she had adored Edgar, and today with this information, about his auntie and his mother, she was more impressed. Yet, he was possessive and controlling. His erratic mood swings showed he was an extremely complicated man. Perhaps emotionally unstable. Margot wondered if she could tolerate his eccentricities. Did she even want to?

For now, she'd accept their pathetic peace. She set it aside, because she had to switch gears and find the brainpower to create Illir's lesson plans.

After washing her face to refocus, Margot got busy, working into the early evening. When she finished, she shoved freshly printed lesson plans into two Beatrice Place envelopes and went to bed before Grey came home. When she put her head on her pillow, that subtle tremor was more apparent than ever. Too tired to worry, she hugged her stomach and dropped off to sleep.

~ 33 ~

CHAPTER THIRTY-THREE

March 13, 2013

"Morning, everyone. Thanks for sending me your updates. They look great. Now, I want to discuss our first test," Jer said.

Cass grimaced and chewed her lips, eager for Peter's response.

"Phishing is great. Right, Cass?" Claudia said.

"Yeah, so far, so good. No sign of detection."

"These big agencies just focus on generating revenue," Peter said. "Damn greedy bastards; these morons won't spend a dime to protect themselves from any intrusion. They're easy pickings."

"It's kind of hard to believe this has gone off without a hitch," Juan said.

"I agree," Claudia said. "Chalk it up to great work. Meanwhile, recon is ongoing, and our antennae are continuous. We'll keep those defenses up."

"So, it's scanning now. Juan, are you ready to find those weak entry points?" Jer said.

"Armed and ready."

"Your time frame, Juan?"

"Two to three weeks."

"Okay. Terrific work. Peter, comments?"

Cass sat up in anticipation. The tension-filled humming in her ears reached a higher pitch.

"Excellent job, everybody," Peter said.

Cass's jaw dropped. Jer's haughty facial expression surprised her, too. He must have talked to Peter and set up this exchange to demonstrate to everyone Peter's reconciliation. Slight relief settled through her stomach. But she was not totally convinced Peter had changed his mind, yet.

"Another thing. I've been making the calls," Jer said. "If you don't hear from me, it'll be because we got problems."

"Explain," Claudia said.

"It's simple. If you don't get a call from me, stop everything and make yourself scarce. Don't call me. Don't call one another."

"You saying that'll be it?" Juan said.

"I'm saying abort."

No one spoke. They didn't have to, because trepidation could be felt through the computer screens. The basement walls were caving in on her. She clawed at her scalp.

Jer ended the call and started checking his emails. He was either an ironman or in denial.

She asked him if he had talked to Peter.

"Yep."

"And?"

"Gave me his word."

"Satisfied with that?"

Jer nodded.

"Are you going to check to see if he's telling the truth?"

"Nope," he said with his face in his monitor.

She shook her head. "Really? Suddenly he's got religion? Just because he says it."

"I can't do any more." He pounded on his keyboard.

"No, that's not true. You can dig into his files, follow his progress, see where he's going. Check his fingerprints."

Maybe Jer didn't know how. The truth? She didn't know either. Claudia and Juan did, although pulling them in could be a poor idea. It might split the team more and skew their focus.

Dammit.

Jer finally looked up from his computer and leaned his head sideways. His eyes were pleading and his voice soft. "Cass, come on. I need you with me on this. Please?"

In the past, she would have melted, but too much had happened. Those days were a distant memory. "Oh, now you need me. You demoted me, in effect, remember?"

"I might be in over my head." He dropped his head with a long sigh. "Let's go outside. I need fresh air."

They grabbed their coats, climbed the stairs, and went out the back door.

The freezing wind ripped at her ears. "I can't stay out here too long. It's freezing." She jumped in place to keep warm. It was unusual for him to say he needed her, unless he was trying to soften her up. She searched his face. "In over your head?"

"I don't know." He blew a thin white cloud of air and scrunched his shoulders toward his ears.

"That's a frightening answer," she said, through chattering teeth.

She watched him clasp his hands on top of his head and turn in slow circles. This was no con. She stopped jumping, realizing he was plain scared. "If we screw this up, doing prison time is the least of our problems. And my teeth aren't clicking because I'm cold. Our benefactors will consider us a liability and eliminate us in an instant. Meanwhile, Peter has undoubtedly already made a pact with them. If so, he'll walk free as a bird."

"Not denying it." He turned his back and bent over, pounding the heel of his cracked leather boots in the snow.

She screamed at him. "Jeremy, you cannot turn your back."

232 ~ DIANN SCHINDLER

He kept pounding, more frenetic now.

"With his first words during our first call, he had you by the balls. He's played you this whole time." Her voice quaked with frustration. "We're in grave danger. I'm sick with worry. I'm done saying it."

She turned and sprinted for two miles. When she stopped, she bent over with her elbows on her knees, crying and retching at the same time. Sweat drenched her quivering body.

Whatever was to happen with Magpie, success or failure, it had wrecked her relationship with Jer. She wasn't crying over a breakup; she had lost a friend. At this point, even that was inconsequential in comparison.

Magpie's goal was to force insurance companies to make healthcare affordable and improve the health of the sick and save the lives of the dying. Now, Magpie teetered on the edge of exacerbating illness and causing death. The irony was devastating and shook her to her core. That's what was making her vomit: killing people.

And going to hell.

Standing up straight, she wiped her mouth with the back of her hand. Her putrid bile filled her nose and started her stomach to clench again. She fought back and rolled her eyes toward the sky. Then, whispered out loud, "Experiencing loss is natural. Affecting loss is unforgivable."

~ 34 ~

CHAPTER THIRTY-FOUR

March 13, 2013

Grey left before Margot got up. She found his note on the kitchen table.

Sorry I had to leave early. I'm behind at work. I'll bring dinner home around nine. Hope that's not too late. Love, Grey.

This was the first time he had used the word *love*. She knew Grey's meaning, though. They had been side-by-side in this trauma because they both loved Andy. She loved Grey, too, although not romantically. Their love was a deep friendship and appreciation for each other. She felt that every day.

To be sure, his leaving early was a reprieve, for a few hours. She had only until dinner tonight to prepare her confession: she had left the door unlocked. A twinge of guilt pierced her stomach because he'd be furious, and rightly so. That wasn't the half of it. Most importantly, an intruder stole the drives and dumped her purse on the sofa, leaving €160.30. No coincidence, this proved their crisis was not over. Knowing Grey's recent behavior, he'd try to convince her otherwise. He wanted to believe they were out of danger. So much so, he refused to see the truth. This would not be a simple conversation.

She was running late and there was no time to wallow in angst. Straightening her back and tossing her hair, her mind went back, revisiting all her work from the night before. She had raked through her ESL files and pulled instructions for verb tenses and articles, along with explanations, definitions, practice sheets, and quizzes. The stack of papers was so thick she had to use both of Edgar's envelopes. Pleased with herself, Margot thought if these comprehensive lesson plans didn't kick up Illir's learning, nothing would.

Now that she had done such excellent work, after her morning coffee meeting with Illir, she'd catch up with Nora and her sisters. The last time she had seen Nora, she was sick, listless, with dark circles around her eyes. Margot hoped she had improved.

Margot made two peanut butter and jelly sandwiches, grabbed three bananas, and stuffed it all in her Sars bag, next to Illir's lesson plans.

She ate a banana before leaving the apartment, securing the door, and trudging up the hill to USAID. The guards greeted her with their typical wide grins. She had met them all, and today it was Berk and Blerta. They pointed, signaling her to enter through the metal door.

As it creaked open and the buzzer began blasting, all the muscles in her body tightened. She barely heard Illir shouting a hello behind her.

He inched forward to open the door and, with a quick bow, motioned her to enter before him.

She said hello back, entered, and closed her eyes to focus on a modicum of inner peace, waiting for the earsplitting blast to stop.

Illir moved past her, flashed his badge at Berk and Blerta, and breezed through the metal detector. He beamed as he waited for her on the other side.

When the door closed and quiet filled the room, she opened her eyes. "I cannot get used to that sound," she said, shaking her shoulders to relax her body. She began the ritual, taking off her coat and placing it on the side table with her purse and Sars University bag. Berk's nod gave her permission to pass through the X-ray cage. Again, as it did nine times out of ten, the alarm sounded.

"Are you sure you don't have a metal plate in your head?" Berk said, chuckling.

"That's a thought," she said, facing him, arms out, and feet shoulder-width apart. When he ran the wand over her body, she wondered why he was doing this instead of Blerta. A female guard was more appropriate.

Welcome to Kosovo.

"I escort Miss Margot," Illir said, omitting the verb.

Margot let out a low, deep-throated growl.

"Oh, sorry. Ah. I will escort," he said, covering his mouth and giggling.

Margot glared back at him and shook her head, indicating this was no laughing matter. Illir dropped his hand and pursed his lips. He understood her message.

"Your belongings," Blerta said, handing her the Sars bag, purse, and coat.

"Thank you. And Illir, nice correction."

As they walked outside across the pavement to enter the next building, Illir said, "Cafeteria in different building. This way."

"Do I need to check with Ganna? I think so."

Illir stopped and shook his head, "No. I call her."

"Yes, let her know I'm here. And Illir, please say, 'I will call.'"

"I will call. Sorry." He wrinkled his forehead and sighed.

Margot cringed at the thought of Ganna hearing Illir omitting his helping verbs. She held her breath as he dialed.

"Ms. Ganna, I am escorting Miss Margot. We will have coffee now." His face turned radiant.

Margot smiled, yet her frustration remained fresh. They entered an empty dining room without talking.

"Please. You are mad. I try and try."

She wanted to tell him the pressure she was under from Ganna and his supervisor and explain she could lose this job. Then, there was the embarrassing failure, letting Grey and the University down, not to mention her other students. And Edgar. And, without income, she couldn't pay her rent. Work was hard to find. She'd have to leave the country. What about Andy? Grey?

Oh my God.

She realized she was talking herself into a panic attack. Her head started spinning and sweat instantly drenched her back. Piercing ringing assaulted her ears, and the light was dimming. She leaned on a table to steady herself.

Illir took her arm. "Something wrong?"

As he helped her sit, the dizziness and ringing stopped. She put her face on the cool tabletop and shut her eyes, repeating to herself, *you're okay.*

"Miss Margot?" he said. "I call doctor."

"No, no." She shushed him and said, "Give me a minute." She let her mind go blank, concentrating on imagined white noise and her breath.

After a few minutes, she sat up, surprised she felt normal so soon.

Illir's squinting eyes, furled forehead, and open mouth telegraphed his grave concern. "No doctor?"

"No doctor," she said, smiling at him. She remembered her mother warning her to pay attention and be aware that our minds and bodies act as one. This incident was a warning sign. Take heed, but how?

"I'm sorry. You work too hard for me. My fault."

"Pfft. Don't be silly." Margot didn't have time to dwell on her near-fainting spell right now. Besides, all her symptoms had disappeared. "Can you order our macchiato? Remember, you're buying."

Tension left his face. "I am buying. Server must come." He raised his eyebrows. "So happy you better. Wait. Are better."

As if on cue, a server appeared.

"*Dy makiato, te lutem*," Illir said.

"Let's get to work," she said, taking the envelopes from her bag. "Here are your lesson plans. I've included answer sheets to the quizzes. Use them after you have completed the work. Don't cheat. Agreed?"

"Agreed," he said, examining the logo. "Hmm. Beatrice Place? I know this business. Very big in Prishtina. Very good. Beatrice Place help many women."

"The envelopes were a gift."

Their coffee came, and they sipped.

"Gift? From Edgar, er, I mean, owner? Nice."

"Yes, Edgar Leeds. Do you know him?"

"No, no." he said, shaking his head back and forth at least ten times. "How is coffee?" He lowered his eyes and dropped his shoulders.

He looked painfully uncomfortable. She ignored his questions, and asked her own. "Have you been to Beatrice Place?"

"Oh, no. Never," he said, straightening his posture. "Very important. Today...is...my daughter's birthday. She is ten today. And she loves cake. We. Will take her to Princesha Gresa Restaurant tonight for special cake. She say. Wait. She said invite you. Come at seven o'clock?"

"Well done. You took your time. I think you get excited and talk too fast. Always take time to think before speaking."

He nodded.

"Yes, of course, I'd love to join you."

"My family. Daughter, Afrodita, and my wife is Albana. I very proud of my family. My wife," he dropped his head, "she was in war. Very difficult life for her. Not so easy for her after the war. I cannot discuss."

Margot didn't know how to respond. She had only seen him smile and laugh. This sad exterior stunned her. "I'm so sorry."

"No, no. I am sorry." He looked up at her with his familiar cheerful face. "Tonight, at Princesha Gresa Restaurant."

"Should we exchange phone numbers in case we need—"

"No, no. Not permitted. Cannot. USAID policy forbids it."

"I see. Well, okay, then. Thank you for the coffee." She took a big gulp. "I'm sorry, I must go now."

"I escort you. Ah. I will escort you."

"Is it necessary?" she asked as they exited the building.

"USAID policy," he said in an apologetic tone.

"For the life of me, I don't understand what requires this much security."

"USAID do many good things for people to recover from war. Help make farms. Education for women business owners."

"That requires armed guards?"

"Cannot discuss. A big hint. Fighting ended twelve years ago. War did not."

She stopped and looked into his eyes. "Did you fight?"

"Oh, yes. All men fight. My brother, too. He was fourteen. Lucky to survive," he said, motioning for her to keep walking.

"We're all lucky you survived as well, Illir. It's too frightening for me to think of you in a battle," she said, patting him on his shoulder. Sadly, hugging was not appropriate. She crossed her arms and dropped her head.

"Many die. Don't be sad. Be happy for the living," he said, opening the door for her.

"A wise man, Illir. You always warm my heart," she said, sensing a gentle flutter in her chest.

His face turned red, "Mine too." He opened the door for her, and they waved goodbye.

She took her time and strolled toward Dragodon, careful to listen to her body and ward off another fainting spell. This gave her time to recall her brief discussion with Illir about Edgar and Beatrice Place. She was perplexed, particularly by his unsolicited reference to Edgar, followed by his emphatic denial. Obviously, he was ill at ease, but she couldn't imagine why. So, she let it go, faulting cultural differences.

When she arrived at Dragodon, she descended approximately thirty steps and spotted the girls sitting on a landing a few yards away. Her heart gripped with delight, and she shouted their names.

They turned and waved to her.

She stepped below, sat next to them, and pulled out their sandwiches. "Hello. *Përshëndetje.*"

"Hello beautiful lady. *Falminderit,*" Nora said as she began eating. Her eyes were bright and clear again, and the gray circles had disappeared.

"Oh, you do like peanut butter," Margot said, putting her hand over her heart. "Thank God, Arita. You were right, Nora is much better."

"*Po.* She better," Arita said.

Nora climbed on her lap, and despite the stench of sweat and urine, Margot's heart swelled.

"Care for a banana?"

Nora looked up at her and smiled. "*Ju lutem.* Euros, nice lady?"

Margot burst out laughing. No matter what, Nora, always the little trooper, did her job and asked for money. "Yes. Po. I have euros."

"Many euro?" Vlora said as her dark eyes widened.

"Yes, many. You must wait. If I give them to you now, you will leave. Finish eating first," she said, swaying Nora back and forth in her arms.

"Okay," Arita said. She rocked with Margot and started singing, "*Nina-nina, more pllum, Flej se nana te don shum, T'i m'u rritsh-o nafak-lum.*"

"It's sweet. It is a lullaby? Do you know the words in English?"

"Maybe. Go sleep, Momma loves you, dream sweet." She shook her head. "English no good."

Margot started singing, "Hush, little baby, don't you cry. Papa's going to sing you a lullaby. Hush little baby, don't say a word. Papa's going to buy you a mockingbird."

The girls squealed and clapped their hands.

Vlora said, "Mockingbird?"

Margot nodded.

"In Kosovo, jackdaws. Many, many jackdaws," Arita said.

"Arita," a sharp voice called from the weeds, causing the girls to jolt.

"Momma?" Margot said.

Nora nodded.

Margot hadn't heard their mother before. Her mind drifted to the night she and Andy were on their way to Valbona's Restaurant. He said mothers crossed into Kosovo illegally and trained their children to look pitiful. They even set them up for sex trafficking. He said people who gave the children money perpetuated homelessness.

Margot reached into her pocket and gave one euro to each girl. She told herself these few euros might prolong their poverty, but these girls, and their mother, would not starve. More importantly, a couple of coins would save them from being lured into sexual exploitation.

Nora scooted off her lap. "*Faleminderit.*"

"See you soon," she said as they ran into the weeds. Margot had fallen in love.

Although she and Andy had fought that night, it turned out for the best because he vowed to develop an organization to help beggar children. She was proud to tell that story to her mother. More importantly, saying it out loud solidified her commitment to achieve his goal herself.

Nora and her sisters always brought joy to her life and today, they had been the sweet, bright light she needed.

~ 35 ~

CHAPTER THIRTY-FIVE

March 13, 2013

Margot changed into her favorite blue dress with the yellow sash. She had been waiting to wear this dress for a long time. The birthday celebration tonight at Princesha Gresa called for fancy clothes. Besides, the pleasure of meeting Illir's family was a much-needed diversion and hopefully would keep that lurking subtle tremor at bay.

She left a note for Grey saying she'd be home by 8:30.

When she arrived at the top of the hill, she ducked under a streetlight to call Golden taxi service. As the phone rang, footsteps crunching on gravel from behind startled her. Edgar's warning of the dangers in Kosovo played in her head. She turned to see. It was too dark. Her breathing neared hyperventilation as the sound of heavy boots on broken asphalt came closer, mimicking her shallow, rapid breaths.

Even before Golden answered her call, she shouted into the phone. "Hello. Oh, yes, I see your car now."

Whoever was walking toward her had to hear her screaming on her phone. They'd realize a car was coming and leave her alone.

The dispatcher answered. "Where to, please?"

A man emerged from the darkness into partial light. He held a huge rifle. Her throat locked.

He said, "Madam, can I help you?"

Now that he was fully illuminated, she realized he was a USAID guard. "Damn." Her voice cracked. "You scared me to death," she said, squinching her eyes closed and berating herself for panicking. She had known all along that guards were here. How could she forget that?

"This is a restricted area after six p.m."

"Oh, I walk through here every day—" She stopped herself from saying she worked at USAID for fear he'd report back to Ganna. And she'd think the worst, of course. "I live two blocks away," she said, pointing to her apartment building. "Can you see?"

"No, I cannot."

"Well, it's—"

"No, madam, I cannot." He showed no emotion. "You should not be here at this hour."

"I understand," she said, pushing her hair out of her eyes.

"Yes, this is Golden taxi," the dispatcher said. "Where are you and where to, madam?"

"I'm at the top of Dragodon. I want to go to Princesha Gresa restaurant," she said into the phone.

"Two minutes."

The connection ended.

Margot put her cell in her pocket and forced a grin. "My name is Margot Hart. I'm meeting friends. Your name?"

"My name is Zamir. I'm here to protect USAID, not you, madam." His tone was sharp, official.

Just then, a white car with the Golden emblem appeared. Zamir opened the door for her, and she slid inside. He slammed the door shut before she could thank him.

The driver said, "Fee is one point five six euros, please."

Margot sat back in her seat, stretched her legs out, and closed her eyes. How could she have allowed a benign threat—footsteps—to thrust her into ridiculous paranoia?

Breathe.

She opened her eyes and peered out her window for the next few minutes to relax. They passed three small, damaged brick structures tucked in between glorious fancy homes. "What happened to those buildings?"

"Still from war," he said. "Government must repair."

"The war ended years ago. Seems a shame," she said, digging in her purse for euros.

The vehicle stopped, the driver got out, and he opened her door.

She scooted out and handed him two euros. To make sure she was home for Grey at 8:30, she asked the driver to pick her up at 8:25.

He agreed, tipping his head.

Illir called to her from the balcony. "Miss Margot. Up here."

She began climbing the concrete stairs, lined with dense, green bushes, decorated with tiny, white festive lights. A chubby girl with long, curly hair, pinned with a red bow, waved from the top of the steps. As Margot got closer, she saw she had Illir's twinkling eyes.

"Miss Margot. My daughter, Afrodita."

"Hello, Afrodita."

"It is lovely to meet you, Miss Margot." She giggled just like her father. "Come, please, meet my mother." She took Margot's hand and led her up another set of stairs to a small alcove. Illir followed.

When Margot saw Afrodita's mother, she nearly gasped. She was nothing like Margot had expected. She was a large woman dressed in a long green paisley skirt and black tennis shoes with white socks, her pink-printed blouse stretched skintight over her massive breasts. She looked to be ten or fifteen years older than Illir.

"Please, meet my wife, Albana," he said, eyes sparkling and bursting with pride.

"Pleased to meet you," Margot said, struggling to find a smile.

Albana blinked a hello and displayed a wide grin that uncovered six or seven dingy yellow teeth. Otherwise, she was toothless.

Margot's stomach turned, and she dropped her head to hide her revulsion. How had Illir chosen this woman for his wife?

"So happy we all together here. My daughter, my wife, and my teacher. Please sit."

"Papa, you said I am to help you learn. You left out are. It is *we are all together*."

Margot was grateful Afrodita had spoken up and shifted her focus away from dwelling on the unkempt Albana. She could look up now and engage again.

"Yes, I know. We are. And we eat cake. Ah. We will eat," he said, shaking his head.

He and Afrodita giggled.

The server approached the table with a plain white cake. No candles and no decorations.

"Let's sing 'Happy Birthday' in English," Afrodita said.

Everyone sang except Afrodita's mother, who stared at the cake. She didn't look unhappy, exactly. More like emotionally neutral.

"My mother doesn't speak English, and she is shy around people who do," Afrodita said, cutting the cake.

Margot wondered if her negative thoughts about Albana were obvious to Afrodita. This little ten-year-old was extremely bright. Was she that insightful? God, she hoped not.

Stop judging.

"I understand. I must say, your English is perfect. How did you learn?" Margot said, pushing herself to be courteous and engage in conversation.

"Thank you. I have English classes at school. But mostly I learned from television even before I started first grade." Pleased with herself, she lifted her chin and raised her eyebrows.

"Amazing," Margot said, taking a bite of cake.

"I explain to you, she my idol," Illir said.

Margot ignored his error. No need to hurt or embarrass him in front of his family.

"Please, Papa. You are my idol. Papa is a good man. Did he tell you he fought in the war?"

Margot nodded.

"My mother stayed with my grandmother and my aunt while our men fought. It was very difficult for them because they were constantly threatened. Beaten and tortured."

"Shh," Illir said, squeezing Afrodita's hand.

She nodded to him and said, "Papa and his brother, Uncle Melos, were in many battles. So many men died because they were the greatest threat to our enemy. Forgive me. We don't discuss the war because we are grateful to God that the women and the men in our family survived."

"Yes, we celebrate every day. I very grateful," Illir said. His eyes glistened as he hugged his wife. She put her head on his shoulder.

Illir clearly didn't see his wife as Margot did: overweight, tooth-less, unattractive.

You are incredibly shallow, Margot.

His affectionate display overwhelmed her and her shameful thoughts about Albana's appearance caused her to tear up.

"Why are you crying?" Afrodita said.

Margot chuckled to disguise her guilt and her envy. "Oh. Tears of joy. You are a lovely family."

"You miss your family?" Illir said.

"Yes, I do. And I want to grow up to be you," Margot said, trying to lift her mood. She choked on a nervous laugh.

Illir and Afrodita burst out laughing.

"Oh. Sorry. I must go now," Margot said, checking her watch. "I'm disappointed we didn't have more time together. Thank you for including me and you're right: your daughter is lovely, smart, a delight. Good to meet you, too, Albana."

Illir and her daughter rose from their chairs while Albana wrapped a piece of cake in a napkin and handed it to Afrodita.

"My father thinks the world of you. He says you are the best possible teacher to have. Here, take some cake home."

"Thank you." She kissed Afrodita's forehead and put the cake in her purse. When she reached over to hug Albana, Albana greeted her with a thin smile that covered her teeth. "*Faleminderit*, Miss Margot. It. Was. Pleasure."

Margot had sense enough to stop her mouth from dropping open, speechless at the warmth emanating from Albana's glowing face. Her thoughts had been downright despicable, and disgusting guilt filled her gut.

"Father, walk her."

"Oh, no, please. My taxi will be here any minute."

Margot made her way to the street, still marveling at Illir and his family, especially his unbridled display of affection for his wife. When she looked back at the balcony, Albana and Afrodita were waving. Illir had his back turned, talking on his cell phone.

She waved back.

Honored to spend time with Illir's family, at the same time she punished herself for her pathetic, ignorant reflections. Illir loved Albana for who she was. He was a good person, a wonderful family man with a strong character. Margot could learn from him.

While the celebration had indeed calmed her tremor, she felt it coming up inside again. The only way to get rid of it, as difficult as it would be, was to talk it through with Grey. She had to if she wanted any peace.

~ 36 ~

CHAPTER THIRTY-SIX

March 13, 2013

A white car pulled alongside Margot as she exited the Princesha Gresa restaurant. She started to open the back door but stopped when she noticed the vehicle didn't have the Golden Taxi emblem on its side.

The driver got out, and she staggered when she saw he wore a mask. His penetrating eyes telegraphed danger. She tried to run, but he rammed her with his shoulder, snapping her head back, stretching her neck muscles beyond their limit.

While struggling to regain her balance, she fell hard backwards into someone behind her. He clamped his arms around her chest in a vicelike grip. Trapped, panic struck her heart, and sweat dripped down her chest.

Her screams muffled to pathetic whimpering as the driver plastered thick tape over her mouth. The man from behind yanked her arms behind her back. A rip tie, pulled tight, tore the skin around her wrists, numbing her little fingers.

With a strong thwack against her hip, they thrust her into the rear seat.

To survive, don't let your captors take you to a different location.

She thrashed her legs with every bit of power she had until the door slammed shut, twisting and cracking her ankles. Someone surrounded her head with a blindfold. She fought, jerking from side to side, dislodging the blindfold. She saw a black tattoo for an instant before it disappeared, as the wrap blocked her vision again. They pulled it tighter, causing hair to rip from her scalp and sting her temples. Her eyes watered, dampening the wrap.

Stale cigarettes and pungent body odor caused putrid bile to mushroom from her stomach. She swallowed to keep Afrodita's sweet vanilla cake from spewing out her nose. With her mouth taped shut, she'd choke to death on the slop.

She remembered reading that choking is a slow death, taking four to six minutes.

The car swerved, slamming her forehead against the window. Hot urine filled her underwear with an eerie sense of relief, just as her brain faded into nothingness.

~ 37 ~

CHAPTER THIRTY-SEVEN

March 13, 2013

Cass stewed. Should she call Maureen? Maybe Jer's reluctance to stop Peter from stealing data was because, in the end, no one cared. Or it could be the opposite and she'd put Jer and herself in serious jeopardy if she ratted.

After pacing an hour in front of her computer, she still didn't have the answers. Her worst thought was she'd let it go and everything would go to hell. And, for the rest of her life, she'd regret she hadn't talked to the only person she trusted.

Her hands shook so hard, she mis-dialed three times. Finally, she got it right.

Maureen answered on the first ring. "Cass, I told you not to call me at this number."

"I have a big problem."

"This better be good."

"First, promise me this is off the record."

"No deal. Maksim Nikitin wants to be in on everything, and I'm bound to that agreement. So, are we done here?"

Cass didn't know what to do. Her mouth fell open. She closed her eyes, searching her brain for an answer.

"Cass?"

"Yeah. I'm begging you to make an exception. Remember, we're cousins."

"Leave family out of it. This is business." Her voice was low pitched, angry. "The clock is ticking. We only have thirty-five days before this thing explodes. Tell me this: Are you talking a delay?"

"No. We're ahead of schedule."

"Now you're really pissing me off. You're supposed to keep me updated. What's the new date?" Maureen's questions skewed her away from her purpose. She became agitated and frantic because she was getting nowhere. Her stomach tightened. "Not sure. It's a moving target right now." She stopped talking when a sharp pain jabbed her groin.

"Oh, that's just great."

"It'll happen before the fifteenth." She doubled over and released a long groan.

"Sounds like your stomach issues are back. Sorry. Think you're cut out for this job? Listen. Unless Magpie has failed, this conversation is over."

Her cousin was damn heartless. "I have information that doesn't affect the project—"

"Fine, then why the secrecy?"

Cass wasn't sure what she said was completely true. "Okay. Wait, er, let me try this: what if we were to go outside the parameters of the cyberattack?"

"Depends."

"Dammit, Maureen, you give me no choice," she said, slapping her thigh.

"So, we're back to where we started. Tell me, and don't forget, I will share this with Nikitin."

Cass could stand erect now but, if prior attacks to her gut were any indication, not for long.

"You might feel better after you tell me. Just saying."

She drew a deep breath, held it, and blew out. "Okay, here goes...."

~ 38 ~

CHAPTER THIRTY-EIGHT

March 13, 2013

A powerful stinging slap on the right side of her face jarred Margot awake. Groggy and eyes still covered, she tried to spew swear words through the tape, but it was glued to her lips. A hoot of snickering laughter transformed her anxiety into a rage, and she let out a throaty growl.

They had bound her wrists and arms, strapping her into a chair. She fought to stand but couldn't. Her ankles were bound, too.

A guy got right up into her face. Despite the cloth over her eyes, she felt the heat from his face. The stench of his stale cigarette breath added to the wretched bile, still stagnant in her throat.

"Disk." His saliva splattered on her cheeks. He ripped the tape off, skinning her lips.

"You fuckers," she screamed, and instantly a large, calloused hand covered her mouth.

"Disk."

She froze and her tears, a combination of determination and dread, streamed down her nose.

"No talk? Okay," he said, pressing her elbow tight against the arm of the chair and blowing smoke in her face. He pressed the cigarette into her forearm, sizzling her flesh. She jerked her head back, screaming until she had no breath. Thrashing her shoulders and chest back and forth only made her neck and head hurt. She stopped when they tacked the tape back over her mouth. The smell of burning flesh filled her nostrils.

A cell phone rang. She prayed it was Grey.

She throbbed and ached all over and imagined blood gushing from her scalp and a deep burn hole, exposing the radius bone in her arm.

When she realized it wasn't her phone, she let out a defeated moan. As the phone stopped ringing, she cocked her head, hoping to hear anything that might help identify her captors. If she survived.

She had nothing to lose, so she bucked and thrashed to get free. The chair legs scooted along the concrete, creating an eerie echo. A breeze kicked up and chilled her back, wet with perspiration.

Were they gone?

Sniffing like a dog, she tried to smell the putrid fuckers. She got a whiff of soil and wet brick, nothing else.

Then, in the distance, she heard footsteps coming closer. Two or three people. Her captors were coming back to kill her like they killed Andy. Her heart pounded out of her chest.

"Beautiful lady."

Margot gasped, cocked her head, and jolted backward.

Could it be?

Someone delicately pulled the tape from her mouth.

"Nora?"

"Yes, Nora. And sisters."

"And Mama," an older voice said.

Margot was dumbstruck as her ankles and wrists let loose, and the blindfold fell into her lap.

It was Nora, Vlora, Arita, and a woman too young to be the mother of these girls. Her face was filthy dirty, and a faded and soiled scarf covered her head. Regardless, her eyes and smile were angelic, even with a front tooth missing.

"Oh, my God. Thank you." Her eyes filled with emotion. Although she felt ready to explode, she held back when she saw fright on the girls' faces.

"Okay. All good now?" Arita said in a delicate whisper, wiping Margot's tears with her soiled sleeve.

"Come," the mother said, holding her elbow to help her up. "Okay to walk?"

Margot nodded, despite knife-like spasms seizing her ankles and neck. "Watch my arm, please," she said, looking at the white circular indentation surrounded by swathes of crimson colored skin. "How did you find me?"

"We sleep here. Hide when men come with you. Watch and wait."

"Thank God for you."

Nora carried her purse and held her hand. They stumbled out of the damaged building with half walls and crumbling brick. When they got to the street, Margot dropped her head and closed her eyes, relying on the girls to take her to safety. She limped as they walked in silence.

It wasn't long before Margot looked up to see they were at Dragodon. She couldn't fathom she had been so close to her apartment the whole time. Tension began draining from her body. At that instant, she heard footsteps approaching. Familiar panic returned, filling her ears with blood gushes through her ears.

Nora dropped Margot's bag on the ground, and in a flash, the girls and their mother disappeared.

"Madam? It's Zamir."

That's why the girls ran. They were afraid Zamir might report them.

"What happened? You look—"

Margot staggered as her legs gave out.

Zamir caught her and helped her to a bench. He leaned his rifle against the seat and retrieved her purse. "It's okay now. You're shivering. Are you cold?"

"Very," she said with her teeth chattering.

"You are in shock. We must get you to a hospital."

Just then her phone vibrated from inside her purse.

"May I," he said, reaching for her phone.

She bobbed her head.

He pressed the green button and held the phone to her ear.

"Margot, where are you?" Grey said.

"Grey. Grey. We were wrong. It's not over."

"What—"

"Please come get me. I'm near. I'm by the—"

Zamir took her phone, "Hello. She's near USAID. This is Zamir. I'm a USAID guard. Come immediately and bring a coat." He ended the call.

"I. I. Two men, I think. Took me—"

"Shh. You're safe now," he said in a soft soothing voice, putting his arm around her shoulder to keep her warm.

Margot leaned on his chest and closed her eyes.

"Margot?"

She recognized Grey's voice. He was out of breath.

"They were going to kill me, Grey," she said, opening her eyes.

He took her hands. "Oh my God. I should have never—"

"She needs to go now," Zamir said. "University Clinic. I'll call Golden."

Grey put her coat over her back and sat beside her. "I'm sorry," he said, sniffing and smoothing her hair away from her face.

They waited in silence for two minutes until Golden arrived.

Zamir helped Margot into the back seat. "You'll be okay."

She didn't answer.

Grey got in beside her. He rocked her, kissed her forehead, her cheek, and her forehead again.

***

As soon as they had entered the clinic, she felt better in a protected environment with Grey at her side. Two doctors and a nurse tended to her right way.

The nurse cleaned and dressed her wounds, shaving her hair and stitching the two-inch gouge on her head. She cautioned her to be aware of infection, especially the cigarette burn on her arm, which would take much longer to heal. "You must wear this neck brace for stabilization and to relieve your strained muscles."

Her jaw still numb, she was grateful she hadn't lost any teeth. Black holes in her mouth would have been the irony of all ironies. Images of Illir's wife Albana's toothless grin filled her mind, and pangs of guilt pulled at her stomach.

A neurosurgeon had tested her vision and reflexes, and even though she had lost consciousness, there were no signs of concussion. She gave Margot strict instructions. "Watch for a persistent headache, lack of coordination, weakness in your arms or legs, and slurred speech."

"Thank you," she said, in a dismissive tone.

"Margot," Grey said. "You have experienced real trauma. It could affect you, psychologically."

She clicked her tongue. "I'm fine."

"Madam," the doctor said, "he is correct. Violent attacks are indeed traumatic. Didn't you say you thought you were going to die—"

"Yeah. But I'm here."

"Nonetheless, denying reality often exacerbates physical injuries. Do not be underwhelmed and minimize the shock to your brain, and to your body. Your physical injuries may take longer to heal. Pay attention to dreams, depression, and intense or prolonged anger. If you have any of these, come see me."

"I understand. Thank you," she said, attempting to stand. She wobbled and slumped back on the bed. "Whoa."

~ 39 ~

CHAPTER THIRTY-NINE

March 14, 2013

Margot dragged herself to the bathroom. She had slept well, although she still ached even three days after her ordeal. When she pulled the dressings away from her wrists, she had dark violet bruises, but the weeping from the torn skin had stopped. The stitches in her head were healing nicely and minute stubbles sprouted from the shaved spots. Plus, her lips were a normal size again.

Grey cracked the door open a few inches. "You decent? Coffee?" He stretched his arm around the door and handed her a cup.

"Yeah. Thanks." She blew on the steaming liquid before sipping, and winced as a sharp pain shot through her face.

"We said we'd go to the FBI this morning. Still up for it?"

"Yeah, give me a few minutes."

Margot showered, dressed, and checked her phone for texts from her mom. Nothing. Her chest sank as she doddered to the kitchen.

Grey sat at the kitchen table. "Wow," he grimaced. "Are you sure you're okay?"

"Yeah. Still a little stiff this morning. Thankfully, no nutty dreams and I'm not depressed," she said, standing taller. "Truth is, I'm angry. Whoever did this to me killed Andy, too."

Grey covered his face with his hands.

"I'm tired of being scared and I'm sick of hearing myself whimper and cry." She squinted, sipping her coffee. "I'm definitely ready to get help from the FBI."

"You sound pretty calm."

"I'm hell bent."

"I can see that," he said with a thin smile. "No neck brace today?"

"Fuck the neck brace," she grinned.

"Well, okay then," he chuckled. "By the way, I can't reach Andy's mom. No answer, and she hasn't set up her voice mail yet. I'll keep trying."

Margot said she'd call her mother later today, no matter how hard it could be to tell the truth.

"It's a new day all right," he said, reaching for their coats and scarves, hooked on the wall. "I called a taxi, and it ought to be here any minute. You ready? It looks breezy, you'll want your scarf."

"One more thing," he said. "As many times as I've been at the U.S. Embassy, I didn't remember FBI. offices. So I checked online. The FBI office in Bulgaria oversees Kosovo. There are three FBI agents here on some special detail about child labor and trafficking laws. They said they'd be in their offices today."

Margot winced as her mind raced to Nora and her family.
***

The driver dropped them off at the U.S. Embassy building and they headed for the entrance.

"I'm nervous. You?" she said.

"Enormous butterflies are having a field day."

She watched his lips twitch. He was sweating and his face had turned purplish pink, his usual overstressed color. She was used to it by now.

Once inside, a guard led them through security and directed them to the FBI office.

Grey took Margot's arm as they walked together through the hall.

A petite, thin woman approached them with a broad smile. "Hello, come in. I'm Special Agent Wilson. How can I help you?"

Grey took out his handkerchief and wiped the perspiration off his forehead and chin. His face had turned its normal color now.

"My name is Grey Valentin, and this is Margot Hart. We're Americans working here in Prishtina."

"Please, take a seat," she said, sitting behind her desk. "Go on." She leaned her elbows on the desk, perching her chin on her folded hands.

Margot nodded for Grey to start.

"Our friend, Andy Stephen, was murdered in Tetovo, Macedonia. We think his murder is related to a cyberattack." He swallowed and cleared his throat. "It's a virus designed to sabotage the United States' health insurance industry. Supposed to happen on April fifteenth." He heaved a long sigh and tilted his head back.

Wilson frowned and cocked her head. "Is that so? How do you know this...this Andy Stephen?"

"Andy is...was my best friend since college."

"And you, Mrs. Valentin, how—"

"No, we're not married. I'm Margot Hart. Andy was my fiancé."

"I see. Your last name, please?" she said, taking a pad and pen out of the top drawer.

"I just told you, my last name is Hart," Margot said, rolling her eyes at Grey. "H. A. R. T."

"Mr. Valentin, spell your name, please."

"V. A. L. E. N. T. I. N."

Wilson kept her head in her notes. "Mr. Valentin, how do you know Mr. Stephen? Stephen spelled S. T. E. F. E. N?"

Margot squirmed with impatience.

"No. It's S. T. E. P. H. E. N. And, like I said, we met in college."

"Mr. Valentin, were you in Tetovo at the time of the murder?"

"No. The police called me and asked me to identify the body."

"Did you?" she said, looking up at him and raising one eyebrow.

He bobbed his head, then dropped his chin to his chest.

"Who called you?" She went back to her pad.

"Officer Dime Pavlovski."

"Excuse me, please." Wilson left the room.

Grey and Margot frowned at each other.

He glanced at his watch and slumped in his chair.

She wrinkled her eyelids.

He scowled.

She leaned forward on her elbows, blowing air, and clenching her fists.

He squirmed and pointed to a camera in the ceiling.

Margot shifted in her chair. She mouthed to him. "Microphone?"

Grey raised his eyebrows and shrugged.

"She's hiding in paperwork because she doesn't have a clue what to do." She said it loud enough for the mic to pick it up, hoping someone was taping them.

"Or we're just nervous," Grey said in an apologetic tone.

"What? You are apologizing for me? Please don't do that."

Wilson stepped back into the office, glaring at them. She shut the door with a loud thwack. "I spoke with Police Officer Pavlovski. He says he has no knowledge of this murder. Says he's never heard of you." She sat on the edge of the desk and crossed her arms. "Are you wasting my time, Mr. Valentin?"

"No. You think I'm making this up?"

"You tell me, sir. Sounds far-fetched to me. Murder? Tsk. Cyber-attack?" She pursed her lips and shook her head. "Who do you work for, Mr. Valentin, and where are you staying in Prishtina?" She settled in her chair again.

Grey's jaw dropped open. Then, he stood and said, "I work with the Chief of Civil Affairs at the United Nations."

"No need to get upset, Mr. Valentin." She didn't look up from her notes. "Sit. What's your supervisor's name and phone number?"

Margot got up from her chair, leaned into Wilson and raised her voice. "It's not relevant. This is serious shit," she said, pounding her fist on the table. "Now, if you want to waste time and hide behind your notetaking, great. In the meantime, I want to talk to your superior." As heat rose from her chest, she loosened her scarf, and a few pieces of plaster fell loose onto the desk. Margot swept them away with a swift jerk of her good arm.

Grey flinched at her flare up.

Wilson rushed to her feet, pointing her finger at Margot. "Sit down. No need for theatrics. I understand you're upset—"

"I will not." Steaming inside, she paused and lowered her voice. "We want to talk with someone with half a brain."

Grey tugged at Margot's coat sleeve, urging her to sit.

Wilson steepled her hands. "You need to—"

"Enough." Margot stepped to the door, stuck her head in the hall, and shouted, "Help. Who's in charge?"

"Margot." Grey whispered through his gritted teeth.

She looked at him, her sneer a signal for him to let her be.

In an instant, three armed guards rushed to her with their hands on their holsters. "What is it, madam?"

"This is bullshit, right here in Agent Wilson's office."

"Ms. Hart, I'm warning you," Wilson said.

"Don't you dare threaten me!"

"Please, don't hurt her. Listen to us," Grey said, sputtering.

A guy in a blue suit sprinted toward them. "Wilson, what's going on here?"

"I want to talk to a competent person." Margot spoke with such force, her neck and shoulder pain returned with a vengeance. She swallowed and rubbed the side of her neck.

"I'm not sure, sir."

"Well, interesting, Wilson. Okay, Ms., what's your name?"

She snapped back. "My name is Margot. Margot Hart. H. A. R. T.." Her voice got louder. "Your agent doesn't listen, and she can't spell. I have an urgent message—"

"I can't talk to you until you settle down."

"Are you anybody, or just another idiot bureaucrat?" Her head throbbed, matching her increasing blood pressure.

"My name is Hawkins. Special Agent Richard Hawkins. I'm in charge. What happened to your head?"

"Funny you should ask. Agent Wilson didn't even notice."

"Is this a domestic violence complaint?" Wilson asked. "We're here in Prishtina, focusing on a myriad of challenges faced by children, often linked to domestic violence."

"Oh my God," Margot said, raising her arms in frustration. "Are you stupid? Have you listened to anything we have said?"

Grey cleared his throat and glared at Margot before looking back at Agent Hawkins. "I'm Grey Valentin. Some men abducted Margot three days ago. If you are truly in charge here, you need to listen. Hear us."

"Agent Wilson, I'll take care of this," Hawkins said. His eyes signaled for her to back off.

Margot got a closer look at Hawkins. He was strikingly handsome, with a no-nonsense, open face. Lean, tall, around six feet five inches.

"Get me your notes, Wilson. You're dismissed."

"Yes, sir." She dropped her head and skulked away.

Margot noticed Wilson and Hawkins avoided eye contact with each other. She sensed Wilson had been out of favor before now, and the thought warmed her heart.

"We'll talk in the conference room." He motioned for them to follow.

"Ah. You're a basketball player?" She was testing to see if he'd engage on a personal level or just be another Wilson and keep his distance.

"What makes you think that?"

"You're tall, in great shape."

"Oh, I see. Not because I'm black?" He squinted.

She detected a sliver of a smile. "No, your championship ring." She pointed to his hand. "You played for the Bulls?"

"Oh, yeah." He held his hand up and curled his lip. "Those were the days."

She liked him.

As they followed him into the room, the guards were in close pursuit. Then Wilson joined them and handed Hawkins her notepad.

"Please, sit. The officers here, Gil and Bradley, will stand outside, just in case you get confused, Ms. Hart. You understand."

Margot gave a quick nod.

The officers left the room, and when Wilson stayed behind, Hawkins dismissed her again.

Hawkins reviewed her notes. "Not much to go on here. Ah. Murder? Hm. Denied by Pavlovski. How do you explain that?"

"Can't. Although, we think it's connected to the cyberattack," Grey said.

He checked the notes again. "Nothing here regarding a cyberattack."

"I told Wilson. Here, read this." Grey handed him Nadia's letter from his coat pocket.

Hawkins scanned it and said, "You speak Russian?"

They both shook their heads.

"A friend translated it for us. Basically, it says—"

Hawkins held up his hand, a signal to stop talking.

They waited.

Hawkins' no-nonsense approach impressed her, but it also increased tension in the dead silence. She wiped her wet palms on her jeans.

Hawkins leaned back in his chair and steepled his hands on the top of his head. He exhaled as if this was just another day in his life as an FBI agent. "I know Officer Pavlovski and I'm fully aware of the goings on in Macedonia: their involvement in hacking. Besides myself, I have two agents here. Wilson and Elliot. Elliot is our tech agent, and she has been instrumental in our investigations in Macedonia."

Margot breathed easier.

"Can you help us?" Grey said.

"Well, where's the disk? This letter says there's a disk in a music box."

"The disk wasn't in there. We took the whole thing apart. Nothing," Margot said.

Hawkins shrugged. "Tsk. Not much to go on here. This all you got?"

"No," Grey said.

Over the next three hours, they told him everything. Their words tumbled from their lips like water from a broken dam, spilling every tiny detail and immersed in waves of emotions. The stranger at her door, the break-in, the storage unit in Peja, Ismet's attack, and her captors.

Hawkins took copious notes and asked follow-up questions to fill in missing pieces.

When they finished, Margot dropped her head to her chest. "Dear God, let us be wrong." Her heart pounded in her ears.

"We'll assume you are correct until we find out otherwise. On the surface, it sounds implausible. Thing is, you two are very credible. Can't imagine you burned yourself or banged your head open. I can confirm with the clinic if need be, but I figure you aren't whackos."

"We're not mental. Yet," Margot said, intentionally shifting her attitude. Hawkins was listening now.

"We got work to do, though." Hawkins pointed to a calendar on the wall. "If April fifteenth is accurate, we have four weeks."

"You mean, it could be wrong?" she said.

"Nadia wrote the letter on July twentieth. Could be a change in eight months. Target date could be later or earlier, and we'll need to consider that variance."

Margot and Grey looked at each other.

"Let's start with Andy. Give me his full name, birth date, and the day you arrived in Prishtina." Hawkins slid his pad over to Margot. "His most recent address in the States, and you said he's a graduate of Stanford?"

"Yep. We were at Stanford together. Then we worked for the Croatian government. In Zagreb."

"Just the two of you?"

"We had a third guy with us. Michael Gorkey. I haven't seen him in a few years. Rumors are he traveled to Macedonia."

"U.S. citizen?" Hawkins said.

"Yeah. Oh. Wait. I think I still have his phone number. I can call him—"

"No, do not call him. Give me his number."

Grey took his phone from his pocket. "Yeah, here it is. Why can't I call?"

"Cause," Hawkins said, jotting the number on his pad, "we don't know what we don't know."

"Great. Just as I thought you were going to help us make sense of all this." Margot shook her head and sighed with exasperation.

"I'm trying to help. Until we connect the dots, do not call him," Hawkins said with a stern frown. "So, listen, there's no use for you two waiting here. I think we have what we need for now unless you can give us anymore."

"That's everything," Grey said.

"Wait," Margot said, pursing her lips and taking a deep breath. "Someone got into the apartment and took the flash drives."

Grey choked.

"I didn't have time to tell you, I'm sorry."

"Someone broke in?" Hawkins said.

"Not exactly." She cleared her throat preparing for Grey's wrath. "I was in the shower, and I thought I heard Grey in the kitchen. When I checked, no one was in the apartment and the flash drives were missing. The door was open." She scratched her neck and swallowed. "Either I forgot to lock it, or they had a key."

"God, Margot," Grey said in a loud whisper.

She couldn't look at him, but when she heard the disappointment in his voice, she winced.

"Are you referring to the drives you found in the storage unit?" Hawkins said.

Margot blinked an affirmative.

Hawkins exhaled. "Got it. Listen, I want to talk to this Ismet Lokaj fella. Can you give him a heads up?"

"I'll tell him," Margot said as she and Grey stood to leave. "And, you'll check Andy's mom, Nadia Stephen, and Andy's father, Kostas Stephen?"

"Yes. My driver will take you home in an unmarked car. He'll drop you off a couple of blocks away. We don't want anyone to know you've been here."

"You think someone is following us?" Margot bit her lip.

"Possibly."

Icy fear filled her chest. She tightened her scarf.

"We'll be surveying your place. Go along with your normal routine."

No one spoke.

"Here's my cell phone number, if you remember more or if you need me."

"I've decided we're okay and we're going to work through this," she said, straightening her posture and lowering her chin for effect. "I'm determined."

"I can see that." He opened the door and told Gil to take them home. "Drop them off two blocks from her apartment."

They started toward the exit but stopped before leaving the building, staring at each other.

She realized they were thinking the same thing: They were finally getting the help they needed.

They teared up and hugged in a long embrace.

"Cold?" he said, adjusting her scarf.

Margot's heart swelled at his sweet attention.

That night, she suggested they sleep together.

~ 40 ~

CHAPTER FORTY

March 10, 2013 (4 days earlier)

When Michael arrived at Union Café, Dugal was waiting in his car. Michael threw his duffel bag in the back seat and got in the front passenger's side. "The cash?"

Dugal pitched a wad of money in his lap.

"Damn, you're a condescending bastard," he said, counting the banknotes.

"Hey, man," Dugal said, pushing Michael's head. "You're bleeding."

"Get your hands off me." He shoved Dugal's hand back and touched his head. It felt like a slight cut, not worth mentioning.

"You got your ass kicked," Dugal said, snickering. "You better clean that off." He pointed to a box of tissues on the floor. "The boss doesn't like blood. So, my friend, did you kill him?"

Michael took offense at Dugal's *my friend*, but he let it go and grunted a no. When he pressed a tissue on his cut, it burned, and Dugal was right. It was still bleeding.

"Damn good thing for both of us. I'd have hell to pay."

Curious, Michael frowned. "Why you? You act like he'd hurt you. For something I might have done? Makes no sense."

"Well." He swallowed and took a long drag off his cigarette. "He'd never kill me. We've been through too much together."

Michael hadn't said anything about killing. It sounded weird. He had a feeling that Dugal was hoping Edgar would never kill him, and was surprised Dugal used that word.

Dugal said his boss had saved his life when he got him out of prison. "I was dying in there. Of course, I can get him mad. He's made me suffer plenty. He can punish you till you wish you were dead. Take it from me. I was there."

It was clear, Dugal was damn scared. "He's a candy ass and I get a charge out of pissing him off. Funny to watch him get flustered," Michael said.

"I'm warning you, Michael."

"Aw, relax, Dugal. Don't get your panties in a twist." Michael was more interested in Dugal's Peja trip and what it had to do with their work. "Tell me, this Peja thing."

Dugal seemed happy to change the subject. "Took me the whole damn day. I had to follow a car to a storage business in Peja. One of the boss's guys told him they put a box in their trunk. It's in the back seat. He said not to open it, but I did anyway. Couldn't stand it. You'll never guess what I found inside." He took a puff on his cigarette and threw it out the window. "Two tubes of lipstick. He'll go bonkers."

"Oh, shit. What color?" He grinned, thinking lipstick was perfect for the prissy ass.

Pausing, they looked at each other with their mouths open, then cracked up.

When their hilarity faded, Dugal coughed and choked on his words. "This is bad: I opened the box, and you got your ass kicked." He wiped his face and squinted. "I'm telling you. We're going to have hell to pay," he said, sucking air in between his teeth.

"All right. Knock it off," Michael said, raising his voice. He didn't want to listen to any more of Dugal's misery. While he didn't think Dugal's boss would do him harm, he wasn't a moron. He could decide he knew too much and hire a thug. Michael hated the thought of having to look over his shoulder all the time, especially if the boss had the edge in their wrangling.

Twerp pisses me off.

He needed a good story. No way he'd admit he lost the wrestling match and failed to leave the message. That was the easy part, for today. More troublesome, the boss said if he didn't do his every bidding, he'd turn him in to the Tetovo police for Andy's murder. But Michael didn't trust him and was totally convinced honor among thieves was bullshit. No matter what he did or didn't do, the jerk would rat on him at the slightest tickle up his little proper ass.

He had to get the hell out of this quagmire...on the sly.

~ 41 ~

CHAPTER FORTY-ONE

March 14, 2013

"Sleep together?" Grey said, "Well. Ah."

"Yeah. Wait. Let me explain—"

"I will. First, I want to call Michael."

"Michael Gorkey? What are you going to say?"

"Nothing. If he answers, I'll end the call—"

"Then, why? You remember what Hawkins said."

"I can't see the harm. Look. He can't know where I am. My area code is Massachusetts. Besides, maybe his number is no longer working." He pressed the call button and put on the speakerphone. It rang five times and stopped.

"Now, can we go back to our conversation?" She bit her lip. "Or do you have another delay?"

"No." He displayed a sheepish smile and tilted his head. "I am very fond of you—"

"Oh, my God, Grey. Before you go there, let me explain. It's not complicated. A simple request for comfort and a sense of safety, that's it." She stood back and held up one hand for him to wait. "I may screw this up. Anyway, here goes. You are a wonderful—a fabulous friend. I'm happy you are here in this apartment, and I love our friendship just the way it is."

Grey opened his mouth to speak but closed it when she continued.

"I need to. What I want. Well. Can you hold me and nothing else?" She made her frustration audible by expelling one long breath in a rapid succession of mouth flutters. "No sex."

"I see—"

"Okay, excellent. Because I'm petrified." Perspiration glistened on her forehead.

He stared at her with his mouth hanging open.

She shoved her hands in her jeans. "If it's too much—"

"Of course not. Honestly, I could use a nice all night long, well...hug. I'm afraid, too. I thought you were going to say you wanted sex," he said with an uncomfortable stutter. "And, that's a lot of pressure." He took a breath. "Anyway, you didn't look petrified when you shouted in the hallway at FBI headquarters. Damn gutsy, I'd say."

"Yeah, crazy." She slapped her hip, happy he'd changed the subject. "Ballsy is a better word." She crossed her eyes for effect.

His up roaring laughter filled the room.

Warm mucus plopped from her nose onto her top lip. Proof she was jumpy.

Margot got two tissues, one for her and one for Grey.

"Here, your head is shiny." She teased.

He wiped the sweat off his head, then they both blew their noses in unison, which made for more crowing.

When the howling subsided, Margot said, "Whew, I needed that. Can't remember the last time I laughed this hard."

Grey nodded in agreement. "I think we both just let go of nervous energy. Thank God we enjoy the same humor."

"For sure. So now, do we understand the sleeping together? Hope I haven't hurt your feelings. I mean. You know. The man thing—"

"Tsk. Enough, please. Don't worry, you can be vulnerable with me. I won't think less of you."

God, he knows you.

Stomach flip-flopping, she nodded. "That's the petrifying part."

"Well, now, you must realize. I have no trouble being open. In fact, I wear my vulnerability on my sleeve. This is where you and I differ."

She anchored her feet. "I understand being open—admitting vulnerability—is a strength, and I get it intellectually, in my brain. It's just my body and heart trail behind. Or are completely absent."

"It's fine, and, I've been thinking, Andy would have been happy we...his best friend, and the woman he loved...we are coming together, as fantastic friends. Don't you think so?"

Her stomach settled. "I do."

***

An hour later they were in bed, struggling to find a position where they were both comfortable.

Grey let out a nervous laugh.

"I'm wide awake. Let's face each other."

They switched around, Margot's arm under Grey's neck and his arm under her waist.

"Does this hurt?" he said.

She rearranged her hips. "Not now. You?"

"I'm good."

They were practically nose to nose. She expected him to have bad breath. Everybody does, to a degree. Surprisingly, his breath was sweet. She wondered, "Does my breath stink?" She cupped her mouth, blowing and sniffing.

"Nope."

"Would you tell me if it did?"

"Nope."

"Dammit, Grey," she said, slapping his shoulder.

He ducked, and they chuckled again.

The room turned still for a while.

Margot thought he might be asleep. His breathing was louder, deeper, steadier. She wanted to discuss Andy. Compare Grey's perspective about Andy to hers. "Grey." She whispered. "Are you asleep?"

"Almost."

"Can we talk? About Andy?"

Eyes still shut, he said, "Uh-huh, go ahead."

Although her left arm tingled with pins and needles, crushed under his weight, she didn't dare move. It could shift the mood, the last thing she wanted.

"How did you meet? How was he back then?"

"In Psych one oh one, freshman year. Super smart. Dressed like a bum, except for his Malevich scarf. A smart ass, and weirdly thoughtful, which made for an interesting and charming combination. Women loved him."

"Oh, great, thanks for sharing." She wiggled her toes to release anxiety that was creeping into her head. "That's what I want to hear. Lots of screwing around."

"No, no. He was discerning." He finally opened his eyes and rearranged himself, leaning on his elbow, facing her. "I learned a great deal from him. Such a brainiac."

"You're a brainiac."

"Well, yeah. Andy, he was smart, and had big ideas. You know, human rights and government stuff. Everything came easy to him. Me? I had to study. We wanted to help people. I wanted to make money. Andy was altruistic and bighearted."

Margot's heart swelled for both Andy and Grey. "He wasn't interested in money because he had money, Grey. And, you're right: he wanted to make a difference on a larger scale, at the cultural level."

"Yes. I saw it firsthand when we worked on the Croatian project. He realized tending to one person at a time or a small group was too slow. Patience was not his forte. Andy wanted to affect systematic change."

"Yeah, we had slightly different perspectives and had excellent debates. Let me ask you, did he talk about me?" She fidgeted her feet to steady her nerves.

"Yes. You were a frequent topic. I never heard him talk about any other woman the way he talked about you."

"Don't make shit up, Grey." She craved Andy's approval and hearing about it was almost too much to take in. It made her miss him all the more. A single tear seeped out of the corner of her left eye.

"I'm not. Man, he knew you well. He said you were gorgeous, and he called you...let's see. Oh yeah, he said you were irascible."

"What the fuck is irascible?" Now she felt stupid and embarrassed. She hoped it was a good thing. Perspiration stung her armpits.

"Well, you are the definition of irascible. It means *easily provoked*. You have a quick temper. Understand, that's why he loved you. One thing. There were others."

"What others? Tell me, what else? God, this is such pathetic self-indulgence."

"Yeah, it is. You deserve it. He loved your intensity and said you were a woman of substance."

"Damn. Substance. Well, obviously, he was evolved if he figured that out." She poked her finger in his chest.

"Yes," he said, pushing her hand away. "Especially with women. Probably got it from his mom. He could be tough, though. He expected women to stand up for themselves. Said you had it in spades, although sometimes you were misdirected."

"Ouch, that smarted." She searched his face. "How so?"

"Well, he didn't specifically say. But I have my observations. Now, don't bite my head off, but your emotions sometimes take over and you lose perspective." He raised his arm to protect his face.

She grinned. His sweet humor was growing on her.

"Yep, the same thing I admire you for: your passion. Quite endearing."

Margot's heart warmed, and she squeezed his neck. "Thank you, Grey. I appreciate this and now I'm tired. You?"

He nodded.

They both moved around to return to their comfortable position, arms and legs intertwined like a two-person cocoon.

Sleep came fast.

~ 42 ~

CHAPTER FORTY-TWO

March 15, 2013

"This is way too early. Seven o'clock. I want to stay right here," Grey said, nuzzling Margot's shoulder.

"Me, too." She gave him a long hug. "I need to get up. I'm going to see the girls. Do you want to come?"

"Absolutely. I'll make peanut butter sandwiches."

"Grab six coins. And call Ismet. We need to tell him to expect a call from Hawkins. And tell him to meet us for dinner."

She slipped out of bed and got in the shower, where she did her best thinking. This morning, she marveled over Grey, her rock. He never hesitated to do whatever she asked. She said out loud, "Hey, sleep with me, Grey, and no sex. And, oh yeah, I'm scared. And what did Grey say? Sure. Just like that," she said, with an exaggerated head nod.

You're so self-absorbed.

Last night, their first time sleeping together, felt so natural, they didn't even mention it this morning, as though they'd been sleeping together for years. She took her time in the shower, humming, enjoying this sweet bliss.

After she got dressed, she joined him in the kitchen.

He handed her a cup of coffee. "We're meeting Ismet tonight at Restaurant Liburnia. After I meet the girls, I'm going in to the office and I'll be back here. I don't want you going out by yourself."

She nodded and stared at him, leaning forward, very close to his face.

"What?" He frowned and dropped his jaw.

She smiled and pecked his cheek. "Thank you for sleeping with me."

"Damn. For a minute, I thought I was in trouble." He chuckled.

"Never."

He looked stunned. "That reminds me of a line in a movie: Who are you and what did you do with my Margot?"

She punched his shoulder and revealed in his delightful *my Margot*.

"Ouch! That's the Margot we know and love," he said, wincing and grabbing his shoulder. "We're back to sparring again."

They finished their coffee and put the sandwiches in her backpack.

Margot checked her cell for missed calls or texts and familiar gnawing guilt filled her chest when she realized her mom hadn't tried to reach here. "I didn't have time to call Mom yesterday, and it's midnight in Minneapolis. I'll catch her later." She shoved her cell in her jeans just as Grey's rang.

He answered, lifting his eyebrows at her. "Wila. Lovely to hear from you. Wait. I'm putting you on speakerphone. I'm with Margot."

"You may want to rethink *lovely*. I promised I'd call if I got news from my friends in the States," Wila said. "I did, and it's apparent we were wrong." She explained five health insurance companies in the State of Maryland had experienced data breaches. "And they're covering it up. You won't read or see it on the news."

"Any others besides Maryland?" Margot asked, massaging her forehead, trying to get her mind around this overwhelming truth.

"Can't say. My colleagues live in Maryland. The insurance companies are independent, organized by state. Could be across America for all we know."

Margot could hear Wila's breathing signaling her anxiety.

Silence.

"Hello?" Wila said.

"Yeah, sorry," Margot said. "This is stunning information. We're in the thick of it, for sure. It's damn scary." She didn't have the emotional energy to tell Wila about her abduction. Plus, Wila would naturally want more information, the details. She did say they had been to the FBI.

"Thank God for the FBI, Margot. They'll protect you."

"That's what they say." Grey had a hint of skepticism in his voice.

"I'm devastated and so sorry for this ghastly news. I'll keep you informed. Let's rendezvous in Albania when this is over."

The call ended.

She repeated *when this is over* in her head, doubting there'd ever be an end.

Chin on his chest, Grey picked at his fingernails. "Should we call Hawkins?"

She shrugged and rolled her eyes.

"Do you think it's too late now?" He chewed his bottom lip.

"Too late?" She was having trouble focusing because her recent constant companion, the subtle tremor, was plaguing her again, rattling her insides.

"To stop the cyberattack?"

"No clue. By the way, you don't think the FBI will protect us?" She searched his face.

"Gut instinct. Wilson was not impressive, and Hawkins has to prove himself."

"We're on the same page. I don't want to deal with it right now. Let's walk. I'm craving fresh air."

"It's thirty degrees. Get your scarf, the one we found in Peja. I'm tired of picking plaster off the other one."

She went to her chest of drawers and pulled out Andy's Malevich scarf, held it to her nose and inhaled his scent. His blue eyes and blond-streaked hair materialized in her mind's eye.

When Grey opened the front door, she pushed the drawer back in and rushed to catch up with him.

"Let me." He wrapped her scarf around her neck, tucking in the loose ends.

She loved it when he did that. "Are you always this thoughtful?"

He smiled at her but didn't answer.

"I've been selfish. Self-absorbed."

"Not at—"

"Our conversations are always about me. I know nothing about you."

"I'm an open book. Ask away." He locked the door, pointed at the lock, and winked. "Don't forget."

She nodded and took his arm. "Let's start with your parents."

He squeezed her arm. "My dad, Hugo, and my mom, Laura, had me late in life." He said they were intelligent and outstanding parents. "I was their only child, and they coddled me." His eyes sparkled.

"Valentin? French?"

"Valentin is French. My mother was Spanish, and they both worked at Barnard College. Dad was a professor of economics and Mother was the librarian."

"Was?"

"Yes, they died within a year of one another when I was a sophomore at Stanford."

"I'm sorry."

Grey explained his parents had a passion for education and took him on their travels throughout Europe, even at an early age. "They groomed me to enjoy a cultured life, and I spent most of my time with them and their friends. So, back in grade school, I was...well, kind of how I am now." He smiled and lowered his head.

"What? Bald?" She teased with a toothy grin. "Tsk. My feeble attempt at humor." When he glared at her, she said, "Hmm...less than feeble. Sorry."

"Don't be fooled," he said, caressing his head. "Everyone agrees. Bald men are super attractive," he chuckled. "Seriously. You know. Overweight, jittery, and I sweat easily. Plus, I was smart and a perfect prey for unrelenting bullies. So, my parents moved me to a private school in the sixth grade."

Embarrassing cinders burned in her chest because she did know. She could have been one of those shitty kids. In fact, that's exactly what she thought when she first met Grey. He was fat, feminine, sweaty, and pink. Her stomach twisted with guilt.

"My grades shot up, because," he said, grinning and playfully jabbing her with his elbow, "I'm a brainiac. And, I learned to choose my friends. As a result, I have grand friends. People I admire, who I value, and who value me."

"I'm challenged in that arena. Choosing friends, that is."

He pressed his lips together and raised his eyebrows.

She read his mind. "Here we go again. You mean Edgar?"

He smiled and batted his eyes. "You brought it up."

"Correct. So, one last question. Hobbies?"

"Travel and opera."

"Wow. Take me to the opera?"

"Of course."

***

"There they are," she said, pointing to the girls sitting on a landing. When they got closer, Margot watched Grey's face as he saw them for the first time.

His lips parted, and his eyes glistened. "Man," he said, sniffing and shaking his head.

"Nora, Vlora, Arita, please meet my friend, Grey."

Their faces brightened. *"Përshëndetje."*

"Husband?" Arita said, giggling and covering her mouth.

"No. You're adorable, Arita." She sat and pulled Nora onto her lap. Her tiny face was dirty as always, and she smelled her strong urine. She remembered how she gagged the first time she got this close. Now, it had a zero effect on her.

Grey said, "Hello, Vlora. Hungry?" He reached into Margot's backpack for the sandwiches. Arita helped remove the paper towel wrapping and handed a sandwich to each sister.

The girls gobbled their food without a word.

"They are beautiful," he said in a whisper, wiping his nose with a paper towel.

"They saved my life." She blinked, releasing a tear.

"No cry, nice lady. Euro *ju lutem*?" Nora said, cupping her hand.

Margot hugged her. "Yes, first, where's Mama?"

Arita's eyes widened, "She love you."

"I love her."

"She say you good American woman."

Nora pressed her finger on Margot's chest, "Nora love Margot."

"I love you, too. Can I see Mama?"

Nora flipped her head toward the bushes, then back again. "No."

Margot felt guilty for not bringing her food, too. She looked at Grey and rubbed the tips of her fingers together. He nodded, reaching into his front pocket and pulling out six coins. He gave them each two. They scampered away.

"Now, I understand why you are so drawn to them." He took her hand. "How can you not fall in love with them?"

Bittersweet emotions overwhelmed her. Sad because she could do nothing for these children beyond a few coins and a bite of food, and grateful Grey was so moved.

How can you not love someone who loves these children?

"Yes. How can you not?" she said.

***

When Margot returned home, she called her mother right away. Today was the day she would confess to everything. Although she wasn't sure how, exactly, there would be no wavering. "Sorry I haven't called, Mom." Her stomach fluttered as the very first word came out of her mouth.

"No worries. Hey, I might need to cut this short because my neighbor's coming over. I have to tell you, I got the best dog. A rescue. Two years old, a brown-black, short-haired mutt. They're the best."

"Yeah, they are. Send me a pic. What's his name?"

"Well, now, before you go crazy on me, I didn't know his name until after I signed the papers."

Margot couldn't imagine why she'd go crazy over a dog's name. She waited.

"His name is Lester."

"Dad's name and you still took him home?" She flushed with fiery anger.

"Ironic, eh? It was love at first sight. You can't blame him for his name, and I can't change it. He'd have an identity crisis."

She sputtered. "Bullshit, Mom."

"For heaven's sake. Your dad left five years ago."

"Five years feels like yesterday. He left you and he left me. Good riddance to the asshole."

"Stop it. He paid for your college tuition—"

"Let's be clear. Some, not all, of my tuition." Her jumpy stomach paled compared to the hot fury searing the back of her neck.

"Dammit. If he had paid every penny, you'd still find a reason to complain. Why must you dwell on the negative? Wait, let me talk."

Margot sat back and prepared herself for the same tired, overdone lecture. She'd listened to it a thousand times: Her dad was a good man. He loved her. He loved Sam. Same old story from her bleeding-heart mother. "Go ahead," she said, tossing her hair. "Then I got stuff to tell you."

"Your father always was and always will be overly sensitive, an outstanding quality. God, when he loves, he loves beyond what most men—most people—are capable of. He loved me that way. I think he still does. When Sam—"

"Mom."

The silence that followed was painfully awkward, and Margot simply had to change the mood if she was going to get to her confession. She remembered Grey saying she was hot tempered. At the time, she didn't agree. There was denying it now, because the proof gushed in her ears as her blood pressure skyrocketed. *You must stop this.* She inhaled a long gentle breath and surprisingly thought of a clever response. "You'll need a fence to keep Lester from running off....Running off. Get it?"

"Ha. Ha. Ha. Good idea, you stinker."

They both giggled.

"Listen, your dad simply could not handle Sam's death. You must learn to forgive."

Margot was beginning to understand that concept since she was faced with Andy's death. "I'm under a lot of pressure here."

"I hear it in your voice, honey. You miss Sam and you won't admit it, but miss Daddy, too. I'm your mother and mothers know."

"No kidding. The good news and the—"

"Bad news."

Margot waited for her mother to carry on even longer. She didn't. It was time for the confession, and stinging emotion flooded her stomach. "Mom...." She sobbed. Not so much for her dad, but for Andy, the break-in, her abduction, the FBI, her living nightmare.

Thank God for the girls and Grey.

"Your dad loves you. Remember what he always said?"

"Okay, I'll play along. He said, love me, love my dog. Ironic, eh?" She whimpered.

"An excellent lesson—"

Suddenly, Lester was barking and growling.

"Oh my God, he sounds as big as a horse and mean too."

"Must be my neighbor. Lester. Stop it. Hush." She raised her voice to an irritating scream. "I love this undisciplined beast. Got to go. Oh—"

"Wait." She blurted out her words as fast as she could say them. "I've held back from telling you the truth...Mom?"

The connection ended.

Just when you found the courage.

~ 43 ~

CHAPTER FORTY-THREE

March 15, 2013

Grey opened the taxi door. Margot got in and slid over, giving him room.

"Restaurant Liburnia, *ju lutem*," Grey said.

As the driver pulled away, she told Grey that her mom's dog had put an end to the call. "Meanwhile, I had prepared to tell her everything. Damn that stupid dog. Mom managed to get in her overdone you-need-to-forgive-your-dad lecture."

"Hm. What's that?"

"My dad left us after Sam died. He's a jerk."

"Really? You've never mentioned him. When did that happen and who's Sam?"

"I don't want to discuss it," she said, gritting her teeth.

After a long pause, Grey broke the awkward silence. "You asked about my parents, why can't I ask you?"

"Because it's different."

"It's true. My parents didn't leave me, they died. I'd do whatever I could to have another chance to talk to them."

"Dammit, Grey, you're pissing me off," she said, glaring at him.

Neither spoke until they were standing in front of the restaurant.

He opened the entrance door. "I'll wait until you're ready to talk. I'm here to support you."

She scowled at him.

As the door slowly shut, he put his hands on her shoulders and leaned into her ear. With a low voice, he said, "I'm sorry. Given what we're going through, it's silly to hang on to old negative emotions. Life's too short."

She hung her head. "You don't get it. I haven't told you...what he did. He fucked up everything." She pouted and her lips trembled.

Grey lifted her chin and put his hands on either side of her face. A tear escaped from her right eye, and he kissed it off her cheek.

She sniffled on the outside, gasping on the inside, stunned as blood rushed to her vagina. Her clit swelled.

Where'd this come from?

"Look," he said, pointing across the room. "There's Ismet. Come on."

Stupefied at her visceral response, she had to center herself before she could follow him. She lagged behind a few feet.

Ismet stood and helped Margot remove her coat. "Hello, my friends. Happy to see you."

Margot hugged him. "How are you? Your arm?"

They took their seats.

"Fine, good. Everything." He poured red wine in their glasses and raised his glass. "*Gëzuar. Besim.*"

"Cheers," Grey and Margot said in unison.

"*Gëzuar* is Albanian for cheers. *Besim* mean trust, faith. Word of honor. Promise. My promise to you. Me, I man of Besa. You trust Ismet, forever." His eyes twinkled with moisture.

They drank.

Margot could see that Ismet was delighted to see them and seemed more at ease than usual. Perhaps because they were visiting his favorite restaurant, where he was most comfortable.

Consumed with emotion, she said, "Honestly, my heart is melting into warm liquid. For you, Ismet, and you, Grey." She looked into Grey's eyes and tilted her head, signaling an apology.

He blinked and smiled.

Ismet wiped his eyes with his napkin. "Good friends."

"Aha. To good friends," Grey said, sputtering, with a grin. "We have been through a lot together. Thank you for all your help."

Ismet's face glowed.

Margot put her arm through Grey's and tightened her elbow.

"Okay. Restaurant is great. Authentic foods from Balkans." Ismet motioned for a server to come to their table. "I order to show you best foods of my country. *Pitalka, qofte me maze, tavë kosi.*"

"Excellent choices," the server said. "I will translate. *Pitalka* is our wonderful bread. Kosovo's traditional *tavë kosi* is a soft, buttery mix of yogurt, egg, and extremely tender veal. And *qofte me maze* are small lamb meatballs with our special herbs, gently fried to a golden color." He raised his eyebrows as if waiting for approval.

"Fantastic," Grey said.

The server clicked his heels, bowed, and left the table.

"This reminds me of an Old World painting. Dark lighting, thick wooden beams. And look at the wine rack. It covers the entire wall," Grey said.

"Thank you for choosing this charming restaurant. We've had little time to celebrate the culture of Kosovo," she said.

"Much to learn about Kosovo. Not now, please. How is Edgar? Your friend." Ismet said, rubbing his chin and squinting at her. "I must ask. You know because I say I worry about you with him."

"Hmpf. Don't get me started," Grey said.

"We agree," Ismet said with a thin smile.

"Well, I must tell you," she said, pausing.

Both men leaned forward, eyes wide with anticipation.

"He dropped off a box of office supplies last week. I didn't ask for them. Just out of the goodness of his heart."

"No, no goodness in Edgar's heart. He want something."

Margot ignored Ismet's remark and added that Edgar had stopped by the apartment a few times when they were in Dhermi. "He demanded I tell him where I had been. Of course, I didn't. He continued to pry, and when he bad-mouthed you, Grey, it put me over the edge. We argued—"

"Why didn't you call me, Margot?" Grey asked.

She touched his hand. "Eventually, he agreed to keep out of my business. It was extremely tense, and truth be told, I doubt his sincerity." She let go a long sigh of frustration.

"Edgar not sincere man."

She ran her fingers through her hair and jerked her bangs off her forehead, realizing she needed to face the truth, finally.

Ismet said. "Never liked him. I think he bastard."

"Sorry, you guys. You were right all along." She shook her head, disgusted with herself.

"Okay, so...what does that mean? What will you do now?"

She shrugged. "Not sure. Just try to stay away from him, I guess."

"When he come again, keep door locked," Ismet said.

"I'm with Ismet. Promise me you will never let him in, Margot."

She breathed deep and nodded. "Let's drink to that."

Just then, the server brought their food. He took his time to point and explain every dish again.

"Looks beautiful and smells divine," Margot said.

They began eating right away, continuing with light, friendly chit chat.

At one point when Grey was particularly animated in sharing his experiences on the glorious Dalmatia coast in Croatia, Margot was riveted. Not so much at what he was saying. It was how he was saying it. His eyes lit up as he described the Bay of Kotor and the island of Rab. He leaned his body forward and made exaggerated facial expressions. Then, he sat back and laughed.

Honestly, at this point, she didn't give a rip about the Dalmatia coast, Kotor, or Rab. She was incapable of concentrating on his words because she was dying to sit closer to him. How could she not want more after he kissed her earlier in the evening?

Your vagina won't let you forget it.

She shifted in her chair and their legs touched. His thigh radiated lovely, incredible heat. Just then, he moved his leg closer. Their knees touched.

He's feeling the same thing I am. We're in sync.

As Grey engaged more in the conversation, he moved back away from her.

Was his moving his leg toward hers an accident? Unintentional?

Margot went back to her food as a dull, sinking sadness, along with a twinge of embarrassment, colored her mood.

He has no clue and you're an idiot.

Finally, Ismet leaned back in his chair and blew a long sigh. "Very full."

"This is delicious," Grey said.

"Thank you. We needed this time with you, Ismet. It's been challenging," she said, shifting the conversation and her sensibilities.

Ismet lowered his head. "More than Edgar?"

"Much more," she said with a long sigh, still dwelling on her stupidity.

She and Grey unloaded with all the details and nuances of the last few weeks. They explained Nadia's letter, the kidnapping, the kids and their mother, the FBI, and Wila's update. She told him to expect a call from FBI Agent Hawkins.

"Oh, my God," Ismet said, putting his hand on his forehead. "What can I do? You want gun?"

"Shit no." she said. "Er, I mean, no, thank you. I don't know how to use a gun. Do you, Grey?"

"No guns for us. Besides, they are illegal here and that's enough for me. I don't want to land in a Prishtina prison cell."

Margot warned Ismet to be careful, that he still could be in danger. "The man who attacked you in your apartment? That was no coincidence."

Ismet sat straight up and puffed out his chest, "No match for me. And we have FBI. Very important American organization."

"One can only hope," Grey said.

"What? FBI no good?"

"We shall see," she said, raising one eyebrow.

"Police here corrupt or not care," Ismet said. "Without FBI, what to do? Is serious."

"Outstanding question and I agree. Serious," Margot said. The subtle tremor returned. She bit her lip.

~ 44 ~

CHAPTER FORTY-FOUR

March 15, 2013

"**He**'s not who I thought he was," Margot said, as they walked toward the apartment.

"Who? Edgar?" Grey said.

"Yeah."

"Glad you figured him out." He kissed her hair.

There, it happened to her again. Her panties dampened.

"Ismet is an impressive person," he said.

"So are you," she said, catching herself on the edge of swooning. This was shocking and weird. But whatever it was, she couldn't deny she had lusted like a stupid teenager all during dinner. Even after their legs no longer touched, she fixated on his mouth as he laughed, talked, and even as he ate. Her eyes riveted on his top lip and the attractive fleshy skin below his lower lip, dreaming how his lips would taste on hers and remembering his sweet breath.

"Yes, we are all impressive. It was a great evening," he said.

They meandered in silence the rest of the way home.

Once inside the apartment, they continued to their separate bathrooms, both ending up in her bedroom dressed in their usual T-shirts and light flannel drawstring pants. Proper. Discreet.

They crawled in bed from their perspective sides, covering themselves with a sheet and blanket.

Just in the past couple of days sleeping together, they had a pattern. They talked for a bit before rolling over and going to sleep, Margot often spooning with Grey cradling her from behind and always maintaining a proper distance where it counted. They never were so close she could feel his penis and he never touched her breasts. It was—had been—perfect.

Tonight was different. Something had shifted since they last slept together, a mere twenty-four hours earlier. Tonight, she wanted more. Unfortunately, she didn't understand how to make it happen. Their relationship was never a topic of conversation because they did what friends do: just be friends. Romantic couples are always defining their relationships. She and Grey never did that, because their relationship was platonic.

She wondered if she had brought this on herself. Their sleeping together had been her idea because she needed a sense of protection and safety. Grey had given her that in spades. Now, she had another sort of free-flowing anxiety that had little or nothing to do with Andy's death, the break-in, or her capture.

Not fear...lust, for sure. Not love. At least, she didn't think so. No matter, she couldn't define the source of the extra layer of angst. Whatever it was, it loomed large in her mind and now infiltrated her body.

She toyed with the idea of masturbating in the spare bedroom. Getting her rocks off could release body tension, but her desire was greater than visceral; it enveloped her every thought. A solitary climax couldn't change that and it might make it worse. She nixed the idea.

Margot held the covers under her armpits with elbows gripped to her sides and faced the ceiling. She was positive she looked pathetic. And Grey was no fool.

What do you want, you idiot?

"Ismet is a great friend," he said.

"Yes, he is."

"Wasn't that restaurant incredible? Great food, eh?"

"Hmm."

He rolled over, and she sensed his eyes on her. She didn't move, eyes glued to the light fixture on the ceiling.

"Cat got your tongue?"

She puckered her forehead, blinked, and struggled to find a way to introduce sex into their conversation.

"Your hair is covering most of your face."

"So?"

"So, it's hard to talk when I can't see your eyes."

"Brush it back. You do it all the time."

"Yeah, but not in bed," he said as he smoothed her bangs off her forehead. "Are you okay?"

She shook her head.

He exhaled. "Face me. Ahem. I got something to say."

Margot couldn't imagine what. She turned and propped her head up with her elbow.

"Please hold your thoughts until I'm finished."

"If this is about Edgar, please don't."

"No," he said. "Hear me out. I saw you looking at me."

"What?" she moved to a sitting position and folded her arms, embarrassed her behavior had been obvious to him. She wondered if Ismet caught it, too. Heat flushed her face and neck.

Grey sat upright. "I've noticed a few changes, Margot. And you must see it, too. Seems you've let your guard down; you trust me now." He paused and raised his eyebrows, encouraging her to respond.

She didn't know how to answer.

He inhaled and blew air through his thinned lips. "Okay. Here it is." He took her hand. "I want to make love to you. Now. Tell me if it's okay with you."

Her jaw dropped. "Ah. Really? I. Ah. Well, I guess so," she said, flabbergasted.

"Oh, no you don't. No guessing. You got to want it, too. I think you do."

"This is rather abrupt, don't you think?"

Grey slid out of bed and paced around the room, "Yeah. Kind of. I've thought plenty about it the last few weeks. I know, I know. You practically hated me when we first met."

She opened her mouth and was ready to confess her awful guilt just as Grey held up his hand with a clear signal: don't talk.

She closed her mouth so fast her teeth clacked.

"We. You and me muddling through this, this hell. We've leaned on each other, grown to trust one another, and slept in the same bed because we were panic stricken—fearing for our lives. This is real shit, and it can tear people apart. Not us. Through it all, we've become closer. That's huge."

She opened her mouth to agree just as he held up his hand again. He marched at the foot of the bed, back and forth. Finally, he sat in the chair with his elbows on his knees, hands clasped at his chin.

She swallowed.

"Relationships, deep or superficial, are not to be taken lightly. We must honor them, hold them dear. You are of superior importance to me. And, frankly, I don't want to lose it...you," he said, opening his hands. "This right here. What you and I have."

A lump lodged in her throat.

He stood. "So, your guess is not good enough. I want an answer with serious thought. And yeah, emotion behind it. You have to say you want it. If you don't, you must say that, too. Whatever, it's your choice and either way, no questions. I promise you can count on my continued respect. I don't want to jeopardize our friendship."

Her lump had narrowed, and she gulped. "I've been a fool. Pure jealousy when you came to Valbona's Restaurant that night because I wanted Andy all to myself. I held on to that negative crap, dysfunction, forever, looking for reasons to treat you like shit. Until. Well, er, until I couldn't anymore."

He didn't speak.

"I couldn't any longer because of you, who you are, Grey. I'm not guessing." She'd never felt so vulnerable and so safe at the same time. "Believe me. I want you to make love to me."

They stared at each other.

He let out a puff of air and got in bed beside her. She scooted down from her sitting position and pulled the covers over him. He put his arms around her, pulled her closer, and kissed her.

At first, his lips were barely parted. Then, mouth open. His lips were firm, breath sweet. He held her hair back while running his tongue around the inside and the outside of her lips. Soon, her clit started to throb, radiating swirling waves to her inner thighs.

She breathed deeper and exhaled longer.

He whispered in her ear. "I want to touch every part of you. Tell me what you want."

Breathless and heart pounding, she couldn't speak.

She sat up and raised her arms, her eyes locking on his. He sat halfway up and took off her shirt. Then his.

They removed their pajama bottoms. Grey slid her panties off. Before lowering her to her back, he looked at her, "Okay?"

She placed her palm on his cheek. "Yes."

He kissed her neck and caressed her breasts. As her nipples hardened, he pressed against them with his fingertips. When she drew a deep breath, he lowered his head from her neck and licked and sucked her tits. At the same time, his fingers found her clit. Massaging, slowly, gently.

Margot arched her back and panted, opened mouth.

"Wet, soft, glorious," he said.

He had to be listening to her breath because she hadn't said a word. And he was there, where she liked it best, searching around with his tongue, firm and persistent. She pushed her knees to her hips. She was completely open, exposed. Then he spread her legs wide. He licked and sucked her clit.

Margot went wild, waves crashing throughout her body.

He backed off a small fraction.

Sweet torment. The delicious pause extended her bliss.

"Oh God, Grey."

Full mouth on her, he used his fingers to pull her labia back to open her more. Cool air washed over her. The tip of his tongue played with her. Goosebumps covered her butt cheeks and the inside of her thighs. Then he covered her clit with his lips, pulling, sucking.

When she lost her mind again, he didn't stop this time. She curved her spine and opened her mouth. Rapid, short huffs.

Suddenly everything exploded, ecstasy rushing throughout her body. She tightened her butt and raised her pelvis in the air, groaning, long and deep. Tears collected at her temples and ran into her hair. Quiet sobs eked out.

Her afterglow still vibrating, she couldn't wait any longer. She reached and found his cock. She gasped. It was granite. Her clit surged again.

"Margot, I'm ready. Please, let me...."

She let go as he got on his back and pulled her on top. She guided him. Slipped him inside. Let him fill her. She panted and rocked. Slow. Easy.

Grey put his hands on her hips, face beaming. "Been my dream."

She pressed down hard, circling her hips. He felt good. Smooth, stiff.

He raised his arms above his head. His breaths quickened. Suddenly, nostrils flared, he inhaled and stopped breathing. Mouth open.

Warm liquid filled her.

When his breathing was almost normal, she slid off his hips and lay beside him. He put his arm out and she rested her head on his shoulder, her arm across him. His heart pumped in his chest.

Silence.

"Where did you learn that? I mean, you've been told this, I'm sure. This was fantastic," Margot said.

His stomach bobbed with a hearty laugh.

"Damn, that's a legitimate question. What's so funny?" Defensive, she shuffled her feet.

"No, no," he said, as his roar settled to a chuckle. "I'm sorry. I always do this after sex."

"So, you always laugh after you have sex." Her mouth curled on one side, forehead scrunched.

"No, not always. Only with sensational sex." He started laughing again.

"You're delirious."

When he heard that, he roared and coughed. He sat up, caught his breath, cleared his throat.

The sight of him fighting for air tickled her. She slapped his shoulder. He ducked and giggled. She joined him.

"I'm delirious after a long run...."

They howled together.

She got out of bed, sashayed to the kitchen, damn proud of her sexy body. After grabbing two bottles of beer out of the fridge, she uncapped them and returned to the bedroom. He reached for his beer and pulled the cover back for her. Margot crawled underneath, and they clinked their bottles.

They took a swig, their eyes danced, and wide grins spread across their faces.

In their silence and after three swigs, they put their bottles on their nightstands and moved to their spoon position. Appropriate distancing be damned, he cupped her breasts.

"Good night, Margot."

"Hm."

~ 45 ~

CHAPTER FORTY-FIVE

March 16, 2013

Grey laughed after great sex; Margot sank into a dead sleep.

She had slept a few hours when she woke, thinking of her mom. And something struck her as odd...the damn dog. After sliding out of bed, she put on her T-shirt and bottoms. With her mobile phone, she left the bedroom and closed the door, mindful of waking Grey.

Her cell said it was 3 a.m. which meant 8 p.m. in Minneapolis. She accessed her mom's number, pressed the icon, sat cross-legged on the sofa and listened.

In less than a full ring, it forwarded to the voice mailbox, which was full. Her mother must have turned her phone off, and she never turned her phone off. Meticulous, she always returned calls and deleted voice messages.

Margot leaned on her elbow on the sofa and rested her chin on her hand, trying to put her finger on her unease with the last conversation with her mother. Not that she confessed; it had to be something else. After racking her brain, she decided on the abrupt, unfinished ending and her lack of closure.

You didn't tell her you loved her.

She cried quietly.

Eventually, she wiped her face with her T-shirt, sniffed, and gained her composure. She wanted to talk to her mother now, to such an extent she considered calling her dad. As she scrolled her list of contacts, Brooks' number appeared. Perfect, he'd be at work at Afton Alps by now and she'd rather talk to him, anyway. She pressed *call.*

"Margot. God. What a surprise. Are you back in town?"

"No. We're still here." Her stomach twinged because it wasn't *we.*

"I miss you two. You guys been having a good time?"

"Yeah. Hey, have you been over to see my mom?"

"Actually, no. Been busy. Sorry."

"Can you do me a favor, check in on her? I can't reach her on her cell."

"Sure. Ah. You mean go over there?"

"Yeah, tell her to call me."

"Why? What happened?"

"No. I just wanted to talk, and her phone isn't working."

"Not an emergency? Are you two okay?"

"No emergency," she said with a cough, praying it wasn't. "I told you, we're fine. Do this for me? It's late there. Can you check on her in the morning?"

"Will do. It'll be good to see her."

After their goodbyes, she ended the call.

The bedroom door opened, and Grey came to the kitchen. "What's going on?"

"I couldn't sleep and tried to call my mom. When she didn't answer, I called a friend to check on her."

"You worried?"

"Last I spoke to her, the damn dog barking, incredibly loud, halted our conversation. I couldn't hear a thing. She hung up before I finished our conversation." She raked her hands through her hair, growling with frustration. "If something's happened. I...I couldn't live with myself."

"Why think that? And in Minneapolis?"

"Her phone went to voicemail, and the box was full....Oh, never mind. You heard Wila, hacking could be happening in Minnesota. This is international bullshit. Kosovo. Macedonia. Maryland. We're naïve to think this doesn't involve the United States, and that includes Minnesota."

"Yes, hacking, and you're thinking that includes harm to your mom? Margot, your imagination is running wild."

She glared at him.

"I'm not dismissing it, I'm saying it's three o'clock in the morning. Come on," he said, leading her back to bed.

She closed her eyes and concentrated on resting her brain.

Nightmares punctuated her fitful sleep. They were vague, with a wicked sense of doom.

***

The clock on her nightstand said 9:15. As she rolled over to see if Grey was sleeping, the dense aroma of fresh coffee wafted from the kitchen.

Grey tapped on the side of the opened bedroom door, cup in hand and a wide grin on his face. "Morning. Coffee?"

"Yeah. Smells great. And someday I'm going to bring you coffee." She scooted up and leaned against her pillow, knees pulled up to her chest. "Sit with me," she said, padding the bed and taking her cup.

He brushed her bangs back, and pecked her forehead. "Your stitches are healing nicely. Does it still hurt?"

She shook her head.

"Rough night, eh?" he said sitting beside her. "You were pretty active. Arms flailing. Grunts and groans. You called for your dad and your mom."

She sipped and inhaled. "Oh, man. Sorry if I kept you awake."

He huffed. "Not at all. Want to talk?"

"Hm. No, I'd enjoy a break from talking. To you, my imagination is going wild. To me, I'm overthinking. Anyway, whatever. Interested in going to the Cathedral?"

"Great way to spend the day. Let's do it."

Margot took a long shower, letting the water wash over her chafed bottom. The minor discomfort was worth Grey's love and attention. She relived his hysterics, and a giggle rose from her chest.

Thank you, Grey.

Within a couple hours, they arrived at Mother Teresa Cathedral. Nothing had changed much since her last visit. Scaffolding was the same and mesh still covered the unfinished portions. As they walked inside, she drew a deep breath in awe of the gleaming white marble, intricate wood-beamed ceiling, and the brilliant stained-glass windows. Beside the breathtaking beauty, the complete silence never failed to touch her heart.

Grey took her hand. "You're glowing. You love it here."

"I do."

"You pray when you're here?"

"Yeah, I guess so. I mean, in my own way. Do you? Are you religious?"

"I'd say I'm spiritual, I'd say. Similar to you, my prayers are in my own style, so to speak. Doesn't have to be in a church...wherever I might be."

They stood in the quiet.

"*Allahu Akbar, Allahu Akbar, Ash-hadu Alla ilaha illallah...Ash-hadu anna Muhamadan rasuulullah....*"

Chanting voices always caused her to pause. The smooth, melodic phrases were deeply peaceful. Warmth flooded her body and settled in her stomach, soothing her unease. "Wow," she said, closing her eyes.

"Yeah."

The chanting continued. "*Allaahu Akbar, Allaahu Akbar.*"

When it stopped, they didn't speak.

Finally, Margot opened her eyes. "I want to talk about Sam and my dad."

~ 46 ~

CHAPTER FORTY-SIX

March 16, 2013

Margot and Grey had received a call from Agent Hawkins while they were at the Cathedral. She wanted nothing to ruin this day and asked if it could wait until Monday.

"No, I'm sending a car."

"What's he want?" Grey said.

"He's sending a car," she said, shrugging.

When they arrived at the U.S. Embassy entrance, a guard unlocked the door. "Ms. Hart? Mr. Valentin?"

They nodded.

"Come in. You must go through security."

Agents Hawkins and Wilson waved and smiled from the hall. Their gestures didn't ease Margot's angst. No government agency is open on a Sunday. Whatever they had to say, she doubted it'd be encouraging. She steeled herself.

"Come on, think positive. I can hear negativity emanating from your mind," Grey said with a forced grin.

She chewed her bottom lip.

Two security guards stood vigilant. One, a trainee with a plain uniform. The other, back against the wall with his arms crossed, wore an officious frown and a gold name tag: Sergeant William Arnold.

First in line, Margot removed her coat and put it on the conveyor belt, along with her backpack.

"Please, scarf, too," the trainee said. "Empty your pockets and place your items in the basket."

She slapped her pants' pockets. "Nothing, and my Malevich stays right here." She tightened her grip around the ends. "I'm cold." She was in no mood for bullshit.

The trainee glanced at the sergeant and cocked his head.

The sergeant dropped his arms in disgust and stepped forward. "Madam, you'll have it back in a nanosecond." He positioned himself facing the image screen and peered over his glasses at her.

Margot blew air, trilling her lips. She took her time, then placed it on the belt. The belt jerked forward with a loud rumble, then continued moving with a soft hum.

The trainee motioned for Margot to step through the metal detector.

Safe on the other side, her backpack and coat appeared. She claimed both and waited for her Malevich.

The soft hum stopped. The sergeant squeezed his eyes and moved closer to the screen, pressing buttons sending the belt backward and forward again and again.

Margot's back stiffened.

"Step aside, madam," he said, pointing to a rubber floor mat next to a long table.

"What? You're kidding me."

She sauntered to the mat and put her coat and backpack on the table. She sneered while jutting her arms out to her sides. "Wanna wand me?"

Grey's eyes locked on hers. He curled his lip, opened his palms, and mouthed, *What?*

"What's happening?" Hawkins said, stepping to the screen.

When Margot saw his mouth slacken, sweat popped on her top lip. Suddenly, she remembered, this was her Malevich from Peja and the first time she had worn it here.

"Wilson, tell Elliot to get here, now, and bring me a paperclip," Hawkins said. He took her scarf and pointed at Margot. "You. Come with me."

"Why are you angry?" Her heart jumped to her throat. "How dare you point your finger at me."

He didn't respond.

She followed him through the hall to a conference room.

"Sit." He slammed the door. "Did you actually think we'd miss this?"

Dumbfounded, her mouth fell open, and she shook her head.

With the scarf spread out across the table, he tugged at a corner and then rolled the material with his thumbs and forefingers. Then, he held it to the light and focused on the edge.

Wilson came in with the paperclip. A forty-something woman in a dark pants suit followed. Her face and piercing green eyes were etched with concern.

Hawkins pried the clip apart and molding it into one long piece. "Hold this back," he said to Wilson. She spread her palms wide, stretching the material taut.

"What's that label?" Margot said.

"You don't know?" Wilson said.

"Would I ask if I knew? What is wrong with you people?" she said, reaching for the scarf.

Hawkins pulled it back beyond her reach. "It says 'Kostas Stephen.'"

"Andy's father."

As Hawkins worked to maneuver the weaved strands, his face hardened and turned tomato red.

When Margot leaned in, straining to see, she detected a raised area inside the yarn.

Elliot hunched over Hawkins' shoulders. "Oh, I see it now."

Margot poked her head forward. "What is it?"

"Where did you get this scarf? How long have you had it?" Elliot said, straightening her back.

"It's Andy's. It was in the storage box in Peja."

"I didn't see this in the report. Why didn't you tell us?" Elliot asked.

"Thought nothing of it. Never noticed this...whatever it is you're looking at."

Hawkins shoved the scarf to Wilson in a huff and tossed her the paperclip. "You try it. Think we're going to have to cut it out."

Margot jumped to her feet. "Don't you dare."

Wilson hovered, digging with the clip.

"So Margot," Hawkins said, squinting at her. "You are telling me you don't know what this is?"

She blinked and dropped her jaw. "I'm not the criminal here, remember?"

"Can't get it," Wilson said.

Margot reached out her hand. The scarf was so important to Andy and represented his love for his father. Now it was hers. "Let me have it before you ruin it."

Wilson glared at her and didn't move. Elliot folded her arms and widened her stance as if to warn Margot to stay calm.

"Guess you're Elliot. We haven't been properly introduced."

Elliot gave a nearly imperceptible nod.

"Well, listen," Margot said. "It's a damn expensive designer scarf. With, I might add, sentimental value. It was Andy's. I said give it to me. It's mine to examine. With delicacy and care." She held back tears.

Wilson didn't relinquish it until Hawkins waved his hand, giving her permission.

Margot began moving her fingers around the fabric and felt a small square. "Someone sewed it inside."

"It's a computer disk," Elliot said, dropping her arms.

"You're shittin' me." Margot dropped to her seat. "Damn. It has to be cut out. Along a couple of threads. I'll do it."

"Scissors, Wilson, and let Valentin in," Hawkins said.

Wilson left the room as Grey entered.

"What's going on?" Grey said, putting his hand on Margot's shoulder. "You okay?"

"They found a disk," Margot said. "All this time... Andy must have taken the disk from the music box and sewed it inside."

Wilson brought the scissors and Margot made a single slice from the outside edge, cutting along one side of the disk to its top corner. She held her breath. With her thumb and forefinger rubbing the material, the disk wriggled loose.

Everyone stared in silence as it tap danced on the table.

~ 47 ~

CHAPTER FORTY-SEVEN

March 18, 2013

Elliot left the room, disk in hand.

Wilson stretched a piece of tape and stuck it on the severed yarn. "This will stop it from fraying."

"Nice little surprise for us. You had me going for a while. Sorry, Margot," Hawkins said, tipping his head. "While we're waiting for Elliot, let's get started. Wilson?"

"First off, we checked on Michael Gorkey. He arrived by plane—"

"Excuse me," Margot said. "Your investigation started with Gorkey? Why? We don't have time for this. Grey mentioned him because he was curious...nothing to do with—"

"Because we found him easily. Hear me out. Gorkey flew to Prishtina around three months ago from Frankfurt, Germany. He left here on a flight to Vienna three days ago. Then the trail goes dead. He's had a few run-ins with the law in the States; assaults, mostly. As far as we know, he stayed out of trouble while here. At this point, there's no evidence of involvement in the cyberattack."

"Humph, government work," Margot said, shaking her head and flaring her nostrils. "Colossal waste of precious time."

"Lack of evidence doesn't mean he's innocent. Keep that in mind. We can't prove he broke into your apartment, Margot, because you didn't call the police and as a result, we don't have evidence. Let that be a lesson. I'd advise you not to make that mistake again." Wilson raised her eyebrows at her.

"Whatever," Margot said with a twisted, smart-ass smile. "Doubt I'll ever need to connect with the police or FBI again. This is enough in one lifetime."

Elliot burst into the room, face red with excitement. "Got it."

No one moved.

Margot went light-headed. "Tell us."

"Hold it," Hawkins raised his arm and stood. "Only the basics. We've classified much of the information."

"It's the best I can do for now. Someone smarter than me needs to look at this. What I can say is this is definitely malware, malicious and extremely complicated."

"How can you determine that?" Grey said.

"I recognize code. Unfortunately, this is way beyond anything I've seen before. Zombies. Blackhole filtering. Smurf echoing. Lots of tools pulled together." She held the file in the air, "This has the plan. Not the actual cyberattack data. Still, it's a gold mine."

"Fingerprints?" Hawkins said.

"It's a shade above my paygrade. I can't tell who it's meant for—"

"Hey, we got word from an insider, so to speak. A friend who has reliable contacts," Grey said. "Two or three health insurance companies in Maryland found breaches in their websites. That's a fact. So, we gotta believe it's underway."

"Nah," Elliot said, scratching her head. "No evidence of that."

"Health insurance companies won't release that information and ruin their image," Margot said.

"Employees talk." Grey said. "It ekes out—"

"Okay, let's assume that's true, for the sake of this discussion. It's in the early stages of testing. Poking around to find vulnerable areas to penetrate," Elliot said.

"Fingerprints? I don't get it," Grey said.

"Patterns of behaviors in development. Or certain processes automatically link back to a known hacker group. Then, too, malware must contact its command base server to get instruction or to move the stolen data out. End servers have an associated domain registered, which, with a bit of luck, is traceable," Elliot said.

Grey leaned back in his chair, "Incredible, and we're behind already."

"How much time we got?" Elliot said.

"The letter said April fifteenth. Today's March eighteenth," Wilson said.

The air seemed to leave the room and Margot and Grey looked at each other, wide-eyed.

"Four weeks. Is that enough time?" Grey said.

Hawkins put both elbows on the table and cradled his face. "Depends."

"And, remember," Margot said, "you said the target date could shift. And if they're in one state, could be they're in other places. Anyway, the timing is fluid."

"Yeah, our source doesn't have contacts anywhere else," Grey said. "Could be everywhere—"

"Let's not panic," Hawkins said. "We got a really good start, now that we have the disk. Meanwhile, we have pulled in other agencies: Homeland Security, National Security Agency, and others."

Silence.

Margot drew a deep breath. "So, why did you call us here?"

"We want to check your place for bugs tomorrow morning and need your permission." He shoved a form across the table. "Sign on the dotted line," Hawkins said.

"Bugs? What the hell?" Margot covered her mouth.

Grey said, "You really think they've bugged us?"

"Try not to worry. It's a precautionary measure," Hawkins said. "Plus, Wilson's putting together a lineup. We might have your kidnappers."

"Not sure it'll be useful. They wore masks." Margot gritted her teeth, thinking people had spied on her. And listened to sex with Grey.

"Lineup will take place in a week or so. Wait for our call," Wilson said.

She nodded. "Hey, I'm on information overload. So, unless you have vital information you want to share at this moment, we'll be here tomorrow."

"Understood," Hawkins said.

As they began walking toward the exit, Margot said, "We both are working in the morning. Here's my key. I'll need it back, of course. And, this stuff is off limits once we're inside the apartment, eh?"

"Correct. One quick question," Hawkins said, taking her key. "Do you know a Leeds? Edgar Bernard Leeds?"

Margot's knees caved.

***

They didn't speak after leaving the FBI office conference room. Not even during the taxi ride home. Certainly not when they entered the apartment.

Finally, when they were in bed, Grey said, "You okay?"

Margot pulled his arm underneath her neck and turned away. "Yes. Let's spoon."

Once on his side, he bent his knees into the back of hers and cupped her breasts. "Warm enough?"

"Now I am."

"Try to sleep," he said, whispering in her ear.

"You, too."

Throughout the night, Hawkins' question about Edgar ate away at her. She had to assume his mentioning Edgar's name on the heels of finding the disk had everything to do with the cyberattack.

The million questions crashing in her head only mystified her. She wanted to talk to Grey. Someplace safe. Where and when?

~ 48 ~

CHAPTER FORTY-EIGHT

March 10, 2013 (8 days earlier)

Edgar had returned home from his visit to Mother Teresa Cathedral. He sat on his second-floor balcony, next to his office in his three-story home just outside of the Prishtina city limits. Here, he was king, especially when he had a snap of weed, a snifter of Serbian Rakija, and his Thai Ridgebacks, Gertie and Oliver, sleeping at his feet.

He gave himself permission to imbibe at least once a day. Lately, it had been twice or more a day, given the challenges put upon him by his business partners. They had offered him a project with a caveat. If he wanted to continue the work of his beloved Beatrice Place, he had to agree to a project called Magpie.

Edgar had learned the price of doing business in Kosovo the moment he arrived in Prishtina six years ago. Corrupt government had taught him well. He cultivated his connections here and in the Balkan countries to avoid the same failures he had experienced in London and New York City. Beatrice Place would succeed, whatever it took.

His favorite Napoleon quote captured it best: "You become strong by defying defeat and by turning loss and failure into success." He lived by those words.

He glanced at his Rolex and noted he had three minutes to breathe in the evening mountain air before his associates arrived. After sipping his Rakija, he blotted his lips with his handkerchief, and arranged the ash tray and glass pipe in a more orderly fashion, each precisely three centimeters apart. He also placed two envelopes on the table, perpendicular to the ashtray.

Gertie let out a low growl, signaling a car approaching. An automobile engine roared at the base of the driveway. His associates had arrived.

He brushed a cold ash from his left pant leg. After stashing his snap and tucking the envelopes in his vest pocket, he signaled for Gertie and Oliver to follow him to the first floor.

Edgar had trained his dogs well. They executed great harm to the largest of men with a simple raised arc of Edgar's right eyebrow. They also stayed perfectly still until he signaled otherwise.

At the front entrance, he pressed the button on the wall, stepped outside, and watched the massive iron gates open.

Dugal drove past the gates and parked. He and Michael exited the car and stepped up to the veranda. Dugal's disheveled appearance distressed Edgar. His jacket was too large, and his pant cuffs frayed from dragging the pavement. He made a mental note to give Dugal additional money to buy new clothes. "Cheers, Dugal. Hello, Michael. Please come in." Oliver and Gertie wagged their tails with such vigor their entire bodies shook. "Hello, my buddies," Dugal said, rubbing their ears and necks.

"Weapons, please," Edgar said, holding the basket at Michael's chest, knowing he would resist. "I see that useless look of defiance, Michael. I suggest you consider not wasting your energy on trivial matters and surrendering your gun."

Michael frowned with a grunt.

They both dropped their handguns in the basket.

"Thank you, gentlemen. Follow me, please."

When they reached the top of the stairs, Edgar got a closer look at Michael. "Your head is bleeding. Come to the bathroom. Wash that blood off. It is utterly disgusting." The sight of blood, any blood, even from a mosquito bite, made him nauseous. He held his stomach and swallowed the saliva filling his throat and mouth.

Michael splashed water on his face.

"Use soap," Edgar said as he retrieved a first aid kit from the closet.

Dugal leaned on the wall, grinning. "What's the other guy look like?"

Michael jolted.

"Quiet, Dugal. I am confident Ismet suffered a great deal. The bleeding has stopped. Now, let me see." Edgar lifted Michael's chin and dabbed a cotton ball soaked with antiseptic on his forehead. "You have a nice little slice here. Please clean it at least twice daily."

Michael coughed, pushing past Dugal into the other room. "Edgar, how much cologne shit did you put on? It's gagging me. Can we get started? I ain't got all day."

"I'm wearing Tom Ford Eau de Parfum and, of course, a man of your stature...correction, lack of stature...could never have experienced such high-quality cologne. Nevertheless, I choose to avoid taking your rude comment personally. Let's go to the balcony."

Michael snorted and rubbed his nose. "God, it stinks."

Edgar glared at him without comment. *Why waste your breath on the imbecile?*

Dugal had placed the box on the floor next to the table.

Edgar had planned to ask Michael about the cut and Ismet, but the opened box distracted his attention. "You opened it?" Edgar exhaled.

Dugal bit his lip and lowered his head.

"What are the contents?" Edgar squinted at him and slowly ran his fingers over his raised eyebrow. It was a familiar signal. When

Dugal's hands began to tremble, it was obvious he understood his message: disobey and accept the consequences.

Dugal opened the cardboard box, took out the small tin, and held it out to Edgar.

"No, you open it," he said as he dropped his jaw and cocked his head. He was angry, but he also enjoyed bullying Dugal, especially when he showed weakness.

Dugal pulled the top off and emptied it on the table. Two lipsticks fell out and rolled to the floor. Dugal scrambled to pick them up and return them to the table. He put his hands behind his back and hunched his shoulders.

No one spoke.

Edgar felt heat penetrating between his shoulder blades. He detested Dugal's posture. Moreover, the lipsticks were a slap in his face. He seethed.

Damn her.

Gertie and Oliver came out from under the table, eyes glued to Edgar. Gertie whimpered, sensing his stress. Oliver did the same. He patted their heads, and they went silent.

Dugal pulled at his fingernails and put one foot over top of the other.

"Stop picking and stand up straight. How many times must I tell you?" He rushed to his office to retrieve his riding crop from the bottom drawer of his desk. A thin strip of fiberglass, sixty-one centimeters long with a leather handle, the perfect tool for punishing.

Dugal had recoiled in his seat, with his knees up to his chest, arms over his head. A familiar sight that caused Edgar's heart to pound with fury.

"All over a stupid tin can?" Michael said.

Edgar took his time walking toward Dugal, holding the crop in both hands across his chest. He paused for a couple of seconds to create more tension and dread, wrinkling his nose and frowning. Then he attacked, hitting Dugal's head and neck, whack after whack. The more agonizing sounds Dugal made, the harder the whacks.

Chaos filled Edgar's mind, his vision turned a bright red, and drool streamed from the corner of his mouth as he sniffled and gasped for air. He continued hitting.

Finally, Michael jumped, ripped the crop from Edgar's hands and threw it over the balcony. "That's enough. You made your point."

The blues snarled and showed their teeth. Edgar managed a blink, and they stopped instantly.

Gasping for air, Edgar fell into his chair, hands dangling at his sides. His thrashing had fatigued his arm muscles. The dogs sat on either side of him, searching his face. "I am fine," he said, patting Gertie's back.

Dugal was still in his tight little ball, coughing and whimpering.

No one spoke.

Edgar knew he had been out of control, but he had no choice. Dugal was at fault. They had had these incidents, the doctor called them, many times. His doctor described them as a pattern of dysfunctional behavior, noting Dugal represented what Edgar truly believed himself to be: a failure. Beating Dugal symbolized self-flagellation. True or not, the analysis only heightened his need to punish Dugal more.

"Okay, let's stop this mental bullshit. Where are we in this...what do you call it? Your international humanitarian project?" Michael settled in his chair and folded his arms. "I want my money."

Edgar retrieved a handkerchief from his pocket and blotted the perspiration from his face and spittle from his chin. "Pardon me," he said as he turned away, blew his nose, and put the handkerchief inside his vest pocket. He walked over to the liquor cabinet and poured a glass of Rajika and chugged it. With a deep breath, he stood taller, shook out his arms and returned to the balcony. He sat and handed them each an envelope.

Dugal scrambled out of his ball and sat upright. His hair stuck straight up, and his face was splotchy red and white.

"Here is a sizable amount of money. Three thousand euros for each of you."

Michael grunted and peeked inside the envelope.

"I'm sorry," Dugal said, forcing a grin over a harrowing frown. He sniffed, wiped his nose with his palm, and rubbed his hand on his pants.

"Yes, I know," Edgar said with a long loathsome sigh. "I often expect too much of you, beyond your capabilities. Let us move on." He said he had another assignment. "It requires both of you to work together in one last effort to acquire the disk."

"How much?" Michael said, shifting his weight.

"Tsk. Michael, Michael, Michael. It's my little secret." He loved the power of suspense and enjoyed watching Michael squirm. "Wait for my call, Dugal. Thank you, gentlemen. I trust you can find your way out. And Dugal, comb your hair."

Dugal nodded and ran his fingers over his sweaty scalp.

Edgar watched them descend the stairs and exit before he poured another drink. He picked up the lipsticks, twisting the tubes up and down. Margot had to know the location of the disk. He was sure of it. She must be forced to confess. Admittedly, he had grown fond of her. Yet, he could easily have her killed, once he had what he wanted.

In due time.

~ 49 ~

CHAPTER FORTY-NINE

March 19, 2013

In the morning, Margot and Grey still maintained their resolve: they'd only engage in mindless chitchat until the FBI checked for bugs.

"Sleep?" he said.

"Yeah," she lied, for anyone that might be listening. Although, she was positive they had no bugs. It was interesting that the FBI had gone from underreacting—especially Wilson—during their first meeting, to wildly overreacting now.

Stupid waste of time.

They drank their coffee in silence.

Grey looked upset, but his face was not quite his usual overwhelmed crimson color.

She lowered her head and blew a silent kiss. "Orange juice?"

"No. Thanks." He sniffed and forced a thin smile.

"It's a great day out there," Margot said, trying to lift his spirits. "You have a full day today?"

"No. Probably be home by eleven o'clock. You?"

"Classes till noon, then I'm going to see the girls. Join me?" She leaned into his face, flashing a devilish grin and mouthed, "Let's get the hell out of here."

Grey whispered, "This is serious." He circled the Malevich scarf around her neck.

She grabbed his jacket collar with both hands and gave him a firm, wet lip-lock.

His complexion faded to a soft pink flush. He exhaled and planted his own long, delicious kiss.

"Whoa, my friend," she said, opening her mouth and widening her eyes, exaggerating her facial expressions. "You're turning me on," she whispered.

"Tonight?" he said, zipping his coat.

She pressed her index finger to her puckered lips, then grabbed her Sars bag and handed Grey his briefcase.

They stepped into the hallway.

"You think you need to ask?"

Grey locked the door. "I'm planting a seed."

As they descended the stairs, she said, "Oh, great. That'll grow throughout my day." She smiled.

"What if we're bugged?" he said, stopping on a step.

She motioned for him to continue. "Well...I started to say duct tape, but...."

"There's a frightening thought, Margot," he said with a tone of disbelief. "You have a sick sense of humor sometimes."

"Just trying to be funny. This is a bunch of nothing. Mark my words. No bugs."

***

When Margot returned home after her classes, she entered her apartment and Grey stood at the front door. His face was a startling, pasty white.

"How was your day?" he said, holding up a piece of paper with the word *bugged* written in bold letters.

Her eyes widened in disbelief. "Good." She dropped her head, wondering how she could have been so wrong. "How was your day?"

"Mine was fine. Thank you."

Their conversation sounded stilted, like poor actors reading from a lousy script.

Grey narrowed his eyes and handed her a note.

We found 2 microphones. Removed 1 from the master bedroom and left 1 in the kitchen. We added our own in the kitchen, as well. Special Agent Elliot.

As she began reading, her body stiffened. By the time she got to Elliot's signature, she stood paralyzed. It was impossible to grasp the idea that people had been listening to her every moment since....Her mind went reeling. She rewound her memory, like a tape recording, back to the moment she moved in here. Then, fast-forwarding, ripping through hundreds of conversations with Grey, her mother, and Ismet. And private, everyday intimate moments. She was mortified when she remembered her meltdowns in the shower, so painfully personal she wouldn't even share with Grey.

They heard everything.

When Grey touched her elbow, her body fell limp. He slid a chair over just in time for her to plop onto it. Dizzy, crazy, overwhelming chaos filled her head.

Grey gently nudged her head forward between her knees. When he whispered *breathe* in her ear, she couldn't stop her tears from flowing like water pouring from a glass. Huge drops streamed alongside her nose, puddling on the floor. She managed to cry in silence, but the hard lump in her throat was fighting to let loose.

Grey got on his knees and wiped her face with a tissue. He lifted her chin. In what looked to be his best effort to sound normal, he said, "Want to catch lunch?"

Margot didn't answer, knowing her voice would crack.

He put on his jacket and pulled her up from the chair.

She stepped to the kitchen sink and splashed cold water on her face. Grey handed her a tea towel and blinked an encouraging smile, although his eyes were incredibly sad.

They left the apartment and didn't speak until they were a block away.

Finally, she said, "They left one bug and added one. Why?"

He shrugged.

"God, Grey, I'm thinking back, rewinding the tape. It's mind-boggling."

Perspiration glistened on his head, and he pulled his scarf away from his neck. "Who has done this?"

Margot hadn't thought about who was responsible until now. She paused and looked into his eyes. "I hate it, but Edgar does come to mind." Her breath checked and her throat locked.

"That's what I was thinking."

She took in a deep breath, held it, then released it, opening her mouth. "Nix on seeing the girls today. Whoever is listening might spy on us there. I'm not even sure it's safe to talk out here in the open."

"Yeah, somebody might follow us."

"Dammit. I'm claustrophobic." Margot held her throat. "Elliot has some explaining to do. I want answers."

~ 50 ~

CHAPTER FIFTY

March 17, 2013

Germia Park was six miles from Edgar's home. Sixty-two square miles of forests, meadows, and the Rhodope Mountains; a pleasant location to meet with Dugal and Michael and exercise his Blues.

Edgar opened the rear door to his Toyota 4Runner. Gertie and Oliver jumped inside, and he slid in behind the wheel. He drove six miles through Germia's primary entrance, parked in his standard spot, and retrieved two leashes from the glove box, in case he needed them. Although park rules required owners tether their dogs, Edgar only did so when rangers were in the vicinity. His blues instantly obeyed his every command. Therefore, restraints were unnecessary.

Gertie and Oliver moaned with excitement. When he opened the door, they jumped out and sat at his feet. Their tails wagged frantically, stirring up dried, fallen leaves. He gave them each a treat.

His Rolex read 8:55. He had five minutes before Michael and Dugal would arrive.

With a slight nod, Gertie and Oliver sprinted like gazelles. They ran for seventy meters, stopped, turned, facing him, and froze, except for their twitching tails, waiting for permission to continue. Edgar raised his arm, his signal for them to return. His chest swelled with pride.

Animals were easier to control than people. Nevertheless, Edgar always endeavored to train his associates on par with Gertie and Oliver. Unfortunately, Dugal was inconsistent and often failed to follow orders satisfactorily. However, Dugal was a rescue, and Edgar came to accept his defects, although not always. Hence their incidents. Of greater importance, Edgar needed Dugal to do his bidding, especially particular acts which were beneath Edgar's dignity.

Michael was entirely a unique breed, averse to taming. More often than not and most disturbing, he could not complete the simplest of commands. Edgar considered him intelligent, albeit barbaric.

Oliver and Gertie returned to Edgar's side. He nodded, allowing them to race again.

Exactly on time, Dugal drove up with Michael in the car. They parked next to the Toyota.

"Good morning. Isn't this lovely?"

"Sure is, boss," Dugal said.

Michael didn't respond.

"I have a question," Dugal said. "Been meaning to ask you. Why did you call us off that woman? After my cigarette burn, she was ready to spill her guts."

"That's debatable, Dugal. My associates told me you were being watched."

"You had somebody watching us? Who?" Michael frowned.

"I have many compadres." He cleared his throat for emphasis. "Do not forget it, my friend." When he saw Michael wince, he smiled to himself, confident he had shaken Michael's confidence.

"Pfft. You are a piece of work." Michael rubbed the back of his neck.

At that moment, Edgar's phone vibrated in his jacket pocket. It was his Maureen. His heart fluttered. Maureen had been his administrative assistant at his safe house in New York City. After his wife died of a dreadful overdose, he had suffered a severe depression. Maureen never left his side, taking responsibility for his every need. They fell in love.

"Excuse me." He motioned for Gertie and Oliver to stay.

When Edgar moved beyond earshot, he said, "Hello, my dear."

"My darling, a quick update. All is well, with a slight blip. First, let me give you the highlights."

She said the Magpie Project continued in the reconnaissance phase. Scans had revealed target entry points and weaknesses. They had gained privileged access and were moving freely within the environment. "We own them now," she said with a snicker.

"I can barely grasp technological terms and am immensely happy you understand them."

"Yes. We're inside systems in Ohio, Virginia, Idaho...fifteen or more. I've lost count. Maryland was the first. We're on the brink, ready to compromise billing systems in every state throughout the United States, including the territories. Magpie will mangle files and erase others. We have fucked the insurance companies." She cooed. "Now, listen to this. The slight blip: there are debates regarding stealing data. This was not in the original plan. It's a minor conflict and in deliberation as we speak."

"What is Nikitin's view?"

"He's cool. Whether our hackers steal data or not, he and his Russian oligarch compatriots want Magpie completed. That's it. They won't release funds to the team until their squabbling stops and they get back to work."

"Is our money delayed? And is the activation date extended beyond April fifteenth?"

"The date is firm. Although we're early. And, our payment? Not to worry. Nikitin is very pleased with your work. He's happy with our little worker bees in Veles and, of course, my connection in Iowa. So, my darling, I wanted to give you the latest information."

"This is wonderful news."

"Listen. I have a delicate matter."

"Yes." His breath quickened, and he used his handkerchief to blot moisture from his top lip.

"Eris Hoti," she said.

"I owe him, Maureen. He reminds me of that in every way he can." Hoti caused him worry because he was fickle, and he valued his Russian friends more than him. Edgar was a menial pawn in Hoti's view.

"It's blackmail, pure and simple. I regret introducing you to him. He's made your life hellacious."

"Yes, however, he saved Dugal and me from facing child-trafficking laws even before we moved to Prishtina. Prison in England or the United States would have killed us both. But, why bring him up now?"

"Keep in touch with Hoti and shower him with attention. He craves it, and without your coddling him, he could turn on you. A negative word from Eris, Nikitin could lose confidence in you."

"I understand. It is completely degrading." He squirmed.

"You disappointed them when you killed Andrey Stephen. Sorry to lay that on you again. And what about the disk? Have you found it?"

"No. Are you sure it exists?"

"It does, according to sources close to Nikitin."

"You just said the hacking is progressing as planned. Doesn't that make the disk unimportant, or perhaps, obsolete?" Edgar felt lightheaded.

"It doesn't matter. They've charged you with finding it and they have expectations."

Silence.

He was accustomed to pressure, although, when Maureen told him the blatant truth, he often had a delayed visceral response. This time his response came within two or three minutes.

"I can tell I've rattled you. I hope you aren't slipping into one or your spells. Try not to dwell on this. Let's not forget, I can be very influential." She said she'd keep him in Nikitin's good graces, and he was to work on Hoti.

"Just to follow up," she said. "I got those logos sealed on two large envelopes, mailed them to the Tetovo boys. You know, they're in Prishtina now. Did you receive them and give them to your little friend?"

"Yes, I gave them to her five days ago."

"Perfect. That's our insurance, my sweet. I miss you. Let's go away together? Soon?"

Grateful she had shifted their focus, he said, "I miss you, too. Indeed, Magpie has kept us apart too long. You decide on a destination." His head spun. He leaned against a tree for balance.

"Wonderful. I love you. Oh, almost forgot, Brooks says hello. Bye now."

"Send him my love."

She ended the call.

He stood while perspiration flooded the small of his back. With his fingers pressed into his carotid artery, he counted the beats and watched the second hand on his watch. His pulse was 200. This accounted for his vertigo. With his eyes closed, he remained stationary, regulating his breathing, and trying to put Hoti out of his mind. He counted to sixty.

When he felt normal again, he brushed the bark off the back of his jacket and straightened his collar. Then he returned to Dugal and Michael. "I am sorry for the interruption. Gentlemen, we are adjourned."

"Your face is all red," Dugal said.

"Where's my money?" Michael said.

"We are nearing completion and I may need you. Perhaps you can earn more money. Meanwhile, here." He handed them their envelopes.

Michael grunted as usual. Edgar had learned to disregard his vile utterances, although they were especially annoying at this moment and added to his overwhelming stress.

Dugal and Michael got in the car and Dugal drove away.

After letting Gertie and Oliver in the rear of his Toyota, Edgar slid into the driver's seat. He strived to enjoy the surroundings, his Blues, and his Maureen. But nagging thoughts of Hoti and Nikitin were too persistent. He lowered his eyelids, squinted, and clenched his jaw. He couldn't do anything to control them from his position so he shifted his attention to that which he could control. That would be Michael, who had become an evil thorn in Edgar's flesh. He had lied, and saying Michael could earn more money was a simple ploy to keep him close. In reality, he had served his purpose and was superfluous now. Any more he needed, Dugal could manage.

This called for Michael's eradication; however, nothing untidy or too violent.

~ 51 ~

CHAPTER FIFTY-ONE

April 1, 2013

Margot, Grey, Hawkins, and Wilson looked through the one-way glass. They watched six men come in from the side, trudge to the middle, and stand against the back wall. Each had a number tagged to his chest and a small card in his hand. They squinted into the blue, fluorescent light, twisting their heads, straining to see their accusers.

Margot pulled her head onto her shoulders and shaded her eyes, hoping they couldn't see her. She confirmed with Wilson. "You sure they can't see us?"

"Just your shadow."

"Ah. Can they hear us?" Grey asked.

"Not with the mic off," Hawkins said.

All the men appeared guilty, and Margot had the same ugly feeling she had whenever she passed through security. Half wore hangdog facial expressions. Half were defiant, smug. Every one of them twitched and flinched as if they were in a diabolical game of dodgeball. With no ball.

Margot gasped when she thought she recognized one.

"Got one?" Wilson said.

Grey and Margot glanced at each other. He nodded, and she tossed her hair.

"Number two," Margot said, forcing air through her lips.

"Yeah, two," Grey said.

Wilson said, "Grey, were you with Margot during the attack?"

He shook his head.

"Well, then—"

"Do it. Number two." Margot spoke quicker and louder than she intended because Wilson pissed her off for asking dumb questions. But also because she was nervous as hell, possibly facing her kidnapper.

Wilson told Number two to step forward. He didn't move.

"He can't hear you, Wilson," Margot said, pointing to the mic on and off button.

"Oh, sorry," she said, flipping the switch, "Number two, step forward and read your card."

When Wilson didn't turn the mic off, Margot reached over and flipped it for her, shaking her head in disgust.

A wisp of a man shuffled toward the glass. Thirty-something, with small sooty eyes, a buzz haircut, and a mole on his cheek. Mouth half-cocked, he fiddled with the corner of his card.

"Where is the disk?" he said, his voice barely audible. He had a Scottish or Irish accent, too close to call.

"Recognize him?" Hawkins said.

"Not exactly, I was blindfolded," she said.

"His voice?" Hawkins pinched his lips.

"Tell him to stretch his arms toward the glass," Margot said.

"What? Why?" Wilson said. "If they covered your eyes—"

"Oh my God, Wilson. Do it and tend to the mic," Margot said.

"Number two, show us your hands." She flipped the mic off.

When he pushed his fists forward, his shirt sleeves inched up past his wrists.

Margot rubbed the back of her neck. She was right. He had a tattoo. "I saw that tattoo. What is it?"

"A flower. Is he Scottish? Could be a thistle," Grey said.

"And you saw this through the blindfold?" Wilson said in an incredulous tone. "Or you've seen this tattoo before?"

"Sure. I got X-ray vision, Wilson." She gave her a blank stare and
dropped her jaw in utter disgust. "Pfft. It slipped off for a second. I
saw that tattoo. Forgot it till now."

"Grey, you saw it?" Hawkins said.

"No. When we were driving back from Peja, a car passed us and
the guy in the passenger seat stared at her. She said he had a mole
on his cheek."

"He was creepy. We dismissed it. I get it now. This Number two
is the asshole who glared at me from the passing auto, and he's the
kidnapper. Same tattoo in the same place. Same mole. Same man."
Margot wiped sweat off her top lip with her sleeve.

"I remember you mentioning him," Hawkins said.

"Wait." Grey took his phone out of his pocket. "I got the license
plate number. Here it is. Number 04 902 FD."

Wilson scribbled on her notepad. "We'll check it. Do you know
his voice?"

"You've got to be kidding me, Wilson. You must think you're in a
call center, just reading the script, ignoring what's being said. And,
yes, I'm stressed and even may overreact to your stupid mistakes.
But, I'm telling you, he's the guy. Now, tell me who it is."

"Wilson, check the license plate. Let's go to the conference
room," Hawkins said, holding up a folder.

"Where's Elliot?" Margot said.

"She's working on the disk."

"All right. Number two," she said they entered the conference
room. She took a seat next to Grey. Her bug questions could wait.

Hawkins sat across from them, opening his folder. "Got everything right here. Dugal Hetrick. Date of birth: September twentieth,
nineteen eighty. Dark hair, brown eyes. He's five feet, four inches

tall. One hundred twenty-five pounds. Mole on his right cheek. Small tattoo on his left hand: thistle." He looked up at Grey and continued reading.

"Born in Scotland, his mother abandoned him at three, leaving him with his grandparents on a farm outside London. He formed a relationship with his grandmother, who tried to help him improve his aberrant and dangerous behaviors. It says she taught him to knit at a young age to keep him less agitated. His grandparents reported he had a habit of torturing and killing farm animals. Rabbits and goats. Hung the family cat from the barn hayloft."

"Sick," Margot said, covering her mouth.

"You mean similar to Dahmer, the serial killer?" Grey said, his face turning crimson again.

"Oh, the guy from Milwaukee. I remember reading about him," Margot said as her legs trembled.

Hawkins said Dugal's doctors reported he suffered from attachment disorder, among other emotional issues. "Symptoms: no eye contact, withdrawn, angry, violent. Hmm...his grandparents sent him to an orphanage at eight years old and he was later transferred to Lindynne Detention Centre. Fast forward six years, he escaped." He flipped the paper, explaining Hetrick ended up homeless, and officials arrested him for minor offenses. "His illegal habits elevated to more serious crimes. He served time in HM Bedford Prison for breaking into a hardware store, stealing money, and battering the proprietor with a shovel." He ran his finger across the page. "Blah, blah—"

"Stop with blahs," Margot said, raising her voice. "Don't skip over. As hard as it is to listen, I want to know every detail." She squeezed Grey's hand under the table, and he leaned his shoulder into hers.

Without looking up, Hawkins continued. "He was a small man and therefore, easy prey. HM Bedford Prison records document sexual and physical abuse by fellow inmates. For his own safety, prison doctors recommended isolation, but he was allowed to pursue his

334 ~ DIANN SCHINDLER

hobby of knitting hats and slippers. The warden allowed him to spend most of his days knitting in the library, under tight security. Released from prison in two thousand ten. Hetrick is psychotic, a danger to himself and others." He slammed the folder shut, folded his arms, and looked up at Margot.

Margot leaned forward, confused by Hawkins' abrupt actions and stern facial expression. "What?"

"London officials alerted Prishtina police when he got to Kosovo. They've been observing him. We've been watching him, too, because he came here from the States along with his attorney... Well, in England, they're called barristers. Pretty smart guy, he got Hetrick released from prison early on a technicality."

"A barrister?" Margot pursed her lips, praying it wasn't the barrister she knew.

Hawkins slid a photo across the table. "Is this the Edgar Leeds you know?"

Margot looked closer and stopped breathing. The man looking back at her had a sharp nose and wavy brown hair, graying at the temples. She hadn't noticed it before, but saw he had dingy yellow, crooked teeth. His blue eyes she had considered attractive before, now, in this picture, telegraphed a fierce, maniacal man.

"This is my friend." She swallowed hard, resisting her inner voice, which was shrieking at her, telling her again that Edgar was no friend.

"You claim he's your friend? Let's hear it," Hawkins said.

Margot explained they had met at the Mother Teresa Cathedral. "He was kind to me and helped me find a place when I moved from Ismet's apartment complex—"

"To the bugged apartment," Grey said.

"From the apartment that had been burgled?" Hawkins said.

She gawked at Grey as moisture filled her eyes, ignoring the question. "Even got me a job. Without him," she said, tugging at her hair. "I had no one else."

"Margot." Grey said with a low voice, tilting his head and touching her shoulder. "You had me."

She exhaled, blinking at Grey. "You were in Macedonia. Truth is, I needed a friend, and Edgar appeared." She struggled to calm thoughts clanging in her head. "I just thought he was quirky, a control freak." Her voice faltered, and she settled in her chair. At first, she'd believed her trust level for Edgar showed tolerance, despite Grey and Ismet's attitudes. She believed her mother would be proud she had evolved and had adopted more tolerance. And she held on to that belief even though Edgar turned rude, strange, argumentative and demanding.

Why?

Her eyes fluttered in confusion.

"This is what we have," Hawkins said. "He's got a checkered background. No arrests, just scandals, on the fringes of breaking laws. Unethical, for sure. With his shelters for women in London and in New York City, he got caught in the crosshairs with oversight agencies and local government, and it didn't go well. Then, and we're not sure how, he got involved with Eris Hoti. Hoti is well known for his battles with Kosovo government and rumored to be connected with powerful men in Russia—"

"Get to the point." Margot said, as her blood pounded from her heart to her throat, compromising her hearing.

Andy. Could Edgar have....

"Is he connected to the murder?" Grey said.

He had asked the very question Margot desperately wanted answered.

At that point, Wilson entered the room. "The license plate is registered under the name of Edgar Bernard Leeds."

Margot, palms sweaty, squeezed Grey's hand under the table.

Silence.

"To answer your question, Grey, well...." Hawkins rose and propped himself against the wall.

Margot studied his face, fixed on his mouth, waiting for the words.

"As far as we can tell, he didn't know Andy," he said, folding his arms. "Not directly, that is."

"Oh my God. He asked when Andy was coming home, repeatedly. And this whole time...he knew. He baited me, the sadistic son of a bitch." She growled and covered her mouth.

No one spoke.

"Let me ask you this? Do you know a Maureen Mason?" Hawkins said.

Grey and Margot shook their heads.

"Her name keeps coming up. We're not sure except Mason worked for Leeds in New York City. They have a thing if you know what I mean." He scratched his nose.

Margot shrugged. "Lots of people have things. Are you saying we're at a dead end?"

Hawkins shook his head and nodded toward Wilson.

"Got facts and I've added conjecture to explain connections. It's classified, and incomplete," Wilson said, handing her a sealed envelope.

"I don't want to read it now," Margot said, unwilling to admit she'd be too emotional.

"Are you sure? When you go back to your apartment, remember, it's bugged. We'll be listening. And they'll be listening."

"They?" Margot said. "You mean Edgar?"

"We got our suspicions," Hawkins said. "For now, though, it's *they*."

~ 52 ~

CHAPTER FIFTY-TWO

March 17, 2013

As Dugal pulled away from Germia Park, he said, "Want me to drop you off?"

Michael needed to buy different clothes to disguise his appearance. "Mother Teresa Boulevard."

He had to get rid of his guns and knives, but he'd wait until the last minute in case the asshole Edgar had him tailed.

He checked his watch; he had plenty of time to catch the 11 p.m. flight to Vienna.

"What are you checking the time for? Hot date? Hey, wanna go to that strip joint? Get some pussy?"

Dugal's eyes lit up and a goofy grin spread across his face. Michael's stomach turned at the thought of having worked with this lunatic.

"Don't be an idiot," he said, although a little pussy did appeal to him.

"Here you are, my friend," Dugal said, as he drove up to the curb at the Boulevard.

As Michael exited the front seat, he got his bag out of the back seat.

After he'd seen Dugal and Edgar together in their fucked-up bullshit, he pitied Dugal. Their history was a mystery. It had to be some psycho crap. Maybe Edgar had brainwashed Dugal to the point he couldn't think for himself. If Dugal had a mind of his own, he might be a sliver above moron on the IQ scale.

"Where are you going with that bag?" Dugal raised his eyebrows and curled his lip, hinting he wanted in on a secret.

Michael threw his duffel over his shoulder. It was packed with everything he needed for his flight to Vienna: a set of clean clothes, shaving gear, and his Italian Beretta handgun. He strapped his pistol to his ankle and his passport in the breast pocket of his coat, along with Edgar's envelope stuffed with euros. "Hey, man. I'd love to get out of here, but I'm waiting for more easy-money assignments from Edgar." He patted his breast pocket. "I'm going shopping. Money's burning a hole in my pocket. Call me when you hear from Edgar."

He shut the car door and watched Dugal wave as he drove off.

Damn, he was glad to be free of that retard Dugal and that pussy Edgar. From now on, it'd be different. He'd start by celebrating and treating himself to a lavish breakfast at the Swiss Diamond Hotel Restaurant—the best hotel in Prishtina. Hoity-toity wasn't his style. But he was avoiding his usual stomping grounds in case Edgar's so-called *compadres* were following him. No harm in playing it safe. After a quick bite to eat, he'd take a taxi to Albi Mall to buy new clothes and leave for the airport.

When he arrived at Swiss Diamond, three suits greeted him with dainty faggot smiles. He almost lost his appetite. They escorted him to the outside terrace, where he chose a spot in the middle, camouflaged by tables filled with chattering business executives. The server poured a cup of coffee and took his order.

Michael unzipped his bag for his cell to confirm his one-way ticket on Arian Airlines. He also pulled out a notepad and pen to scratch out his escape plan.

Just then, his cell phone vibrated. Somebody calling from the States, although he didn't recognize the area code. So he refused the call and blocked the number. No time for nonsense, he dialed Arian Airlines and confirmed his flight to Vienna.

Before jotting his travel details, he sat back, sipped his coffee, and surveyed his surroundings. Flowers in low concrete planters surrounded the terrace, situated to block any dine and dash strategy. He noticed a guy on the outside, walking alongside the flowers. A big guy, a navy down-filled jacket, head lowered and steady. As he passed by, Michael picked up on his eyes, darting from side to side. Shifty eyes were a sure sign he was in hiding. He could very well be one of Edgar's *compadres*.

Michael quickly planned an attack, should it be necessary. He'd jump the barrier, easy. Grab him. Break his neck. It'd take fifteen seconds. He imagined hearing those tiny bones crunch and snap. Pure joy to his ears.

He drew a breath to refocus his thoughts, then he accessed the Austrian Railways website on his phone. From the Vienna airport, he'd taxi fifteen minutes to the Flughafen Wien Bahnoff train station and catch the first train to Salzburg. Seats were wide open, so he'd buy a ticket on site. To keep the *compadres* thinking he'd be in Salzburg, he'd hop off the train before its final destination.

After scribbling the details, he folded his paper and put it in his breast pocket. The server brought his breakfast. While he ate, he continued scouring his surroundings, on the lookout for the shifty-eyed dude.

Calling the all-clear, he drank more coffee and relaxed. For some crazy reason, a little nothing town in Austria called Steyr popped into his mind. It was a short drive from the St. Polten stop on the train route to Salzburg. He had been there with Sophie Haas. No way could he forget her, try as he might.

They met on his way home after a tour in Afghanistan. He was on a layover in the Istanbul airport, walking around, biding time, when he came to a coffee shop. She was the first woman he ever saw. Well, he had seen women his entire life. They were different: pussy, something to fuck. She was the first woman he saw as a person, a human being.

Damn, she was gorgeous.

Lightning struck his brain and cemented his feet to the floor. She sat at a table, drinking espresso, and reading the travel section of "The Local," an international newspaper. Long, flawless legs crossed at the knees, her red skirt pulled to her thighs. She wore a black turtleneck sweater.

He sauntered over to her and introduced himself. She brushed her dark hair away from her face and asked him to join her. He sat, mesmerized, while she ordered him an espresso. She said she was on her way to her home in Steyr.

They discussed travel, politics, and Europe. Words flowed between them as if they had been friends for their whole lives. Then, she leaned three inches from his face with her soft green eyes locked on his and said he should come with her to Steyr.

Michael swallowed. "Now?"

The edges of her eyes crinkled. "Why not?" She showed him her ticket, pointing to the departure gate. "Perhaps there is a seat available."

Despite Michael drinking coffee, he swore he was drunk with liquor. When he stood up, he grabbed hold of the chair to keep his balance.

Thirty minutes later, he had a seat on her flight and eight hours after that, they were in her living room drinking beer, laughing, talking.

He couldn't stop looking at her. For the first time in his life, he wanted to make love. And that's what they did, morning, noon, and night.

Smart, sweet, sexy, and funny. God, he loved everything about her.

Now, for the first time, he understood what those happily married guys had been yammering about when they mentioned their wives. They said they couldn't imagine life without them. Michael thought they were fucking liars or brainless idiots.

Then Sophia happened. He wanted to be with her every minute. And he wanted to take care of her. The best, she said she wanted nothing, except him.

Over the next few weeks, they planned their lives together. He'd move in with her. They'd get married. He'd work at Steyr Motor Company until he found better work.

They talked dogs, cats, even kids. It was wild, and very real.

Then the time came for him to report to Fort Carson, Texas. Sophia cried so hard his heart broke. In fact, they cried together. He had never cried with anybody, let alone a woman.

They communicated constantly. Letters, phone calls. Skyped every day, often three or four times a day.

His problem, he couldn't leave stateside until he had completed his tour. Then the worst: he had orders to return to Afghanistan. This time, he got shot up bad. They sent him to Germany for surgery and rehab. After that, he received orders to go home. No matter what he did, he couldn't get approval to go to Austria. He had to go to the United States first. He considered going AWOL and decided against it because he'd have to hide forever. Even worse, if they caught him, he'd never see her again.

Time trudged forward. He got stuck in the States and she landed a job as a researcher at the Thalia Bookstore, taking up most of her time.

Conversations weren't the same. She retreated, and, of course, denied it. He couldn't handle it and stopped calling. She did, too.

"Sir," a server said, interrupting his reminiscing. "Care for anything else?"

Michael shook his head, pulled out thirty euros, and threw the banknotes on the table. He gathered his gear and walked toward the taxi stand. His mind returned to Sophia and Steyr again. While it'd been over two years, he swore he could still smell her honey and lavender hair.

Dammit.

He ducked behind a tree, he took a chance, found her number on his cell, and hit call. He shivered like a scared puppy.

When she answered, she said, "Hello, Michael" before he even identified himself. His gimp leg buckled and right then and there, they were in Istanbul again.

She begged him to come home. That's what she said. She said, "Come home, Michael."

Suddenly, he was that man again, the man she loved. God, she made him feel superior. "I'll be home in the morning, babe."

His heart busted out of his chest. He exhaled a satisfying sigh and told himself he could focus on Sophia once on the plane. For now, he had to concentrate and return to his vigilant surveillance.

The taxi dropped him at Albi Mall, and he bought fancy leather shoes, dress slacks, a black leather jacket, and two white dress shirts. He finished it off with black socks and a damn expensive leather belt, but resisted the clerk's effort to sell him ties. Shit, this change was hard enough.

Before he caught the taxi, he changed his clothes in the men's room.

Two hours later, he stood in front of the International Prishtina Adem Jashari Airport.

Everything was happening so fast and without a single hitch.

One last thing to do before he entered the terminal: get rid of his weapons. Where? The place was solid concrete with no outside trash cans.

He darted to the side of the building near a patch of weeds. Stooped on one knee, prepared to run if need be, he unstrapped his pistol from his ankle and stuffed it in a bush. After he unzipped his bag, he retrieved his Italian handgun. As hard as it was to let it go, he tossed it, too. He zipped the duffel bag closed and searched the area. He was alone.

As soon as he started for the front of the building, out of nowhere, someone tackled him from behind and had him in a tight choke hold. Michael was stunned, and it took him a second to get his wits about himself. But then he went into fight mode. He dropped his bag and jammed his right elbow backward into this perp's chest. The guy growled and loosened his grip.

In an instant, Michael twisted himself around. He faced the man and grabbed his jacket by the arms. And in a single action, he pulled his shoulders forward and kneed him in the stomach.

The fucker might be done, but Michael wasn't.

He turned him around backward. His right arm tight around his throat, left hand hard on his chin, Michael dragged him to the wall. He snapped his neck, as simple as you please. Lifeless, the man slid to the ground. It was the guy in the blue jacket. No more darting eyes now.

Panting with his nostrils flared and mouth open, his balls pulsated. Too bad he didn't have time to enjoy the afterglow. He picked up his bag, bolted to the front entrance, and got in the customs line.

His heart raced out of control and his hot, sweaty face and bulging neck likely telegraphed trouble to anyone observing him. While wiping his face with his palm, he slowed his breathing, forcing longer, deeper breaths, and incorporating rhythmic self-talk.

Inhale, easy. Exhale, okay. Inhale, easy. Exhale, okay.

It worked.

Suddenly, his phone vibrated. He brought it out of his pocket. Dugal. He pressed decline, blocked it, and stuffed the cell on the inside of his leather jacket.

As he neared his turn in the customs line, he remembered Kosovars loved Americans, even the guards. When they saw a U.S. passport, they turned into brainless fools, smiling, joking. Critical thinking skills disappeared. He chuckled to himself. The only thing

344 ~ DIANN SCHINDLER

left was that he had to get on that fucking plane. And do it before the police nabbed him for the murder he had committed less than five minutes ago.

Luckily, the guards let him breeze through. In a flash, he got through the gate as passengers were boarding. He could have purchased a first-class ticket, but didn't want to bring attention to himself, in customs and onboard. Still remaining alert to identify enemies, he followed the line of passengers and was inside the plane in his window seat in no time. A few more minutes, and he would breathe easier.

Once airborne, he pushed his seat to the reclining position and closed his eyes. Safe now, his body melted into the seat cushion. He hadn't been this relaxed in months, and looked forward to two hours of sleep.

Thoughts of that pussy Edgar and numbskull Dugal floated out of his consciousness.

As he drifted off to sleep, he imagined Sophia, her green eyes, her honey and lavender chestnut hair.

~ 53 ~

CHAPTER FIFTY-THREE

March 17, 2013

Michael stood on the platform of the Vienna City Center Flughafen Wien Bahnhof Station, waiting for the train to Salzburg. He arrived early because he wanted to study each passenger coming down the escalator. At first, he was alone. Gradually more people came, until a constant flow of travelers filled the departure section. When the last stragglers joined the crowd, he moved back to board car Number thirty-five, continuing his surveillance. He hoisted his gimp leg up, placing the sole of his shoe against the red-tile wall, while bracing himself for the usual stabbing knee pain. Strange, it didn't happen.

Weird. Was it love?

He chuckled to himself, thinking he was going off the deep end. *Tetched* was the word his dad always used.

A little girl, four or five years old, descending the moving stairway, caught his attention. An old man, maybe her grandpa, held her hand. She wore black, patent leather shoes with white, lacey socks. The old man beamed with pride.

Michael wondered if he'd ever have a granddaughter, or even a kid.

Man, you are going simple.

He jerked his head to force himself to concentrate. He scanned again. No one looked suspicious.

His cell phone inside his leather jacket vibrated, startling him. He pulled it out and checked the caller ID: Grey Valentin.

Shit.

Questions filled his head. Was Valentin on to him? Why call now? The caller ID had a Massachusetts area code, although he could be calling from anywhere in the world. Then he remembered Andy had mentioned his name in the Tetovo hotel. Steam and sweat pooled on his back, dampening his new white shirt.

He declined the call and blocked the number. Gritting his teeth, he willed Grey and Andy out of his consciousness. Besides, they were assholes.

Now that he had his phone handy, he'd chance a quick call to Sophia. He pressed the call icon.

"Hello, Michael, where are you?"

Her voice melted the tension and cooled his back. "At the station. Train to Salzburg arrives in a minute or two. How are you?"

"I'm eager to see you, sweetheart...."

An elderly man on the escalator caught Michael's attention. Something felt off about him. He was bent over, using a cane, and had greasy dark hair sticking out of his fedora. His overcoat was too big in the shoulders, with sleeves hanging below his fingers. A positive sign of major trouble. This called for a closer examination.

Michael heard the train coming in the distance, so he had little time to check this guy out. He walked toward the tracks and stopped at the edge of the ochre-color warning strip painted on the floor.

"Wait a minute, babe." He shouted into the phone over the engine, which was roaring louder.

When Michael leaned forward for a better view, it confirmed his suspicion. The man wasn't elderly; he looked to be in his twenties with smooth babylike skin. He was a fraud.

Michael's body tensed into fight mode.

Watch his hands. He might reach for a piece.

His blood pressure soared when he realized he'd failed the sniper cardinal rule: avoid distraction. Like an idiot, he had no gun, no knife, and no fucking plan. He had to go on the defense. It was impossible to kill without detection in this crowd.

"Michael?" Sophia said. The thunderous engine and blasting horn nearly drowned out her voice.

A conductor helped the imposter into a wheelchair, and they kept their distance, staying near the bottom of the escalator. Michael's heart slowed slightly. Still, he didn't take his eyes off the guy's hands.

These two assholes were partners. He'd stay glued to them both.

The train was arriving, brakes emitting an ear-piercing squeal. The horn's clamor jarred his brain. He yelled into his cell. "Babe. Sorry—humpf."

Someone had banged his shoulders hard, knocking him off his feet, and toward the tracks. His cell flew out of his hand, and he thrashed his legs and arms, grabbing at the air for balance.

As if in slow motion, Michael watched the ochre strip slide under his brand new, hundred-dollar black leather shoes, as he floated into the danger zone. He twisted his upper body and turned his head a fraction, just enough to see the massive train charging at him.

Strange, the engine and horn were silent.

In the last second, Michael understood. The man in the wheelchair and the conductor were decoys.

You're fucked.

~ 54 ~

CHAPTER FIFTY-FOUR

March 22, 2013

Cass knocked three times before Mrs. Bloom answered the door.

"Oh, I'm sorry, Cassandra. I was in the laundry room. Come on in. Jer didn't say he had a meeting today."

"Good morning. He called me and told me to come right over." He hadn't told her what this was about, but his voice was intense, stressed.

Jer bounded up the cellar stairs and slammed the door. "Let's go." He looked wild, eyes blazing and sweat pouring down his face.

"Lordy, Jeremy. What's gotten into you?" his mother said, jamming her hands on her hips. "You been jumpy since this morning. It's three o'clock and you haven't eaten a thing."

Jer opened the back door and shoved Cass outside. She hooked her right arm around the porch column to stop from falling into the holly bushes.

"Jeremy? Answer me," her mother shouted as the door shuddered closed.

Cass was scared. Maureen probably called him and ratted on her. Now what was she going to do?

She followed Jer as he shoved his hands in his pockets and stomped into the field without speaking. Then he turned and stared at her, posture threatening, and jaws clamped shut.

She waited, bracing for his diatribe. Her response would be that he gave her no choice but to seek Maureen's advice.

He continued staring, his eyes narrowing, jaw muscles rippling.

The anticipation was too great. She had to fill the quiet space with something, anything, to break the menacing tension. "Do you think you should have left the stalks through winter instead of plowing them under before the fields froze?"

Stupid question, but....

No answer.

The silence was so toxic it settled in the weakest part of her body: her stomach. She pressed on. "Guess you didn't have time. Do you think you'll get corn—"

"Shut the fuck up," Jer said, growling through his clinched teeth. He turned away from her.

She closed her eyes in relief, although she doubted Jer was finished. Not yet.

He paraded in a square in front of her, jerking his shoulders, turning at each corner like a robotic soldier. As his elbows battered against dry stalks, yellowed particles flew to the ground, dotting the shallow snow.

Suddenly, out of the corner of her eye, Cass saw the crow. Without making a sound, he swooped in and gently perched himself on sturdy dead corn stalk ten feet away.

Jer didn't waiver from his idiotic pacing.

"What are you doing, Jer? Looks kind of nuts."

Cass had never seen him this furious. They used to play Army and march around the chicken coop when they were kids, but this was ridiculous, and it struck her as funny. She covered her mouth to muffle her laughter. She wanted to stop him. Ask him what had caused him to be so upset. She watched him go around one more time. When he got close enough, she whispered to him. "Did you fuck it up?"

Jer stopped flat. He opened his mouth, raised his arm back, and struck her face with his open palm.

She fell, rolling in blistering agony. His powerful slap jarred her brain. Eyes squeezed shut, she saw red turn to black and back to red again. She wanted to wail, but she sucked it up. He didn't need to see her in pain. See her as vulnerable, weak.

Jer took her arm and pulled her upright. "Shit. I'm sorry." Perspiration leaked from his chin.

With her head still spinning, she leaned forward and put her elbows on her knees to keep her balance.

"I shouldn't have hit you, but you pissed me off."

When she wiped her nose, blood smeared on her hand. Shooting back pain stopped her from standing straight. She choked and barked. "Peter, eh?" she said, without looking at him. God, she wanted to ridicule him more.

He didn't answer.

"Tell me, you asshole." Hatred gripped her chest.

"Peter sent me a text."

"Yeah?" She worked through her agony and stood erect, eyes still fixed on the ground.

"He texted a single word: *abort*."

With her back to him, she started walking toward home. The crow followed, gliding and hovering around her. She didn't duck because nothing surprised her anymore. His wings thudded as he landed atop a dry stalk fifteen feet ahead of her. As she got closer, he cocked his head, aligning his eye with hers.

When Cass looked back at him, he let out a soft caw. She nodded and kept walking.

Jer shouted after her. "What are you going to do?"

Cass didn't answer. He didn't need to know she had decided the instant he hit her.

Whatever it took, she'd survive, and she'd never go to prison.

CHAPTER FIFTY-FIVE

April 2, 2013

When Margot awoke in her bed, it was dark, and she was alone. A glimmer of light from the kitchen streamed under her door. She saw tiny, illuminated dust particles, propelled by warm air rolling from the furnace, whirling in the narrow beam. They were like little stars, dancing to their own music. Comforted, she lay for a time delaying the start of another, likely dreadful day.

Light flooded the room as Grey opened the door. "Coffee?"

"In a minute." She put on her robe, brushed her teeth, and doddered to the kitchen table. He poured their coffee and sat across from her. She noticed a letter on the table on official FBI stationery, signed by Special Agent Hawkins, dated April 1, 2020.

Obvious from Grey's drawn facial expression, he had read it. When she searched his face for more clues, she detected nothing.

They didn't speak until Margot had finished half her coffee. After a long, loud sigh, she said, "Did you see the date? It's April Fool's day."

"To my knowledge, that's not recognized in Kosovo."

"But you and I know it."

He waved her comment off and motioned her to read it.

"All right. Guess I can't put it off any longer." She read silently, knowing the microphones were picking up every word.

Edgar Bernard Leeds DOB 6/27/1973

Born in London, England, to Beatrice Marie Leeds, a single parent (fifteen years old).

Marriage: 2003–2006 Loretta Lumani (deceased).

In 1979, Beatrice Leeds left Edgar in the care of her sister, Minerva Price (1923–1993). Price, a wealthy, childless widow, highly educated, well connected to upper class London, dedicated her humanitarian efforts to women and orphans. She served as a founding member of Lindynne Detention Centre in Hertfordshire, England.

Minerva Price died when Leeds was a student at the University of Cambridge.

He continued his studies and became a barrister.

Leeds went on to establish safe houses for women in London, New York City, and Prishtina, Kosovo, in succession, each named Beatrice Place. He used a quote from Price as the business slogan: Let your past guide you, not decide you. Claim your future.

London government officials cited Leeds for lack of compliance in a variety of areas, e.g., lack of required HVAC, lack of proper food safety, failing to file required paperwork, and, in addition, a myriad of Department of Health and Social Care citations. Beatrice Place was fined and often forced to close temporarily. Ultimately, the legal battles were too costly, and Beatrice Place closed permanently in 2003.

That same year, Leeds moved to New York City, opened Beatrice Place, and married Loretta Lumani. Again, he faced the same legal issues he had experienced in London.

He was forced to close Beatrice Place in New York City in 2010, and soon after was reportedly seen fraternizing with Eris Hoti.

Hoti is thought to have financed Leeds' relocation to Prishtina.

354 ~ DIANN SCHINDLER

He presented him to prominent and unsavory people in Kosovo who funded and facilitated a circuitous route to set up Beatrice Place.

Dugal Hetrick: Leeds met Hetrick at Lindynne Detention Centre. They formed a close relationship. Later, when Hetrick was serving time in HM Bedford Prison, Leeds facilitated his early release in 2010, and has employed him in a variety of positions since that time.

Despite challenges to Beatrice Place in Prishtina, women residents appear to thrive, therefore allowing Leeds to enjoy a revered reputation with locals.

Our investigation is not complete.

Margot scooted the report across the table, mouthing, "How could I be so wrong?"

Grey lowered his eyes. "I'm sorry. Ismet and I warned you."

"Great. Thanks for reminding me I'm a poor judge of character. Screw you." She scoffed.

He got up, leaned against the kitchen sink, and sipped his coffee, staring at her.

Grey was right, but she wanted nothing of it. She was grieving the loss of her friend...who really had never been her friend. Edgar had used her, and just because she was coming to grips with that reality, the loss and humiliation weren't any easier. She chewed the inside of her cheek, struggling to keep her emotions in check.

"I'm here for you, always. You know that," he said, shifting his weight. "And, as your devoted friend, I have to be honest."

Someone banged on the front door, jolting Margot from her new reality. She jumped to her feet and in a voice just above a whisper, said, "Who is it?"

Grey bolted to the door and looked through the peephole. He turned to her, eyes wide. "Edgar."

"Margot. Open up," Edgar said, grumbling in a deep baritone and continuing to pound on the door. His vicious voice and brutal blows were unlike the Edgar she knew, who was always cool and in control.

"Give me a minute." She put her fist in her mouth, pantomiming her terror for Grey to see.

Grey nodded acknowledgement. "Morning, Edgar. We'll be right there."

She sprinted to the bedroom to change out of her pajamas.

"Grey, let me in," Edgar said, using an opposite voice: even and calm.

Margot sensed he had shifted his tone because he realized she was not alone. She threw on a sweatshirt and jeans and ran to the kitchen. After pursing her lips and inhaling through her nostrils to gain composure, she opened the door.

Edgar's appearance shocked her. He wore wrinkled jeans and soiled tennis shoes. His unshaven face was wild, lips agape, blazing eyes. She couldn't imagine what had caused this wild behavior. One thing for certain, something dreadful was about to occur. To hide the fright filling her every pore, she commanded herself to stay quiet.

"Hello, Edgar," Grey said with a shaky half smile. "Coffee?"

Edgar tramped through the kitchen to the sofa, flashing his intense, bulging eyes at them. With his feet apart, he swayed side to side, with nostrils flaring.

Just as Grey motioned for Edgar to sit, Margot spotted the FBI report on the kitchen table. She inched over, slowly slid it off the table, folded it behind her back, and shoved it into her jeans' rear pocket.

"I do not want coffee." He gritted and bared his crooked, dingy teeth.

With her most even and cheerful inflection, she said, "What brings you here this morning?" Her knees wobbled as her mind went to the picture Hawkins had showed her. Now his eyes were maniacal, like in the photo. She glanced at Grey as he squirmed and vibrated.

Edgar rushed her, gripped the neck of her sweatshirt and pulled her face to his, so close, she saw his pupils constrict and his blue eyes turn a dull gray.

He roared at her. "You. You have ruined everything."

She fluttered her eyelids and gagged as his caustic breath blistered on her face.

"You are not making sense," Grey said. His pink face flushed purple.

Edgar didn't respond. He glued his eyes to hers. "My Dugal. You had him arrested." A glob of spit foamed on his chin as he wagged her neck and head, raising her up on her toes.

She held herself steady from choking by holding his wrists.

Will he strangle me?

"I love him. He is the only family I have left," Edgar said.

Grey said, "Why don't you sit and tell us, Edgar?" His eyes darted and squinted at Margot, signaling he had a plan.

Edgar wagged his head with a fierce *no*.

"We want to hear. Please. I want to know, Edgar." When Grey motioned for him to sit a second time, he released Margot and perched himself on the edge of the sofa. His right cheek twitched, and his breath rushed from his gaping mouth.

Margot fell into a chair, rubbing her neck. "Please, Edgar, talk to us," she said, coughing and gasping for air.

"I love Dugal as if he were my child. He needs me," he said, sniveling and sobbing. "They beat and sexually abused him at the orphanage. It's called Monster Mansion. Can you imagine?" He looked up at them, pleading. "My young, frightened Dugal. I could not allow it."

"What did you do?" She held still, fearing any movement might shift Edgar's mood. Suddenly she remembered the FBI bug. They'd be here any moment.

"I rescued him." Edgar seemed to relax. His eyes returned to their normal blue color, his breathing steady, lighter.

"You saved his life, Edgar," she said, smiling at him and confident the FBI would arrive any moment.

Stall.

"I believe I did. I am all Dugal has. I am his protector. He cannot return to incarceration." He stared, focused somewhere inside his mind. Then, instantly, he began slapping his skull repeatedly, gnashing and spitting. "It is my fault. It is my fault."

"No," Margot said. "It's going to be fine." She touched his shoulder. "It's going to be fine."

He jumped to his feet, towering over her, tugging his shirt collar, drenched with sweat. He shoved his right hand in his jacket pocket. "I demand you retract your statement, Margot. I blame you." He quickly slid his hand out of his pocket and held a pistol inches from her face.

Grey snarled and lunged, slamming into Edgar's ribs, causing his body to veer away from Margot.

A shot blasted, echoing through the apartment.

Grey groaned and fell face-first to the floor.

In the silence that followed, Margot couldn't move, her eyes riveted to Grey, slumped on his side. Dark blood trickled from his chest. She crawled beside him, calling his name. His face, distorted and jammed in the carpeting, grew pale; his lips, pasty. He lay quiet and motionless.

"You shot him." Instinctively, she leaped to her feet and pushed Edgar's shoulders with both hands. "You killed him."

He staggered for a moment but remained upright. Two fisted, he pointed the gun at her stomach, mumbling nonsense.

Hot urine escaped into her panties. "Edgar, no."

The gun rattled in Edgar's hands as his entire body trembled.

Her eyes searched the room for a weapon. The Tiffany lamp. She grabbed the pole with both hands. Lifting the massive base, she groaned, swinging it backwards. The glass shade flung away and shattered on the kitchen floor.

The sound must have startled Edgar because he dropped his arms. Only for an instant. Yanking them up, he pointed the barrel at her stomach again.

Margot heaved the lamp at his face. Her aim was too low. The base skimmed his arms, and he dropped the gun. The weight of the lamp flung her off balance. As she fell to the floor, Edgar planted his foot on her forearm. She wriggled loose and thrust her body into his knees.

His bones popped and cracked, and he screamed, toppling to his back and struggling to grab his knees.

Margot scrambled to her feet, took the lamp base and hoisted it above her head.

"Margot, don't." He whined, shielding his face with his arm.

His whimpering caused her to pause, the base poised in midair. But then he strained, reaching for the gun. Just as he got it in his hand, she slammed the base, smashing his forehead with a sickening thud.

A shot rang out.

Margot froze in complete confusion, then collapsed. Drool streamed from her lips as she lay on her back, waiting for her brain to reboot. An odd sensation developed on her arm and caught fire. She didn't move her head, just her eyes. Her upper arm was mangled and bleeding.

The front door splintered open and three people with helmets, goggles, and rifles bolted through.

"Grey is dead. He's dead," she said, her voice failing.

One person bent on one knee said, "We were on our way."

She recognized Wilson's voice.

"Fuck you," she said, barely audible. She watched as Wilson placed two fingers on Grey's neck.

~ 56 ~

CHAPTER FIFTY-SIX

April 2, 2013

The hospital waiting room was chilly, dim, and seedy. The floor, uneven and broken tile, was soiled to a permanent discoloration and gnarled with notches and dents from years of heavy equipment rolling through the halls. Harsh fluorescent lights exposed the uneven paint and cracked plaster on the walls. Worse, nothing smelled medicinal.

Even if Grey were alive, Margot had little faith he'd survive, given these conditions. She couldn't imagine any qualified doctor working here, with the obvious lack of attention to cleanliness and repair.

Hawkins and Wilson sat with her in silence. She had lost all sense of time after they tended to her arm. A flesh wound, the nurses said.

Too filled with despair and fatigue to talk, Margot's mind found a deep, black hole. She gladly escaped into this comfort zone and pushed thoughts and emotions away. But suddenly, reality swooshed back in, flooding her with the knowledge that she'd suffer endlessly, her life forever altered, having lost both Andy and Grey.

Her thoughts returned to the first time she met Grey. From that moment, she envied his friendship with Andy. They were close friends. So, naturally she detested him, his bald head, his double chin, that pinkish complexion and his unease, which caused him to sweat profusely. Even his superb intellect annoyed her. And when he continued to treat her with kindness, that had pissed her off, too. Did she know she was an asshole? Of course she did. All the more reason to despise him because he brought out her worst behaviors.

Then Andy's murder had thrown them together. They mourned, and they suffered. And, when she no longer noticed his imperfections and her attitude began to shift, she fought it. Why? Because she enjoyed detesting him. And throughout the difficulties, Grey had been there, persistent, thoughtful, and understanding, despite her surly, abusive, petty bullshit.

No wonder Andy loved Grey.

She exhaled, thinking how she had frivoled the time away when they could've been happy together. And now he was gone. She could never tell him how sorry she was and how much she loved—

"Ms. Hart."

Jolted from her mental machinations, Margot raised her head. Two doctors asked her to follow them. She nodded for Hawkins to come with her. Wilson, too, even though she had been a total shit to her. She needed them now.

As they walked through the hall, the sound of their collective footsteps, out of sync, reverberating against the blemished walls, was an eerie match to the chaos colliding in her brain. She felt detached and when she teetered, Hawkins took her hand. "I got you."

Despite being on the fringes of reality, Margot sensed they were taking her to a private place. They entered an office with velvety carpeting and walls painted a pleasant, soft green, a stark contrast to the waiting room. The lighting cast a serene warmth across the room.

What better space to tell her Grey had died?

The first doctor sat behind the desk. The other one stood. Margot, Hawkins, and Wilson sat across from them. Wilson handed her a box of tissues.

"Ms. Hart, Margot, I am Dr. Smythe," the first doctor said with a German accent. "This is my colleague, Dr. Helmet. Agent Wilson tells me you are not related to Mr. Valentin. Correct?"

Margot couldn't find her words. She pressed her lips together.

"Agent Wilson, we should tell you. We agreed."

Margot noticed the doctor's lips moving, but the words tumbled and echoed. She didn't understand what they were saying, and she didn't care.

"Ms. Hart. Are you listening?"

She hummed a response.

"All right," she said, leaning closer. "Mr. Valentin has suffered serious injuries, with a single bullet, at close range. When it entered his body, the trajectory ascended from the point of entry, causing considerable damage to his left side. The bullet lodged between two ribs—"

Dr. Helmet nudged Dr. Smythe. "Allow me." He cleared his throat. "As luck would have it, there is no damage to vital organs. With excellent care and physical therapy, Mr. Valentin will recover. He's a strong—"

She lowered her voice. "You mean, he's alive." She swallowed and mopped her nose.

Dr. Helmet bowed his head. "He's been asking for you; however, he's heavily sedated now."

"But he didn't move. The blood," Margot said. She was dumbfounded, and white noise filled her brain.

"We were able to remove the bullet and repair the surrounding tissue. Now infection is the greatest threat, you understand."

Margot thought she had no more tears. Wrong. She bellowed. Legs weak, she struggled to stand, and when finally upright, Dr. Smythe took her uninjured arm and guided her to Grey's room.

Margot paused at the doorway, scanning every inch of Grey. His eyes were closed, and his face was a light pink color. He had a tube in his nose and lines coming out of his arm, tethered to machines. She moved closer and took his hand, covering her mouth to muffle the sobs rising from the deepest part of her body.

No one spoke as the minutes passed.

"I'm sorry, Grey," she said, eyes riveted on his face. She felt her consciousness normalizing and her hearing and vision improving. "When can he come home?"

"If it goes well, and his markers are normal, three or four days. Be aware, however, his injuries require constant care. Will he have someone—"

"Yes. Me." She bit her lips with determination and whispered she was sorry in Grey's ear again.

The heart monitor beat at a steady tempo.

Finally, Hawkins said, "You must be exhausted. We'll take you home."

She squeezed Grey's hand. "Let's get you well." As she walked toward the door, she said to the doctors, "I thought he. I mean. You saved his life. I will forever be grateful."

They nodded.

Leaving the hospital, Wilson said, "Your apartment is secure now. We scrubbed everything. And, we removed the bugs."

"Grey saved my life."

Wilson didn't respond.

"Leeds is in the hospital, in custody. Can't hurt you," Hawkins said. "You gave him quite a blow. He keeps quoting Napoleon. I think it's Napoleon."

"How's that?" she asked.

"Something like, 'Victory belongs to the most....' What was it, Wilson?"

"The most persevering. 'Victory belongs to the most persevering.'"

Margot did not know what that meant, and she didn't have the energy to ask.

"Don't worry. He's delirious and he'll be out of commission for a long time."

***

Margot must have fallen asleep because suddenly she realized Wilson was helping her get in bed.

"Are you in pain? Does your arm hurt?"

"No. Still numb. Is Hawkins here?"

He tapped on the door, "Okay to enter?"

Margot nodded.

"You need to rest," Wilson said.

"I need to talk to you," she said, willing herself to find renewed energy. "When can I get a full report? Who? Why? How? And what's with the cyberattack?"

"It's complicated," Hawkins said. "We'll fill you in."

"Resolved?"

"No. We're close. It's incredibly elaborate. International. Quite a few actors and phenomenal intelligence—"

"I'm sorry. I thought I could talk, but my brain is fried." Margot fought to keep her eyes open.

"For sure." Wilson said.

"One last thing I'm compelled to share before I drift to sleep." She pulled her head up off the pillows. "You should have been at the apartment as soon as you heard Edgar banging on my door. If you were listening. If you weren't, that's an unspeakable error."

Hawkins said, "Margot, we—"

She held up her hand. "I'm done."

~ 57 ~

CHAPTER FIFTY-SEVEN

April 5, 2013

It had been three days since Edgar wounded her and Grey. Margot walked around her apartment in a daze the first day, balancing her thoughts between reliving every detail to pushing them out of her mind. And, of course, she wallowed in negative self-talk, punishing herself for misjudging Edgar. She wanted her mother, of course, and called repeatedly, only to be disappointed when she couldn't reach her. Brooks didn't answer his phone either.

Thank God her visits to see Grey were the highlight of her days.

She called Hawkins and told him to meet her at the hospital, adding she needed a favor and had questions.

***

Margot bought a coffee just as Hawkins and Wilson walked into the cafeteria.

"Have you seen Grey? He looks great," Margot said, as they sat at a table.

"Hope to this morning. How are you doing? How's the arm?" Hawkins said.

"Hurts like hell," she said. "Movement is constricted, and I took off work this week. Anyway, as they say, you should see the other guy. So, how is Edgar?"

Hawkins said he's suffered brain damage and severe leg injuries. "Docs said it was tricky there for a while."

She felt a sharp spear of guilt. "Shit, he almost died?" She covered her open mouth. "I didn't mean to, er, I didn't fully realize what I was doing. I thought he had killed Grey. God, I'd die if I thought I killed a human being. Fuck. I'm not making sense." She bent forward, clutching her stomach, trying to hold her thoughts together.

"Yes, you are, and you didn't kill him," Hawkins said. "Even if you had, it'd be self-defense."

"Doesn't matter...if I had taken a life," she shook her head and bit her lip.

In the silence that followed, Margot's mind retreated to the living room, where Edgar held the gun to her chest. She remembered waiting for the agents to come while Grey lay dying and she faced death herself. In an instant, she was back there, in the terror of that day. Her face turned feverish with anger. "You should have been there. None of this would have happened." She glared at them. "What took so long?" Spittle flew out of her mouth.

Hawkins waited, then blinked a sad apology. "Shift change, but that's no excuse. We've cited the officers responsible."

"God dammit, Hawkins," she said, dropping her head in her hands. "You are in charge," she said, looking up at him again. "You should be cited." She tossed her hair. "I'm sending you our medical bills. That's the least you can do."

He nodded with a blank stare.

They sat quietly, long enough for Margot to regain her composure. After sitting up straight and wiping her face, she said, "Edgar was crazed because I had identified Dugal. How did he know that?"

Hawkins tilted his head, pausing before he spoke. "We let him make a call and he must have called Leeds."

Margot asked where Dugal was now.

Hawkins said that they considered Dugal a flight risk and acted on a handful of local charges to hold him. "He went berserk in his cell. As a result, they placed him in the psychiatric ward in a facility in Prizren that specializes in mentally ill offenders."

She exhaled a long breath. "He and Edgar are a pair."

"The best news is the cyberattack has been foiled."

"I don't believe it." Margot said, shaking her head.

"True. The hackers got nothing."

"That simple?" Margot said with an incredulous tone.

"Hardly. Don't want to overwhelm you with a bunch of details. Lots of agencies worked together, including the Secret Service, a variety of independent cyber security companies, and state and local police."

"You positive? I mean, I've read viruses can go dormant, waiting for the right time to appear again."

"Positive," Wilson said.

"Who was it?" Margot said.

"The cell, the source of the cabal? You'll never guess this. Kids. Well, people in their twenties. It spread across three states and the leader lives in Iowa, of all places," Hawkins said, curling his lip and shaking his head. He explained that the hackers started by infiltrating the United Association of Insurance Officials, which lists every insurance company in each state and territory, their personnel, email addresses, and websites. "Maryland was the tip of the iceberg."

"I still don't understand. The disk didn't reveal how, or who, right?"

"Once those Maryland insurance companies admitted breaches in their systems, we had what we needed. We pulled in the best of the best from Homeland Security, and they entered their systems, which led us to David Jackson, aka Peter Johnson, our tipping point. He's well known and was once huge in Anonymous." Hawkins leaned back in his chair with a look of self-satisfaction. "You, Grey, and the disk were key."

"And Andy, too," Wilson said, squinting, then smiling. "We're sorry for your loss. For both you and Grey."

It was a lot of information to take in and Margot had enough answers for now. "Listen, before we go to Grey's room, I have a favor." Margot explained how she hadn't been able to reach her mom, including the abrupt ending to their last conversation, and her calling on Brooks for help. "Can you contact her? Here's her information."

After taking down her mother's address and phone number, Wilson got on the phone at once and ordered the local FBI to contact the Minneapolis office and follow up.

"Do you want an update on Andy?" Hawkins said.

A ripple of angst appeared in Margot's chest. The number one question which had been baked in her mind for months was *why did Andy lie?* She couldn't bring herself to ask it out loud because she was afraid of the answer. But, it was time.

"I do and Grey will want to hear it, too."

***

"Andy did not have a job with the State Department. He wasn't honest with you, but then again, his motives were good. Let me explain," Hawkins said.

Margot sat on the bed beside Grey, holding his hand, bracing herself for more truth. She nodded for Hawkins to continue.

"First, we followed your tip regarding the Maryland insurance companies. Then, we used the data on the disk—Andy's disk—to foil the attack."

"Andy protected you," Wilson said. "He had a meticulous plan to destroy the virus and the hackers. Our informants in Veles, Macedonia, said Andy got copies of the disk to the right people." She explained the cyberattack was so highly sophisticated it took much more time to analyze the data and determine a method to stop it.

"Everything pointed to April fifteenth as Zero Day," Hawkins said, looking at his watch. "Look, it's April fifth. They infiltrated insurance companies weeks ago. Again, the Maryland information was key."

"Andy was a hero," Wilson said.

"So true," Grey said. "He was kind, generous, and always wanted to help."

Margot sniffed and sputtered. "He devoted himself to people who were mistreated by corrupt governments. It was even more complicated because of his emotional involvement. He also did this for his parents. Especially for his dad. I think he did it to reclaim their relationship."

"Yeah, they were estranged for many years. Guess he wanted to make it right," Grey said.

"Why health insurance companies?" Margot said. "I mean, it's common knowledge, insurance companies are ripping people off. However, that's not from corrupt government."

Hawkins answered, noting the insurance companies don't care about people. "The greed is staggering. Lots of fingers in the till, from pharmaceutical companies to lobbyists to our elected officials."

"Elected officials benefit, financially and politically," Wilson said.

"Wait, though. He ended this cyberattack," Margot said. "The irony is he'd be on the side of the hackers. Under the condition, of course, they didn't include sabotaging patient files."

Grey kissed her hand. "He took on a monster this time. We loved him, didn't we, Margot?"

Suddenly, as if she had been holding her breath for months, air emptied from her lungs. Turning away from the bed, she covered her face in her hands and sobbed.

Everyone waited in silence.

Once she regained her composure, Margot said, "We did...I'm sorry. Not sure where that came from. Whew."

Grey squeezed her hand.

Finally, she said, "One more thing. We're talking around this. Explain to me, who was pulling the strings?" She sniffed. Wilson handed her a tissue, and Margot wiped her nose.

"It didn't start in the United States," Hawkins said.

"Shit," Margot said, "if not the U.S., where?"

"Russia?" Grey said. "Isn't that what Nadia said in her letter? Did you find confirmation?"

"Wait, where does Eris Hoti fit in here?" Margot said.

"Hoti, Leeds, and Hetrick, of course, and authorities nabbed a Maureen Mason in New York City. They're facing charges under the Computer Fraud and Abuse Act. Although it might be hard to stick to Hoti and Leeds, don't worry, they've committed other crimes. Nadia Stephen mentioned Russian oligarch Maksim Nikitin. It's unfortunate; he's well protected, and we may not bring him to justice," Hawkins said.

"We'll get him eventually," Wilson said.

"Leeds was a puppet under Hoti's thumb. And, let's not forget, we're in conversations with Officer Dime Pavlovski. While we may never discover Andy's killer, we'll do everything we can to have those involved pay for their actions," Hawkins said.

"So, I want to back up. You're saying Edgar is entangled in Andy's murder?" Margot asked.

"Hetrick put us on to that. There's a lot we don't know," Hawkins said.

"This shakes me to the core. People from all over the world took part. How do people gain this much power?" Margot said.

"They are only powerful when we fail to take action. Some people get involved with intent; others, unknowingly," Wilson said.

"Brooks, too," Margot said, shaking her head in disbelief.

Hawkins raised his macchiato cup. "To Andrey Orlo Stephan."

The sound of his full name filled Margot's chest with pride.

Grey's eyes moistened, and he smiled at her as they drank. "I have a couple more questions. Did you find Andy's dad or his mother?"

Hawkins leaned back in his chair and took a deep breath, "We understand his mother found her husband in *Džepčište*, a small village near Tetovo. They were safe there, for a while. Sad to report, Kostas Stephan died in a car accident in Tetovo. Reportedly, an accident."

"You think otherwise?" Grey said.

Hawkins nodded.

Margot gasped.

Silence.

"Before the cyberattack was foiled? I mean, do you think Andy knew?" Margot said.

Wilson shrugged, shaking her head.

"Can't imagine the pressure he suffered," Margot said. "Mrs. Stephan? Dear God, hope she's alive."

"Yeah. Sorry, we're late getting back to you on this. She's vanished." Hawkins said.

"Dead, too?" Grey said, frowning and ducking his head.

Hawkins rubbed his chin.

"Dammit, tell me we're finished." Margot jumped up and leaned her hands on the bed, waiting for their response. When they didn't answer, Margot glared at them.

Grey tugged at her sleeve to sit back down. She ignored him. "Listen. I'm just a girl from Minneapolis, not equipped. It's—"

"It's too much," Wilson said. "You're not trained. We are. And to be honest," she looked over at Hawkins, "I personally am overwhelmed with your persistence and all you have gone through. You are quite a woman, er, Well." She cleared her throat. "That's coming from me. Woman to woman."

"Okay. That's enough, Wilson," Hawkins said, standing. "We're done here, and we'll be in touch as more develops. Get well, both of you."

"Wait. I got something to say," Margot said, taking a deep breath. "I get that I've been difficult—"

Hawkins cleared his throat with exaggeration and grinned in agreement.

"Yeah, and I'm sorry. But only for when you did not deserve my ire. Some you had coming." She raised her eyebrows to Hawkins. "To tell the truth, I formed an opinion as soon as I saw you guys. It's a weakness I'm working to correct. Thing was, I wanted immediate, accurate answers to questions. To questions I didn't even know how to ask."

She shifted her feet and held her hand up when Wilson started to speak. "And for you, Wilson. I was very hard on you, especially at first. I'm asking myself now. No, I'm kicking myself and wondering, would I have treated you the way I did if you were a man?"

Wilson bit her bottom lip, raised her eyebrows, and shrugged.

"If I'm reading you, your silence, correctly, I'd say, woman to woman, you are being kind to me."

Wilson grinned.

"Throughout it all, you've taken my criticisms very well. Frankly, that made me even more furious," Margot chuckled. "Welcome to my world of dysfunction. Thank you very much." She raised her coffee cup. "And I hope I never see you again." She flashed a wide smile.

~ 58 ~

CHAPTER FIFTY-EIGHT

April 7, 2013

Grey had been in the hospital for five days. When Margot brought him home and put him to bed, he said he wanted to talk. She sat beside him.

"We haven't had a moment alone, forever. God, I've missed that. Tell me, how are you?" he said.

Grey's insistent concern for Margot, amid his life-threatening injuries, overwhelmed her. "Man. Here you are...asking how I am? Who are you, anyway? How is it you...my hero...came into my life?"

"Funny. You think I'm Wonder Man. I think you're Wonder Woman."

"Let's say...mutual admiration?"

They stared at each other.

Gratitude warmed her entire body, and an involuntary grin spread across her face.

"You look radiant."

She felt radiant.

"Let's celebrate with a glass of wine."

"Doc said no alcohol," she said, wagging her finger.

"Screw 'em. Couple of sips won't kill me."

She rolled her eyes and got a bottle of Sauvignon Blanc from the rack, along with two glasses and an opener.

She opened the wine. He poured.

He raised his glass. "To our mutual admiration."

A massive lump entered her throat and stuck there, nearly cutting off her air. She put her glass on the side table and swallowed repeatedly.

"Damn. You okay?"

Her mouth quivered. "I thought...." She put her hand over her heart. "I thought you were dead. I can't begin to describe how that felt," she said, opening her mouth and blowing air. "The dread and the enormity of it suddenly hit me...again. Phew. Not sure what came over me....Sorry."

Grey handed her a tissue.

Her cell vibrated in her back pocket. After she pulled it out and looked at the caller ID, she jumped off the bed.

"Mom, thank God."

"Honey, I'm sorry." Her voice shook and was higher than normal.

"Are you all right?"

"I'm okay. There...Well, I'm okay now. I didn't have my phone."

Margot waited for more. She only heard her mother's breathing. "Mother?"

"I'm here. I've been in the hospital. They say I can go home soon."

Margot wanted to scream at her, demanding she explain what had happened. She couldn't because her mom sounded so feeble. "Are you alone?"

"No. Nurse and doctors. And...wait. He wants to talk to you."

"Hello, Ms. Hart? She's much better now." He spoke in a gruff whisper.

"Who are you?"

"Name's Meyer. Dave Meyer. I'm an FBI Special Agent from the Minneapolis office. Agent Wilson notified us. Your mother suffered an attack in her home. And. Well, I'm not a doctor. You must talk to them. An agent from the Prishtina office will contact you with the details. Wait, Mrs. Hart wants to talk to you."

"Margot, don't worry. I'm going to be fine. I need to sleep now, honey."

"Mom?"

The connection ended.

"Dammit. She sounded terrible. I told you, Grey. They got to her." She paced.

"Let's not jump to conclusions."

"Don't give me the coincidence bullshit, Grey," she said, squeezing her eyes shut and pounding her fists on her thighs. "I knew it...I knew it." She dropped to the bed and bawled.

Grey stroked her hair.

Minutes later, Margot stood, blew her nose, and swallowed. "I'm calling Hawkins," she said, dialing his number.

Hawkins answered at once. "Hello, Margot. Is this a good time for you? We're at your front door."

***

"No." Margot jumped up and slammed her palms on the kitchen table. "Brooks?"

Hawkins opened his folder. "Yes, Brooks Pap attacked Sherry Hart. They arrested him at the scene."

"Brooks attacked her? I can't believe it. He's a harmless, lazy-ass twerp. Shit, I asked him to check on her. I sent him to her house. My God. He's been a friend to the family...dinners over our house."

"Were you aware?" Hawkins said. "Says here his parents are Serbian. Immigrated to the U.S. at an early age. Big Serbian community in Minnesota. Law-abiding people, but, as in any community, you find a few rotten apples."

Margot fell to her chair, "He and Andy were friends. How could I not know? Such a betrayal." She cupped her mouth.

"Your friend Mr. Pap hooked up with Serbian Nationals and who were right in there with Russian oligarchs. The dots are connecting now."

"Listen, I'm not going there. Tell me about my mom. Her injuries. She's been unconscious? For how long?"

"I spoke with her doctors," Wilson said.

"Doctors, plural?"

Wilson nodded. "A neurologist and....She fainted, and it took them a while to determine why. No actual head injuries. It puzzled the doctors at first. The oncologist. Ah. I'm uncomfortable. You need to talk to the doctor."

"Tell me," Margot screamed, her face full of terror. "She's got cancer?"

"Yes, leukemia. I have it here." She combed through her papers. "Here it is. Chronic lymphocytic leukemia."

When she heard leukemia, her mind bolted to death sentence. And a four-hundred-pound weight landed on her chest. She understood oncologists helped people die from cancer. "Grey? I can't lose my mother. I can't."

"I'm here, Margot," he said.

"Call her doctor. Here's his number. He's expecting your call," Wilson said.

"We're taking off now to give you privacy," Hawkins said as they walked out the door.

"Shall I dial?" Grey said.

"Yes, yes," she said, raking her hands through her hair and bouncing on her toes as anxiety completely attacked her body. "Go ahead." She splashed water on her face in the kitchen sink.

Grey dialed and asked for Dr. Bartholomew in oncology.

Margot sat beside Grey, trying to hold still. He pressed the speaker icon and sat the phone on the table.

"This is Dr. Bartholomew."

Margot identified herself and explained why they were calling, rubbing her face on a kitchen towel.

"Chronic lymphocytic leukemia, CLL. Your mother has a non-diffused pattern of bone marrow involvement. While she shows signs of chromosome thirteen deletion, there are no other chromosome abnormalities. Questions?"

"Translation?" she said, frowning at Grey.

"Of course, forgive me. Her CLL is at Stage Zero. We'll be watching her closely for more indicators."

"How many stages are there?" She pursed her lips.

Grey squeezed her hand.

"Five, zero to four. Zero is low risk."

"So she's not going to die?" Margot said, blurting her words.

"Ms. Hart, we all are going to die. CLL at Stage Zero is slow growing. I'd release her tomorrow. Unfortunately, she's experiencing shoulder and back pain. I'm consulting with Dr. Edwards, her GP, and she's keeping her for a few more days." He added he had arranged for home care and physical therapy for the following two weeks. "Meanwhile, I'll continue testing and follow up. Anything else?"

"No, I mean...."

"Your mother told me to tell you not to rush home," he chuckled. "She's very good at giving orders, Ms. Hart."

The call ended.

Margot and Grey sat in silence.

Margot was taking it all in. Another crisis for her mother and for herself.

"Good news, right?"

"It's better than I expected.," Margot said, staring up at the ceiling. "My poor mom. Sam, my dad...Can there be more?"

"They're taking excellent care of her."

"She doesn't know about Andy."

"Or what happened to you?"

Silence.

"Or to you, Grey."

"Or us, Margot," he smiled and pecked her cheek. "Feeling better?"

"Yeah, but, I swear, trauma is our way of life."

"We're coming down the other side."

"Yeah, at least no one is hunting us. Grey, what would I have done without you?" She scooted her chair closer, wrapped her arms around his shoulders and squeezed.

"Ouch."

"Oh, crap." She pulled away. "Sorry."

"I'm kidding. Do it again." He cackled.

She growled through her teeth. "I want to punch you so bad." She hugged him tenderly this time.

"Honestly, I'd rather we make love."

"That'd be great," she said. "Could smart, eh?"

"Meh," he grinned.

"Well, it's not the loving part. It'd be your laughing. Belly laughing, a painful afterglow."

"It'd be worth it."

"Might tear your sutures," she said, tilting her head.

"Pain and pleasure are closely related." He raised his eyebrows.

"Let's find out." She took his hand and led him to the bedroom. They crawled into bed.

"Don't say I didn't warn you." She inhaled and kissed him, long and hard.

He gulped as she yanked the covers back and carefully opened the fly of his pajamas.

"Does this hurt?" she said as she gently drew out his cock.

Eyes closed, he moved his head back and forth, spreading his knees wider apart.

"Damn, you're hard. Wow." She puffed air.

He shoved his pelvis forward as she put her lips on the tip of his rod, using her tongue to draw tiny circles.

They gasped in unison.

Then, suddenly, she stopped, "Promise you won't laugh too hard?"

Jaws open, he thrust his penis toward her. "Don't concern yourself. I have a high pain threshold." He shut his eyes again.

She took him in her mouth.

~ 59 ~

CHAPTER FIFTY-NINE

March 25, 2013

Turkish Airlines Flight Number 4850 from Prishtina, Kosovo, arrived in Bangkok, Thailand at 7 a.m. local time. USAID training location was in the Athenee Tower, thirty minutes' drive once outside the Bangkok Suvarnabhumi Airport traffic.

Illir Goxilli walked with his briefcase to the luggage carousel, retrieved his suitcase, and proceeded through customs. He had to make one stop before going to the Athenee Tower. He hailed a cab, got in the back seat, and handed the driver a card with the address.

The driver read the card and returned it to him before pulling out into the traffic. He weaved through thick, drab smog billowing from cars and motorbikes, all amassed at the curb, with drivers struggling to claim passengers.

The taxi driver took the highway to Bangkok's Old City, also known as Khaosan, passed the Grand Palace and Wat Arun, to Khao San Road. He slowed the vehicle to a crawl and craned his neck to see the side streets.

Finally, the driver turned onto a narrow street lined with vendors cooking on their portable makeshift stoves. Hordes of people buying breakfast spilled over into the center of the road. The driver maneuvered around the crowd, pulled to the side, and stopped. He pointed toward an outdoor laundry with clothes hanging on plastic cords sagging with too much weight, stretched twelve feet across the entrance.

Illir leaned forward and held his hand up, signaling for the driver to wait. The driver bobbed his head, put the car's automatic transmission in park, and lit a cigarette.

Illir grabbed his briefcase, exited the back seat, and waited on the pavement, wiping perspiration off his neck with his handkerchief.

Cassandra peeked out from behind a faded red curtain behind the plastic clothes lines. "Mr. Goxilli?"

He nodded.

"Come," she said, flipping the wet clothes and shoving the drape aside. They passed three rumbling washing machines and approached an emaciated old man sitting with his bare legs crossed at his knees and a grubby chartreuse flip flop dangling from his big toe. Shoulders hunched over, a fist full of cards in his lap, and his elbow leaning on a green plastic table, he dragged on his hand-rolled cigarette. He squinted at Illir, spit a piece of tobacco from his lip to the dirt floor, and returned to his Solitaire card game.

As Cass waited, her mind went back to Jer and her promise to herself: she'd never go to prison. She had managed that well, working with Maureen to enlist those Macedonia kids again just in the nick of time for her to leave the country and disappear. And before that bastard, Peter, was caught. Jer, in all their years together, had never given her the credit she deserved. He'd pay for that in spades. Deservedly so. She brushed her long bangs off her face, barely able to contain her triumphant defiance.

Illir placed his briefcase on the table, unlocked it, and retrieved two manila envelopes. After placing them in front of the old man, he closed his case and removed it from the table.

Thick blue-gray cigarette smoke streamed from the man's nose and mouth. He dropped his head in a modified bow and with a snap, placed a queen of diamonds on a king of spades.

Maureen entered from the back alley. She took one envelope and with her long, red thumbnail, lifted the edge of a blue and yellow sticker attached to the top right corner, peeling it back just enough to satisfy her. She exhaled.

"Is it there?" Cass said.

Maureen pushed the sticker back down with the heel of her hand. "Yep, check the other one."

Cass's heart raced as she repeated the procedure. "We're good." She handed her envelope to Maureen. Her chest filled with pride.

They watched Illir slip around the red drape and duck under the clothes.

When he was out of earshot, Maureen held the envelopes next to her cheek, almost swooning. "Amazing how much data are in such tiny chips."

"Very true," Cass said, with a haughty grin. "Those kids ramped Magpie back up again with a technology that was first took place in 1996, when Panix, one of the oldest internet service providers, was knocked offline for several days by a SYN flood."

Maureen held her hand up and Cass stopped talking. "Please, Cass, I love that you love this stuff, but I have no idea what you are talking about. So, spare me."

"Yes, but it's important to understand that Vis and Bestar created even bigger botnets." Her voice trailed when Maureen shook her head.

"I get it, Cass. They are cutting edge. What that means to me is that we're going to need to keep them flush with money for a very long time or they'll flip on us."

Cass scrunched her shoulders and exhaled. "It's all about the money."

Maureen pursed her lips and nodded.

They watched Illir enter the cab.

Cass reached into her cargo pants pocket for the old man's payment. She handed him a wide wad of baht. Thirty-two thousand baht, the equivalent of $1,000, would go a long way in Thailand.

"*Kapunkap*," he said, bowing his head over his steepled hands and slowly blinking his eyes.

Illir slammed the door shut. "Athenee Tower, *kruṇā*."

When the taxi was out of sight, Maureen turned to Cass. "Keep the blonde hair and hang out in Thailand until you hear from me."

~ 60 ~

CHAPTER SIXTY

September 7, 2013 (6 months later)

"Where did you meet her?" Margot said.

"In San Sebastian, Spain, at an outdoor restaurant, listening to a young woman on the street, accompanied by a six-piece orchestra, singing Puccini's *O mio babbino caro.* Can you imagine? I noticed a woman sitting in front of me. Her long hair quivered, and I realized she was shivering from the cool air. I tapped her on her arm and gave her my scarf," Grey said.

"How gallant and romantic, Mr. Valentin."

"It didn't start that way. Romantic, that is. Anyhow, we hung around the entire day. Madeline told marvelous stories, and her fascination with architecture and its relationship to culture, climate, and history captivated me. Especially in San Sebastian, known both for its traditional and avant-garde architecture. For the following two weeks, we explored the city and eventually I became enamored. I kept it to myself, positive she'd never entertain such nonsense with me."

"Why not?"

He explained he was twenty years younger than her. "She took me to her apartment for dinners and ultimately we started discussing sex. They were intellectual discussions regarding sex positive behaviors."

"Sex positive? Never heard of it." She wondered if Madeline had completely fooled Grey. Seduced him.

"New to me, too. As its name implies, sex positivity is based on the notion that sex is a natural part of life. Nothing to be ashamed of or embarrassed by. Rather, it is having a positive attitude and respecting others' sexual preferences. There's more to it."

"Question. Did you wonder? A woman twenty years your senior taking you home and talking sex? I mean, they'd arrest her in the States."

"I was of age. And, your question is a perfect example of sex negative. And proof you grew up in the United States, where we learn sex from watching porn and reading magazines. We're not taught consensual sex is healthy. Pleasurable—"

"Coffee?" the flight attendant said. "Last call. We land in Minneapolis in fifteen minutes,"

"Orange juice and water, please," Margot said.

Grey shook his head.

"I'm sorry, Grey, I didn't get it and probably a bit jealous."

"Don't be silly." He said he and Madeline had four glorious months together. Then, she became ill. "I mean, tragically ill. Pancreatic cancer. She refused to see me...said she wanted me to remember her as a vibrant woman, not frail, suffering, and dying."

Silence.

"I never saw her again. I fell into a deep depression," he said, sniffing, "for a long time."

"It's horrible. I don't know what to say," she said, taking his hand.

"I got a letter from her three months later. She said she could die knowing we were the best together and claimed I was beautiful." He choked. "She said I did everything for her when, in reality, she changed my life. She taught me to be proud of who I am, inside and out." He closed his eyes and covered his mouth, sobbing.

She leaned on his arm and waited a few minutes before speaking. His pain stabbed at her heart. "A lovely, but difficult story."

"OJ and water," the flight attendant said. "Three dollars, please."

"Oh, I forgot." Margot unbuckled her seat belt, moved her hips up and dug in her pocket for change. "Here, thank you."

"Yes. Bittersweet." He inhaled and blew his nose on a napkin. "I'm incredibly grateful to her."

Margot sipped her orange juice and offered her water to Grey. He declined.

Neither spoke.

"Did she teach you to laugh?" Margot smiled, gently shifting the mood.

"Actually, I never laughed until Madeline. She said during orgasm, your brain is working overtime to produce a slew of different hormones and neurochemicals, including dopamine...which makes you experience pleasure."

Margot nearly spewed her orange juice. "How clinical."

They chuckled.

"Yeah, a brilliant woman."
***

Margot finally arrived at her home in Minneapolis. While Grey and Lester, the dog, napped on the living room couch, she and her mom had retreated to the bedroom for girl talk. They lay on the bed on their stomachs, resting on their elbows.

"You're skinny," Sherry said, slapping Margot's butt.

"You've lost weight, too." Margot patted back.

"Well, I'd say we've both been through quite an ordeal. I regret I couldn't be there for you."

"I just kept thinking 'I want my mom.'" She sniffed. "I needed you...phew. Listen, I don't want us to sit here and cry," she said, sniffling. "Let's keep upbeat. No dwelling on the negative."

"Agreed. We have plenty to be thankful for. And, oh, by the way, you said sell Myrtle."

"Boy, I'm thinking that was stupid. Grey and I are going back to Kosovo, but my Myrtle, I loved that car. I keep telling myself: life is about connections, experiences, memories. Not possessions."

Sherry tilted her head, rubbing against Margot's.

"Mom, tell me, how are you, really?"

"I'm fine." Sherry said she was diagnosed with chronic lymphocytic leukemia, noting they had caught it early. "No cure, however, it's treatable. Don't you worry." She smiled, "And, I have Brooks to thank."

"God, Mom. Brooks might have killed you! You certainly have a way of finding a pony in a pile of horseshit."

"Look, without Brooks' effort, my leukemia would have gone on unchecked, for who knows how long." Sherry sighed. "I will survive. And you will, too."

"For sure," Margot giggled. "We're bitchy survivors," Margot giggled.

"Like your Myrtle."

"Hm." Margot picked at her fingernails.

"Precisely why I didn't sell her."

"You're kidding me." Margot practically squealed, jumping up on her knees.

"Couldn't." Sherry tittered.

"Mom, you're the best."

"Well, then, since you admit I'm the best, this is perfect timing. You remember our conversation about your dad?"

"Yeah, Lester the dog and Lester the dog. Damn."

"Ha. Ha. hilarious. Lester, the dog, saved me from Brooks. Your father came to the hospital and, well, we reconnected."

"Oh my God, Mom. In an instant? Where's he been? And how 're-connected'?" Margot dropped her head.

"Lester, your father, took care of me when I got home from the hospital, when I needed him the most." Sherry cocked her head and looked at her with sad eyes. "Honey."

Margot shook her head and pouted her lips. "Mother."

"Takes time to come around, and you will. He's in my life again and we both are thrilled. You just got to keep opening your heart, as you have with Andy and Grey."

"Hey, ladies?" Grey said, rapping on the door.

Sherry and Margot vaulted to their feet.

"We're coming," Sherry said. "We'd better get out there. Nice, catching up. By the way, I told your daddy he could come over later."

"You're kidding." Margot's back stiffened. "That's not fair. Too much too soon."

"Nope, you have a couple of hours to prepare. I'm counting on the adult Margot being here," Sherry smiled and squeezed her hands. "He's very proud of you."

Silence.

Margot was conflicted. She wanted to please her mom. And she truly wanted to punish her dad. She scratched the back of her neck.

"I'm counting on you."

She tossed her hair. Sherry hugged her and they moved to the living room.

"Your house is charming, just as I expected. And the fire is great," Grey said, looking at the family photos on the mantle. "Is this Sam? She's adorable. I see the same devilish grin on Margot's face every so often."

Sherry nodded, "Yes, she was a pistol."

"I'm sorry," he said.

"No, no. I think we're on the other side of the dreadful loss." She explained they had reached the point where they could enjoy and celebrate her and her time with them on earth.

"I must tell you, Mom, Grey helped me understand something extremely important. We had a long conversation, and I told him the complete story about Sam. Thing is, I thought my guilt was totally wrapped up in forcing Sam to go home in a terrible snowstorm. While there's truth to that, I repressed my shame. I was ashamed I didn't drive. Alice would still be alive. I could have been with Sam, and we would have died together."

"Together? Oh my God! Don't even say it. Lose my only two children at the same time? Margot, we promised to stay positive today."

"It is positive. Before, it was complete self-destructive. My memories of Sam are no longer torturous. I love thinking of her now."

"Wow, Grey, I'm beyond happy you came into Margot's life."

Grey rubbed Lester's ears. "We're an outstanding team."

Margot beamed.

They sat quietly.

"Can I ask? You said you'd be returning to Kosovo. Do you have specific plans? Will you work for USAID again?"

"Might. We have a bigger goal," she said, smiling at Grey. "We plan to carry on Andy's idea and create an NGO to help children. Get kids off the street in safe homes with access to education."

"You were destined for an outstanding and meaningful future. I'm bursting with pride."

Lester stirred and barked.

"We got company," Sherry said. "Back in a sec."

"Oh my God. I think that's my dad. Shit. Hug me."

"Really? This is great. I'm glad, Margot. You need to let stuff go. Life's too short."

She pulled Grey close to her, and they were in a tight embrace, nose to nose, when two official-looking gentlemen entered the living room with her mother.

Relieved it wasn't her dad, Margot sniggered. "Who are you? Why the somber looks?"

"This is Agent David Meyer. Remember? You spoke to him over the phone," Sherry said with a shaky voice, biting her bottom lip.

Meyer didn't move and his intense stare made Margot nervous. She raked her fingers through her hair. "Good to meet you in person, Mr. Meyer."

He didn't respond.

Burning wood snapped and popped in the fireplace, and Lester sat at attention at Grey's feet.

Grey said, "You have a message?" He wrinkled his brow and Lester perked his ears.

"You guys know Hawkins?" Margot said, exhaling to release the angst building in her mind.

They didn't answer.

"Tsk. Well?" Margot stomped and put her hands on her hips. "Spit it out, fellas."

"Margot Evelyn Hart, you are hereby under arrest for conspiracy and wire fraud under the Computer Fraud and Abuse Act," Agent Meyer said, displaying his badge. "This is Agent Crawford."

Crawford pulled her arms behind her back and slipped handcuffs around her wrists.

Sherry gasped and slumped onto the sofa. When Lester growled, she pulled him toward her. "Shush."

Gobsmacked, Margot's mind went reeling, searching for meaning.

"You have the right to remain silent. Anything you say can and will be used against you in a court of law. You have the right to an attorney—"

"What the fuck are you doing?" Grey said, eyes wide and moist. His complexion had turned crimson.

Margot's jaw dropped in disbelief. "I get it. Hawkins put you up to this, didn't he? It's insane." She tried laughing. No sound came out because her fear, like desert sand, dried her throat.

"If you cannot afford an attorney, one will be provided for you. Do you understand the rights I read to you?"

Margot looked at Grey and tossed her hair. His crimson had turned white.

"Ms. Hart, do you understand?" Meyer said.

Margot shuddered and her chin quivered. "You're making a terrible mistake." She wiped her eyes with her shoulder.

"I know Hawkins," he said, pulling a cell out of his breast pocket. He pressed a button to dial, held the phone to his ear and waited. "Here she is." He pushed the speaker icon.

"Margot?"

"What the fuck is going on?" she said, spittle flying out of her mouth.

"My sentiments exactly," Hawkins said.

"Whatever! You screwed up royally this time," she said, her forehead slick with perspiration. "This is wrong."

Sherry rushed to Margot and wrapped her arms around her shoulders.

Hawkins said, "I need to ask you."

"Yeah?"

"Do you know a Goxilli? First name Illir?"

ABOUT THE AUTHOR

Diann Schindler traveled for four years as a solo nomad exploring 45 countries in six continents. Her experiences in Prishtina, Kosovo inspired her to write "Claim Denied."

"My creativity went wild and compelled me to write about murder, villains, cyber-espionage, and of course, love."

"Claim Denied," her first thriller, follows her coming-of-age novel "Just A Girl" and her nonfiction book, "The Essential Guide to a Life of Travel: the ABC's of International Travel."

She is writing her third novel, the sequel to "Claim Denied," which follow Margot's next chapter in a small town on the Eastern Shore of Virginia. Publication: Winter, 2022.

Diann lives in Madeira Island, Portugal. When she isn't writing, podcasting, swimming, playing guitar or traveling, she is drinking wine with friends.

*****

For more information about Diann about her books, go to
www.DiannSchindlerAuthor.
And for more about her travels, go to www.DiannAbroad.com.
Subscribe to her newsletter, distributed via email, usually on a
monthly basis or when the mood strikes her,
and to "In the Know!" her podcast show.

Email her at DiannSchindlerAuthor@gmail.com.

BOOK CLUB QUESTIONS

1. Talk about the characters, both good and bad. Describe their personalities and motivations. Are they fully developed and emotionally complex? Or are they flat, one-dimensional heroes and villains?
   Margot, Andy, Grey, Edgar, Ismet, Illir, Sherry, Ganna, Hawkins, Wilson, Vis, Bestar, Cassandra, Jeremy, Mrs. Bloom, and any others.
2. What do you know...and when did you know it? At what point in the book did you begin to piece together what happened?
3. Good crime writers embed hidden clues, slipping them in casually, almost in passing. Did you pick them out, or were you...clueless? Once you've finished the book, go back to locate the clues hidden in plain sight. Did you find any buried?
4. Red herrings: false glues to lead you astray. Did you find any red herrings that threw you off track? If so, were you tripped up?
5. Comment on references to blackbirds, crows, jackdaws, and Magpie. Any significance to you?
6. Comment on the settings: Prishtina, Kosovo; Iowa; Tetova, Macedonia.
7. Talk about the twists and turns—those surprising plot developments that throw everything you think you've figured out into disarray. List them. Did they enhance the story, add complexity, and build suspense? Were they plausible or implausible? Did they feel forced and gratuitous; that is, inserted merely to extend the story?
8. Let's discuss ratcheted suspense. Did you find yourself anxious, quickly turning pages to learn what happened? A what point does the suspense start to build? Where does it climax...then perhaps start rising again?

9. Comment on the hackers' plot. Did it keep your attention?

10. The ending: did it ease up on tension, create more? Did it tidy up all loose ends? Any left hanging?

11. Is the conclusion probable or believable? Is it organic, growing out of clues previously laid out? Or does the ending come out of the blue, feeling forced or tacked-on? Perhaps it's too predictable. Can you envision a different or better ending?

12. Point to passages in the book—ideas, descriptions, or dialogue—that you found interesting or revealing, that somehow struck you. What, if anything, made you stop and think? Or maybe even laugh.

13. Overall, does the book satisfy? Does it live up to the standards of a good crime story or suspense thriller? Or does it somehow fall short?

14. Comment on the cover. Did it reflect important aspects of the novel?

15. Compare this book to other mystery, crime, or suspense thrillers that you've read.

16. Would you recommend to others? Why or why not?

***

Is your book club interested in reading and discussing
"Claim Denied"?
Diann would be please to set up a conference call to join in the discussion and/or answer any questions.
Please email her at DiannSchindlerAuthor@gmail.com.

CLAIM DENIED

More books by Diann Schindler

"Just A Girl"

"The Essential Guide to a Life of Travel:
the ABC's of International Travel"

found on Amazon and Ingramspark

CPSIA information can be obtained
at www.ICGtesting.com
Printed in the USA
LVHW081056160721
692885LV00012B/294

9 780999 137529